HARDYBOYS ADVENTURES™

3-BOOKS-IN-1!

#1 SECRET OF THE RED ARROW
#2 MYSTERY OF THE PHANTOM HEIST
#3 THE VANISHING GAME

FRANKLIN W. DIXON

D0132625

ALADDIN   New York London Toronto Sydney New Delhi

This book is a work of fiction. Any references to historical events, real people, or real places are used fictitiously. Other names, characters, places, and events are products of the author's imagination, and any resemblance to actual events or places or persons, living or dead, is entirely coincidental.

ALADDIN

An imprint of Simon & Schuster Children's Publishing Division

1230 Avenue of the Americas, New York, NY 10020

This Aladdin paperback edition June 2016

Secret of the Red Arrow text copyright © 2013 by Simon & Schuster, Inc.

Mystery of the Phantom Heist text copyright © 2013 by Simon & Schuster, Inc.

The Vanishing Game text copyright © 2013 by Simon & Schuster, Inc.

Cover illustration copyright © 2013 by Ben Sowards

All rights reserved, including the right of reproduction in whole or in part in any form.

ALADDIN is a trademark of Simon & Schuster, Inc.,

and related logo is a registered trademark of Simon & Schuster, Inc.

THE HARDY BOYS MYSTERY STORIES, HARDY BOYS ADVENTURES,

and related logo are trademarks of Simon & Schuster, Inc.

For information about special discounts for bulk purchases, please contact Simon & Schuster Special Sales at 1-866-506-1949 or business@simonandschuster.com.

The Simon & Schuster Speakers Bureau can bring authors to your live event.

For more information or to book an event contact the Simon & Schuster Speakers Bureau at 1-866-248-3049 or visit our website at www.simonspeakers.com.

Series designed by Karin Paprocki

Cover designed by Steve Scott

Interior designed by Mike Rosamilia

The text of this book was set in Adobe Caslon Pro.

Printed and bound in India by Replika Press Pvt. Ltd.

2 4 6 8 10 9 7 5 3 1

Library of Congress Control Number 2016933430

ISBN 978-1-4814-8553-1 (pbk)

ISBN 978-1-4424-4619-9 (*Secret of the Red Arrow* eBook)

ISBN 978-1-4424-2238-4 (*Mystery of the Phantom Heist* eBook)

ISBN 978-1-4424-5982-3 (*The Vanishing Game* eBook)

These titles were previously published individually by Aladdin.

CONTENTS

CONTENTS

SECRET OF THE
RED ARROW

THE HOLDUP 1

FRANK

T'S FUNNY TO THINK ABOUT HAVING ENEMIES. Not funny ha-ha. Funny strange.

I was standing in line at the First Bayport Bank on Water Street. Dad had sent me here on an errand, explaining that the Hardy household believed in banking in person, not online. Mistakes were less common, he said, when the tellers had a face to remember. Even plain old Frank Hardy's face.

I knew it was just an excuse to get me out of the house. "You're spending too much time cooped up in front of a computer screen." Dad, Mom, Aunt Trudy, and my brother, Joe, each told me that at least five times a day.

Well, they weren't the ones who had to give a speech. That's right: In one week, yours truly had to get up in front of the entire Bayport High School student body to present my American history paper on civil liberties, which my teacher, Ms. Jones, had called "exceptional." I'd been really happy about that until I realized it would lead to mandatory public speaking. Thinking about it gave me turbocharged butterflies. I was embarrassed to admit it, but if there was one thing I truly hated, it was public speaking. D-day was right around the corner, and I didn't even have a final speech yet. I pretended to be "researching," but the reality was that I was turning into Joe: a world-class procrastinator.

The line in the bank was long, and the wait was boring. It had rained all morning, which meant drippy umbrellas inside. My sneakers were soaked through from the walk.

I took out my cell and texted Joe. We were going to meet up later at the Meet Locker to study. (That's a coffee shop, in case you were wondering. A popular hangout, it's open late, and they serve a mean Maximum Mocha.)

NO SIGNAL.

Typical, I thought. Bayport had become notorious for its spotty cell reception.

Staring down at my phone, I accidentally bumped into the person in front of me in line. "Sorry," I said. The guy glanced back. Then, eyes widening, he turned to face me.

It was Seth Diller, Bayport High's very own Quentin Tarantino.

"Oh. Hey, Seth," I said.

He studied me with his strange, unblinking, pale-blue eyes. He looked very highly charged for some reason, like

4

he'd beaten me to the Meet Locker and drunk about twelve espressos. A few inches shorter than me, Seth was wearing a black turtleneck so tight it made me wonder if his brain was being deprived of oxygen. Finally he dipped a nod in my direction. "Frank," he said quietly.

I didn't know Seth very well. But he always had a camera in his hand. He was president of the Bayport High AV Club.

His specialty was monster videos. I'd seen a couple on the club website. Lots of fake tissue damage and gross-out effects. Joe appreciated that Seth took the time to make all his effects "in the camera"—meaning not digitally. No CGI for Seth. He was a purist. Joe was a fan, me not so much.

"Working on any new monster masterpieces?" I asked, just to be friendly.

He nodded. "Yes . . . in fact, I'm cooking up something really special."

"Really?"

He smiled. "That's right. I'm hoping this new movie will break my record of eleven thousand four hundred fifty-six views on YouTube."

I guessed that was impressive. "What's it about?" I asked.

He frowned and gave a shrug. "It's hard to describe."

I figured he didn't want to talk about it, so I just wished him luck and changed the subject. "Hey, how's your brother doing?" Tom Diller, Seth's older brother, had been badly wounded while serving with the marines in Afghanistan.

Seth grew quiet, and I was starting to feel sorry I'd brought up such a personal subject. That's when we heard the screams.

"Everybody stay where you are!" a voice yelled.

Three men with guns, each wearing a mask from a recent slasher movie, had entered the bank. They were moving fast, pistols in their outstretched hands. One disarmed the security guard, dropped the guard's gun in a trash can, and forced him to lie on the floor. Another locked the front doors. The third came toward us.

I'm not going to lie: I was shocked, and a little scared. I could feel my heart hammering in my chest like it was trying to break out. The truth is, I'd been in far stickier situations than this one, but you don't exactly expect to run into a bank robbery on a Saturday morning in a sleepy little town like Bayport.

Seth, standing right beside me, stiffened and made a panicky sound in his throat. Seeing his fear brought me back to my senses. "Stay calm," I whispered to him. "Do whatever they ask. Everything will be fine."

He was fumbling in his pocket. Glancing over, I saw him take out his smartphone. Hands shaking, he hurriedly tapped the screen until a wobbly image of his own feet came up. He had enabled the video cam.

He was going to record the robbery.

"Seth, listen to me very carefully," I said in an urgent whisper. "Do not do that. These men are wearing masks for a reason. Just put your phone away."

But he wasn't listening. He cupped his hand so the phone was partway concealed and held it low against his leg, angling out at the room, capturing the heist in action.

"Empty your pockets and your purses!" the third gunman yelled. He was my height and thin, wearing a bulky army jacket that didn't fit. "Nice and calm, people. No sudden moves. We don't want to hurt anybody."

The gunman who had locked the doors joined him. "But we will shoot anyone who gets in our way!" he shouted. He rushed to one of the tellers' windows and proceeded to collect money from behind the counter.

Army Jacket began taking valuables from the people standing in line. Rings, necklaces, and wallets disappeared into a canvas bag he was carrying. He made quick work of it. My mind was racing. What would be the reaction of the gunmen if they saw Seth recording them? It would depend on a million factors. How experienced they were. How nervous. How desperate. Were these men killers?

Army Jacket reached Seth, standing right by my side. I held my breath. The gunman paused only for an instant while Seth dropped his wallet and wristwatch into the canvas bag in one movement. He hadn't seen Seth's phone in his other hand. I breathed a two-second sigh of relief. Then Army Jacket was facing me.

Something strange happened then. Army Jacket just stood there, letting the moment drag on too long. He didn't say anything. He didn't take my watch or my wallet. He didn't even seem all that threatening. He was just . . . staring at me.

Did he know me? It was possible. Even though my brother

and I are supposed to be officially "retired," we'd put away a fair share of criminals in our time. Maybe this guy had been sent to prison, courtesy of Frank and Joe Hardy, and had just gotten his release.

See, our dad, Fenton Hardy, was once a world-famous detective. Growing up, Joe and I would help him on his cases. Then we began tackling mysteries on our own. We were proud of our successes. But after one too many close calls, things started to get a little out of hand, for reasons having to do with private investigators' licenses (we didn't have any), insurance (none of that, either), and the threat of being sued by every hoodlum we ever put under a citizen's arrest. Which is not how my brother and I wanted to spend the remainder of our teenage years, provided we're lucky enough to survive them. Some of us even have hopes of college one day . . . of a scholarship . . . of a normal life.

So with a few phone calls, including references from our principal and assurances to the police chief and state attorney general, we "retired." Officially, it stays that way—for all the Hardys. Our dad writes books on the history of law enforcement. And Joe and I go to high school.

That cozy arrangement, a.k.a. "the Deal," lasted about a month before Joe and I started going crazy. Maybe being a detective is something in your blood. I don't know.

Since then we've started taking the occasional case for a good cause or to help a friend, but we try to keep it confidential. And we deny everything. We don't consider it lying, just being prudent. We haven't told our dad, which makes me feel a bit guilty, but I get the feeling he suspects.

Not that it mattered right now. All that mattered was that Army Jacket's arm had slowly fallen to his side. His gun was pointed at the floor. Like he'd forgotten about it. Now was my chance.

I was about to grab the gun and wrestle it out of his hand, but his accomplice hollered, "Hey! What are you doing?"

Shocked back into the moment, Army Jacket raised his gun again. My chance was gone. I'd blown it. I could see the tiny mouth of the black barrel, aimed between my eyes. He was about to fire!

2 SEEING DOUBLE

JOE

I **WAS STARING INTO A FACE I'D KNOWN MY ENTIRE** life: my big brother Frank's. For a dizzy second or two, I forgot where I was and what I was doing.

It had totally slipped my mind that Frank had been sent on a phony errand down to the bank. Everybody in the Hardy family agreed he had been spending way too much time on the computer lately, and that he needed to go out and get some exercise and fresh air. The rain shower was just a bonus. Besides, Mom and Dad did all the household banking online. It is the twenty-first century, after all.

When I saw Frank, I almost blurted out his name. I caught myself just in time. But there had to be some way I could let him know it was me in the Michael Myers mask (the one from *Halloween*, you know). How could I signal to him? How could I let him know?

For a second, I thought about speaking to him in sign. Frank and I are both pretty fluent in American Sign Language. I could keep it simple: B-B G-U-N.

Letting him know, first of all, that I was just holding a BB gun. An unloaded one at that. It was the most important thing to communicate if we were going to stop these idiots!

But I'd better back up a little bit. You're probably wondering how Joe Hardy came to be holding up a bank in the company of two hardened criminals in the first place.

I had been on my way down to the Locker to meet Frank. (It's actually called the Meet Locker, which I think is kind of a stupid name. Most kids seem to agree and just call it the Locker.) Frank was all worked up about his speech, which was (as he had told me a million times) exactly one week away. Anyway, I was supposed to help him with it.

As I walked past the alley behind the bank, a big guy in a Michael Myers mask—just like the one I was wearing now—darted out from behind a car and yanked me off my feet. Now, before you call me a wuss, I do know judo (I'm a green belt). But the business end of a nine-millimeter Glock was pressed right up against my gut, so I played along.

It was not the first time I'd had a gun trained on me by some hoodlum. Frank and I had been solving crimes since we were little. We had to keep it on the down low nowadays, of course, because we kept getting sued. But the situation wasn't completely unfamiliar to me.

Mr. Glock dragged me over to a van. The door was wide open. Inside, a woman was squirming and whimpering, and when I took a closer look I recognized Mrs. Steigerwald, the owner of Bayport's bowling alley, Seaside Lanes. A big guy was holding another gun and had a hand clamped over her mouth, but he lifted it just long enough for her to shout, "Joe! Help m—"

She was wearing a baseball cap and these big, 1970s-style sunglasses—her usual getup—and she was so terrified, her glasses seemed to be fogging up. It was awful. The other gunman told me I had to help them rob the bank . . . or she'd "get it." Their partner hadn't shown up, he said, so they were a man short. Then the first guy tossed a big, greasy-looking army jacket at me and handed me another *Halloween* mask and the BB gun.

I racked my brain, but I couldn't see any way out. Poor Mrs. Steigerwald was about to hyperventilate.

"Don't worry, Mrs. S," I assured her, putting on the army jacket and the mask. "It'll all be over really quick. Then I'll come right out to check on you."

"All r-right . . . J-Joe," she answered through chattering teeth. Which surprised me, since she normally called everybody plain old "you." I didn't think she knew my name. I was always "You—the blond Hardy." But I let it slide, thinking she was just terrified.

Sixty seconds later, I was a felon.

Have you ever tried to hold up a bank with the sole aim of keeping anyone from being hurt? It's quite a high-wire act.

"Hey!" one of my accomplices barked at me now, snapping me back into the present. I'd been staring at Frank, trying to figure out how to communicate with him. "What are you doing?" he demanded.

There was no chance to team up with my brother at the moment. It was too risky. I just needed to get this ordeal over with as soon as possible. I took Frank's wallet and moved on.

The next customer in line brought me to a halt. This time I couldn't hide my shock.

"Um . . . Mrs. Steigerwald?" I said. My voice was muffled through the mask.

Mrs. Steigerwald looked freaked out—and mad. She wasn't wearing her hat and glasses now, and her bright-red hair stuck out at crazy angles. Her green eyes—a really memorable shade—stared at me suspiciously. She clutched her purse, getting ready to hit me with it. "What do you want, you?" she asked.

Now I was really confused. How was Mrs. Steigerwald standing right in front of me? If she was in the bank, who was out in the van being held captive? How could she be in two places at once?

"Were you just outside?" I asked her.

She looked confused. "When?"

"Like, two minutes ago."

"No," she replied. "I've been here for the past half hour, discussing Seaside Lanes's bank loan with Tom Baines." The color started returning to her cheeks as she got going. "Which I wouldn't need to do if the young people in this town would tear themselves away from their screens once in a while for some good, clean, healthy bowling!"

I took a deep breath, set my gun on the floor, and stepped away from it. Then I raised my hands over my head.

Frank nearly knocked the wind out of me when he tackled me and wrestled me to the ground. My brother looks skinny, but he has some power. I didn't resist. The bank erupted in chaos. People screamed. I caught a glimpse of the other two robbers ducking out the side door. The security guard ran over and put a knee in my back.

Frank ripped the mask off my face. To his credit, he didn't say anything. He just frowned.

"There's a really good explanation," I said.

"I bet there is," Frank answered.

Before I could get that explanation out, though, Bayport's finest were on the scene. Our town might have lousy cell phone reception, but I guess the landlines worked just fine.

I was in cuffs and out the door before I could say another word.

Frank offered some good parting advice: "Joe, don't say anything until Dad and I get to the station."

I nodded and gave him a behind-the-back thumbs-up.

The police cruiser was waiting at the curb. The officers put me in the back, slammed the door, and took off.

Now, I know Frank told me not to say anything, but I didn't see any harm in being friendly. I'm a people person. Besides, I was just relieved the whole ordeal was over without anyone getting hurt. I figured together, we would sort this whole thing out.

So I said, "I know it sounds funny, but I am so glad to see you guys."

They didn't answer. No problem. For the present, I was a robbery suspect, caught in the act. Not the kind of person most cops would want to be friendly with. I wasn't offended.

Then a thought occurred to me. "How did you guys get there so quick?" I asked. "Was there a silent alarm? Or were you just passing by?"

Unsurprisingly, they kept up the silent routine.

As we cruised down Orchard Street, my gaze shifted out the window to a familiar yellow scooter, parked in a driveway. I felt a little tingle in my chest. She was home. Janine Kornbluth, that is.

The police cruiser took the corner at Starboard and Main. We were a block from police department headquarters. I began preparing myself for booking and getting my mug shot taken. (Sadly, this was not the first time I had been inside a jail cell.) But instead we sped up.

"Hey," I said. "You missed the turn."

We passed the station, gathering speed. Main Street

leads straight out of town and becomes State Road 17. We passed the last houses. Then there was nothing but pine trees growing tall and straight all around us.

Was I being kidnapped? I stared hard at the police officers, then noticed a detail about the hefty one behind the wheel. He had a scar on the back of his left hand—kind of a pink crescent moon. One of the guys in the bank heist had had the same scar! I should've noticed it sooner.

These guys weren't the police—they were the bank robbers!

Now I realized what had happened: The gunmen must have been wearing these police uniforms under their jackets. They had rushed out of the bank, dumped their masks, jackets, and the loot, and then dashed right back in to "arrest" me. No wonder the cops had been so quick.

My ordeal wasn't over after all.

A sharp pain in my wrists made me wince. I made an effort to relax my arms. I'd been straining at my handcuffs. Crazy, I know, but I was just starting to realize how mad I was.

These hoods had hijacked my morning, scared a bunch of innocent people witless, robbed a bank using me as a dumb accomplice, and now were getting clean away. And who knew what they planned to do with me now? What if their cruel tricks weren't over?

At Satellite Road, five miles outside the Bayport city limits, the cruiser slowed to a stop. The gunmen got out, pulled me out, and uncuffed me. "Start walking," the hefty one said. He pointed back into town. "That way." They got back in and drove off in the opposite direction.

I followed them. Admittedly, not very fast. But I was jogging along well enough.

Ahead of me, the cruiser stopped. The reverse lights came on. They backed up until they were beside me again. The driver's-side window rolled down.

"What do you think you're doing, kid? We told you to walk the other way."

I stared back at them without answering. I didn't open my mouth. I didn't even blink. I was done cooperating with these clowns.

They looked at each other and shrugged. "He'll never keep up on foot," the skinny one said. "Not if you gun it."

The hefty one nodded and stomped on the accelerator. The cruiser spit gravel and shot away. Within ten seconds it was gone from my view.

I sighed, turned, and began the slow walk back into town. Oh well, at least it had stopped raining.

When I got home, dirty and tired, the real cops were waiting for me. Luckily, after I told my story I avoided the booking, the mug shot, the taking the laces out of my shoes. I was told I wouldn't be charged with anything, and they left.

After they were gone, waiting for me on the kitchen table was a treat from Aunt Trudy: some kind of delicious sauce on top of homemade, ribbony pasta. I didn't know what it all was, but it was terrific.

Aunt Trudy lived in a little apartment above the garage. We called our aunt Green Thumb Trudy because she was crazy for gardening. She went to meetings on the subject of gardening and belonged to several gardening societies in the area. She also had a wicked sense of humor. My late lunch had come with a note attached: *For the Jailbird.*

Frank sat with me and gave me the final pieces of the puzzle while I ate.

After all I'd been through, here's the kicker: It all turned out to have been some sort of prank!

Mrs. Steigerwald was never under any threat. The woman I saw in the van must have been a double who'd gotten hold of a similar baseball cap and sunglasses. She may have even been wearing a bright-red wig. I'd been completely fooled.

All the loot from the holdup was found in the alley next to the bank in a cake box with a note that said, *Just kidding! LOL!* The police would return all the personal items and cash once they'd had a chance to dust for fingerprints.

Frank watched me as I finished up my lunch special and rinsed my plate. "Are you okay?" he asked after a moment. "You must have had a crazy day. I was worried about you."

Sometimes it's nice to have a brother.

3 CONSEQUENCES

FRANK

AFTER THE FIFTH SIGH, I PUT THE photos down. "Okay, what's wrong?"

Joe had been looking through the Frank Hardy Known Criminal Index, a collection of mug shots and wanted posters I kept in my briefcase. But his eyes had glazed over, and his leg was bouncing in place.

"Did you ever stop and ask yourself *why*, Frank?"

"Why what?"

"Why people do the things they do . . . Why the Earth revolves around the Sun . . . Why we get involved in every kind of crazy trouble that crops up around here . . ."

I couldn't hear the rest of his answer. The decibel level in the Bayport High cafeteria was, as ever during lunch period, at the hollering point.

Joe toyed with his meal for a bit. He'd ordered his usual: the special of the day. I don't think he actually prefers one dish over another. He just likes variety.

I knew something was bugging him. After the cops left Saturday, he'd been in typically high spirits. But later, his mood had shifted, and he'd barely spoken two words since.

My blond-haired, blue-eyed brother is an unlikely one to sulk. In fact, he's one of the sunniest people I knew. But every once in a while something would get under his skin. He wouldn't bring it up right away. First he'd talk about something else. Finally he'd work his way around to what was really going on in his head. I knew I didn't have long to wait.

I was right.

He had been staring at a stack of photos of various white males between the ages of twenty and forty, but I could tell he wasn't really seeing their faces. (We'd been hoping he would be able to identify the phony cops who had briefly kidnapped him after the bank holdup on Saturday, but so far no luck.) All at once, he looked at me in alarm and said, "Am I a major-league sucker or something? Sort of Mr. Gullibility?"

"No."

"Do I have a sucker's face?"

I wanted to laugh. But I didn't. "A sucker's face? No. Why?"

"Well, look what happened: First I got taken in by a bunch of phony bank robbers. Then I got tricked by someone pretending to be Mrs. Steigerwald. And then I let myself get busted by fake cops!"

So that was it.

I was about to tell him I didn't think he was any more gullible than I was, whatever that was worth, but a voice interrupted our conversation:

"Dude, that was sick!"

Laughter echoed from the table next to ours. I looked up and saw a bunch of football players staring down into somebody's smartphone screen. As I looked, one of the players—Neal "Neanderthal" Bunyan—glanced up and met my eye.

Uh-oh. Neanderthal, Joe, and I were not exactly friends.

"Yo, Frank!" he yelled now, grabbing his friend's phone and holding it up so I could see it. "You seen this? It's your big movie debut!"

Big movie debut? I looked at Joe, who seemed to share my sense of wariness. Last I'd checked, I didn't have a feature film in production.

"What do you mean, Neander—er—Neal?" Joe asked.

Neanderthal got up from his table and walked over, still holding the smartphone. "Someone just messaged this link to my buddies," he said, holding it up so we could see the screen. It was a YouTube clip. He hit play, and Joe and I frowned at each other and watched.

The second the picture came up, my mouth dropped

open. It was me—at the bank yesterday. First I was shot from behind, standing in line, minding my own business. Then the screen moved to capture the "robbers" entering the bank, brandishing their "guns." Everyone screamed, and the bank robbers yelled at us to stay calm, then that they'd shoot anyone who didn't cooperate.

After a few more seconds, the screen dissolved to black, and then words flashed up in bright-red capital letters:

WHAT WOULD YOU DO?

And then:

PANIC PROJECT!
COMING THIS SUMMER!

I frowned again and looked up at Joe. He looked just as puzzled as I felt. "What was that?"

"That," I replied, handing the phone back to Neanderthal, "is what I think is supposed to become a viral video."

Neanderthal was laughing. "So, let me bet on what happens next," he said, turning around to make sure his buddies were watching. "Frank, I'm going out on a limb to say you pee your pants. Sorry, maybe I should have said 'spoiler alert.'"

I avoided Neanderthal's eyes as I wiped my mouth, tossed my napkin on my tray, and stood up. "Let's go, Joe."

"Awww, don't be embarrassed," Neanderthal chided,

chuckling. "I'm sure I would have been real scared if the same thing had happened to me. I mean, not as scared as you look, but scared."

Joe was still working on his special of the day. "Really?" he asked. "We're done with lunch?"

I nodded. "Really."

Joe looked disappointed, but he grabbed his tray and followed me away from our table. "What's up?"

I was looking around the cafeteria. "We need to find Seth Diller."

Joe looked around too. "Why?"

"Because he took that video."

I wasn't seeing Seth anywhere around the cafeteria. Then I remembered that some of the AV Club kids ate in the AV room. And Seth, as you might imagine, was big into the AV Club. Like president-three-years-running big.

Joe looked confused. "Wait, he shot that?" he asked. "Seriously? How would he have known to do that?"

I shook my head. "Not sure. He shot it with the video camera in his phone."

Joe furrowed his brows. "But . . . that makes it seem like Seth was involved. . . ."

"And he staged it all," I finished. "Like one of his stupid monster videos. Come on." I grabbed Joe's arm and led him up the back staircase toward the AV room. I don't usually have much of a temper—I'm a thinker, not a fighter—but I have to admit, the closer I got to Seth Diller, the more I wanted to punch him in the face. Had he really staged an entire bank robbery for the sake of some dumb movie project? Hadn't he ever heard of actors? Hadn't he ever heard of scripts?

Sometimes I think reality television is ruining our culture.

"Hey," I said, plowing through the door to the AV room. Seth sat with his AV cronies on a set of stairs near the back, surrounded by a maze of DVD players and old-school televisions on carts.

He looked surprised to see us. "Hey, Frank," he said, looking a little nervous. I understood his wariness. I mean, Seth and I had probably exchanged five words, total, in the entire year before the bank robbery. Now I was hunting him down on his "turf."

"My brother and I need to talk to you," I said. "Privately."

After a few seconds, Seth nodded. "Ah—okay."

He got up and walked over to us, and I held the door open for him to pass through. Then I walked over to a quiet corner of the hallway, by a window, and gestured for Seth to follow.

"What's this about?" he asked quickly, looking uncomfortable.

"It's about the video you shot on Saturday," I replied, crossing my arms. "Of the robbery. Remember?"

Seth looked at me blankly. I don't think the expression in his pale-blue eyes changed at all. "What do you mean?"

I sighed. So we were going to do it this way. "I'm talking about the video you took on your phone," I said, and then paused to wait for the recognition to spark in his eyes. But none came. "Come on, Seth. I saw it."

Seth gulped. It was nearly unnoticeable but for the lump traveling down his throat. "I didn't shoot anything. Is that all? Because we were kind of in the middle . . ."

Joe gestured at Seth's pocket, where the outline of his smartphone was clearly visible. "Then you won't mind if I borrow it for a sec?" he asked.

Seth frowned. "What?"

"Your phone." Joe gestured at Seth's pocket again. The top of the phone was peeking out. "I have just remembered that I need to call our aunt Trudy and remind her to buy some zucchini for dinner tonight, because I'm having a craving. Okay?"

Seth looked unsure how to react. Yes, this was a ridiculous request, but his phone was in plain sight. He was caught. "I really don't have time. . . ."

"It'll only take a second." Joe held out his hand.

Seth looked from Joe to me and back again. He didn't lose his composure, but very deliberately reached into his pocket and pulled out the phone. He looked at the screen for just a moment before Joe pulled it out of his grasp.

Joe moved closer to me and held out the phone so I could see it. The background was a particularly gory scene from one of Seth's most popular flicks. Joe didn't even bother pretending to make a call. He went straight to the "Videos" folder and clicked on it. A list popped up:

Roadkill cat.mov

Cool sunset.mov

Bankheistraw.mov

"That's it," I said, pointing.

Joe clicked on the video, and after a few seconds of buffering, it came up. The same video of me at the bank that Neanderthal had shown us just moments before.

Seth swallowed again, then looked down at the floor.

"Check his sent e-mails," I suggested on a whim. Joe pulled them up, then chuckled.

"There it is," he said, showing me the screen again. Sure enough, it was the same e-mail containing the link to the Panic Project trailer.

I looked up at Seth, whose eyes looked slightly buggier than usual. Other than that, he gave no outward indication of fear.

"Maybe we should go somewhere more comfortable," I suggested. "I think you have a lot of explaining to do."

4 HARMLESS

JOE

"**W**HAT I DON'T UNDERSTAND," PRINCIPAL Gorse was saying as he crossed his good leg over his bad one, "is why you couldn't tell people what was going on. We've all seen movies, Seth. They have actors, scripts. If you know the ship on-screen isn't really sinking, does that make *Titanic* any less sad?"

Seth took in a quick breath. He looked like he was struggling to keep his composure. "Principal Gorse, I mean . . . come on."

The principal looked to the rest of us—me, Frank, and Officer Olaf, who had been sent in when the Bayport PD heard that we'd learned something about the bank robbery—for support.

"I think what he's trying to say," I jumped in, "is that real emotions are always more interesting to watch than fake ones. That's part of the appeal—that there is no script. Anything could happen."

Seth looked at me and smiled. "Exactly. I was performing a cinematic experiment. How would people react when they were put in these crazy, seemingly dangerous situations? What would happen?"

"And what happened in this case," Officer Olaf said, moving from his spot leaning against the front of Principal Gorse's desk, "was awfully lucky for you, Seth. Nobody got hurt. Nobody panicked and had a heart attack." He paused, standing right in front of Seth and looking down at him with serious brown eyes, running his fingers over his droopy mustache. "But you realize that was just luck, don't you?"

Seth looked up at Officer Olaf, defiant. I could tell he wasn't going to back down. "I didn't hurt anybody, Officer Olaf. It was never my intention to hurt anybody. It was just a harmless prank."

Frank, who was sitting next to me on a bench against the wall, huffed. "But you did kind of rob a bank," he pointed out.

Seth glared at him, surprised. "I did not," he insisted. "I staged a bank robbery, but we gave everything back."

"But in that moment," Frank said, getting to his feet, "I, and everybody else in that bank, really believed we might die. Make the wrong move, and you could have shot us full of holes. I'm sure lots of people were wondering whether they would make it out of the bank alive."

Seth frowned. He looked down at the floor for a second, then back into Frank's eyes. "I told them afterward that it was just a joke."

"But what if something had gone wrong?" Principal Gorse asked. He leaned across his desk. "Seth, you don't seem to get it here. Bank robberies are serious business. People panic. They act violently if they think it will save their lives. They feel terror that doesn't go away just because you leave a note saying it was only a joke."

Seth shifted uncomfortably, but his expression didn't change. "I take risks for my art," he said simply.

Officer Olaf sighed and turned to Principal Gorse. "Do you want to tell him what his punishment from you is? Because I'm about ready to take this kid down to the station house and straighten him out there."

Seth frowned again. Now he was looking a little nervous. "I'm being charged with a crime?" he asked.

Principal Gorse took a deep breath and said, "Seth, I'm afraid I have no choice but to suspend you for three days for cyberbullying your fellow students."

Seth jumped to his feet. "Cyberbullying?" he cried. "What?"

Principal Gorse gestured to Frank and me. "These two gentlemen were in your video."

Seth glared at me. "But they weren't even—"

"I'm afraid it's school policy."

Seth bit his lip, still glaring. He looked from me to Frank to Principal Gorse. "This is—"

But Officer Olaf didn't let him finish. "Now you have to come with me, Seth," he said, standing up. "You have the right to remain silent. Anything you say . . ."

Officer Olaf continued to read Seth his Miranda rights as Seth looked from him to Principal Gorse, stammering. "But—but—I didn't—"

"Criminal mischief," Officer Olaf said, moving close enough to Seth to wave a pair of handcuffs in his face. "You created a major disruption this weekend, Seth—diverting the police force and panicking citizens. I get that you didn't really rob a bank. But it turns out, pretending to rob a bank is pretty bad too." He jingled the cuffs again. "I'd rather not use these. Think you can walk out with me like a big boy—no trouble?"

Seth was still glaring at Officer Olaf, but his lower lip was starting to wobble. He took one last look around the room, and when he spotted me, his face flushed with anger. "Darn it, Joe! I thought you liked my videos! I thought you were cool!"

I sighed. I mean, I did feel bad for the kid. In his warped way, he was pretty talented. "Listen, Seth, if putting me in cuffs and making me hitchhike back from miles out of town—not to mention the whole issue of having to rob my brother—if that's how you treat a fan, I'd hate to see what you do to your enemies." I paused and tried to smile, but Seth wasn't having it. I gave up. "Seriously, dude. You went too far."

Seth pulled his lips tight, then turned and allowed Officer Olaf to lead him out of the office. The officer nodded at Principal Gorse on the way out. "Thanks, Hank," he said, glancing briefly at me and my brother. "Boys."

Then he turned his head and walked out the door, and he and Seth were gone.

Principal Gorse sighed. "Sometimes, boys," he said, "I think the world is changing too fast for me. Can either of you explain the appeal of that movie to me? Watching people get scared out of their minds for no real purpose?" He shook his head and shrugged.

"I think it's about shock, sir," I said. "In this day and age we've been desensitized to trauma, crime, horrific happenings. It takes more and more to shock your audience. Look at movies like *Saw* or *Hostel*—they go much further than the classic Hitchcockian horror of the past."

Principal Gorse nodded, looking bemused.

"So the natural next step," I went on, "the final frontier, if you will, is real emotion. Instead of trying to shock his audience, Seth is allowing them to share in the real shock of his unknowing participants."

Principal Gorse blinked. He was a nice guy, really; dressed like he always was, in a slouchy cardigan sweater, along with his usual corduroy pants and brown shoes. He had a kindly face with sort of messy brown hair and glasses. He looked like—well, like a kind of hippieish high school principal. A youngish man, maybe only forty years old, except that he also walked with a fancy hand-carved cane, which was the result of a bad skiing accident five years earlier.

You would probably have been able to pick out Mr. Gorse's car in the teachers' parking lot just by looking at him: It was an orange 1970s Karmann Ghia. Pure beatnik. Even its engine—it made a singular *put-put-put* sound—reminded you of him, so that wherever you were in Bayport, if he was passing anywhere within earshot, you were aware of him through that unique *put-put-put*. *There goes Mr. Gorse,* you would say to yourself.

We considered Mr. Gorse a friend—he'd been my band teacher in middle school. I knew he liked us. He'd been really nice to Frank and me when the Deal was being negotiated. Now he tilted his head, giving us both a concerned look.

"How are things going, Hardy Boys?" he asked. "I understand the legal problems you boys have had this past year. As a matter of fact, I received a note from the state board of education about you both."

Joe and I shifted uncomfortably in our chairs.

Mr. Gorse opened the letter and started reading. "Apparently, I'm to understand that—as part of a plea agreement with the state attorney general—you are both subject to 'instant recourse.'" He looked up at us. "I guess that's a little bit like probation." He continued reading. "Which, if you are found to engage in any kind of 'independent ama-teur law-enforcement-type activities,' will result in the pair of you being sent to"—here he brought the letter close to his eyes—"the J'Adoube School for Behavior Modification Therapy on Rock Island."

He wasn't telling us anything we didn't know. But it was not pleasant to hear it spoken out loud. "Are you meeting regularly with your legal adviser?" he asked.

Joe and I nodded. Our lawyer was Uncle Ben—Ben Hardy, our dad's brother—a Hartford tax attorney who had been given the thankless job of dealing with all the legal problems we'd accrued in the past year.

"Good. Well, what I wanted to say to you was that all this stuff . . ." He waved at the letter. "It doesn't change anything as far as I'm concerned. The world needs fighters, boys. People with the courage to stand up for what's right. But you can't accomplish your goals if you're locked up in juvenile hall or if your transcripts show half a dozen suspen-sions. Am I right?"

We nodded.

"Just remember, I'm in your corner. And my door is open, day and night."

Just then, his door actually opened.

"Oh, I'm sorry," a woman said. It was Yukiko Collins, one of the school's art teachers.

Mr. Gorse brightened. It was rumored that he and Ms. Collins were dating. Nobody wanted to pry, on account of

Mr. Gorse being a widower. (His wife had died in the skiing accident that had broken his leg.) But Joe and I liked the idea of Mr. G and Ms. C being an item, because they were our two favorite people at Bayport High.

"That's all right, Ms. Collins," Mr. Gorse said, rising to his feet, a smile on his face. "We were finished here."

As we passed outside, Ms. Collins smiled. She always wore crazy, mismatched clothing with horizontal stripes, and men's hats, and today was no exception.

Everybody loved Ms. Collins. She was one of those teachers who had the knack for always making you feel enthused and entertained. Joe and I had our own reasons for loving her: She had written the recommendation letter that kept us from being sent to the reform school Mr. Gorse had mentioned: J'Adoube—a really notorious place on a tiny, isolated island twenty miles out to sea. All kinds of rumors existed about the place. Rumors about strange "behavior modification therapies" with names like "Swarm" and "Funhouse Mirror." It was also rumored that several kids died each year trying to escape.

Today Ms. Collins seemed troubled. "I hope you boys are careful about talking on your cell phones," she said.

Smiling at this haphazard warning, I said, "You don't believe that stuff about their causing brain cancer, do you, Ms. Collins?"

"No, but I think mine's been hacked or something. . . ."

That sounded odd. I wanted to ask her more about it.

But Mr. Gorse invited her in. She said good-bye to us with that same uneasy air, and the door shut behind them.

In the lobby, Principal Gorse's secretary, Connie, smiled and held up two green late passes. "How's Trudy, boys?"

Connie knew Aunt Trudy from their gardening club. Together, they'd helped make an untended plot in back of the school into an overflowing vegetable garden. The cafeteria even used the fresh veggies in its daily special. (Not that you could tell, really. If only Aunt Trudy would teach some cooking classes down there!)

"She's good," Frank said with a smile. "We'll tell her you say hi."

Connie nodded. "I'd appreciate that. Have a good day, boys."

I'm not sure Connie needed to bother with the late passes. Frank and I both had study hall in the cafeteria next with Coach Gerther, who barely glanced at the passes before grabbing them out of our hands and gesturing vaguely at the rows of tables. "Take a seat."

Coach Gerther was rumored to have lost 80 percent of his hearing in the Vietnam War, which made him the perfect teacher for study hall. The din regularly reached rock-concert levels. It was literally impossible to get any work done in there, unless your "work" involved studying the effects of loud noises on hearing over time. Frank and I settled at a table in the back, and Frank pulled out a notebook.

"So . . . ," he began. "About the speech . . ."

"Yo—Hardy boys!"

I looked up to see Sharelle Bunyan standing over us. Well, *looming* over us was more like it. She was the queen of pep. Although she was an old friend of mine from junior high, we'd drifted apart in high school. She was very popular (not that we were *un*popular—but she was definitely in the alpha group).

It was actually nice to see her. She had the same red curly hair she'd had as a kid, only now she wore her cheerleader uniform, with the Bayport High colors of green and gold and the school mascot—Bill the Bulldog—pictured snarling on the front.

"Hey, Sharelle. Long time no see. What's up?"

"I was hoping," she said, "that you guys would be able to volunteer for the blood drive." She sat down next to us. As she did, she accidentally dropped a clipboard she was carrying. It clattered to the floor. "Shoot!" She picked it up and dusted it off, then held it out under our noses. Apparently, we had no choice but to sign up. "Ball of energy" is how people used to describe her in junior high. I saw that the description was still applicable.

"Um, sure, Sharelle."

"Yeah, we're always happy to bleed for a good cause."

We were starting to add our names to the list when she spoke to us under her breath. As she did, her whole demeanor changed. She sounded panicky.

"Look, guys—I need your help," she whispered. Something about her mood was contagious. We lowered our voices to match hers and kept our heads down.

"What kind of help?" Frank asked.

"You know . . . with a *mystery*."

A mystery. There it was. You have no idea how a reputation as a teenage detective can complicate your life. Frank started to answer, but I gave him a nudge. He picked up on my wariness and stayed silent. The truth was, although it sounded harmless and kind of fun, this wasn't an innocent topic for us anymore. There were serious consequences for us involved with anything remotely connected to sleuthing. Consequences that Frank and I didn't talk about, because . . . well, we didn't like to *think* about them. Not that they would stop us. But we still had to be more careful now than we used to be.

"Why ask us?" I said cautiously.

"Oh, come on," Sharelle said. "Don't give me that. Everybody knows you guys are, like, Sherlock Squared. You're both packing heat, right?"

"Don't believe everything you hear, Sharelle."

"Well, anyway—I need help. Or . . . well, Neal needs help." She was the only person in school who did not refer to her older brother as Neanderthal Bunyan—yes, the same charming fellow who'd introduced Frank to his impending Internet fame this morning. He was also the star linebacker of the BHS football team.

"Is he all right? Did something happen to him?"

"Yes. He's . . . fine, more or less. Physically at least. But . . ."

She glanced around the hall. Clearly, she was uneasy discussing this out in the open. "Look, I'm going to ask for a bathroom pass. Can you guys follow me, and we can talk about it out by the vending machines?" It would be quieter there. Apparently, the blood drive had been a cover story to make contact with us.

She got up to lead us out of the cafeteria. I was cautious but curious. I started to follow her, but Frank said, "We'll meet you there in five."

Sharelle seemed puzzled. She looked like she wanted to say something, but instead she just nodded and walked off.

Frank watched her go up to Coach Gerther, get her pass, and head out the door. Then he turned to me, his expression dark. "Neanderthal Bunyan—asking us for help," he said. "That doesn't seem odd to you?"

The truth was, it did.

It was six or seven months ago—before we had to retire. Joe and I had tracked down a drug ring. What we didn't know or anticipate was the series of busts around town that would follow—the consequences of our investigation, including the arrest of the former star linebacker for the Bayport High School football team, Neal "Neanderthal" Bunyan, all-state three years running, who had apparently been abusing steroids.

Neanderthal Bunyan had good reason to enjoy seeing Frank and me humiliated. Would he even accept our help?

"Let's just be careful," Frank suggested.

It might be a challenge, in some classes, for two brothers to get bathroom passes for simultaneous bathroom trips. But fortunately, Coach Gerther had stopped caring a long time ago, possibly before we were born. He grabbed two passes from a big coffee can he kept on his desk and waved us away.

We found Sharelle waiting where she said she'd be, by the vending machines. Frank and I took a seat on either side of her.

"So what's going on with Neanderthal?" I said.

"Okay," she said in an excited whisper. "This, like, totally *insane* thing has been happening. . . ."

MONITORED 5

FRANK

'M NOT SURE WHO WAS THE LEAST COMFORT-
able when Sharelle led Joe and me into Neanderthal
Bunyan's bedroom that afternoon. Neanderthal was lying
back on his bed, all his attention focused on the football-
themed video game he was playing on the TV that hung
on the wall.

"Get out, Sharelle," he said without looking up, but when
three people walked in, and not one, he sighed, hit a pause
button, and looked up.

"Oh," he said, looking startled and not pleased. "It's—"

"You need help, Neal," Sharelle said in a bossy voice. I
had a sudden premonition of what it might feel like to have
Sharelle as a sister, and a chill ran down my spine. "I asked
these guys to come over because I knew you never would."

Neanderthal didn't say anything. He was staring from me to Joe with a curled lip, like he smelled something horrible. "I don't need any help from these two," he said, and picked up the game controller again. He unpaused the game and turned his attention back to the screen. "You can show yourselves out," he finished.

Fair enough. I touched Joe's arm and started heading for the door. We weren't supposed to be doing any investigation right now . . . so why waste time trying to convince a guy who didn't even want our help? But Joe seemed to hesitate, looking to Sharelle. Suddenly she jumped forward, grabbing the controller from her brother's hand.

"HEY!" Neanderthal yelled.

"HEY YOURSELF!" she shouted back, matching him on volume. She gestured to me and Joe. "I asked these guys to come over today because even though you don't have the best history, they're the only ones who can help you," Sharelle finished.

Neanderthal pursed his lips. Clearly, he didn't like the direction of this conversation. But I could tell that Sharelle's words were making a dent. He let out a groan and looked down at his New York Giants comforter. Then he crossed his arms and settled back against the head of his bed, still scowling, still not looking at us.

"Do you want to tell them what happened?" Sharelle asked, moving closer to the bed.

Neanderthal shook his head. "You tell them," he muttered.

Sharelle turned back to face Joe and me. "Okay," she said. "About a week ago, Neal started getting some very weird e-mails."

I nodded slowly. "Weirder than the e-mail this morning with the link to the movie trailer?"

Neanderthal gave me a contemptuous look. "Dude, way weirder than that," he said. "What do I care about you guys getting robbed in some bank? No, this was . . ." He trailed off, staring off into the distance, fear invading his expression.

Not sure how to proceed, I looked to Sharelle. "This was?" I prompted.

Sharelle looked at Neanderthal, as though waiting to see whether he could pull himself together and finish the story. When he didn't move for a few seconds, she sighed and turned back to us. "This was really creepy," she said. "The address was one he didn't recognize, and the e-mail itself was just a link. No signature, no message."

I looked at Joe. This was sounding familiar. "Okay . . . and?"

Sharelle paused and looked at her brother. "Tell them, Neal."

We both turned to face Neal. He was staring at the black television screen, and as we watched, he seemed to shake himself off and looked down at his comforter. "The link went to a video," he said, then swallowed. "The video was . . . it was of me sleeping," he said quickly, then shook his head again.

I looked at Joe. He looked just as confused as I felt. "Sleeping?" he asked. "As in . . ."

"As in right here, in this bed," Neanderthal said, patting

the mattress beneath him. "I don't know when it was taken. Or how. Or by who. But whoever made it . . ." His voice wavered. "They were watching me all night."

I met Joe's eyes. "Wow. That's really . . ."

"Creepy," Joe finished. He shivered a little. "Man, I think I have the willies now."

Neanderthal looked a little relieved. "Yeah?" he asked. "It's freaking me out too. I just don't know who would want to watch me sleep—or why."

"That's not all," Sharelle added.

"It's not?" I asked.

Neanderthal was shaking his head. "No," he said. "The really creepy thing is, it's happened more than once. I've gotten three videos e-mailed to me over the last five days."

I frowned. "So whoever's watching you sleep—they might be doing it a lot."

Neanderthal nodded. "And it looks like—I mean, this really creeps me out, but it looks like you can watch the video feed live on the web. They e-mail me links to the recordings, but there's also a link to watch the live video." He paused. "I just don't get it," he said finally. "I don't know who would want me monitored. I don't think I have any enemies—I mean, besides you guys."

Touché. I looked at Joe.

"Can we see them?" he asked.

Neanderthal looked a little uncomfortable, but he nodded. "Yeah, let me just fire up my computer."

While he walked over to the desk on the left side of the room and opened up a blue laptop, I took a quick scan of the room, looking for anything suspicious and cameralike. Nothing stood out, though. Neanderthal had a surprisingly minimalist decorating style. Whoever had hidden a camera in here must have really tried hard.

After a minute or so, Neanderthal called us over to his computer. He had a web browser open to his e-mail. "Here it is."

He clicked on a message from youreup@fastmail.net. There was no subject, and when the message opened, it contained only a link.

Neanderthal clicked on the link, and a grainy black-and-white video started up.

It took me a minute to figure out what all the shapes were in the dim light, but then I could make out Neanderthal, in his bed, tossing and turning, then lying still.

The video was silent apart from the sound of Neanderthal breathing and the occasional creak of the springs in his mattress.

"Whoa," muttered Joe.

"Have you looked for a camera?" I asked. I turned in the direction the video was shot from; it looked like the camera had been on Neanderthal's shelf of sports trophies.

"That's the really creepy thing," Neanderthal said, clicking back to the web browser and opening up another e-mail. He clicked on that link, and another grainy black-and-white video started up, this one shot from a totally different direction. It looked like this camera had been posted just above his door. What the . . . ?

"Every time I get a video, I look for the camera," Neanderthal explained, "but I never find anything. Not even anything they might have hidden the camera inside. It's like each time they film me, they're sneaking in a camera, then coming back in, taking it out, and . . ."

"And uploading the video and sending you the link," Joe finished.

Neanderthal nodded. "I keep searching my room," he said. "Every night before bed, I look for a camera. But I never find it. Lately . . ." He stopped and rubbed his temples. "Lately the videos start after I'm already asleep. I feel like they're sneaking in . . ."

"While you're sleeping?" I asked. Super creepy!

Neanderthal sighed and nodded. "I can't believe it either," he said. "The last couple nights, I've set my alarm to wake up at one in the morning, and then again at three. I figure I'll get up and check the web, figuring that if the video's running, I can at least find the camera."

I nodded. "And how's that worked out?" I asked.

Neanderthal and Sharelle exchanged a concerned look. "It hasn't," Neanderthal admitted. "I wake up in the morning and find that someone turned off the alarm."

A chill went down my spine. "Wow."

"We tried to set up our own camera the other night," added

Sharelle, "but when we tried to watch the footage, it was two hours of Neal sleeping, and then it just went black. It was like someone disabled the camera without ever being seen."

Joe's mouth was hanging open. "That is . . . wow."

Sharelle turned to me. "We have a burglar alarm," she said. "My parents set it every night when they lock the door, which is hours before Neal goes to bed. It monitors all the doors and windows. But lately we've noticed after each time, the alarm has been turned off somehow."

Joe shook his head and let out a low whistle. "How're they doing it?" he asked.

I looked around the room, then walked over to the windows, giving them a little jiggle. Everything looked really secure.

"Is there anyone outside the family who has the code to the alarm?" I asked.

"No way," Sharelle scoffed. "Mom guards that code with her life. She wouldn't even give it to either of us till we turned sixteen."

I nodded slowly, looking at Joe. He looked just as lost as I felt.

"Okay," I said, trying to gather my wits. "I'm glad you reached out to us, Sharelle, because I think we can help. Here's what we're going to do. . . ."

6

THE ARROW

JOE

I HAVE TO ADMIT THAT I WAS A LITTLE STUNNED when Frank started with the "Here's what we're going to do." Because I had no idea what to do. Whoever was monitoring Neanderthal had reached a level of creepy I had only encountered in horror movies and bad dreams. I was no fan of the guy, but even I had trouble imagining what he could have done to deserve this.

When Frank explained further, though, it started to make sense. Whoever was monitoring Neanderthal was good. Clearly, he—or she—knew how to break into a secure house, plant a camera, feed all the footage to the Internet, and do it all without being caught—despite Neanderthal and Sharelle both knowing that this was going on.

It didn't make sense to try to beat that person at their

own game. As Frank explained, all we could do, for now, was try to observe the monitor.

I yawned as Frank fired up his laptop and got on the web.

"Really?" Frank asked, smirking. "Already? It's ten o'clock."

I shook my head. "That was a stress-relief yawn," I said. "I'm tense. Animals yawn to release tension."

Frank looked skeptical. "Either way, maybe I should take the first shift while you take a nap."

I blinked, watching the screen as Frank opened up the e-mail that Neanderthal had forwarded to us and clicked on the link. Nothing was up yet—just a big black box that said WATCH FOR COMING ATTRACTIONS!

"I can watch with you for a while," I said, making myself comfortable with some pillows on Frank's bed. "So hey . . . do you think Seth Diller is involved in this?"

Frank frowned as he stared at the screen. "That was my first thought too," he admitted. "It just seems like too much of a coincidence. Neanderthal comes to us about this strange, video-related trouble, the same day that . . ."

"Seth Diller gets arrested for causing trouble with his video camera," I finished.

Frank nodded grimly. "But it seems a little . . ." He paused, searching for the right word.

"Sophisticated?" I suggested. Seth's movies were endlessly entertaining . . . but sophisticated they were not.

Frank sighed. "I was going to say sinister," he finished.

That made me sit up. "Sinister?" I asked. "You don't think making me commit a felony and then kidnapping me was sinister?"

"Seth knows you," Frank explained, and at my incredulous expression, added, "Well, a little bit. He knew you could handle what he was dishing out."

"And Neanderthal?" I asked. Neanderthal had never struck me as a delicate flower.

Frank shivered. "This is just creepier. I don't know that anyone could handle what he's getting."

I didn't say anything to that. After a few seconds I yawned again.

Frank didn't lift his eyes from the computer. "I don't know. Might be torture to watch someone sleep while you're sleepy yourself."

"I don't know what you're talking about," I said. "I'm very perky."

Frank snorted, and then the black box on the screen suddenly filled in with the darkened image of Neanderthal's room. Neanderthal lay in a big lump on the left side of his double bed. The comforter was pulled up to his chin, and his breathing was regular. But there was something off about him. He looked weirdly stiff.

"He's awake," I said.

"Wouldn't you be?" Frank asked.

Well, yeah. It actually impressed me that Neanderthal was getting any sleep at all these days. I would have a really hard time forgetting that someone was about to break into my room and broadcast my sleeping form on the Web. You'd have to count a lot of sheep to fall asleep under those circumstances, I figured. I thought of my own tried-and-true trick to get myself to sleep: counting, naming, and picturing the crooks Frank and I had put away, one by one, starting from the earliest and moving on toward the most recent. There was Bruce Fishkill, the kid who'd stolen the class hamster in first grade. Nasty little kid—and I know it's not nice to call children nasty but really, this kid was something else. When we went out for recess after it rained, he would run around stomping on all the worms who'd been flooded out of their holes. And that still doesn't even come close to what he did to Jeannie Gilbright's chocolate milk that one time. . . .

"Joe. JOE!"

I was startled awake by a swift kick from my brother.

"Not in the milk!" I mumbled, blinking and shaking my head.

Frank was pointing at the computer screen. "Get serious, bro. We've got action here."

I swiped the backs of my hands over my eyes and sat up, feeling dizzy. Frank was pointing at the picture of Neanderthal sleeping—and he did really seem to be sleeping now.

"What's up?" I asked. "I don't see any—OH, CRAP!"

My brother and I have seen a lot of things, and generally, I think you'll find, we're pretty unflappable. But sometimes you see something and the only proper human response is OH, CRAP!

Like when you're watching live video of one of your class-mates sleeping and a figure dressed all in black, and wearing one of those rubber Halloween masks—Jay Leno, I think—suddenly pops into the bottom right corner of the image and waves at the camera.

"What is he doing?" I asked, thinking out loud. I have a nasty habit of doing that when I'm under stress. "What is he doing there? Is he going to—OH, CRAP!"

Another figure appeared in the bottom left corner, this one wearing a Conan O'Brien mask, and also waved. Then they both turned and started advancing toward Neander-thal.

Frank grabbed his phone off his nightstand. "That's it. I'm calling the police."

I didn't argue.

"I thought this was a prank," I said as Frank dialed 911. "It was creepy, sure, but I thought it was harmless."

The moment the word "harmless" left my mouth, Jay Leno grabbed Neanderthal's sleeping form, lifted him from the pillow, and—BLAM!—punched him in the face.

Frank's mouth dropped open. "Oh my— Hello? Yes, I'm calling to report a break-in and assault at 83 Hillside Drive. . . ."

There was no sound in the video, but Neanderthal was definitely awake now, and I could see him let out a scream before Conan pulled out a few inches of duct tape and stuck it over his mouth.

Together, Jay and Conan pulled Neanderthal off the bed. He was out of frame, but I could see the two masked intruders railing back to punch him again.

Frank was finishing up his call. "Okay. Okay, then. Thank you."

He clicked off his phone and looked at me. His expression was serious. "They're sending the police." Then he reached over to his desk and grabbed the car keys.

"Let's go save a football player," he said grimly.

A police cruiser was already sitting in the Bunyans' driveway when we arrived, lights flashing.

Frank and I jumped out of the car and ran up to the front door. Through the window, we could see quite the little convention gathered in the brightly lit living room: Sharelle, her mother, two officers . . . but I didn't see Neanderthal.

A big, burly man with wild gray hair and a bushy mustache pulled open the door and regarded us suspiciously. "You two called the police?" he demanded, in a not-exactly-grateful tone.

The door behind him swung open another inch, and I could see Neanderthal standing there. He was okay! He had a black eye and he looked—well—uncomfortable, but he was still standing.

Frank nodded. "Yes, sir. Neander—Neal asked for our

help with his problem, and we saw that someone had broken into his room. I called the police right away."

Neal's father let out a snort and walked away. *So much for gratitude,* I thought.

Actually, I realized as I scanned the room, nobody looked exactly happy to see us. Least of all Officer Olaf, who was standing next to his new partner—a rookie—and frowning at us.

"Neal here seems to think you overreacted," Officer Olaf said, tapping the tip of his pen against his notebook. "He says what you witnessed was some sort of football team prank. Right, Neal?"

We turned to face Neal, who was wearing a fleecy blue robe with flannel pants and looked supremely uncomfortable. "That's right," he said, but he wasn't quite meeting my eyes—or Frank's. He was looking past us, at the wall behind our heads. He made a face and shrugged. "It was a joke. You know, no big deal. The guys took off when they heard the police. They were really freaked."

Frank looked at Officer Olaf. "And you didn't chase them?"

Olaf glared at him. "Your friend here seems to think no crime was committed," he says. "The window was open. His friends snuck in to play a prank."

Instinctively, I turned to Sharelle. She was looking at her big brother, concerned, but she wouldn't meet my eyes either (or Frank's). I glanced at my brother, who looked just as confused as I felt. What was going on here?

Frank cleared his throat. "Well, gosh, we're sorry to waste everyone's time," he said, staring daggers at Neanderthal. "We sure could've sworn we witnessed a violent assault on Neal that was broadcast over the Internet. But maybe we were misinterpreting."

Neanderthal still wouldn't look at Frank. He crossed his arms in front of his chest and looked at the carpet.

I had an idea. "Hey, Neal, I think I left my phone in your room when we were here earlier," I said. "You wouldn't mind taking us back there so I can grab it? Maybe you can explain what happened, too."

Officer Olaf sighed deeply and shoved his notebook at his rookie partner. "Gosh!" he said, clearly mocking us. "Oh, golly gee! We're the Hardy Boys, and we sure are sorry to waste the taxpayers' time and money." He stomped toward us and paused to glare at my brother, then me. "Typical," he muttered, shaking his head. "When are you two going to learn to mind your own business?"

He stomped past us, out the door. His rookie partner looked befuddled, then smiled nervously at everyone and followed him. "Um, good night. Sorry to barge in on you all."

Neanderthal nodded at Frank and started walking down the hall toward his room. We both followed. Behind us, Neanderthal's parents looked at each other, shrugged, and started turning off the lights.

Once we were back in Neanderthal's room, I closed the

door behind us. "You want to explain to us what the heck just happened?"

Neanderthal sighed. He moved around his bed, picking a pair of socks up off his floor and throwing them into his hamper. "I'm sorry you guys misunderstood," he said quietly.

"Misunderstood?" said Frank. He stepped forward. "Neal, come on. We agreed to help you, and you just made fools of us." He paused and looked around the room. "Where's the camera? Or did they take it back?"

Neanderthal didn't answer. He was rubbing his shoulder thoughtfully. His eyes kept going to this one spot on the floor.

"Are you hurt?" I asked. He wasn't obviously bleeding or anything, but Jay and Conan might have done all kinds of damage before the police showed up.

Neal shook his head. "I told you," he said. "It was just a joke. No big deal."

I could tell that my normally coolheaded brother was starting to get frustrated. "Was this some kind of warped revenge thing?" he asked, moving closer. "Is that it? Because—"

Suddenly Frank reached out and yanked down the sleeve of Neanderthal's robe. Neanderthal jumped and grabbed at the sleeve, but not before we saw his shoulder and the top of his arm—which were covered in bruises.

"Neal!" I cried, moving closer. "That doesn't look like my idea of a joke."

Neanderthal backed away, yanking his robe back on and

crossing his arms. "You guys, come on. I think you should leave."

"Not before you explain what's going on," Frank insisted. He lowered his voice. "Why are you lying?" he asked. "What really happened tonight? You can tell us."

Neanderthal didn't respond, just stared at the floor and shook his head. After a few seconds of silence—during which we didn't leave—he finally raised his eyes to meet Frank's.

They were full of fear.

"Please," he said finally, in a low voice. "If you know what's good for you—or me—you will forget that Sharelle ever asked you here. It was a misunderstanding, okay? I don't need your help."

Frank frowned, then turned to me. I shook my head, mystified. What could it take to scare Neanderthal Bunyan— one of the biggest meatheads in school—this badly?

"Okay," I said after a minute or so. "We'll take your word for it, Neal. If you want us to leave, we'll leave."

I looked at Frank and raised my eyebrows, like, *Shall we?* Personally, I was done trying to make nice with Neanderthal. Obviously, something was going on with him. But if he didn't want to tell us about it, so be it.

Frank hesitated before nodding. Before he moved, though, he turned back to Neanderthal and lowered his voice. "If you ever want to tell us what's really going on," he said, "we're here."

Clearly, Frank has more patience than I do. I was already fantasizing about my nice warm bed and the four or so hours of sleep I could still get if we hightailed it home. But when we turned to walk out the door, something jumped out at me.

It was right over Neal's bedroom door—just above the center of the door frame.

A tiny red triangle with what looked like little legs coming out of it. Painted on, like with a stencil.

It definitely hadn't been there when Frank and I had come by earlier.

In fact, it was shiny. Was the paint still wet?

I pointed. "Neal—what the heck is that?"

Neal's reaction was brief but intense. His face turned scarlet and his eyes widened like a ghost had appeared behind us. But then he looked down at the floor and shook his head, and when he faced us again, he looked totally nonchalant.

"What do you mean?" he asked. "That red thing? Just something stupid Sharelle and I painted up there when I was little."

Frank stared at the symbol. "I could swear that wasn't there be—"

But Neal kept talking, drowning him out. "We were into Native Americans. Arrowheads. You know."

He walked around his bed toward us, then opened the door and raised his voice. "Well, bye now. You two sleep well."

My brother and I regarded each other warily. Neanderthal's parents could clearly hear us now. No way he was going to reveal anything else.

"Okay," I said, strolling through the door. "Well, good night."

Frank didn't look terribly eager to leave, but it was clear he got the message too. We walked down the hallway to the living room and the front door. As we were about to leave, a figure jumped up off the couch in the darkened room, startling us.

Sharelle.

She walked over, not quite meeting our eyes. "Good night, guys," she said, and then, lowering her voice so only we could hear her, "Sorry."

Frank leaned closer and lowered his voice to match hers. "I don't suppose you want to tell us what's really going on?" he whispered.

Sharelle looked up at him. Her eyes were full of regret. "See you around," she said, in her normal tone.

I sighed. "Right," I said, walking through the door behind my brother and closing it behind us. "See you around."

PANIC PROJECT 7

FRANK

I DON'T KNOW ABOUT JOE, BUT I DIDN'T GET much sleep when we finally got home from our aborted attempt to save Neanderthal Bunyan's life. Something about the way he'd looked at me—*If you know what's good for you, or me*—with his eyes full of fear. It was an emotion I normally didn't associate with football players. It just creeped me out.

In the morning, as I drove to school, Joe suddenly piped up. "It was revenge," he said decisively.

"What?"

"The whole deal at Neanderthal's house last night," he said. He was looking out the window thoughtfully, watching Main Street fly by. "It has to be some cockamamie plot of his to get revenge for being put away somehow, I've decided."

I snorted. "Well, if you've decided, it must be true," I said sarcastically.

Joe turned away from the window. He looked stung.

"Sorry," I said. "I'm just not so convinced."

"What else could it be?" Joe asked, holding out his hands in a beseeching gesture. "I've run though everything in my head. The Mafia. Zombies. Killer robots."

"I think it could be killer robots," I muttered, pulling into the parking lot. But he wasn't paying attention, which was sort of why I'd said it. I didn't think there were killer robots. In Bayport.

"Unless you believe there's a force out there that could scare Neanderthal Bunyan into total submission," Joe went on, "which I don't . . . the only logical explanation is revenge."

I pulled the car into our usual parking space, put it in park, and turned off the engine. Neither one of us made any move to get out of the car just yet.

"It could be Seth Diller," I said finally.

Joe wrinkled his nose. "Pfft," he said. "Seth Diller."

I looked at him. "You were the one who thought he was sinister enough to pull this off."

Joe was staring out the windshield now. "That was before last night," he said.

"Before the beating?" I clarified.

"Before I saw Neanderthal Bunyan with the poop scared out of him," he corrected me.

I looked out the windshield. A bunch of freshman cheer-

60

leaders were running around with "spirit boxes" they'd made for the football players. They contained cookies, usually. I noticed Sharelle among them, carrying a shoe box decorated in the BHS colors. Maybe it was just me, but it looked like some of the pep had been sucked out of her. She seemed to walk a little more slowly and carefully, like something was pressing her down from above.

Maybe Neanderthal's situation—whatever it was—was weighing as heavily on her as it was on us.

"We should still talk to Seth when he's back," I said, unbuckling my seat belt and grabbing my backpack. The first bell was going to ring in three minutes. It occurred to me that since the bank "robbery," I'd made absolutely no progress on my speech.

Detective work and schoolwork never mixed well. Which was part of the reason for the Deal.

Joe sighed and unbuckled his seat belt. "Great," he said, taking his turn at sarcasm. "I'm sure Seth will be really psyched to talk to us."

"Hey, Seth."

Joe and I had caught up with our favorite prankster in the hot-food line in the cafeteria. When he was back three days later, he seemed to be torn between the ravioli and the meatballs.

"Go for the special of the day," Joe advised. His tray was already piled high with it.

Seth looked at both of us like he'd just lost his appetite. He looked at Joe's tray and his expression worsened. "What is it?" he asked Joe.

Joe looked down. "Mostly peas," he replied neutrally.

Seth sighed and shook his head, turning back to the line. "Ravioli, please," he asked the lady behind the trays.

"Bad choice," Joe said, looking disappointed. "Did you hear about when Winnie Maxwell found a tooth in her ravioli?"

Seth grimaced. "A human tooth?"

Joe looked at him frankly. "Does it matter?"

We had made it to the cashier now, and Seth paid first, then promptly tried to lose us by running off to a table in the back. The Hardy Boys are pretty quick with cash, though. We paid and were able to catch up to Seth within seconds.

"We need to talk to you," I said, not interested in wasting any more time.

Seth looked straight ahead. "I'm not interested in talking to you," he replied.

"Come on," said Joe. "In my opinion, you still owe me for making me walk all the way home from where that police cruiser dropped me off."

Seth glared at him. "And in my opinion, you can never repay me for making me spend four hours in jail last night."

Four hours? What an amateur. "What, your parents wouldn't pick you up?"

Seth sighed and nodded. "My dad is not talking to me this century," he said. "As of yesterday. Thanks to you."

"Really, thanks to you, Seth," I pointed out. "As I have mentioned before, you did kind of rob a bank."

"And as I have mentioned before," Seth replied, "it was a harmless prank."

Hmm. The three of us had reached the end of the cafeteria, but stubbornly, Seth made no move to sit down, probably not wanting to invite a long conversation. I gestured to the table behind us. "Shall we?"

But Seth shook his head deliberately back and forth, like a kindergartener. "Can you just say what you need to say and we'll be done with it?"

Joe was frowning, thinking about something. "Hey, how did you get access to the cruiser?" he asked.

"What?"

"The police cruiser," he clarified. "For your little harmless prank."

Seth raised his chin defiantly. "I know people."

Interesting. "What kind of people?" I asked.

"Important people," Seth replied. "City people."

"And they were willing to go along with your dangerous prank?" I asked. "Who was this?"

"I'll never tell," Seth replied. "I protect my allies. Look, can we get to the point?"

I glanced at Joe. "Neal Bunyan," I said simply.

Automatically, Seth's eyes went to the table toward the front where the football players—even former ones like Neanderthal—always sat. But Neal wasn't there today. He hadn't come to school. I wasn't sure whether to be worried about that.

Seth looked confused. "What about him?"

I put my tray down on the nearest table, pulled out my phone, and went into my e-mail. I still had the message Neanderthal had forwarded to me the day before, with the link to the video footage. I clicked on it and held it up for Seth. "See that?"

Seth squinted, then frowned. "Is that Neal?" he asked. "Sleeping?"

"Someone's been breaking into his house to film him sleeping and broadcast it on the Web," Joe explained.

"What? Why?" said Seth.

"I don't know," I said, giving Seth an accusing look. "Why?"

"Wha-what are you . . . ?" Seth looked down at the video again. "Why would I want to film Neal Bunyan sleeping?"

Joe leaned closer, lowering his voice. "Maybe so that when a couple of masked goons broke into his bedroom last night and beat him up, you'd get the whole thing on video."

Seth stared at Joe, stunned. "What?"

"Tell us the truth, Seth," I said, leaning in. "Is this part of the Panic Project? Are you hoping we'll see Neal's beating on the big screen someday?"

Seth looked at my phone, horrified, and shook his head. "No!" he insisted. "Look, we might disagree about the bank heist prank, but I would never plan a prank for Panic Project that involved someone really getting hurt."

"How do we know you're telling the truth?" Joe asked.

"Well, for one," Seth said, "I was at the police station until midnight last night, and then my parents took me right home." He paused. "As you might imagine, they were keeping a pretty close eye on me. I think they'll vouch for me being home all night."

Hmm. The beating had started a little after midnight. Admittedly, it would be pretty hard for Seth to get out of jail, put on black clothes and a mask, and run to Neal Bunyan's house to beat him up.

But Joe looked less than convinced. "That doesn't mean you couldn't have gotten someone else to do it," he pointed out. "Maybe one of the important people you know?"

He had a point. "What else have you got?" I asked.

Seth sighed. "I—I—" He stopped and looked at the screen on my phone. The video had stopped. He put his tray down, reached over, and restarted the video. Then he smiled and pointed. "Aha!"

"Aha?" asked Joe.

"That's not my camera," Seth said, pointing at the video. "It's way higher quality video than the one I have. This was made with a pretty expensive camera. See?"

He pulled out his own phone and played the bank robber video. Indeed, it was much grainier and less sharp than the video of Neal.

But Joe still looked skeptical. "That doesn't mean you only have one camera," he said.

Seth sighed. "Look," he said, pulling up his website on his phone. "Watch any video. Any movie I've made. I guarantee you, none of them will match the picture on this video."

We clicked through a few. Seth was right. Some of the video quality was better than his phone's, but none of them were as sharp as the video of Neanderthal.

"And how do we know you didn't buy this camera especially for the Neal project?" Joe asked. But I could tell from his tone that his heart wasn't in it. Seth had convinced him.

"That's, like, a thousand-dollar camera," Seth replied. "You can ask my parents. For real, I don't have that kind of money. If I was saving up for a camera like that, they'd know."

I looked at Joe. I could tell we were both thinking the same thing: Seth was telling the truth.

"Okay," Joe said finally. "We believe you. I guess the Panic Project is dead."

"As a doornail," said Seth bitterly. "Thanks to you guys."

"But let me ask you something." Joe put his tray down and grabbed his napkin. Then he pulled a pencil out from behind his ear—a Joe-ism, to make sure he always has something to write with in school—and sketched something on the napkin. "Do you know what this symbol is?"

Joe held up the napkin and I swear, Seth paled visibly. I grabbed the napkin to get a look myself and realized that it was the triangle-with-legs symbol we'd seen over Neal's door last night. Or early this morning, technically.

Seth seemed to pull himself together with effort. "Nope," he said finally. "Anything else?"

"You sure you've never seen that symbol before?" I asked, pointing at the napkin. "This one right here?"

Seth swallowed hard and shook his head. "Nope. Well, gotta go."

"Never?" asked Joe, seeming to pick up on Seth's reaction too.

Seth looked from Joe to me, his expression squirrelly. He was kind of a squirrelly guy in general, but this was a particularly squirrelly moment. "You guys have never seen that symbol before?" he asked.

"What does that mean?" Joe asked.

"What does what mean?" asked Seth. He gave an exaggerated shrug. "Where did you see it?"

"Over Neal's bedroom door," I said.

Recognition sparked in Seth's eyes, as if what we were telling him suddenly made sense. But just as quickly as it appeared, Seth buried it. "Well, I don't know what it is," he repeated. "Look, if you'll excuse me, I want to eat my ravioli now." He picked up his tray, and before Joe or I could decide whether to stop him, took off in the direction of the AV room.

SECRETS

8

JOE

"YOU SAW IT, RIGHT?" I ASKED MY BROTHER as we finally settled down at the table in the back of the cafeteria with our food. My peas were cold.

"What am I, blind?" asked Frank, poking at his turkey sandwich. Frank has this inexplicable distaste for the hot food in the cafeteria. He doesn't know what he's missing, in my opinion. "Of course I saw it. He was scared. The minute you showed him that symbol, whatever it is, he got scared."

I forked a few more peas, then tapped them against the tray. I was about to respond when Janine Kornbluth walked by on her way out of the cafeteria. When she saw me, she smiled and gave a little wave. I stared after her, unable to pull myself together enough to wave back.

I'll admit it wasn't the first time I'd been distracted by the thought of Janine Kornbluth. I'd noticed her a few weeks ago, her dark hair and pale face with the little crease between her eyebrows that meant she was thinking. We were in the same French class. I liked how quietly she did everything. Right down to the way she closed her locker, which she did quietly, instead of slamming it like I always did.

Good sense told me she was completely out of my league. I was too noisy, for one thing. But still, there had to be some way I could "sell her" on Joe Hardy. Although the perfect idea hadn't occurred to me yet, I was actively brainstorming.

"Joe?" Frank was saying. "JOE? HELLO?"

"Right. Sure. Triangle with legs," I responded, hoping he hadn't totally changed the subject and started talking about electrons or something. (This was Frank, after all.)

Frank looked amused. I was pretty sure he'd seen Janine pass by. "So we'll take a cab ride this afternoon," he said, and took a sip of lemonade.

Cab ride. Oh, *right*. "Sure," I said.

A cab ride was definitely in order to get to the bottom of this whole triangle business.

After school, Frank and I parked the car near the bus station, then hoofed it over to the cab stand. Bayport's bus station is not exactly a metropolitan hub, so it was quiet, between buses, and Frank and I were the only ones waiting for a cab. We had to wave away a couple (that is a surefire way to annoy a cabbie, by the way) before the cab we were looking for, from the Red Apple fleet, medallion number N567, pulled up to the curb.

Frank slid into the backseat, and I followed.

"One conference fare, please," Frank said as I slammed the door behind us.

The driver pulled the cab back onto Main Street, then drove slowly out of the downtown area, toward the more woodsy part of town where houses were few and far between.

"What can I help you boys with?" Professor Al-Hejin said after about ten minutes.

Professor Al-Hejin has been a trusted friend and confidant to Frank and me since we were just starting out this investigation thing. As a full-time cabdriver, the prof hears all the town's most salacious dirt. He knows everything about everything in Bayport. And he's usually willing to share it with Frank and me, because he knows we'll use it for good.

"If I show you a symbol," I said, "can you tell me if you've ever seen it before?"

Professor Al-Hejin met my eyes in the rearview mirror, thoughtful. "I believe so," he said. "Shall I pull over so you can hand it to me?"

I nodded. He pulled into the driveway of an abandoned house, as though he was going to turn around, then idled near the overgrown lawn. I pulled out my triangle-with-legs sketch from lunch that day and passed it through the glass divider to the prof.

Professor Al-Hejin held the napkin up so he could see it. He made no reaction at all. He didn't jump, or gasp, or turn around. In the rearview mirror we could see that his eyes were serious, completely focused on the drawing.

After a few seconds he took his hand off the wheel and very carefully folded the drawing in half. He handed it back to me through the divider, sketch on the inside, not meeting my eyes.

He put the cab in gear and was back on the road, headed back into town, before I could get the question out.

"Professor Al-Hejin? What is it?"

He didn't answer for a few seconds. I could see that his expression was grave, his mouth pulled into a tight line. "I will drop you back off at the bus station," he said quietly.

"What? Why?" asked Frank.

Silence. The woods whizzed by.

"Professor Al-Hejin, please talk to us," I begged as we drew closer to town.

More silence. I looked at Frank, and he looked as confused as I felt. What was going on?

"Professor Al-Hejin," said Frank, "if we insulted you, we didn't mean to. We're just trying to figure out what this symbol means."

"We have no idea," I added.

Professor Al-Hejin remained silent. After a few seconds, though, he pulled over to the side of the road. He sat still for a moment before catching my eye in the rearview mirror.

"Where did you see this symbol?"

I leaned forward. "Over the doorway to our friend's bedroom," I replied.

He looked stung, like that was terrible news. He shook his head, reached into his shirt pocket, pulled out a handkerchief, and wiped his forehead.

Frank and I were quiet for a while, wanting to give him whatever time he needed.

Finally he cleared his throat. "This is a bad symbol," he said simply.

"But what does it mean?" Frank asked.

The prof just shook his head. "Bad men," he said.

"What bad men?" I asked.

Professor Al-Hejin sighed loudly and took his foot off the brake. Within seconds we were back on the road to town.

"Professor," I pleaded as we sailed past factories and warehouses, "whatever you know, you can tell us. Whatever you're afraid of, we don't know anything about."

"We're just hoping to find out what the symbol means," Frank added, "so we can help our friend."

Professor Al-Hejin seemed to think that over. After a minute or so, he looked in the rearview mirror again. "Do you know what it means," he said quietly, "to be marked?"

"Marked, like, for punishment?" I asked. "For death or—I don't know—"

"Your friend is marked," the professor said, just as quietly. "You had best steer clear of him."

I met Frank's eye: *What?*

"How do you know about being marked?" Frank asked. "Were you marked?"

The cab jerked as Professor Al-Hejin suddenly pulled into a gas station. He pulled up to the convenience store and hit the brakes.

"You get out here," he said simply.

I looked at Frank. I had never seen the professor like this. He usually answered all our questions without hesitation. He knew us.

But now I didn't even think it was worth arguing. I'd never seen the professor so spooked.

"Okay," said Frank. He dug a few of Aunt Trudy's famous homemade health bars—these were cranberry with cashews and sesame seeds—out of a pocket in his backpack and handed them through the divider. The prof never let us pay him for the ride. But we liked to give him something for his time and trouble.

Now he hesitated, looking at the bars, then out the window. Frank pushed them forward again, as if to say, *Take them.*

"Please," Frank said. "I'm sorry if we made you uncomfortable."

Professor Al-Hejin slowly took the bars, then caught Frank's eye in the mirror and nodded.

"Bye, Prof," I said, opening my door and scooting out.

The professor nodded again and bit into one of the health

bars. As soon as Frank got out and shut the door behind him, the cab pulled off.

"I guess we're walking back to the station," I said, watching the cab disappear.

"I guess so," said Frank. "Good thing we're only a mile or two away."

I nodded. Slowly we made our way out of the gas station and started walking down the street in the direction of downtown.

"So what do you think?" I asked after a few minutes. We'd both been silent, lost in our own thoughts.

"I think," Frank said, looking serious, "that whatever this is, it's a lot bigger and more dangerous than what happened to Neanderthal."

THE DARK SIDE 9

FRANK

MY BROTHER AND I HAVE ALWAYS HAD kind of a Don't Ask, Don't Tell policy with our father about investigation, or at least we did up until the Deal went into effect. We never told him about cases we were investigating, nor did we ask for his help or advice based on his years of experience as one of the area's top detectives. In return, he never grilled us about how, exactly, we were spending all our free time, or whether we were breaking any laws to do whatever it was we were doing.

As Joe and I returned from our Cab Ride to Nowhere, however, we were both feeling like it might be time to get some advice from Dad. He was nothing if not plugged into the town of Bayport. If this triangle with legs really was as sinister as the professor had implied to us, surely Fenton Hardy had run across it at some point during his career.

When we got home, my mom was in the kitchen, frowning at some photos of a house she was getting ready to show. "No, no, no!" she was saying, circling things in the photo with a black Sharpie. "Not enough lighting! Too much clutter! People, get your shoes into a closet!"

"Got a tough one on your hands, Mom?" Joe asked gently. We Hardys all seem to be Serious about Something. Dad is Serious about the Law. Aunt Trudy is Serious about Food. Joe and I are Serious about Justice. And Mom is Serious about Real Estate.

Mom looked up with a smile. "Boys!" she said. "How have you been? Is your friend feeling better today?"

We'd told our parents that we left in the middle of the night to check on a classmate who'd been in a car accident and was rushed to the hospital. Broken leg, concussion, nothing serious.

"Yeah, great," Joe said. "Already hobbling around on crutches. Hey, Mom, is Dad around?"

Mom gestured to his study. "In his study with the door closed," she replied. "He's been in there all day. Says he's wrestling with a chapter on the Articles of Confederation. It's fighting back, I'm afraid."

Great. So Dad would be in a terrific mood. "Thanks, Mom." I gave her a quick kiss on the cheek, and Joe and I walked over to Dad's study and knocked on the door.

"Come in!" Dad's tone was smack in the middle between

Leave me alone and *Oh please, please, come in here and distract me from this horrible mess.*

"Hi, Dad," I said, pushing open the door and walking in with Joe behind me. Dad was sitting behind his desk, his shirt rumpled, his hair looking like he'd recently been trying to tear it out. (He doesn't have much, either, so that's just an indication of how tough this chapter must have been.)

"Boys," he said, sighing and leaning back in his chair. "Oh, why did I decide to make my career in writing? What demons were possessing me?"

Joe and I were silent. Actually, our dad had left his long career as a detective and taken up writing as part of the Deal. So arguably, the demons in question were Joe and me.

Which didn't exactly make us feel great.

"Dad," I said, deciding to get to the point, "I think Joe and I need to ask you something."

Dad looked at me, suddenly serious. I don't think we'd come in to "ask him something" in a long time . . . probably not since the legal troubles we'd had leading up to the Deal. He sat up straight in his chair, pushing his mouse and keyboard away.

"Sounds serious," he said. "What is it, boys?"

I looked at Joe and nodded. Slowly, he pulled out the napkin he'd sketched the triangle-with-legs symbol on and unfolded it, then pushed it to my father's side of the desk. Dad looked down at it, recognition dawning on his face and then, just as quickly, fear.

"Where did you boys get this?" he demanded in a tight voice.

I cleared my throat, suddenly nervous. "We saw it painted on the wall at a friend's house."

Dad took in a breath, and relief seemed to wash over his face. He grabbed the napkin, balled it up, and threw it in the wastebasket under his desk. "Then this is not something to concern yourselves with."

I looked at Joe. *What?*

"What if we think it's . . . um . . . causing problems for a friend?" Joe asked.

"Who is this friend?" Dad asked, turning his Detective Laser Gaze on my brother. "What has he—or she—gotten himself involved in?"

"Does it matter?" I asked, and then instantly regretted it when the Laser Gaze was pointed at me. I cleared my throat and then continued, more gently, "Is this symbol . . . is it a punishment of some kind? Does it mean someone's marked you?"

Dad sat back in his chair and sighed. He ran his hands through his hair, making it stick up more. "Every town has its dark side," he said, looking up at the ceiling and then back at us. "Why are you asking? What's going on with you boys? You're not investigating again, are you?"

"Of course not," Joe said quickly, reflexively.

I shook my head. "We understand the Deal," I said, not meeting Dad's eye.

"It's just . . ." Joe sat forward in his chair, beseeching Dad.

"This friend of ours. Bad things are happening to him, and he doesn't know why. Is it because of this mark?"

Dad leveled his gaze at Joe, his face neutral. "It could be," he said quietly. Then louder: "Listen, boys, under the circumstances, and with the troubles you're already facing, it is extremely important not to let it get around town that you're asking questions about this . . . this issue. Okay?"

"You mean the triangle with legs?" Joe asked.

"The wha—?" Our father stopped himself and laughed, seeming to get it. Then, just as quickly as it had appeared, the smile was gone. "I'm serious, boys. This is very, very serious business. Some things are best left alone. Uninvestigated. Do you understand? And one of those things is the Red Arrow."

Joe looked at me. *The Red Arrow,* he mouthed. So the triangle with legs had a name.

And our father knew it. And didn't want to talk about it.

Which, for Fenton Hardy, was pretty unusual.

"But, Dad, if the Red Arrow exists," I said, "and it's that terrible—so terrible that no one can even hear you talking about it—shouldn't someone do something about it?"

Dad looked at me. Hoo-boy. This look was even worse than the Laser Gaze. This was the Son, I'm Disappointed in You, But I'm Going to Let My Eyes Do the Talking Gaze.

"Well, Son," he said calmly, "you're assuming that someone hasn't already tried."

I took that in. My mind was reeling with questions: Does

that mean . . . ? Is he saying . . . ? But before I could decide whether even one of them was safe to ask, we were interrupted by loud, tinny music.

"Hit me baby one more time . . . !"

Joe sat up and reached into his pants pocket, yanking out his phone. "I like the classics," he told me sheepishly as he clicked the talk button. "Hello? Yeah, this is he . . . Yeah . . . No, that's . . . Oh no. Oh, man. Okay. Yes."

He clicked off the phone and looked up at Dad and me. "Um," he said awkwardly, "well, thanks, Dad, and point taken. Listen, I think I need to talk to Frank."

Dad nodded and waved us out of his study. "All right, I need to get back to this chapter. Remember what I said, boys."

We assured him that we would and stepped out of the study. Joe closed the door behind us and turned to me with a frantic expression.

"That was Sharelle," he whispered urgently. "Neal was hit by a car today. He's in the hospital!"

THE PAST

10

JOE

HOSPITALS ARE NOT HAPPY PLACES UNDER the best of circumstances, but when we spotted Sharelle in the lobby of the Bayport Memorial ER, we knew something big was up. Her face was streaked with mascara-y tears, and she was clinging to her cell phone like it was her only friend in the world.

"Frank! Joe!" she cried when she saw us come in. We ran over to her.

"What's going on?" Frank asked urgently.

Sharelle shook her head. "Oh, gosh," she breathed, closing her eyes. A couple more tears squeezed out of the corners, following the trails down her cheeks. "I don't know exactly, except that Neal was hit by a car downtown. It was going fast for the city, and he was unconscious when he came in. The hospital called our house, and I was the only one home. My parents are on their way from work in the city. The doctors are working on Neal now." She paused, then swallowed and squeaked, "I hope he's okay."

"I'm sure he will be, Sharelle," I said, putting my arm around her. I didn't know at all, of course, but I know a person who needs comfort when I see one. I glanced at Frank over Sharelle's head. His expression was as grim as I felt.

Someone had hit Neal with a car? After he'd gotten beat up last night? It couldn't be a coincidence.

We sat down in the uncomfortable plastic chairs that every hospital must buy from the same catalog. Sharelle was sniffling, digging soggy tissues out of her pocket and swiping at her eyes. Frank pulled a handkerchief—yeah, a handkerchief, he gets it from our dad—out of his pocket and handed it to her. Sharelle thanked him and pressed it to the corners of her eyes.

"Sharelle," Frank said in what I knew was his gentlest tone, "can you tell us what really happened last night?"

Sharelle sobbed, pressing the handkerchief to her eyes and then slowly, with shuddering breaths, calming herself. "I'm so sorry, you guys," she said, looking up at Frank and then me. "I know we put you in a really bad spot."

"You can make it up to us by telling us the truth," I suggested.

She took a deep breath. "Right. The truth." Rubbing the

handkerchief between her fingers, she stared down at it and started talking. "It was the police sirens that woke me up. By the time I got out of bed, the police were already at the door, talking to my parents. I didn't hear those guys break in or start beating up Neal. I wish I wasn't such a heavy sleeper. . . ."

She trailed off and stopped. Frank and I just watched her patiently, and a few seconds later she began again.

"As I walked out into the hall, Neal's door opened. He looked awful. Beat up, but more than that, more scared than I had ever seen him. Ever." She looked from Frank to me. "You guys are brothers. You know . . . when you grow up with someone, you see them at their best and their worst."

"You mean you'd seen him scared before," Frank said.

She nodded. "Right," she said. "Like, he hates roller coasters. Or you should have seen him when we rented *Paranormal Activity*. . . ." She shook her head. "Terrified. But this was way worse than that. This was like . . . he'd seen the ghost from that movie right in his bedroom. Like he'd seen the worst thing he could possibly imagine, and nothing could scare him worse."

I looked at Frank. It probably goes without saying, but that level of fear did not sound like it was caused by a football players' prank.

"I asked him what had happened," she said. "I was really worried about him. The police were there. I knew it had to be serious."

Frank nodded. "What did he say?"

She stopped and took in a breath, shaking her head. "He just said, 'Don't worry about it.'" She looked at me. "Can you believe that? Of course I was like, 'What?' and he said it again, 'Don't worry about it.'" She paused and bit her lip before continuing. "Then he took me by the shoulders," she said. "He looked me right in the eyes, and I could see how terrified he was. He said, 'Sharelle, if you care about me at all—don't worry about it. Okay?'"

I frowned. "So what did you do?" I asked.

Sharelle shrugged and looked at me again. "What could I do?" she asked. "I was really freaked out. I said okay. And then Neal said that no matter what happened, I had to back him up, and I said I would. I had never seen him like that."

I looked at Frank. I knew that he, too, was thinking about the conversation we'd just had with our dad. *Some things are best left alone.*

It seemed like Neal Bunyan certainly believed that. Even as terrible things were happening to him. What scared him—and Professor Al-Hejin, and my dad—so much? What could be worse than someone sneaking into your house in the middle of the night and beating you up?

As I was pondering this, a nurse came over. "Miss Bunyan," she said, gently touching Sharelle's shoulder, "your brother is resting in a room and ready to see you now."

Sharelle jumped up, turning back to gesture for Frank and me to follow her. "Let's go."

The nurse gently stopped her. "I'm sorry, it's immediate family only."

Sharelle stopped and regarded the nurse. She was, as I might have implied previously, not someone who was easily dissuaded. "These are my brothers," she said simply.

The nurse looked from Sharelle—who resembled a red curly-haired fireplug—to serious, dark-haired Frank, to me. I have been told I look like a young Owen Wilson without the nose. And with a chin. Which I guess means I don't look much like Owen Wilson at all. But anyway, my point: I don't look all that much like Frank, and neither one of us looks anything like Sharelle.

The nurse seemed to get this, but as quickly as she registered it, I could see that she was making a decision not to ask. "Okay," she said, and smiled sympathetically at all of us. "Please come with me."

Neal was already set up in a shared room on the third floor, but the other bed was empty. He looked bad. His right leg was in traction, he had a jagged, stitched-up cut along his right arm, and he had two black eyes. The right side of his face was all scraped up, like he'd been dragged along the street.

Looking at him, all I could think was, *Ouch.*

"Neal!" Sharelle cried, running right to his side.

Neal looked happy to see her for just a few seconds before his eyes turned to Frank and me, and his expression darkened. "What are these two doing here?"

Sharelle gave her brother a frank look. "Neal, come on. I'm not playing around anymore. You could have been killed today."

Frank stepped forward. "Look, Neal, if someone is after you, don't you think you should tell someone about it?"

Neal glared at him. "It was an accident," he said stiffly.

Sharelle looked at him in disbelief. "Are you kidding me?" she asked. "After what happened last night, you expect me to believe this was random?"

Neal looked away. "I don't care what you believe," he said. "It was an accident. Just an accident."

There was silence for a little while, and in that silence I had an idea. "Hey," I said, turning to Sharelle, "how old were you when you and Neal got into arrowheads?"

Sharelle looked at me like I was out of my mind. "What?"

Frank caught my eye and nodded. "You know," he said, stepping forward. "When you painted that little figure above Neal's bedroom door? It looked like . . ." He gestured to me. I grabbed a notepad that was on the nightstand and started drawing, pushing the pad toward Sharelle when I finished.

Her jaw dropped.

"The Red Arrow?" she asked, turning toward Neal, who was already gesturing for her to lower her voice. "You got Red Arrowed and you weren't going to tell me?"

Neal shook his head. "*Shhhh!* Keep quiet, Sharelle."

"I'm not going to keep it quiet!" Sharelle glared down at him. "You know how freaking serious this is, Neal!"

Neal sighed and looked at his sister. It was clear from his expression that he did, indeed, know how freaking serious this was.

"Um," I said, raising my hand like I was in class. "Not to interrupt, but Sharelle, could you explain to us how freaking serious this is?"

She looked at me, unamused. "Come on," she said in a low voice. "You guys have lived in Bayport your whole lives, haven't you?"

I looked at Frank, who nodded. "More or less," he agreed.

"Then how do you not know about the Red Arrow?" she asked.

I sighed. "I'm realizing that we may be the last people in town who don't know," I admitted.

"But no one will talk about it," added Frank.

Sharelle looked grim. She seemed to be gearing up to tell us what she knew, but before she could begin, Neal broke the silence.

"It's like a curse," he said weakly, staring out the window. "It's been around forever. Nobody knows where it comes from or who's behind it. But if you find the mark of the Red Arrow on your stuff, your life is basically over."

Over? I looked at Frank. "You mean, they'll kill you?"

Neal didn't respond for a moment. "No," he said finally, "or I mean, not necessarily. Maybe your business will dry up. Maybe your boss will fire you the next day. Maybe the love of your life will suddenly decide she needs to move to Reno to find herself." He stopped and looked over at us. "Maybe a couple of masked guys will break into your house and beat you up. Or maybe someone will plow into you with their car while you're crossing with the light."

I frowned, confused. "That seems like pretty serious stuff," I said. "Why not report it to the police?"

Neal scoffed. "The police!" He shook his head. "Everyone who's ever reported it to the police . . . something worse happens to them before the police can do anything."

"You mean someone on the police force is in their pocket?" Frank asked.

Neal shrugged. "Maybe." He paused. "I don't know how far up this thing goes, but nothing would surprise me. The police. Firefighters. City officials. This has gone on forever, and sometimes it stops for a few years, but it never goes away."

Hmm. I was still taking all this in. Neal was basically telling me about a criminal organization that had been operating right under our noses for our entire lives. Was it possible that the Red Arrow had always been part of Bayport, and somehow escaped Frank's and my notice?

"Neal," Sharelle said, "why do you think this is happening to you? What did you do to tick someone off?"

Neal sighed. "I don't know," he said. "I've been trying to think about it. The only possibility I can come up with is . . . Pyro Macken."

Frank raised his eyebrows at me. Pettigrew "Pyro" Macken was a notorious troublemaker, the son of a wealthy blueblood family whose father was busted years ago by our dad. Frank, in turn, busted Pett a few years ago for arson (hence the nickname "Pyro"). He was sent to juvie. Now Pett's out, and he's mostly a harmless eccentric, quarreling with his family. I don't really think he's that dangerous. But Frank thinks otherwise. "Pett Macken is a grenade with the pin pulled," he told me once. "The fuse may burn for years. But one day he's gonna go off."

"Um . . . what did you do to Pett Macken?" he asked now.

Neal sighed. He looked like he wasn't proud of what he was about to tell us. "I kind of stole his girlfriend," he said. "I mean, not really. But at this party, I met a girl he'd been seeing for a few weeks and, well, we kind of ended up kissing." He shrugged. "And then she kind of told Pyro she didn't want to see him anymore. And we dated for a few weeks."

I could see the gears turning in Frank's head. "You think he was mad enough to hurt you?" he asked. I could tell that, in Frank's estimation, it wasn't exactly outside Pett's wheelhouse to cause somebody bodily harm.

Neal looked at Frank like it was clear. "Yeah. I mean, he's kind of crazy." He stopped and fingered the long, jagged cut along his arm. Then he added, almost as an afterthought, "He really hates you two, by the way."

PETT 11

FRANK

FTER THE WEAKLY LIT GLOOM OF THE
hospital, the bright sunshine and vibrant
sounds of Main Street were almost too
much, too overwhelming. It seemed strange
that life could go on, people could still be
shopping for groceries and doing laundry and paying parking tickets, when a shadowy criminal organization was terrorizing our town.

"What do you think?" Joe asked, crossing his arms and looking up at the sky. He seemed as startled by the bright, cool day as I felt.

"I can't believe this Red Arrow thing has been going on for years and we never knew," I replied.

"I can't believe Dad knew," Joe added.

"Maybe he was protecting us," I mused, looking up and down the street. "Hey, can I say something I'm pretty sure will surprise you?"

Joe shrugged. "Sure," he said. "It seems like a day for surprises."

"I don't think Pett is behind this," I said. Joe turned to me, an eyebrow cocked. "It's too sophisticated," I went on. "Pett is a psychopath. If he was going to go after you, he would hit you over the head with something big and heavy, douse you in gasoline, and set you on fire. There'd be none of this psychological torture kind of thing."

Joe seemed to consider what I was saying. "I don't think Pett even knows the word 'psychological,'" he agreed.

"This just seems too big for him," I concluded. "Not that he couldn't be involved."

Joe sighed. "Which leaves us back at square one," he said. "If it's not Pett, who could it be?"

I sighed. It had been such a long day. I didn't have the energy to reply. And I knew I didn't need to. Joe and I know each other well enough that I knew we were both feeling the same thing.

"Hey," I said, pointing at the restaurant across the street. "Do you see that?"

"What?" Joe followed my gaze.

"Over the doorway there," I said. "Come on."

I led Joe over to the crosswalk, where we waited for the light and then crossed. (*Although that didn't help Neanderthal,*

I thought grimly.) Then we walked over to the restaurant I'd seen, which looked like it was in the process of being renovated and wasn't currently open.

Over the door, a small triangle-with-legs symbol had been painted.

"The Red Arrow," Joe and I breathed at the same time.

"So what do you think?" Joe asked. "Did the owner tick off the same person as Neanderthal?"

"Or maybe someone different, but who's involved in the same criminal organization?" I suggested. "How big do we think this thing is?"

"Neal said it was big," Joe pointed out. "Really big. Remember—he wouldn't be surprised if there were city officials involved."

I frowned, thinking that over. "Let's take a walk," I suggested.

Joe followed me as I led the way down Main Street. We took a meandering route, wandering along the side streets, through the parking lots, past city buildings.

"Look," Joe whispered, pointing at a bulkhead that led into a basement under On Second Read, the town bookstore. A tiny Red Arrow symbol had been painted there—and was already fading.

We saw another one stenciled over the window of an apartment on the second floor of a building on River Road. And a third—very tiny—painted on a bike chained to a rack in Heller Park.

"It's everywhere," I said. "Has it always been everywhere? Have we just not seen it?"

Joe shook his head but didn't reply.

"What kind of detectives are we?" I asked. "These have been hiding in plain sight for how long?"

Joe walked over to a bench and sat down. I sat down next to him. Together, we looked back at the main square of the town we'd grown up in, the town we'd almost derailed our whole future investigating and trying to clean up. Was it possible that Bayport was still keeping secrets from us?

The side door of the library opened up, and out stepped Seth Diller.

Joe groaned.

Seth didn't seem to see us as he hustled across the street and into the park. He was nearly right on top of us before his eyes narrowed in recognition and he stopped short.

"Oh," he said, not looking very psyched to see us. "Frank and Joe Hardy."

"We meet again," Joe said, nodding.

"Neal Bunyan got hit by a car," I said, not even saying hello. "We were just visiting him in the hospital."

Seth's eyes bugged out. "Are you kidding?" he asked.

I shook my head. "I wish I were," I admitted. "But it's true. It seems like someone really has it out for him."

Seth nodded slowly. It looked like there was more he wanted to say, but he didn't.

"Seth," said Joe, pulling out the sketch I had drawn in the hospital, "are you sure you can't tell us about this symbol? Neal seems to think it's related to what's happening to him."

"Really?" Seth looked surprised. But his expression quickly returned to neutral. "I don't know anything about it."

"You've never seen it before?" I pressed.

Seth looked away. "I have to go." He pushed his backpack up on his shoulder, fished some car keys out of his jeans pocket, and started walking toward the parking lot. I glanced quickly at Joe, who nodded, and we both stood up and started walking with him.

"Seth," Joe said, "man, I'm a fan of yours. We go way back. You can tell us the truth!"

"Neal told us a little bit about it," I added. "We just want to know as much as we can. We're not accusing you of anything."

Seth was speeding up. We had to work to keep up with him. We reached the parking lot, and Seth clicked the button on his keys. A *beep* sounded from a nondescript silver coupe parked near the dog run. He hustled over to it, and Joe and I followed.

About ten feet away from the car, Seth stopped short. Joe and I didn't realize at first, and we almost went plowing into him.

"Oh my—oh," Seth stammered weakly. His face was paper white.

I looked at Joe and then followed Seth's gaze to the car. Within seconds I saw what was causing Seth's distress. Something was stenciled on the driver's-side window.

The Red Arrow.

RUMORS 12

JOE

SETH TRIED TO PLAY IT COOL, LIKE HE wasn't worried, but I could see him shaking as he walked over to the driver's-side door and opened it.

"Seth, come on," I begged, moving closer. "We saw the Red Arrow. We want to help you. Let us."

He climbed into the car and put the key in the ignition.

"Seth!" I yelled, moving around and banging on the windshield. "Come on!"

Seth looked at me through the windshield, his jaw set, his expression grave. "You guys can't help me," he insisted, looking from me to Frank, who was trailing a few steps behind. "Not with this."

Without another word, Seth slammed his door and

96

turned the key in the ignition. I backed away from the car just in time for him to throw it in drive and peel out of the parking lot.

Frank looked as worried as I felt. "What do you think will happen to him?" he asked.

I shrugged. "Hopefully, it won't be as bad as what happened to Neanderthal," I replied. "But I'm not feeling optimistic."

Frank sighed. "Let's go home," he suggested.

Home—and a nice home-cooked meal from Aunt Trudy—sounded pretty great right now. The sun had just gone down, and the streetlights made a warm glow against the inky-blue sky. It was the kind of night that made you want to be safe at home, tucking into a bowl of spaghetti or something.

Mmmmm. Spaghetti.

That's when I heard the *WEE-OO, WEE-OO* of a police siren right behind us.

I turned around and groaned. A cruiser had pulled up right behind us, as quiet as a mouse. Clearly, whoever was inside was looking to startle us.

The driver opened the door and climbed out, and I can't say I was surprised.

Officer Olaf. As Neanderthal had said of Pett earlier, he really hates us. Our investigations haven't exactly made Frank and me the most popular kids in town.

What's Officer Olaf's deal? I'm not really sure. Secret

insecurity about his mustache? Not enough affection from his mother? Possibly both of those, and more. But his problem with Frank and me seems to stem from the fact that we've caught a lot of crooks in this town—a lot more than he has, frankly. And I don't think he likes that. I don't think he likes looking like the ineffective cop he is.

"Look who it is," he said now, a smile hovering insincerely below his droopy mustache, "the Hardy Boys!"

"You seem happy to see us," Frank said. He nodded politely to Olaf's rookie partner, who was sitting in the passenger seat, looking like he'd prefer to be spared this whole sordid scene.

Officer Olaf grew serious. "Happy to have found you, yes. Happy about what I have to say? No." He furrowed his bushy eyebrows. "There are rumors around town that you boys have been asking about the Red Arrow."

Gulp. Who had told Olaf? I guess it didn't matter. It's impossible to keep a secret in a town like Bayport, where everybody knows everybody else's business. You sneeze and someone three houses down says, "Bless you."

Frank shot me a surprised look, then turned to Olaf. "Huh. Who told you that?"

At this point, I was distracted. From my viewpoint I could see, behind Olaf and his cruiser, the stores of Main Street. Specifically, I had a pretty good view of the restaurant that had the Red Arrow over the doorway. As I watched, an older man with glasses, wearing a sport coat, walked up to the door, carrying a box filled with what looked like pots and kitchen stuff. He put down the box, grabbed a key from his coat pocket, and unlocked the door. Then he disappeared inside with his box.

I'm not sure why this stood out to me, but something just seemed off with this guy. I'd been curious about the owner of this restaurant and what he might have done to anger the Red Arrow. This guy didn't look like a troublemaker or anything. He looked like he might be a math teacher. Or an accountant.

"Ohhhh, I see," Frank was saying. I'd missed whatever Olaf said to explain how he'd heard about our investigations. "No, what you heard about isn't an investigation at all. Joe and I are working on a project for our civics class."

Olaf looked dubious. (To be honest, I thought it was kind of a stretch too. Frank and I aren't even in the same grade.) He leaned his elbow on the hood of the cruiser. "About the Red Arrow?" he asked. "Your teacher approved that?"

Frank didn't miss a beat. "It's taught by Coach Gerther," he said quickly.

I saw movement back on Main Street that caught my attention. Looking frustrated, the man with the glasses exited the restaurant and sighed, looking down the street, maybe toward his car. It looked like he'd forgotten something. He scurried off in that direction, not bothering to lock the door behind him.

I turned back to Olaf, who seemed to understand now.

Clearly, he was acquainted with Coach Gerther. "I see," he said. "Well, you boys know the Red Arrow is just an urban legend, don't you?" He laughed in a forced kind of way. "Do you also believe that alligators live in the sewers in New York City? Or that Pop Rocks and soda killed that kid from the Life cereal commercials?"

Frank and I started chuckling too. "Of course not," I said. "But the Red Arrow definitely has a . . . presence in this town, wouldn't you say?"

Olaf stopped laughing. "If you mean that teenagers love to whisper about the horrible things he's supposedly done, and paint that stupid symbol all over town, then sure." He stood up from the cruiser and stepped closer to us, eyes intense. I'm pretty sure he was hoping to stare us down, but that's impossible, because Olaf is a couple of inches shorter than both of us. "But let me tell you this. There's no such thing as the Red Arrow. It's just a stupid myth that encourages vandalism and distrust of the authorities. I don't want you boys legitimizing this story by asking around about it. And I especially don't want you boys investigating." He leaned even closer and dropped his voice to a whisper. "We all know what happens if you boys are caught investigating, don't we?"

I was opening my mouth to answer when it happened.

BOOOOOOOOOOOOOOOOOOOOM!

An earthshaking sound engulfed the whole center of town, so loud and startling that Frank grabbed both Olaf and me and dragged us to the ground.

Chaos erupted, people screaming and running out of buildings to see what had happened. Olaf jumped to his feet and turned to Main Street in shock.

The restaurant with the Red Arrow over the door was on fire. Well, what remained of it.

It had exploded!

A CALL FOR HELP

13

FRANK

I DIDN'T SLEEP WELL THAT NIGHT DESPITE BEING
exhausted, having gotten only a few hours' sleep the
night before. I lay in my bed and stared at the ceiling,
working the facts over and over in my mind, trying to
find a way to make it all make sense.

I like for things to make sense.

An electrical fire. That was the official finding of the
Bayport police and fire departments regarding the restaurant
we'd watched get blown away before our very eyes. The Red
Arrow stenciled above the door had been dismissed as graffiti. A teenage prank, Olaf had hissed at us, his expression
practically begging us to argue with him.

Which we couldn't, of course. Joe and I were caught in
a major catch-22 here. Tell the police what we knew—and

why we knew it wasn't a coincidence—and we'd be admitting to doing some real investigating, therefore breaking the Deal. The J'Adoube School for Behavior Modification Therapy on Rock Island beckoned.

But that meant accepting—or pretending to accept—the Official Explanation. The restaurant's owner, a mild-mannered guy named Paul Fumusa, certainly seemed to accept it. He even admitted that he hadn't had the electrical systems inspected yet, thereby leaving him open to mishaps like this one.

But really. Let's be realistic for a second here. Bad wiring and weird electrical connections cause fires, sure.

But explosions? Big and loud enough to blow half the roof off the place, and clear the town?

Then there was the guy's face. Paul Fumusa's, I mean. His expression was a combination of shell shock and resignation that I'd seen only once before—on Neanderthal Bunyan when we showed up at his house after the beating.

Yeah. This whole scenario had Red Arrow written all over it.

Exactly what—or who—was the Red Arrow? When Joe and I had talked briefly before we hit the hay, I reminded him that when Officer Olaf scoffed at the existence of the Red Arrow, calling it an urban legend, he'd referred to the Red Arrow as "he." What if there was one person, some kind of criminal mastermind, behind the strange events of the last few days? But we'd been too exhausted to discuss this new possibility.

I sat up in bed and then climbed out, padding out of my room and down the hall to Joe's room. I pushed open his door to the sound of loud snoring.

"Seriously?" I asked, flipping on Joe's desk lamp.

Joe did not respond. He was curled up in the fetal position, hugging his comforter like a teddy bear. His mouth was open. A puddle of drool glistened on his pillow.

"JOE!" I shouted, moving closer to the bed. He jumped like he'd gotten an electrical shock. Sputtering, he looked around and spotted me sitting on the end of his bed.

"Wha?" he asked, leaning back against the headboard and wiping his mouth.

"I wanted to discuss the case," I said.

Joe stared at me, his expression going from confused to incredulous to . . . uh-oh. Kind of murderous.

I may have misjudged this one.

But luckily—I guess—for me, we were interrupted by Britney Spears.

"Hit me baby one more time!"

Joe jumped again and scrambled for his phone on his nightstand. Grabbing it, he clicked it on and held it to his ear. "Uh . . . hello?"

He scrunched up his eyebrows as he listened to whoever was on the other line. I was stumped. Who would call at this hour? Unless . . .

Joe met my eyes. "Okay," he was saying. "Okay, Seth. I know. We'll meet you at your place."

I heard squawking from the other line. Seth didn't seem to like that idea.

"Okay, okay," Joe said, nodding. "Sure. I got it. The walls have ears." He paused. "Yeah, I know where you mean. Okay. See you there in ten."

He clicked off the phone and turned to me, holding up one finger. "One," he said. *Do not ever wake me up in the middle of the night to discuss a case.*"

I was feeling a little sheepish, I must admit. "Understood," I said with a nod. "Sorry about that."

Joe nodded. "Two," he said, holding up a second finger, "we have to meet Seth Diller in the woods behind the football field. He wants to talk about the Red Arrow."

Seth had sounded totally freaked out, Joe explained as we drove through the deserted streets of Bayport for the second time in two nights. He was afraid his house was bugged, his phone was bugged. That's why he wanted to meet in person.

"Did something happen to him?" I asked, wondering what had prompted this sudden cry for help.

"I don't think so, not yet," Joe said, pulling into the parking lot behind the football field. We got out and started following a narrow path through the woods, toward a little clearing maybe half a mile in. The clearing was a popular hangout for kids to do all sorts of activities, not all of them legal. Joe and I had gotten to know it well during our investigative career.

When we reached the clearing, we saw Seth sitting on a big rock that had been covered in graffiti as long as I'd been alive. He looked nervous.

"Hey, Seth," I said, nodding in greeting. "I'm glad you called. We want to try to help you."

Seth stood. He still looked freaked. In fact, his eyes looked particularly buggy tonight. "Thanks, guys," he said. "I'm glad you showed up. I'm ready to talk about the Red Arrow."

That was weird.

"You don't have to shout it," Joe said. "The walls have ears, rememb—OOF!"

Suddenly a dark figure appeared out of the woods and tackled both Joe and me, pushing us to the ground. I wasn't able to brace myself with my hands, and I went down hard on my chest and had the wind knocked out of me. I struggled to get my bearings.

This was a setup.

I could hear the thud of fist hitting muscle as the attacker pummeled Joe, and Joe fought back. I pushed myself up and the woods spun. I could see Seth standing nervously behind our attacker, looking every bit like the weasel he was.

"This is the thanks we get for trying to help you?" I managed, still struggling to get my breath.

But then I heard a buzzing sound and looked over at my brother and the attacker. He was wearing a David Letterman mask. And he had a Taser!

"No!" I shouted as I leaped forward, grabbing the thing out of his hand right before he applied the electrical current to my still-struggling brother. That got the attacker's attention. He immediately turned to me, lunging to get the Taser back, but he only succeeded in knocking it out of my hand. He threw his whole weight on me, pinning me to the ground. I used all my best self-defense training (Dad insisted, back in the day) to get free, but this guy was all arms. I placed a few well-aimed punches, but at my odd angle, I was able to land only a few.

I could tell the guy was tiring out, though. Maybe whoever had sent him hadn't mentioned that there would be two victims. He crawled forward, and I could tell he was going for the Taser.

But then Joe suddenly stood up behind him, the Taser in his right hand! He was panting, still trying to catch his breath from his own struggle with this guy.

Joe pressed the sides of the Taser, and the electrical current sizzled, bright blue-white.

"You want to tell us what the heck's going on?" he asked. "Or would you like to meet my friend Mr. Sparky?"

MISCHIEF 14

I DO NOT LIKE GETTING WOKEN UP. I MEAN, REALLY.

Aunt Trudy used to wake us for school in the mornings, but after a few well-aimed pillows to her head, she bought me an *extremely loud* alarm clock and said I was on my own.

So when I was woken from a sound sleep for the second night in a row—by Frank, technically, and I had not forgotten that, but really by that weasel Seth Diller—I was getting answers.

The Taser felt almost too good in my hands.

"Did you hear me?" I demanded, holding the Taser closer to our attacker and letting the current crackle. He shrank back.

I turned around and held the Taser out to Seth. I hadn't

forgotten he was back there. "Or you?" I demanded. "You seem depressed, Seth. Maybe some nice electroshock therapy would help?"

"Hey, hey, hey." Frank suddenly stood beside me and gently—very gently—reached out to take the Taser. "Why don't we all just calm down? Nice and calm. Totally nonelectrically calm." He held out his hand, and reluctantly, I dropped the Taser into it.

"I want answers," I whispered to my brother.

"Let's not get arrested," he hissed back.

Seth and Dave (Letterman) still looked pretty freaked, though. Seth's eyes were the buggiest I'd ever seen them. And Dave was shaking.

"Take off the mask," I ordered Dave, hoping that just knowing we had the Taser now would be enough.

It was, apparently. The attacker reached up and pushed the mask back over his head.

I saw his face and gasped.

Pett Macken!

"Neanderthal was right!" I cried. "This wasn't too sophisticated for you after all!"

Pett's dull eyes drilled into mine, mystified. "Sophisticated?" he asked.

Frank held out his hand. "Slow down, slow down," he said, stepping forward and gesturing for Pett and Seth to sit down. "Why don't you two tell us what happened—in your own words?"

The two boys sat, Seth sighing deeply.

"I don't know exactly what happened," he said, running a hand over his face.

"Tell us what you know," I urged.

"Okay." Seth looked at the ground. "I saw the Red Arrow on my car this evening, when you guys were there. You saw it with me."

Frank nodded. "Why do you think you were targeted?"

Seth shrugged. "I'm not sure," he said. "Really. My best guess, though, is that I'm being punished for talking about it with you two."

That had me pretty skeptical. "Talking about it with us? How would anybody know?"

Seth glared at me. "You really are naive, aren't you?" he asked. "It's like I told you just now. The walls have ears. I'm sure somebody is listening to this conversation as we speak."

I'm not proud of this, but those words sent a little chill down my spine.

"Okay," said Frank. "So you see that you're targeted. What then? How did we get here?"

Seth looked down at his hands. "I was woken up in the middle of the night by a phone call," he replied.

"Sounds familiar," I said. "And?"

Seth shivered. "It was this creepy voice," he replied. "Distorted, like someone talking through a pipe. It was from a number I'd never seen before. The voice told me that if I did something for him—if I helped him get you two—he'd let me off. The Mark of the Red Arrow would be lifted."

I glanced at my brother. So the Red Arrow knew about us. They—or he—knew enough to want to stop us.

That wasn't good.

I turned to Pett, who was sitting there like a bump on a log (literally). "What about you?"

Pett looked up, like he'd just remembered he was part of this conversation. "What about me?"

"How did you get involved with the Red Arrow, Pett?" Frank spelled out slowly.

Pett shook his head. "I don't know," he said. "I don't know what I did to make him mad. I came home one day, and there was a mark on my motorcycle."

"You have no idea what you did to prompt it?" I asked.

Pett shook his head.

"Pett probably does all kinds of despicable things every day," Frank said quietly to me.

I sighed. Man, I was tired. "Okay, okay. You don't know why you got Red Arrowed. But how did you get here?"

Pett looked confused. "I rode my bike?"

Frank groaned. "Why did you beat us up, Pett?"

"Oh!" Pett, seeming to grasp his place in this investigation at last, sat straighter on the log. "Well, a couple of months ago, I got a call like Seth here," he said, gesturing to Seth. Seth shrank back, like he didn't want to be associated.

"Same distorted voice?" Frank asked. "Same unfamiliar number?"

Pett nodded. "The voice told me that I could avoid any further punishment—that's what it said—by doing some jobs for him." He paused. "Or her. It could be a her, I guess."

"Odd jobs?" I asked. "Like pummeling people?"

Pett nodded again. "I beat some people up, sure," he said. He held up his left arm and flexed it. "I guess I'm lucky I've got some muscle."

Frank caught my eye. I could tell he was disgusted. "And that's why you came here tonight?" he said.

"That's right," said Pett. "I got a call telling me I had another odd job. And then it turned out to be you guys." He grinned.

"That was lucky," I said, trying to interpret the grin.

"Sure," said Pett. "It was a job I enjoyed, after what you boys did to me."

Frank held up the Taser and sparked it, once. "Didn't exactly turn out great for you," he pointed out.

Pett just glared at him, then looked away.

I closed my eyes for a moment. "All right," I said, holding up my hands. "I think we're done for the night, gentlemen. Let's all go home and get some sleep."

Seth looked surprised. "That's it?" he asked.

I was about to say yes—or *We'll talk about it in the morning*—when I was interrupted by the blaring of a police siren.

Seth's eyes widened. "Uh-oh."

It was coming from the parking lot. I looked at Frank.

"Uh-oh," he whispered.

Before we could move, I heard footsteps running down the path.

"Freeze!" Olaf's voice came through the trees before he even surfaced at the path's end.

I looked at Frank and slowly held up my hands. He followed suit. No need to anger Olaf in the wee hours of the morning, I figured.

Again. We were having a really banner week.

Olaf appeared at the end of the path, his rookie partner behind him. Both were brandishing weapons.

"Hands up!" Olaf yelled. Frank and I were way ahead of him, but Seth and Pett slowly followed suit.

Olaf moved in and slowly circled the four of us, casing the location. "Okay," he said after a few seconds. "I'm going to march you all back to the cruiser, and you're coming back to the station with me. Understand?"

"What?" Pett asked in a surly tone. "Why? For what?"

Olaf glared at him. "Oh, it's you," he said snootily. "Back to jail so soon? We've received noise complaints about a fight going on out here." He paused and looked me right in the eye. "We're taking you all in for criminal mischief."

Criminal mischief. A charge that can conveniently encompass basically any reason a cop might take a dislike to you. Frank and I had been brought in for criminal mischief before. Most likely, we'd be brought in again . . . and again. And again.

That didn't mean our parents liked it much, of course.

As we all marched behind Olaf and his partner back to the cruiser, I caught Frank's eye again. He cocked an eyebrow. "Does this seem like a place with a lot of neighbors to you?" he whispered.

He was right. The reason kids could get away with all kinds of various activities in these woods was that they were completely secluded . . . from everything. The nearest houses were at least a half mile away. Too far to hear the fight we'd had.

So what was really going on here?

A TIP 15

FRANK

WAS STARTING TO GET RED ARROW VISION. Everyone who appeared in front of me, I imagined as the Red Arrow. Officer Olaf. Chief Gomez. Even Hattie, the kindly longtime receptionist at the Bayport Police Department.

Clearly, I was losing it.

Joe and I were almost immediately ushered into Chief Gomez's office as Pett and Seth were led into a different room.

He didn't exactly look thrilled to see us. But then, we rarely met on happy occasions.

"Boys," he said, inclining his head and looking from Joe to me.

"Chief Gomez," Joe said, "this is all a big misunderstanding."

Gomez laughed. "Oh, sure. I've never heard that from you boys before."

"It's true," I threw in. I didn't actually expect him to believe me, but it was worth a shot. "We were just having a conversation with Pett and Seth when Officer Olaf showed up."

Gomez rolled his eyes at me. "Just a conversation," he said, deadpan. "At three o'clock in the morning. In a deserted part of town."

"That reminds me," Joe piped up, sitting a little straighter in his chair. "Who called in the noise complaint? There aren't any houses anywhere near those woods."

Chief Gomez's expression turned hard, like he was tired of humoring us. "That's classified information." He leaned forward. "Listen, boys, I thought we had a deal." He lowered his voice. "The Deal. Sound familiar?"

I looked at Joe. Time to get serious. "Of course it does, sir," I said, putting on my best altar-boy face.

Gomez sighed, like he was just as tired as we were. "I've been hearing rumors that you boys are doing some investigative work around town," he said. "That would be unfortunate, wouldn't it? After we worked so hard to get the Deal in place."

Joe leaned forward. "We haven't been investigating, sir," he said, "but we have been asking a few questions about the Red Arrow."

Gomez looked at him. "The Red Arrow," he repeated, no emotion in his voice.

"It's a symbol we've seen a lot around town," I said. "Some

people seem to think it's related to a . . . a curse, of sorts."

Gomez looked at me hard, then cleared his throat. "Listen, boys," he said, "I'm not thrilled about the Deal either. I want you boys to be safe, but you've contributed a lot to the town over the years, and I . . . well, I'll admit it. Sometimes I miss your input on a case here or there." He paused. "But I certainly don't enjoy hearing that you boys are jeopardizing your future over some urban legend. Some ghost story teenagers tell each other at slumber parties."

Joe shot me a nervous glance. "But what if . . . what if, without investigating, Frank and I stumbled on some information implying that the Red Arrow is very real?"

Chief Gomez looked from Joe to me, shaking his head. "I'd say great," he said, lowering his voice and moving closer. "Care to tell me what it is? And how you got it?"

I looked at Joe, subtly swiping my hand across my neck. Cut it out. Catch-22. "No, sir," I said.

"Listen." Gomez smacked his meaty hand on the top of his desk. "I want this to end. I don't want to be called into the station at three a.m. to give you this warning again." He gave us another serious look. "Stop sniffing around. Follow the Deal. Don't put your whole future in jeopardy."

Just then the phone on his desk rang. The chief frowned at us as if to say *Quiet!* And then picked it up.

"Yes? . . . Okay. Okay. Yes, understood."

He hung up the phone and gave us an insincere smile. "Boys, after consulting with your father, we have decided to drop all charges against you." He leaned forward. "But you'd better stay out of trouble from now on. Understand?"

"Absolutely, sir," I said, standing up. Phew! Fenton Hardy comes through again.

Chief Gomez led us out of his office, grabbing his jacket on the way out. "I'm going home to get some sleep," he told us.

Sleep. Much as I'd struggled with it earlier that night, it sounded divine. Gomez led us out to the lobby, where Hattie informed us that our aunt Trudy was on her way. I glanced at Joe, wondering if that was a bad omen.

"Is Dad going to kill us?" I whispered, taking a seat on an uncomfortable chair.

Joe shrugged. "I think we have a fifty-fifty shot," he replied.

I'm not sure how long it was before Aunt Trudy showed up. Truth be told, I may have dozed a bit. Joe too. Joe did ask about Pett and Seth, and was told they'd been released about half an hour before us.

Before I knew it, Hattie was calling, "Boys?" and Joe and I startled awake. Aunt Trudy was standing before us, smiling tensely.

"Hi, Aunt Trudy," Joe said. "We really appreciate you picking us up. Are Mom and Dad, um . . . ?"

"Apoplectic?" Aunt Trudy supplied, her smile warming. "You'll have to ask them. Your dad came up to wake me and ask me to come get you, then holed himself up in his study. I didn't get much besides 'boys' and 'police station.'

And 'again.'" You mother went to bed early not feeling well, and doesn't know yet."

I looked at Joe. "Uh-oh."

He nodded. "That doesn't sound good."

I stood up and chatted with Aunt Trudy about her garden while Hattie passed our belongings back to us, and Joe ran to use the men's room. When he came back, he grabbed my arm. "Maybe you should use the restroom too before we leave," he said, giving me a meaningful look.

I looked at Aunt Trudy. "That's not a bad idea," I said.

She waved her hand. "Sure, sure, go ahead. It's not like my bed is calling for me or anything."

Joe gave her a smile. "We owe you big-time, Aunt Trudy. What if Frank and I cook dinner tonight?"

Aunt Trudy grimaced. "Ugh. What have I done to earn such punishment?" she asked.

Joe shrugged. "Well, we'll figure out something. I'm, ah, going to grab a drink from the water fountain."

He followed me back down the hall to the restrooms, then grabbed my arm again. "Check it out."

He was holding out his wallet, billfold open to reveal a note written in thick black marker on yellow lined paper.

CHECK OUT THE RESTAURANT.

"It was in my wallet when I picked it up," Joe whispered. I looked at him incredulously. "It had to have been left by someone in the police department," I whispered back to him.

Joe nodded. "Or someone who was arrested, maybe."

I shook my head. "They wouldn't have access to people's belongings."

"Either way," Joe said, "we need to get over there. We'll need something to distract Aunt Trudy."

I nodded. "On it," I said. "Operation Trudy Distraction, in full effect!"

"Ouch!" I cried as I fake-stumbled down the last step from police headquarters to Main Street. "Oh, ow! Man! Hold on, you guys. My ankle."

Joe and Aunt Trudy turned around, Aunt Trudy looking concerned, Joe impressed.

"What happened, Frank?" Aunt Trudy asked.

I made a big show of hopping around, like my ankle was injured. "I think I twisted it," I said, then sighed. "Oh, man! It's going to be a struggle to get down the steps to the parking lot."

Aunt Trudy looked grim. "Do we need to take you to the hospital? Do you need an X-ray?"

"No!" I cried, and noticed that Joe seemed to just stop himself in time from shouting it with me.

"I'll just put some ice on it when we get home," I added. "This happens to me a lot. I must have weak ankles."

Aunt Trudy pursed her lips. "Well, if you say so. I

suppose I'll need to get the car and bring it around for you."

I nodded. "That would be great, Aunt Trudy. Thanks."

Aunt Trudy turned to Joe. He seemed to realize after a few seconds that she was waiting for him to go with her.

I moved closer to Joe and leaned on his shoulder. "It would be great if Joe could stay with me," I said. "To lean on."

Aunt Trudy shrugged. "Well, I guess so," she said. "I'll be right around with the car. You boys stay put."

We waited until she was halfway down the stairs to the parking lot, then dashed down the street to the remains of Paul Fumusa's restaurant.

The blown-out windows had been masked with plastic, and scorch marks covered the exterior. It was pitch-dark inside, but the Hardy Boys come prepared. I pulled out a key chain with a super-bright flashlight on the end and shone it into the restaurant.

We could make out charred remains of tables and chairs. Debris. What looked like a burned umbrella handle.

But nothing that meant anything to us. Nothing we could point to and say, *Here's the key to the secret identity of the Red Arrow!*

Which is sort of what I'd been hoping for, I admit.

"Do you get it?" Joe asked, watching me aim the flashlight back and forth.

"No," I admitted with a sigh. I had no idea what was going on here.

Beep, beep! We both turned around to see Aunt Trudy in her little hybrid, looking surprised—and annoyed—to see me walking just fine.

We ran over to her and jumped into the car.

"I bent my ankle this one way and then totally recovered," I said, feeling my cheeks burn at the lie. "It's a miracle!"

WATCHED 16

JOE

I T WAS CLEAR, BY THE TIME WE GOT HOME, THAT it was going to take a lot more than dinner to get back on Aunt Trudy's good side.

"You'd better go in and talk to your father," she huffed as she got out of the car and slammed the door.

They were the first words she'd spoken since Frank had told her about his miracle recovery.

I looked at my brother, and we both sighed. What a long, miserable night. Upsetting our beloved aunt Trudy was just the icing on the cake.

But there was still more to come. We had to talk to Dad.

We went into the house and slowly approached his study, then knocked quietly.

"Dad?" I called.

"Come in," he replied in a gruff voice. I looked at my brother.

"Here goes," I whispered, and pushed the door open.

"Dad," Frank said before we even crossed the threshold, "we can explain."

"Can you?" asked Dad, standing up and walking around the desk. "Can you? Really?"

Without another word, he brushed by us and out of his study. We had no choice but to follow him down the hallway, through the foyer and to the front door, which he opened.

"There," he said, stepping out and pointing up over the doorway.

I had a sickening realization before I looked. It couldn't be. But of course it was. It only made sense. . . .

There, stenciled above our front door, was the Red Arrow.

"Dad," I managed. But no more words would come.

He looked hard at me, then Frank. "Let's go back to my study."

We followed him back through the door, the foyer, the hall, to his study. He closed the door behind us, and Frank and I dropped exhaustedly into the chairs facing his desk. Dad picked up a mug of probably cold coffee and took a swig. (He still drinks it long after it's gone cold. Frank calls this "gross." I call it "hard-core.")

When he'd finished, he put the coffee cup down and sat

down behind his desk, looking at both of us through hooded eyes. Dad looked as tired as I felt.

"I thought," he said after a few uncomfortable moments, "we had an agreement."

I took a deep breath.

"We did, Dad," Frank said, sitting forward in his chair. "But look, Joe and I believe—you taught us—that if something wrong is happening in this town, and people are getting hurt, then we should do everything within our power to fix it."

Dad stared at him. "Really? Up to and including putting your own family in jeopardy?"

Frank shook his head. "We didn't mean to do that."

"I thought I was very clear the last time we talked," Dad went on, his voice low. "Some things are better left alone. And you didn't leave this alone."

Neither one of us answered. Our father eyeballed us for a moment more, then dropped his gaze to the desk.

"It makes me wonder," he went on, "how much I can trust you two in general anymore. For example, keeping up the Deal." He looked up at us.

Frank and I didn't say anything. It was sort of an unspoken agreement between us that he, Dad, and I never mentioned the Deal. Honestly, it hurt too much. I don't think any of us liked to be reminded of what we had lost in the Deal—or at least, lost the right to do openly.

But at the same time, the Deal was the only thing securing

us a decent future. College and a job and a family and kids one day. Without the Deal, it was the J'Adoube School for Behavior Modification Therapy on Rock Island. Which was not the kind of future anybody wanted.

For a few minutes, nobody spoke.

Finally Dad leaned across his desk. "As I have told you," he said, "there are powerful forces at work here. I really don't think you boys know what you're getting into. If you care about me, if you care about your own future, please just leave well enough alone."

"But, Dad," Frank said, "how do you know? Were you Red Arrowed before?"

Dad was quiet for a few seconds. "No," he said. "I was never that unlucky. But I've had clients who were."

I looked at Frank. There was a question forming on my tongue, but I was almost afraid to ask it.

Fortunately, my brother and I think alike—and he is sometimes braver than I am. "What happened to them?" he asked.

But my father never got the chance to reply.

He was cut off by a bloodcurdling scream from upstairs. Aunt Trudy!

Aunt Trudy stood in my room, my backpack dropped before her on the floor.

"It's watching me," she whispered when the three of us appeared. "It's watching. . . ."

"What's going on?" My parents' bedroom door opened and out stumbled my mother, hair tousled, wearing her signature satin pajamas. She looked from Dad to me to Frank to Aunt Trudy. "Who was that screaming? What are you all doing up?"

Dad turned to look from Mom to Aunt Trudy. "It was Trudy screaming," he said. "It's a long story. But, Trudy—who's watching? What do you mean?"

Aunt Trudy backed out of my bedroom, pointing at a plastic robot on my bookshelf. I built it in the second grade. His name is Mike the Robot.

But behind Mike the robot . . .

A red light blinked. And a lens pointed.

Watching.

Waiting.

"We're being videotaped!" Aunt Trudy cried.

FRANK

IT'S A PRETTY HUGE KICK IN THE PANTS TO have to go to school on the day after two sleepless nights, after being beaten up, arrested, chewed out by your father, marked for punishment by the mastermind of a shady criminal organization, and monitored in your own home.

It's an even bigger kick in the pants to have to go to school on the day after two sleepless nights, after being beaten up, arrested, chewed out by your father, marked for punishment by the mastermind of a shady criminal organization, and monitored in your own home . . . only to have to give a speech on civil liberties that you have not prepared for in any way!

That's right. I, Frank Hardy, Extreme Public Speaking Fraidy-Pants and Meticulous Student Extraordinaire, was now facing my worst nightmare: giving a speech. In front of more than three hundred students. Did I mention I hate public speaking?

"Maybe you can tell Ms. Jones the truth and ask for more time," Joe suggested as we pulled into the school parking lot.

Yes. That had every chance in the world of working, with the week I'd been having.

"Which version of the truth?" I asked. "The one where I was distracted by the shady criminal organization no one will admit exists in this town?"

Joe nodded, his face grim. "Yeah. Better to just fake your way through it, I guess."

Oh, to be my brother sometimes. To be a person for whom "just faking your way through" a speech in front of three hundred people is an option. I sometimes wonder what happened with Joe and me where he got the exact opposite genes that I did. I mean, except for the sleuthing gene.

And admittedly, we both have pretty good hair.

We'd managed to disable the video camera we'd found last night, but we were still very aware of the Red Arrow mark on our heads, so we tried to lie low all morning. We didn't really expect that anyone would try anything during school hours, but really, who knew?

"Ready for your speech?" Ms. Jones asked with a big smile when I walked into American history class third period.

"I'm a little nervous," I admitted.

"Oh, you'll be fine." She gave me a little pat on the shoulder, then paused. "You're not . . . going to say anything unusual, are you?"

Unusual? What did that mean?

"I have a section written in Martian," I replied with a smile. "Is that too weird?"

Ms. Jones looked confused for a moment, then chuckled. "Oh, Frank," she said. "I'm sure you'll be fine."

Funny how everybody who was not me was so sure of that.

My speech was to take place at 11:20 sharp—fourth period. I tried to lose myself in Ms. Jones's lecture about trench fighting during World War I, but I couldn't concentrate. Later, when I looked back at my notes, I found a sketch of a noose with *HELP ME* written all around it.

I had to ask for a bathroom pass four times in forty-five minutes.

Then, all too soon, the bell rang.

Ms. Jones smiled at me like I'd just won the lottery. "Well, class," she said, "let's make our way to the auditorium, where we'll hear your classmate Frank Hardy's brilliant presentation on civil liberties!"

There were some cheers, some groans. A football player exercised his civil liberties by throwing an eraser at my head when Ms. Jones walked out the door. "Brownnoser," he hissed.

Oh, if only those were my only problems. If only I'd be crying myself to sleep that night because the football players didn't like me, and not because I'd wet myself in front of three hundred people.

I followed Ms. Jones to the auditorium like a dead man walking. People talked to me, greeting me, I guess, or wishing me luck, but I didn't hear any of it. Keeping up a steady stream of pep talk, Ms. Jones led me around the gym to the backstage entrance to the auditorium, which would lead me onto the stage.

She opened the door, and I could hear the dull roar of my three-hundred-some classmates, none of them (except for Joe, of course) prepared for the meltdown they were about to witness.

I tried not to look out into the audience. Ms. Jones walked up to the podium, which had been set in the middle of the stage, to introduce me, talking about why she had chosen my "exceptional" paper to be presented to the entire school. It was something about the importance of preserving our civil liberties, even in this day and age, blah, blah, blah. I couldn't make out much beyond the sound of blood pounding in my head.

But I could tell she was winding down.

"And without further ado," Ms. Jones went on, "let me present to you . . . your classmate, Frank Hardy!"

There were a couple of random boos—to be expected, really—but mostly polite applause. I forced my feet to move one after the other and carry me onstage. The applause intensified. I managed to smile at Ms. Jones and make it to the podium without passing out.

I looked out at the packed auditorium. Hundreds of faces stared back at me. I tried to locate Joe in the crowd, but it was impossible. My breathing sped up, and I remembered the top piece of advice Joe had given me: Imagine everyone in the audience in their underwear.

It didn't help much.

I touched the microphone, tapping it gently to make sure it was on, and then pulled it close to my mouth.

A deep, shuddery breath reverberated throughout the auditorium.

"Civil liberties," I forced myself to say, smoothing the paper with my notes out in front of me, "are a crucial element of our democracy."

Creeeeaaaak.

The heavy double doors at the rear of the auditorium slowly opened, and light from the lobby flooded in behind a dark silhouette, which leaned on a cane. The silhouette moved forward, and the lights of the auditorium illuminated Principal Gorse. He noted that I was staring at him and nodded encouragingly in my direction. His kind brown eyes crinkled at the corners. He stepped forward, slowly, and the bright lights flashed off the cane in his hand. It was shiny silver metal; it looked like something NASA might have designed. Totally different from his old hand-carved cane. When had he gotten it?

Someone in the audience coughed, "Narc," and I startled back to attention. ("Narc" is the affectionate nickname bestowed on Joe and myself by some of our classmates—mostly, the friends of people we've busted.) I realized I'd been silent for about thirty seconds and smoothed my paper again. Sheesh, my hands were sweaty.

"Civil liberties," I said loudly, "are . . ."

And then, suddenly, it hit me like a bolt of lightning.

The note that had been slipped into Joe's wallet: *CHECK OUT THE RESTAURANT.* And the charred umbrella handle.

It hadn't been an umbrella handle. It had been a cane.

Principal Gorse's cane!

I hated the thought that our kindly principal might be behind the terrible things the Red Arrow had done, but the more I thought about it, the more sense it made. Neal, Seth, and Pett had all brought shame to Principal Gorse—in some small way—by being busted for a crime while attending Bayport High School. I had no idea what Paul Fumusa had done to him, but surely there was more to Principal Gorse's life than the little bit we saw at school. Maybe Paul Fumusa had flirted with Ms. Collins or rear-ended the Karmann Ghia or told Principal Gorse that turtlenecks with sport coats were over.

I was paralyzed, standing there.

"Narc says what?" someone finally hissed from the second row.

It was enough to shake me out of my thoughts.

"Civil liberties," I began, "are . . ."

A farce in this town, I thought.

I put my elbows on the podium and leaned on them, suddenly feeling . . . angry.

"You know what?" I barked suddenly into the mic, startling the people sitting closest. "This whole speech is all kinds of bull, because the biggest threat to our civil liberties in the town of Bayport is the one no one will talk about." I leaned right into the mic, enjoying the feeling of the words slipping out of my mouth. "The Red Arrow."

I could see people in the audience looking shocked, sitting a little straighter, a *Did I just hear that?* expression on their faces. That's when I spotted Joe. He was sitting on the aisle, about midway back, and his jaw was hanging open.

"There, I said it," I went on. "Is everyone scared? Is lightning going to strike me from above? Because that's how he keeps his power, you know. No one will talk about it. No one will talk about what the Red Arrow is doing."

People were squirming now. I looked back at Principal Gorse, and his face wore an expression I'd never seen on him before: pure rage. He was turning scarlet, his eyebrows drawing harsh lines over his eyes, which bugged in horror.

He began marching down the aisle—as fast as he could manage with the space-age cane.

"So let's talk about what he's doing," I went on. "He's beating kids up. Forcing them to do his bidding. Even spying on their cell phone conversations."

Principal Gorse reached the foot of the stage and began

struggling up the three stairs. Having no idea why he was climbing up, I'm sure, Ms. Jones rushed forward to give him a hand.

"Who knows how far up his influence goes?" I asked. "Is the Red Arrow connected with the police? With town officials? Even . . . school officials?"

Principal Gorse lurched up the last step and immediately lunged in my direction. I actually had to swerve away to avoid being tackled by the man. He looked like a hungry wolf, like he would have happily chewed me up and spit me out right there if he could.

Instead he grabbed the mic. "This speech is over," he panted. "I need to meet with Frank . . . immediately."

The din in the auditorium immediately rose to study-hall levels, all the students wanting to know what was happening, what I had done. Ms. Jones ran over, brows furrowed in confusion.

"Simon?" she asked, touching Principal Gorse's shoulder. "What's . . . happening? Are you . . . ?"

Joe, who'd jumped up in his seat the minute Principal Gorse took the mic, ran up the aisle and onto the stage. "I'll go too!" he blurted, running to my side. "I . . . I . . ."

"I suppose we all have a lot to talk about," I said, giving Principal Gorse a meaningful look.

He nodded. "Come with me," he said, moving off toward the wings of the stage.

With Ms. Jones still mystified, and the teachers in the

audience struggling to regain control of their students as chaos broke out, Joe and I followed Principal Gorse through the wings and out a door that led to a quiet hallway behind the gym.

When he turned to face us, Principal Gorse's face was completely different. The rage was gone. In its place I thought I saw regret.

"Okay," he said, his voice low as his eyes darted around the hallway. "Clearly, you boys are in need of . . . answers. Answers I think I can provide."

I nodded. "Go on."

He took a breath and stopped. "I would like to do this somewhere private," he went on. "I promise, when I finish what I have to say, I will leave myself at your mercy. Looking back, I see where I have gone wrong. I know that I must be punished. Understand?"

Joe looked from the principal to me, and I could tell he was mystified but going to play along. He nodded.

I nodded too, turning back to the man I believed to be the Red Arrow. "Principal Gorse, you know we've always respected you. I don't want to make this more difficult than it needs to be." I paused. "But I think I need to call the police now. I hope you understand."

I pulled out my phone and started dialing the Bayport PD's number. Before I could get past the first digit, Principal Gorse silently put his hand on my phone and stopped me.

"Do you want to know the truth or not?" he asked evenly.

I looked at Joe. He looked as surprised as I felt. Of course we wanted to know the truth. But I wanted to be safe, too.

The principal lowered his voice. "Come with me," he said, "and I'll tell you everything. Call the police now, and I'll cooperate, yes—but I won't answer their questions. I won't give you any of the answers you want."

Joe widened his eyes at me. I didn't know what to do. I knew we shouldn't trust Gorse . . . but I needed to know what the Red Arrow really was. Why such a seemingly nice man had done this.

Principal Gorse eyed me sympathetically. "You may keep your cell phone on, of course," he said. "If you feel uncomfortable at any time, the police are just three digits away, no?"

I swallowed and looked at Joe. It sounded reasonable. Maybe we weren't going to get to the bottom of the Red Arrow without taking a risk.

"Okay," I said finally.

Gorse gave an abrupt nod. "I appreciate that, boys. If you'll follow me . . . I know a place where we can talk privately."

He took out a key and led us through a small doorway and down a flight of steps. We were entering the fabled Bayport High School basement. Depending on who you talked to, the bodies of failing seniors were buried down there, or the secret room where teachers kept all the answer keys, or a forgotten dungeon. Unlike the Red Arrow, though, those were actual urban legends.

Principal Gorse paused before a metal door and then pushed it open. Blinding sunlight streamed in. We walked out onto the football field.

To the right was an area that had been under construction for the past few months. Rumor had it that we were getting a new gym and locker rooms, but right now the place just looked like a mud farm with some construction equipment and storage containers. Principal Gorse approached one of these containers and pulled out a key.

"This has been my secret office for some time," he said quietly. "I've come out here whenever I was doing something I didn't wish for anyone to witness. I keep a laptop in here and make all my phone calls on a disposable cell phone."

How long had this been going on? I wondered. Had Principal Gorse always been the Red Arrow, even when our dad was struggling with it? I hoped we'd get the truth once we stepped inside.

The principal unlocked the heavy padlock, pushed the heavy metal door open, and walked inside. The room was narrow, rectangular, and dim, with a tiny bit of light filtering in from a hatch in the ceiling that was open just a crack.

I looked back at Joe and followed Principal Gorse inside. Joe was close behind. We stood in the room, blinking as our eyes slowly adjusted.

The room was cold, and totally empty. Then I spotted

something strange. The end of a hose had been fed through the narrow opening of the hatch. At that moment, Principal Gorse suddenly lunged at me, swinging his cane at my head.

"AAUUUGH!" I ducked just in time, but the tip of the cane cracked Joe, who'd been rushing to my defense, in the nose. Blood spurted in all directions.

"What the—?" I managed, as Principal Gorse brought the cane back and swung it again.

I careened to the side, but it still hit me flush in the shoulder, knocking me to the ground and making me moan with pain.

Principal Gorse aimed a quick, nasty kick at Joe's leg and sent him tumbling to the ground too. He stood over us, brandishing the cane like a baseball bat.

"You idiot Hardys," he hissed in a gravelly voice I'd never heard before. Did our principal have multiple personalities? Or was this all a sleep-deprivation-induced hallucination?

No. He stumbled over to the door, kneeling down to turn something just out of sight. Immediately I heard water trickling into the hose. Within a few seconds, a steady gush poured out of the hose into the container.

"This storage container is completely watertight," Principal Gorse went on.

He grabbed two chairs, then pulled us up roughly, slamming us into our seats, and started tying us up with rope that was lying nearby. "You'll note there's no drain in the room.

No, this container is going to fill up slowly, leaving you boys plenty of time to ponder your last breath and how you got to this point."

I was able to reach into my pocket for my cell phone and quickly dialed 911.

Nothing happened.

I looked at the screen. No!

NO SIGNAL.

Principal Gorse chuckled. "I've made note of the various places around the school where cellular service drops out," he said. "There are so many of them! It's almost as though someone was tampering with the signal."

He walked through the door, grabbing the edge to slam it.

I tried to lunge to my feet, but I couldn't really move, thanks to the pain and the rope. Gorse let out an eerie laugh as the metal door shut behind him. I heard him replacing the padlock on the chain, leaving Joe and me trapped inside.

GUSH 18

JOE

I'D NEVER REALLY HAD A FEAR OF DROWNING until that door clanked shut behind Principal Gorse. It's a pretty terrible way to die, when you think about it. First off, you have plenty of time to realize that you're dying. Plus, from what I have gathered, slowly running out of air is not really a comfortable way to go.

"How do we get out of here?" I asked Frank, struggling against the rope. Already the floor was nearly covered by a growing puddle. The water was coming in fast.

Frank groaned. He wriggled around and managed to work his way out. "That cane felt like a baseball bat," he muttered, making his way over to me.

"Maybe that's why he got the metal upgrade," I suggested. Frank worked at the rope and got me free. I winced as I stood up, rubbing my shoulder. I paused. "For real, Frank, how did you figure out that Principal Gorse is the Red Arrow?"

"It was the cane." Frank stood with a groan. "I remembered the debris we saw in the restaurant. There was something that looked like an umbrella handle—remember?"

Riiiiight. "Yeah. When we got that note we couldn't figure out."

"It wasn't an umbrella handle," Frank went on. "It was a cane. Principal Gorse's old cane."

Aha. "And Neal, Seth, Pett—they all got in trouble while at Bayport High."

"Maybe they disgraced him in some way. I don't know," Frank said. "And I haven't figured out how Paul Fumusa plays into it. But clearly, Principal Gorse has been hiding a lot from us."

He stopped and looked around the room. "Do you see anything we could use to stand on to reach the hose?"

I looked around. The room was really dark, lit only by the light seeping in from the opening around the hatch. "Not really," I admitted. "This thing is pretty tall."

The water was deepening, up to our ankles now. The stream from the hose splashed into the pool. My feet were soaked, and it was getting harder to walk around.

"Hey, Frank," I said.

He turned around, curious.

"That was a great speech."

He let out a short laugh and shook his head. "I hope it doesn't turn out to be my swan song."

I could tell he was getting nervous. Truthfully, I was too. We'd gone up against a lot of nasty characters before. But the Red Arrow had been operating in Bayport and avoiding detection for years. Even Fenton Hardy feared him. Was he smart enough to defeat us? Had the Hardy Boys met their match?

That's when I heard banging on the door.

"What the . . . ?" Frank muttered.

I sloshed over to the metal door. "Hello?" I yelled.

I could barely make out the voice on the other side over the rushing water.

"Frank? Joe? Is that you?"

The voice was nasally. Female. I looked at my brother.

Sharelle!

"Sharelle, are you out there?" I shouted. "Please help us! Can you open the door?"

I heard grunting and clanking as Sharelle yanked on the chain. "It won't budge!"

"Gorse has the key!" I cried.

"I knew you were acting weird during your speech, Frank," Sharelle called. "I snuck away from my class and followed you and Principal Gorse out onto the football field. I knew something strange was going on when he led you in here. What's going on?"

I shook my head. Sharelle Bunyan. Our hero?

"It's filling up with water!" Frank shouted. "This is some kind of old holding tank. He left us in here to drown!"

I leaned against the door. "Sharelle, can you call the cops for us? Listen. This is very important. You have to talk to Chief Gomez. Okay? Nobody but Chief Gomez. Tell him that we're trapped in here. Tell him it's urgent—this container is filling with water!"

"Okay," Sharelle replied, "but I'm going to have to go back to the school to get service. This whole field is a dead zone, and I don't want anybody to see me."

"Fair enough," I replied, "but tell them to hurry. And you hurry back. Please!"

The water was up to our knees now. Once the water level rose, it wouldn't take long to push all the air out of the room. We didn't have a lot of time.

"Okay!" Sharelle ran off.

I looked at Frank. He looked like he didn't know what to do. "Let me try standing on your shoulders," he said.

I moved closer and bent down so he could try to climb up. It was hard to see in the faint light, and with the water level rising higher and higher. Soon it was up to our waists.

Frank climbed up my back and tried to steady himself as he carefully placed his feet on my shoulders. With him holding on to my head, I tried to straighten up slowly, and then Frank started to move from a crouch to a standing position.

He was close enough to the hatch to make a swipe at the hose.

I watched, breathless, as his hand pushed at the hose, but it just swung back and forth. It was wedged beneath the heavy hatch door.

"Darn it!" Frank shouted as his right foot slipped. I tried to grab my brother, but he tumbled into the water, where he splashed around, trying to find his balance.

"It's wedged in there anyway," he said when he stood up, holding his head. "I don't think I can push the hose out."

I checked my phone again, which I'd moved to my shirt pocket to keep it dry. "Nothing," I said with a sigh. "I can't take this. There has to be something we can do!"

Frank's eyes kept going back to the door. "Do you hear anything?" I asked. I had to admit, I was wondering how much we could trust Sharelle. Even if she had really run out to call the police, it was entirely possible that it would just take them too long to get here. The water might have filled up the container by then. And Frank and I . . .

I couldn't think about it.

Just as I was losing hope, I heard Sharelle's yell.

"They're coming! I called!"

I sloshed over to the door. "Did you talk to Gomez?"

There was a pause. "He wasn't available," Sharelle said finally. "Or at least that's what they said. I talked to the officer who came to the house the other night. Olsen?"

"Olaf," Frank corrected her with a groan.

Officer Olaf was not exactly the cop I'd choose to hold my fate in his hands. He, well, hated us. And he'd tried so hard to convince us that the Red Arrow was an urban legend. Was he connected somehow?

There was nothing to do now but wait. The water was at our chests now.

No sign of the police.

"Sharelle," Frank shouted, "can you go out front to look for the police and bring them right to this container? I don't want them to waste any time."

"Of course," Sharelle said. "Are you—are you guys okay in there?"

I looked at Frank. I had the unsettling sense that he was sending Sharelle away because, if worse came to worst, he didn't want her to have to listen to us drown while she was stuck on the other side of the door, helpless.

"We're just ducky," I replied, but it was hard to force levity into my voice. "Quack, quack."

I could feel her hesitation. "Okay," she said after a moment. "I'll be right back with the cops. Don't worry!"

I looked at Frank.

"Help me get on your shoulders again," he said simply. "We might as well try."

I crouched down under the water, holding my breath—not really easy with a broken nose. Frank grabbed my shoulders and tried to scramble up. We were both shaking, though, scared and amped up on adrenaline, and this time he didn't even get both feet onto my shoulders before he pitched forward into the water, taking me with him. As he fell, I accidentally inhaled, and water flooded my nose and mouth. I was disoriented and scrambled around with my hands, finally finding the floor and standing up.

"I didn't like that," I said, sputtering.

"Let's try again," Frank said, not looking me in the eye.

We tried again. This time he got up onto my shoulders and took another swipe at the hose before losing his balance. The hose stayed put.

The water was nearly up to my neck.

"Frank," I said.

He wouldn't look at me. "Again," he said. "We have to keep trying."

"Frank," I said again, feeling my throat burn, "what if the Red Arrow's bested us?"

That's when I heard it. Sharelle's voice.

"They're here!" she yelled through the door. "Frank! Joe! Are you okay?"

The next few minutes were a blur. Finally grasping the dire situation we were in, Officer Olaf used his pistol to shoot out the padlock. A few seconds later, the door was yanked open, sending a flood of water cascading onto the grass.

Immediately the water level sank from where it hovered beneath our chins.

We were saved!

. . .

"I suppose I owe you two an apology," Officer Olaf said later that afternoon, as Frank and I sat, still wrapped in blankets, across from his desk at the police station.

Chief Gomez really was out that day, it turned out. His three-year-old daughter had the stomach flu, and he was staying home with her, since his wife had to be out of town on business.

Now Officer Olaf stared down at some paperwork he was shuffling across his desk, as if to avoid looking Frank or me in the eye.

"You do?" Frank asked, raising an eyebrow at me.

Olaf sighed. "It's possible," he said, "that I may have taken your accusations about the Red Arrow less seriously because of my personal . . . well . . ."

"Animosity?" Frank supplied.

"Burning hatred?" I suggested.

Olaf rolled his eyes. "Deeply held suspicion," he said finally, "of you two. But it seems that everything you've told us about Principal Gorse is true. After we got him at the school, we have been interrogating him for a few hours, and he's confessed to being the mastermind behind Bunyan's attack, the blackmailing of Pettigrew Macken, and the explosion at Paul Fumusa's yet-to-be-named restaurant." He paused and looked down at his notes. "He had his connections set up hi-tech surveillance and carry out the actual attacks, since he couldn't."

"See, that's the one I don't get," Frank said, shrugging

and leaning back in his chair. "Why Paul Fumusa?"

Officer Olaf looked at him. "Because he wouldn't pay a 'protection fee' to the Red Arrow to avoid these types of attacks," he said, and sighed. "Which is apparently a form of extortion that the Red Arrow has been pulling in Bayport for years."

I leaned forward. "Has Gorse always been the Red Arrow?"

Officer Olaf signed a paper and frowned. "Well, we still aren't positive the Red Arrow actually exists."

"You said he confessed to everything," I pointed out.

"Correction. He confessed to everything *he* did," Olaf clarified. "He won't talk about the Red Arrow. At all."

Just then we heard the door to the interrogation room open, and two police officers led Principal Gorse out in handcuffs. He had a strange expression on his face that I can only describe as disturbed. He was staring at his clasped hands like they held the secrets to the universe, and I was just waiting for him to rub his hands together and cackle, Mr. Burns–style.

Olaf startled and looked at us. I got the distinct sense that Principal Gorse was not meant to see us there.

He looked up and caught sight of Frank and me, still damp, but very much alive. His eyes bugged, and he pointed one bony finger at us (dragging the other hand with it because, you know, handcuffs). "You!" he shouted, in that low, gravelly voice from before.

The cops leading him tried to hustle him along, but

Gorse dug in his heels. "You think you've stopped it," he said, "but the Red Arrow cannot be stopped. Cut off its head, and another will grow in its place. It's only a matter of time, boys. I wasn't the first, and I won't be the last!"

The cops had succeeded in dragging him down the hall by then. But Gorse twisted his neck to fire one last parting shot.

"Good luck sleeping tonight," he said, his voice a snake-like whisper. Then the cops dragged him around the corner to the lockup, and he was gone.

I looked at Frank. Seriously, had the whole kindly principal thing been an act?

"Yeesh." Sometimes there are no other words.

Frank nodded. He looked at Olaf. "Do you believe us about the Red Arrow now?"

Olaf was still focused on his paperwork. He took out an actual rubber stamp and brought it down on the top of a form. The corner of his mouth quirked up as he replied, not lifting his eyes, "I suppose anything's possible in this town."

RETIRED 19

FRANK

YOU WANT TO OPEN WITH A JOKE," JOE suggested, leaning back in his chair and taking a sip of his Maximum Mocha. We were at the Meet Locker, trying to get some studying done. "It disarms the audience. Puts them on your side."

"As opposed to whose side?" I asked, my pencil hovering over my notebook. *What do flies wear on their feet?* I wrote, just beneath the title of my newly assigned speech. Answer: Shoos.

Joe leaned over and read what I'd jotted down. "I'd keep thinking."

Right. Well, luckily, I had a whole two weeks left to work on this one. Ms. Jones had forgiven me for going off on a tangent during my last speech. She understood that I was trying to vanquish a longtime Bayport menace. She hadn't completely let me off the hook, though. I'd been assigned a new speech.

Topic: Justice.

Joe suddenly grabbed his phone from where it sat on the table. "Ooh, ooh, ooh," he said, staring into the screen. "I just got service! Look, I have a voice mail."

"Some people ignore their phones while they're studying," I pointed out.

"Some people weren't on the receiving end of a wink from that cute Daisy Rodriguez in algebra this morning," Joe fired back, going into his voice mail. "Why yes, Daisy, I would be willing to explain parabolas in a closer setting. Oh."

Joe wrinkled his nose and replayed the message on speakerphone. We were the only two people in the Locker's back room.

"Hi, Joe. Listen, this is Megan Willensky. You know— Spanish class? Anyway, I'm calling because I have a problem that I think, um, you and your brother could help me with." She paused and dropped her voice to a whisper. "I heard what you did for Sharelle Bunyan?" Her voice rose back to a normal level. "Anyway, call me back. We can meet and I'll, um, tell you all about it. Thanks."

Joe looked at me unhappily. Principal Gorse was in jail, awaiting trial. It took some convincing, but Seth, Neal, and Pett had all gone on record with their stories. Olaf came through with some forensic evidence that tied Gorse to the explosion.

That was all good news, of course. The bad news was that Frank and I had been called into Chief Gomez's office with our dad to go over the Deal again in excruciating detail. We were being watched now, he told us. No more shenanigans. And absolutely no more investigating.

We were well and truly retired.

I looked at Joe sadly, then glanced at the time on his phone. "We'd better go," I said. "Aunt Trudy's making eggplant curry tonight. And you know she's still mad at us for lying to her about my ankle."

Joe nodded and wordlessly put his phone in his pocket. I picked up my notebook, and as I was putting it into my backpack, a tiny piece of paper fluttered out and landed on the table.

It landed faceup, staring back at us like an accusation.

The Red Arrow.

I looked at Joe. Neither of us said anything for a minute. Was this real? Or was somebody messing with us?

"Who?" he asked.

I shook my head. "Could be anybody," I said. "I had this notebook at school all day. Every class."

His brows furrowed. "It has to be a stupid joke. Right?"

I didn't say anything. I grabbed the paper and tossed it in a nearby trash can. I wanted to make a statement, in case anybody was watching.

Frank and Joe Hardy were not controlled by the Red Arrow.

"Let's go," I said to Joe.

Together, we hoisted our book bags onto our backs and sauntered out through the main room and into the sunny air.

Joe pulled his phone out of his pocket and kept playing with it the whole way to the car. Clicking it on, clicking it off. Checking for more messages. Fiddling with the volume.

When we climbed into the car and shut our doors, I put the key in the ignition and turned to him.

"You going to call her back?"

Joe looked at me, hopeful. "Should we?"

I nodded.

There was no use denying it. Sleuthing was in our blood.

Joe grinned and dialed the phone. He waited a few seconds for an answer, then said, "Hey, Megan, it's Joe Hardy returning your call. I heard you have a problem that my brother and I might be able to help you with?"

MYSTERY OF THE PHANTOM HEIST

KEYED UP

1

FRANK

"YOU'VE GOT TO SEE THIS, FRANK!" JOE said. "You too, Chet. It's totally sick."

Help, I thought as my brother held up his prized possession, a tablet, for the gazillionth time. Not another lame clip on YouTube!

It was the last thing I wanted to look at as we sat inside the swanky Peyton mansion. I wanted to check out the two slick cabin cruisers docked outside the bay window!

"Will you give us a break already, Joe?" I told him. "I think we've seen enough skateboarding squirrels and break-dancing babies to last a lifetime."

Our friend Chet Morton cracked a smile. "Yeah, but those rapping sock puppets you showed us before were pretty sick," he admitted. "Got any more of those?"

Joe shook his head. "Check it out—it's serious stuff," he said, practically shoving the tablet in our faces.

"You, serious?" I joked. "Since when?"

Joe knew what I meant. Our ages were only one year apart, but our personalities—worlds apart. Joe was always high-strung, fast-talking, and unpredictable. Me—I'm more the strong, silent type. At least that's what I like to think.

"Will you look at the clip already?" Joe urged. "I can't keep it on pause forever." He hadn't put down that fancy new tablet since he got it for his birthday. I couldn't really blame him. We couldn't have smartphones until we were in college, so the tablet was the next best thing. It surfed the Web, got e-mails— even took pictures and videos. Speaking of videos . . .

"Okay," I sighed. "But if I see one squirrel or sock puppet— it's over."

Chet and I leaned forward to watch the clip. There were no skateboarding squirrels or sock puppets—just a clerk at a fast-food take-out window, handing a paper bag to a customer. The clerk looked about sixteen or seventeen. The person behind the wheel had his back to the camera, which was probably being held by someone in the passenger seat.

"Bor-ing!" Chet sighed.

"Wait, here it comes," Joe said. He turned up the volume just as the clerk said, "Six dollars and seventy cents, please."

The driver reached out to pay. But then he yanked the lid off his jumbo cup and hurled what looked like a slushie all over the kid at the take-out window!

"Keep the change!" the driver cackled before zooming off. I could hear another voice snickering—probably the creep filming the whole thing.

I stared at the screen. "Definitely not cool," I said.

"And a perfectly good waste of a jumbo slushie," Chet joked.

"Not funny, Chet," Joe said with a frown.

"How did you find that clip, Joe?" I asked.

"Lonny, a guy in my math class, forwarded it to me," Joe explained. "Lonny was the poor clerk who got slushied."

"Did they ever find the guys who did it?" Chet asked.

Joe shook his head and said, "The burger place called the cops, but so far the slushie slinger's still on the loose."

"You mean it's a—cold case?" Chet joked. "Cold . . . slushie—get it?"

"That's about as funny as those skateboarding squirrels, Morton," I complained. "What we just saw was someone's idea of a dumb prank."

"Yeah, but whose?" Joe asked.

This time Chet heaved a big sigh. "Time out, you guys!" he said. "You promised your dad you were going to slow down the detective work, at least for now."

"Slow down?" Joe asked. "From something we've been doing since we were seven and eight? Not a chance, bud."

Of course, what Joe didn't mention was that we were one wrong move away from reform school. No one knew about the Deal except our family, the police, and our former principal—who had his own issues to deal with now!

"Yeah, but a promise is a promise," I said. "So put that thing away already, Joe."

"Before somebody comes in and sees it," Chet added.

"What would be so bad about that?" Joe asked.

"Because," Chet said, smiling, "surfing clips on YouTube isn't the thing to be doing in the parlor of one of the über-richest homes in Bayport."

Glancing around the posh room we were sitting in, I knew Chet got the über-rich part right.

"Check out the pool table, you guys," I said.

"As soon as I finish checking out those little beauties," Chet said, nodding toward a nearby table. On it was a silver platter filled with fancy frosted pastries.

"Don't even think of taking one," Joe said, pointing to a portrait hanging on the wall. "Not while he's watching us."

I studied the portrait in the heavy wooden frame. The subject was a middle-aged guy in a blue blazer and beige pants. His hair was dark, with streaks of gray, and he was holding a golf club. I figured he was Sanford T. Peyton, the owner of the house, the boats, and the pastries.

I didn't know much about him, just that when the multi-billionaire dude wasn't living large in Bayport with his wife and daughter, he was opening hotels all over the country and maybe the world. The guy was crazy rich. And right now, crazy late!

"We've been waiting in this room almost half an hour," I said as I glanced at the antique clock standing against the wall. "Can someone please remind me why we're here?"

"Gladly!" Chet said. He stood up with a smug smile. "My friends, we are about to be interviewed by Sanford T. Peyton for the honor of working the hottest party of the decade—at least here in Bayport."

With that, Chet turned to another portrait hanging on the opposite wall. This one showed a teenage girl with light brown hair, wearing a white sundress and holding a Cavalier King Charles spaniel with huge eyes.

"His daughter Lindsay's Sweet Sixteen!" Chet declared, pointing to the portrait with a flourish.

"Cute," Joe said with a grin. "And I don't mean the dog."

Chet and Joe were definitely psyched about this party. Too bad I couldn't say the same for myself.

"You guys, we weren't good enough to be invited to Lindsay's Sweet Sixteen," I said. "So why should we work it?"

"Two words, my friend, two words," Chet said with a smile. "Food and—"

"Girls!" Joe blurted out.

"Got it!" I said with a smirk.

The only thing I knew about Lindsay was that she didn't go to Bayport High with Chet, Joe, and me. Which was no surprise.

"Most of the kids at this party will be from Bay Academy," I said, referring to the posh private school in Bayport. "And you know what they're like. Total snobs—"

Chet cleared his throat loudly as the door swung open. Joe

and I jumped up from our chairs as Sanford Peyton marched in, followed by his daughter, Lindsay. Walking briskly behind Lindsay was another girl of about the same age. She had long black hair, and her dark eyes were cast downward at her own tablet she was holding. As she glanced up, she threw me a quick smile. I caught myself smiling back.

Hmm, I thought, still smiling. *Maybe this job isn't such a bad idea.*

"Have a seat, boys," Sanford said as he sat behind his desk, facing us. Lindsay and the other girl stood behind Sanford, looking over his shoulders at us.

As we sat back down, I could see Sanford studying the applications we'd filled out.

"I see you all go to Bayport High," he said gruffly.

"Yes, sir," I said.

"Daddy, they're cute, but not gladiator material," Lindsay cut in.

The three of us stared at Lindsay.

"Say what?" Joe said under his breath.

"Gladiators?" Chet said. "I thought you needed waiters. You know, to pass around the pigs in blankets."

"There will be no pigs in blankets at this party, boys," Sanford said.

"What kind of a party has no pigs in blankets?" Chet asked.

"Daddy." Lindsay sighed as she checked out her manicure. "Just explain."

Sanford folded his hands on the desk.

"You see, boys," he said, "the theme of Lindsay's Sweet Sixteen is No Place Like Rome. Four strong young men dressed as gladiators accompany Lindsay into the hall as she makes her grand entrance."

"You mean Empress Lindsay," Lindsay emphasized. "And the gladiators will be carrying me on a throne designed just for the occasion."

Joe, Chet, and I stared at Lindsay as she flipped her hair over her shoulder. Was she serious?

"Got it, I think," Joe said. "But you'll still need waiters, right?"

"For sure," Lindsay replied. She turned to the girl with the tablet and said, "Sierra, make sure you get the music I want for my grand entrance."

"'Hotter Than Vesuvius,'" Sierra said, tapping on her tablet. "Got it."

So her name was Sierra. Nice name for a nice-looking girl. I watched Sierra busily taking notes until Sanford's voice interrupted my thoughts.

"If we do hire you as waiters," Sanford said, "there'll be a dress code."

"That's no problem, sir," I said. "Joe and I own suits."

"Oh, not suits," Sanford said. "Togas."

"Togas?" I repeated.

"You mean those sheets the guys in ancient Rome used to wrap themselves up in?" Chet asked, wide-eyed.

I glanced sideways at Joe, who didn't look too thrilled either. Was this Sweet Sixteen really worth it? But when I turned to look at Sierra, I got my answer. You bet!

"I'm sure we can get togas," I said.

"Or some white tablecloths from our mom," Joe added.

Lindsay tapped her chin as she studied us one at a time. She pointed to me, then to Joe.

"Those two can be waiters," Lindsay said.

"Just me and Frank?" Joe asked, surprised. "What about Chet?"

Sanford didn't even look at Chet as he went on with the party details.

"The Sweet Sixteen will be held this Sunday night, being that the next day is a holiday," Sanford said. "That gives us a whole day on Saturday to prepare food, the decorations—"

"My outfits!" Lindsay cut in.

I could see Chet making a time-out sign with his hands. "Excuse me," he said. "But what about me? Aren't I going to work this party too?"

"Maybe," Lindsay said. She turned to Sierra. "Put that one on the B-list. We can always call him if we get desperate."

"B-list?" Chet muttered.

Sanford looked at Joe and me and said, "Well? Don't you want your job instructions?"

I glanced over at Chet, who looked like he'd just been kicked in the stomach.

"No, thank you, sir," I said, standing up. "It's either all of us or none of us."

Joe stared at me before jumping up from his seat too. "Yeah," he said. "Come on, Chet, let's go."

"Are you guys crazy?" Lindsay cried as the three of us headed for the door. "Do you realize how amazing this party will be? You never know who you might meet!"

"If the kids are anything like you," Joe mumbled, "that's what we're afraid of."

I wasn't sure whether Sierra or the Peytons had heard Joe, and I didn't want to find out. All I wanted to do was get out of that house ASAP!

"B-list," Chet kept repeating once we were outside. "Why do you think Lindsay put me on the B-list?"

"*B* for 'bodacious,' dude," Joe said, laughing. "That's you!"

Chet cracked a smile.

"Forget about Princess Lindsay, Chet," I said. "I heard Bay Academy kids can be snooty—but that one takes the cake."

"Wrong!" Chet declared. He pulled a squished iced pastry from his jacket pocket. "I took the cake—on our way out!"

"Oh, snap!" Joe laughed.

As we walked to my car, I had no trouble forgetting about Lindsay, but Sierra kept popping into my head. Then, as if Joe had read my mind . . .

"I saw you watching that Sierra, Frank," he said with a grin.

"You never miss a beat, do you?" I smirked.

Joe shrugged and said, "Just saying!"

Leaving the sprawling Peyton mansion behind us, we walked down the flagstone path toward the private parking lot. I could see my car in the distance right where I'd parked it. But before we could get to my secondhand fuel-efficient sedan, we had to pass a parking lot full of luxury SUVs and sports cars.

"Boats and cars," I sighed. "How many fancy toys can one family have?"

"Not enough if you're a Peyton," Chet said. "Which ride do you think is Empress Lindsay's?"

Joe pointed to a red sports convertible whose vanity plate read LUV2SHOP. "I'll take a wild guess and say that one!" he chuckled.

Chet whistled through his teeth as we went to check out the shiny car. The top was down, so we got a good look.

"Black leather seating," I observed as the three of us walked slowly around the car. "MP3 output . . ."

"Yeah, and I'll bet that's a heated steering wheel," Chet added.

"That's not all it has, you guys," Joe called.

Glancing up, I saw my brother staring at the car door. He didn't look impressed. Just dead serious.

"What's up?" I asked.

Without saying a word, Joe pointed to the door. I turned to see what he was pointing at. That's when my jaw practically hit the ground—because scratched across the gleaming red door were the angry words:

RICH WITCH!

BAD APPETITE

2

JOE

THE THREE OF US GAWKED AT THE DOOR
and the message. I had seen keyed cars before—
but never scratches as deep as this.

"Whoa," Frank said. "A keyed car has got to
be the worst kind of prank."

"Worse than a million hurled slushies," Chet agreed.

The word "slushies" made me remember the YouTube
video—and the clueless punks who starred in it.

"You guys," I said. "What if this was done by the same
slushie-slingers we saw in the video clip?"

Frank gave it a thought, then shook his head. "I don't
think so," he said.

"How come?" I asked.

"Because I think it was another Sweet Sixteen reject,"

Frank explained. "Who knows how many kids Lindsay dissed by putting on the B-list today?"

"And watch out," Chet joked. "When provoked, we B-listers can get pretty ugly."

I ran my finger along the deep scratches. Frank was probably right.

"It wasn't one of Lindsay's friends, because they're probably rich too," I thought out loud. "It probably *was* a reject like us."

"Hey, you guys weren't rejected from working that party," Chet reminded us. "You can still be fitted for your togas, you know."

"Thanks, but no thanks," Frank said. "Lindsay's Sweet Sixteen may be the party of the decade, but it's not worth the humiliation."

"And who needs all that fancy-schmancy food when you can get the most awesome burgers and fries at Chomp and Chew?" I added.

Chet's eyes lit up at the magic words. "Chomp and Chew, huh?" he asked with a smile. "Could that be a hint?"

Frank shook his head as he pointed to the scratches on the car door. "Wait a minute, you guys," he said. "What are we going to do about Lindsay's car?"

"What do you mean?" I asked.

"I mean, should we tell Lindsay about the scratches?" Frank asked. "She really ought to know."

I glanced back at the Peyton house. Sure, I felt bad for

Empress Lindsay and her trashed car. But the thought of facing her and her dad again practically made my skin crawl.

"Nah," I said. "She'll find out soon enough."

We took one last look at the scratches before walking away.

"What do you think Lindsay will do when she sees her keyed car?" Chet asked.

"Get Daddy to buy her a new one?" I said with a shrug.

The Chomp and Chew was only a fifteen-minute drive from the Peytons'. You couldn't miss the place, with its giant neon burger spinning on the roof. It may have been super tacky, but the burgers were tastier than filet mignon. . . . Not that I'd ever tasted filet mignon.

By the time we were cozy in the booth next to the window and under the TV, we had forgotten all about Lindsay and her keyed car. All we could think about were the burgers we were chomping and chewing: guacamole burger for me, Western burger for Frank, and the everything burger for Chet.

"Our favorite burgers and our favorite booth!" Chet said, popping a pickle chip into his mouth. "Are we lucky or what?"

My mouth was too stuffed to answer, so I gave Chet a nod. As my eyes began to drift up toward the TV, I spotted someone I knew from school. It was Tony, a Bayport High senior like Frank. But Tony wasn't happily chomping or chewing like us. He was crazy busy clearing dirty dishes and glasses from a nearby booth.

"There's Tony Riley," I whispered to Frank and Chet. "I didn't know he worked as a busboy here."

We watched as Tony picked up his tip. He looked at it, rolled his eyes, and murmured something under his breath.

"The guy definitely looks overworked," Frank whispered.

I felt bad for Tony and wanted to cheer him up. So I waved and called, "Yo, Tony! I'll bet free burgers come with the job, huh?"

Tony dropped his rag on the table and walked over to our booth.

"Who cares about that?" he said in a low voice. "After working in this place almost all day, the last thing I want is a Chomp and Chew burger."

"Wow," Chet said, shaking his head. "This place must really be a sweatshop for you to pass up a Chomp and Chew burger."

Tony snorted and said, "Working in a sweatshop would be a breeze compared to this place. A kid in the last booth just wrote his name on the table with ketchup!"

"What was his name?" I asked.

"Al," Tony replied.

"At least it's only two letters," Frank said.

"He wrote his full name, guys!" Tony sighed. "Alexander!"

"Bummer," I said. Maybe that sweatshop *was* a better deal.

"If you hate it that much, Tony," Frank said, lowering his voice, "why don't you just look for another job?"

"Part-time jobs aren't so easy to get, Frank," Tony explained.

"And I'm saving up for a new phone, so I can't quit now."

Frank nodded as if to say he got it.

"Frank and I can't even have fancy phones yet," I said. "But this is the next best thing."

"What is?" Tony asked.

"Glad you asked," I said, pulling out my tablet. "Tony, my man, when was the last time you saw a skateboarding squirrel?"

"Spare me, Joe," Frank groaned.

But Tony finally cracked a smile. "Squirrels on skateboards—no way!" He laughed. "Let me see that."

I was about to search for the clip when a voice shouted, "Yo, busboy! Why don't you start earning your minimum wage?"

Tony froze. So did we. Who'd said that?

Turning my head, I saw a bunch of guys in a nearby booth laughing it up. They were wearing polo shirts and khaki pants. One of the guys had on a Bay Academy varsity jacket.

"Bunch of jerks," Chet said. "Who do those guys think they are?"

"They're Bay Academy kids, that's who," Frank whispered. "No doubt they'll be going to Lindsay's Sweet Sixteen."

"Yeah," I scoffed. "But they won't be passing around barbecued hot wings and punch."

Looking at Tony, I could tell he was trying hard to keep his cool.

"No problem, guys," he called back. "I'll be there in a minute."

"A minute isn't good enough!" the guy with a maroon polo shirt and wavy blond hair boomed. "This table here is pretty messy."

His friends snickered as he picked up a half-full glass of chocolate shake and poured it all over the table!

Tony's face turned beet red, but he kept his mouth shut. Not me . . .

"Hey, losers!" I shouted toward the booth. "Why don't you clean up your own mess?"

"Yeah, well, why don't you shut up?" the guy with the biggest mouth snapped.

"Game over," Frank muttered as he stood up.

He looked like he was about to go over to the Bay Academy booth, until we all saw someone in a police uniform heading up the aisle.

"Sweet," I said. "Somebody must have called the cops on those guys."

As detectives, Frank and I knew all the officers in Bayport. Sometimes we'd ask them for advice on a case we were working on. Sometimes they'd even ask us for advice, which was really cool.

Most of the officers were great guys—minus one named Officer Olaf. His beef with Frank and me was that we were always trying to do his job. Lucky for us, the cop at the Chomp and Chew was Officer Schroeder.

I expected Officer Schroeder to stop at the Bay Academy booth. Instead, he walked right past them, straight to us.

"Boys," he said with a nod. "The chief wants you to come to the station right away."

Frank and I traded confused looks.

"We've retired from investigating, Officer Schroeder," I said.

"It's not about a case, Joe," Officer Schroeder said. "It's about the gash on Lindsay Peyton's car."

"Oh!" Frank said with a nod. "Does the chief want to know what we saw?"

Officer Schroeder's mouth became a grim line. "No," he said. "The chief wants to know what you did."

MISINFORMED 3

FRANK

THIS DIDN'T LOOK GOOD.

"Excuse me, Officer Schroeder," I said. "Does the chief think that we keyed Lindsay's car?"

The officer heaved a sigh. I could tell he wasn't thrilled with the situation. All the cops had known us since we were little kids.

"You can ask all the questions you want at the station," he explained. "Come on, guys, pay your bill and let's go."

"Okay," Chet said. "But can we at least get our burgers to go?"

"Chet, just pay," I murmured.

Quickly and quietly we laid our money on the table before we left. By now all eyes in the Chomp and Chew were on us as we followed Officer Schroeder up the aisle.

I knew we weren't criminals, but I sure felt like one.

"Good luck, guys," Tony whispered as we walked past him. "Whatever this is all about."

"Thanks," I whispered back.

I could hear snickering as we passed the Bay Academy booth. I tried not to look at the creeps until one of them sneered, "Bad day, burger boys?"

Without even looking, I knew who it was—the idiot who'd tipped over the chocolate shake.

"Surprise, surprise," Joe said, loud enough for the whole booth to hear. "I thought they didn't allow animals in here."

"Will you quit it, Joe?" I muttered. "The last thing we need is more trouble."

Once outside, we followed Officer Schroeder to the squad car. He walked a good few feet ahead of us, giving us some privacy.

"I knew it," I murmured. "I knew we should have told Lindsay about her car."

"Frank, I just had a weird thought," Joe said quietly.

"What?" I asked.

"What if they dust the car for fingerprints?" Joe squeaked. "I ran my finger along the scratch—about three times."

"You think that's bad?" Chet said. "I snatched a pastry on the way out. What was I thinking?"

All I knew was that this was serious stuff.

"Look," I said. "When we get to the station, we'll just tell Chief Gomez the truth. He's known for being fair."

"Um . . . FYI," Chet said. "I heard Chief Gomez retired about a week ago. Some other officer at the station was just promoted to chief."

"Which one?" I asked.

"How should I know?" Chet said. "You're the detectives."

"Well, that explains it, then," I said. "This new chief, whoever he or she is, probably wants to be extra thorough. You know, cover all the bases."

"If you say so," Joe said. "I just hope covering all the bases doesn't mean fingerprints!"

We left my car in the Chomp and Chew parking lot, and Officer Schroeder drove us to the station. Joe and I were glad he didn't run the siren—the last thing we wanted was more attention.

The ride to the station was only fifteen minutes but felt like fifteen hours. When we arrived, Officer Schroeder led us to the receiving desk. I was almost anxious to see the chief and get this over with. If he or she was as fair as Chief Gomez, we'd be out of here in a matter of minutes.

"I've got the Hardy brothers and the Morton kid," Officer Schroeder said.

"Okay," the officer behind the desk said. "Chief Olaf said he'd see them right away."

Chief Olaf?

I stared at Joe, who looked about as sick as I felt. If the new chief of police was Officer Olaf, we did not have a chance!

"Yo, Frank," Joe whispered as we followed another officer down a long hallway.

"What?" I whispered back.

"Do you think they have wi-fi in the slammer?" Joe asked.

"Whatever," I mumbled.

The new chief of police, Olaf, was sitting behind his desk as we filed into his office. He looked up at us and immediately scowled.

"If you Hardys think you're off the hook because your father was a private investigator, well, think again!" he barked.

"We weren't planning on playing the dad card, Officer— I mean, Chief Olaf," Joe said.

"What exactly is this all about, Chief?" I asked carefully.

"Didn't Schroeder tell you?" Chief Olaf demanded. "Something nasty was scratched on the door of Lindsay Peyton's very expensive car."

"We know about that," Chet blurted.

"You bet you know," Chief Olaf said. "You boys were at the house at the time of the incident. Someone even saw you hanging around Lindsay's car in the parking lot."

Someone? I wondered who had gone to the police about us. Was it Sanford Peyton? Lindsay herself?

"We were at the house, Chief, that's true," I said. "But we were there to apply for a job, not to make trouble."

The chief leaned forward. "And this job would get you into one of the biggest parties in Bayport, right?"

"Lindsay's Sweet Sixteen," Joe said with a nod.

"Well, you didn't take the job, did you?" Chief Olaf asked. "In fact, you left the place pretty steamed, am I right, boys?"

"They called me B-list material!" Chet blurted. "How would you feel?"

I gave Chet a quick but subtle elbow jab. He had a habit of stuffing his mouth—and running it too.

"Well?" Chief Olaf asked, leaning back in his big leather chair. "So what's the story?"

"Chief, you know we're detectives," I said.

The chief raised an eyebrow. "Last I checked, your dad and I discussed that you should concentrate on other things."

"Okay, we *were* detectives," I said quickly.

"We solved crimes," Joe added. "We don't commit them."

"Then what about that guy?" the chief said, leaning over to point at Chet. "Mr. Peyton said he stole a pastry!"

"Rats!" Chet hissed.

I took a deep breath, trying to keep my cool. "Chief Olaf, we had nothing to do with Lindsay's car being keyed," I said. "We can even prove it if you just give us a little time."

"I think this prank had something to do with another one that happened yesterday," Joe said.

"Show him the video, Joe!" Chet urged.

But the second Joe took out his tablet, the chief held up his hand as if to say, *Stop*.

"This is nothing new," Chief Olaf said. "Those pranks have been going on around Bayport for weeks."

"Weeks?" I said, surprised.

"Then you'll definitely want to look at this, Chief," Joe said, holding out his tablet.

"Why? So I can watch Katy Perry, or whoever it is you kids like these days?" Chief Olaf growled. "And as for you guys working on another case—give me a break. My best officers can't even catch those punks."

"Those punks?" Chet said hopefully. "As in . . . someone else?"

"So you believe us when we say we didn't key Lindsay's car?" I asked slowly.

Chief Olaf narrowed his steely blue eyes straight at us. "Let's just say I'm letting you go with a warning," he said.

I could hear Chet sigh with relief. I, too, was relieved. We were finally off the hook . . . or were we?

"But just remember that I'm keeping my eyes on all you kids," Chief Olaf said sternly. "Even you so-called detectives."

So-called detectives? Ouch! Technically, we weren't supposed to do any more investigating after our last adventure (if you call having a crime gang coming after you an adventure), but since we helped put away the Red Arrow, Dad and Chief Olaf made us a deal that if we checked in and made sure to follow a few guidelines, we could still catch a few bad guys every now and then. Most important, we wouldn't be sent to the notorious J'Adoube School for Behavior Modification. And it looks like we might be catching bad guys sooner than expected.

When the chief opened the door, we couldn't get out fast enough. We walked quickly up the hallway, not looking back.

"So-called detectives," Joe scoffed. "He's just jealous because we're good at doing his job."

"Joe, keep it down!" I warned. "The last thing we need is more trouble with the new chief."

"But Olaf practically said we're clean!" Joe insisted.

"Let's just get out of here," I said as we stepped into the waiting area.

"Are you sure you want to leave?" Chet asked.

"Yeah, why?" I asked. I followed Chet's gaze to the long wooden bench against the wall. Sitting on it were an elderly woman, a middle-aged man, and . . . Sierra?

My eyes widened as the pretty, dark-haired girl stood up and smiled in our direction. It was Sierra, all right. But what was she doing at the station, of all places?

That's when it suddenly clicked—and when my admiration turned into anger. The person who'd gone to the cops about us wasn't Sanford Peyton or Lindsay.

It was Sierra!

CLUED IN 4

JOE

I DIDN'T HAVE TO READ FRANK'S MIND TO KNOW he was thinking the same as me—had Sierra told on us to the cops?

"So you're the informant," Frank said as Sierra walked toward us.

"Informant?" she asked with a smile.

"Let me put it in plain English," I said. "Did you come to the cops to tell them we keyed Lindsay's car?"

Sierra's smile turned into a frown. "I saw what happened, and it's such a bummer," she said. "Lindsay adores that car."

"I believe that," Frank said. "So why didn't the chief look totally convinced that we didn't key it?"

"I believe you," Sierra said, tilting her head and looking

all flirty. "You're not gladiator material—or vandal material, for that matter."

"Did you tell that to Mr. Peyton?" I asked.

"How could I?" Sierra said, her eyes wide. "He was already on the phone with the chief."

Okay. That explained who'd called the cops, but it didn't explain what Sierra was doing at the police station.

"So, do you come here often?" I joked. "Must be the free coffee and doughnuts."

"I happen to drink tea," Sierra said. "And I'm here because Mr. Peyton wanted me to make sure the Sweet Sixteen had the police presence he requested."

Frank looked relieved to find out that Sierra wasn't the snitch. "If you ask me," he said, "that party is going to need the whole force."

"What do you mean?" Sierra asked.

"With all those kids from Bay Academy," Frank said, "the place will be oozing with bling, fancy watches, and state-of-the-art phones."

"Hey, no fair," Sierra said, faking at being insulted. "I go to Bay Academy."

I could practically hear Frank gulp.

"Awkward," Chet said under his breath.

"Um—you do?" Frank asked, turning red. "I had no idea. You don't seem like . . . I mean—"

"It's okay," Sierra laughed. "Oh, and FYI, I wasn't invited to Lindsay's Sweet Sixteen either."

"You weren't invited?" I asked, surprised. "And you don't mind doing all this grunt work for the Peytons?"

Sierra shook her head.

"I'm interning for the head event planner of the party. It's what I want to do after I graduate college, so it's really good experience," she explained. "Although walking Lindsay's yappy little dog was definitely not in my job description."

Frank laughed, a little too loudly. He blushed when the officer behind the desk cleared her throat.

"So you go to Bay Academy," Frank said, lowering his voice. "I guess that means you don't date Bayport High guys."

Whoa. Frank wasn't exactly smooth when it came to girls, so for him to make a move, he'd have to be pretty serious.

Chet and I turned to Sierra for her reaction. She flashed Frank a sly smile before pulling out a pen. Then she picked up Frank's hand and wrote her name and number on his palm.

"Why don't you call me and find out?" Sierra said with a grin.

Man, I thought. *If Frank wasn't already crushing on this girl, I might!*

Chet glanced at Frank's scribbled-on palm. "If you do go out with Frank . . . Sierra Mitchell," he said, "you won't be sorry, that's for sure."

"What do you mean?" Sierra asked.

"Yeah," Frank demanded. "What do you mean?"

"Because Frank is the best detective in Bayport, that's what I mean," Chet said. "Other than his brother, Joe, here, of course."

"We're a team," I added quickly.

Sierra tilted her head to study Frank, then me. "Detectives?" she asked. "Seriously?"

"Not only that," Chet went on, "Frank and Joe are going to find out who keyed Lindsay's car if they have to turn this jerkwater town upside down!"

"We are?" Frank cried.

It was news to me, too, but the most surprised seemed to be Sierra. Her eyes lit up like headlights as she said, "You are?"

Frank stared back at Sierra. Then he smiled and said, "Um . . . yeah, sure."

"I guess that means we're on the case," I said.

"Okay, kids," the officer behind the desk snapped. "This isn't a bowling alley—time to socialize somewhere else."

"We were just leaving, Officer," Frank said.

"And I'm here on business," Sierra told her.

Frank gave Sierra a little wave before we headed out of the station. We had to walk along the road back to Frank's car, still parked at the Chomp and Chew. It was a long walk, but we were just happy to get out of the station. As for Frank, he looked just plain happy!

"Who knew getting arrested would be a great way to meet girls, huh, Frank?" I teased.

"We weren't arrested, we were just warned," Frank said. "And all Sierra did was give me her number, so the ball is in my court."

"Yeah, right," Chet chuckled. "Just make sure you don't wash that hand, dude."

We were having a good laugh when I heard the fired-up engine of a speeding car. I turned just in time to see a shiny black Benz barreling down the road. Frank, Chet, and I stopped to watch the car as it came our way. A car window came down and . . . *CLUNK!!* An empty soda can was hurled out the window, barely missing Chet!

"Hey!" Chet yelled.

The Benz kept going, so fast I didn't see who was inside. But I could hear them laughing—and it sounded exactly like the guys at the Chomp and Chew!

"Jerks!" I called after the car.

"Hey, Chet," Frank asked, "are you okay, buddy?"

"Yeah, sure," Chet said with a nod. "Who do you think those guys were?"

"It had to be those Bay Academy losers," I said angrily. "The ones who were giving Tony a hard time at the Chomp and Chew."

Chet kicked the can away. "What's with those Bay Academy kids, anyway?" he wondered aloud as we continued walking up the road. "I mean, why are they being such morons?"

"Come on, Chet," Frank said. "Not all Bay Academy kids are bad news."

I raised an eyebrow at my brother.

"Hmm," I teased. "And does her name happen to be Sierra?"

Frank gave me a little push. "Okay, you guys," he said. "Now that we're on the case, we've got to get serious about Lindsay's car. Who do you think could have done it?"

"I still think the punks who slushied Lonny are the punks who keyed the car." I patted the pocket holding my tablet. "And if that stunt goes viral—we'll know for sure!"

"No games at the dinner table, Joe," Mom said as she placed a platter of lasagna inches away from me. "You know the rules."

I looked up from my tablet and said, "But it's not a game, Mom. I'm looking to see if any more pranks went viral."

"We're working on a new case," Frank explained. "Somebody scratched up Lindsay Peyton's car. We want to find out who did it."

Dad stopped piling lasagna on his plate. "Are you sure that's a good idea, guys?" he asked. "After what happened today with Chief Olaf?"

We had already told Dad about being called to the police station. He wanted to call Chief Olaf, but we begged him not to play the dad card.

"Dad, we're not going to stop working on cases just because the chief thinks we're detective wannabes," I said.

Dad nodded as if he understood. Fenton Hardy had

worked as a detective for decades. He did some occasional consulting still, but was focused on writing full-time.

"Plus, the faster we find the real culprits," Frank said, "the faster the chief will stop blaming innocent kids around Bayport—"

"Like us," I cut in.

"Okay," Dad said, taking a helping of salad. "Then go for it."

Mom cleared her throat to get my attention.

"You may have won Dad's argument, Joe," Mom said, narrowing her eyes at my tablet. "But you didn't win mine."

"Okay, okay," I said, putting it away.

Our mom, Laura Hardy, was a star real estate agent in Bayport. She could convince anyone to buy a home—or put away their tablets at dinner.

I was just about to pile some lasagna on my own plate when I saw Frank sniffing the air.

"What's that smell?" Frank asked, wiggling his nose.

"Grated cheese?" I guessed.

"No," Dad groaned. "It's your aunt Trudy burning those smelly scented candles again."

"But Aunt Trudy lives in the apartment above the garage," I said. "How can we smell them all the way over here?"

"Because that's how potent they are," Dad said. "If you ask me, they smell more like rotten eggs than spring rain and patchouli."

"Eggs—that reminds me," Mom said. "Someone at work told me there was a prank at the library last night."

Prank? My ears perked up like a dog hearing a whistle.

"What kind of prank, Mom?" I asked.

"Something about someone throwing eggs down the book drop," Mom said, shaking her head. "A half dozen books were totally ruined."

Frank shot me a look across the table. Another prank in Bayport? Now I really wanted to check out YouTube to see if it had gone viral. I had a feeling Frank did too.

The two of us practically inhaled our lasagna. As soon as we were excused, we raced up the stairs to my room. We sat down on the floor—but not before I tossed aside a bunch of dirty socks, a hoodie, some notebooks, and a half-eaten banana.

"Sometimes I can't believe we have the same DNA." Frank sighed. "When are you going to clean up this place?"

"I just did," I said. "You should have seen it before."

"How are we going to find it?" Frank asked. "There are millions of videos on YouTube."

"We could search 'egg pranks,'" I said as I turned on the tablet. But before I typed in a search, I had another idea. "Or . . . we could find the user name for the slushie video."

"What good would that do?" Frank asked.

"We can do a search of the user name and see if he or she posted the egg prank," I explained.

"Go for it," Frank said.

It didn't take me long to find the infamous slushie-slinger clip. It was posted by some guy who called himself "slickbro13."

"Slickbro13, slickbro13," I repeated. "What do you think the number thirteen stands for?"

"Bad luck?" Frank guessed.

"It was definitely bad luck for Lonny," I said as I searched for more slickbro13 clips.

It didn't take long to find what we were looking for. Not only did we find a clip of the egg drop crime at the library, we found other videos of window smashings, Dumpster tippings—even more slushy slingings at different fast-food places. And all of them posted by slickbro13.

"This must be the vandalism Chief Olaf was talking about," Frank said. "The ones that happened over the last few weeks."

I checked to see the dates on some of the clips. They had been posted during that time.

"Who are the kids in the videos?" I wondered.

To get a better look, we switched over to my computer. There I was able to enlarge the videos, even pause them at certain points. It helped, but not enough.

"The vandals are wearing dark bandannas over their faces," Frank pointed out. "The videos were also shot at night, which makes it extra hard to identify them."

"Why do you think they posted their pranks, Frank?" I asked. "On YouTube of all places, for everybody to see?"

Frank shrugged and said, "Probably to show off. Or maybe as a message to the cops to catch them if they can."

The cops made me think of Lindsay's vandalized car. After a quick search, I found a video of that prank too. But since all we could see was the vandal's hand scratching the car, it was even harder to make out.

"Great," Frank complained.

I reran the video, carefully watching the hand as it used a key to scratch out the words RICH WITCH.

For some reason this prank had been pulled during the day, not night. Not only could I see the color of Lindsay's car, I could make out the color of the vandal's sleeve—dark green with gold trim. Colors I had seen many times before.

"Frank," I said, "that sleeve has our school colors on it!"

Frank leaned forward for a better look. He turned to me and said, "That's our school varsity jacket. I'm almost sure of it."

"That's what I thought," I said. "We may not know who those viral vandals are, but we know where they are."

"Yeah," Frank said with a deep frown. "Our school!"

FOUND 5

FRANK

AS I DROVE TO SCHOOL THE NEXT MORN-
ing, I kept my eyes on the road and my
mind on the case. We now knew that one
of the viral vandals went to Bayport High.
It didn't tell us who the culprit was, but it
was a pretty good start.

"Here's the plan," I said, stopping at the light. "We're
going to check out every kid in our classes for clues."

"Every kid?" Joe said from the passenger seat. "What do
we look for?"

"Varsity jackets, for one," I said. "Then there are those
dark bandannas."

"As if the vandals are going to wear bandannas over their
faces at school." Joe rolled his eyes.

"Just keep your eyes peeled, that's all I'm saying," I said as I drove around the corner. Bayport High School was halfway up the street. As I pulled up to the school, I noticed a bunch of teachers and kids crowded around the basketball court.

"A game so early?" I wondered out loud.

"Maybe it's practice," Joe figured.

I parked in the student parking lot. As Joe and I made our way to the court, I could see Principal Vega. He was shaking his head slowly as he spoke to the big guy in a beige suit. At first I thought it was Mr. Sweeney, the history teacher, but as we got closer, my stomach did a triple flip.

"Principal Vega is talking to Chief Olaf," I groaned under my breath.

"Do you think the chief is here about us?" Joe asked.

"Doubtful," I said. "Maybe Chief Olaf figured out that the vandals go to our school."

Joe and I joined Chet and his sister Iola near the basketball court. Iola Morton was the same age as Joe and just as fearless. She didn't look much like Chet, but their appetites for burgers were practically identical.

"What's up?" I asked.

"Check it out," Chet said.

I looked to see where Chet was pointing. Sprayed across the basketball court in red paint was the word "Scaredevils."

"Scaredevils," Joe read out loud. "Sounds like some kind of gang."

"Yeah," I said, staring at the tag. "A gang of viral vandals."

"Chet told me about the slushie clip," Iola asked. "Were there more?"

"We found a YouTube video of the car keying," Joe explained. "The vandals might be Bayport High students."

"No way," Chet said.

"Does Principal Vega know?" Iola asked.

"He will as soon as we tell him," I said. "Chief Olaf ought to know what we found out too."

"You're going to deal with Olaf again?" Chet groaned. "Good luck."

"Thanks, dude," Joe said. "Something tells me we're going to need it."

Joe and I squeezed through a crowd of kids to get to the principal and Chief Olaf. The chief frowned when he saw us.

"Principal Vega," I said, "Joe and I might have some information about this tag."

"And it's not about us!" Joe said, looking straight at Chief Olaf.

Principal Vega was new to Bayport High, but he knew we had done detective work in the past.

"All right, then, boys," Principal Vega said. "What do you know?"

The other students crowded closer to hear. Just in case some of them might be Scaredevils, I kept my voice low.

"We think some of the vandals go to Bayport High," I said.

Joe nodded at the tag on the basketball court. "Like that Scaredevils gang," he said.

"Gang?" Principal Vega shook his head and said, "That's highly unlikely."

"Why?" Joe asked.

"I may have been here only a few weeks," Principal Vega said, "but I know that Bayport High School has no gang activity—and never will, if I can help it."

"But—" I started to say.

"Don't you have a class to go to, Hardys?" Chief Olaf cut in.

"Don't you want to know what we found out?" Joe asked.

"Sir," I quickly added.

Chief Olaf opened his mouth to say something, but Principal Vega piped up.

"Thank you, Frank, Joe," the principal said. "But the chief and I have got this covered."

Joe and I sulked away from the basketball court. I wasn't surprised that Chief Olaf didn't believe us, but Principal Vega wouldn't even hear us out!

"Well, that was a total waste," I grumbled.

"I'll bet some Scaredevils were nearby having a good laugh too," Joe said.

We were about to walk back to Chet and Iola when Joe suddenly said, "Frank—look over there."

"What?" I asked.

Joe nodded toward the street. "That black Benz outside the school," he said. "Didn't we see that car some-where?"

I turned to look at the car. It did look familiar, and right away I knew why. . . .

"That's the car that soda can was thrown from," I said. "The one that almost hit Chet."

I recognized the pugnacious face staring out of the car window too. It was the Bay Academy guy from the Chomp and Chew.

"What's he doing at our school?" I asked. "That's what I'd like to know."

"Seeing how the other half lives?" Joe scoffed.

The driver glared at me, then at Joe. He then grabbed the wheel and drove away, tires squealing.

We hurried to the curb to watch the car take off.

"Why would a Bay Academy kid care what was going on at our school?" I asked.

"Unless he had something to do with the tag on the basketball court," Joe said. "And the other pranks around Bayport."

"Too bad we don't know his name," I said.

"We might know more than you think," Joe said. "I caught the guy's vanity plate as he took off. He goes by—are you ready? Awesome Dude!"

"Awesome Dude?" I said. "Give me a break."

We still didn't know the driver's real name. But his vanity plate was a start.

· · ·

Throughout the day, Joe and I gave ourselves the same assignment: to ask questions about the viral videos and the mysterious "Awesome Dude" in the black car.

Joe and I weren't in the same classes, but most of the kids we questioned didn't have a clue about the videos or the vanity plate. Some knew a couple of "awesome dudes," but they didn't drive expensive black cars. After school Joe was happy to check out his tablet for more viral videos. It didn't take long for him to find what he was looking for.

"Ta-daa!" Joe sang. He held up the viewing device triumphantly. "Slickbro13's clip of the basketball court prank."

This clip showed some punk waving a spray paint can as he tagged our basketball court. His back was to the camera, making his face unidentifiable.

"First Awesome Dude, now slickbro13," I said. "How can we find out who he is?"

Joe shrugged. "We can contact YouTube," he said. "Maybe they'll give us slickbro13's real name."

"Not a chance," I said. "No company would give that information out so easily—especially one as big as YouTube. They probably wouldn't even know."

"Maybe we'll have more luck with Dad," Joe said, pocketing the tablet. "It pays to have a private investigator in the family, even if he is supposed to be retired."

The word "retired" wasn't in Fenton Hardy's vocabulary. Even though he was supposed to be writing a book about the history of law enforcement, occasionally he went back to doing what he did best—fighting crime!

We ended up walking to Dad's office downtown. Even though he'd retired, he kept it for writing purposes. Sometimes (well, a lot of the time) the house isn't exactly quiet.

"Hi, guys," Dad said when he saw us.

"Hi, Dad," Joe said, plopping down on the cushy leather sofa. "What's up?"

"You tell me," Dad said. "How was school today?"

"Not great," I replied. "Some creeps spray painted a gang tag on our basketball court."

"Vandals again?" Dad said. "Do you have any leads?"

I nodded and said, "Some suspicious-looking kid was hanging out in front of the school this morning. He drove off before we could find out more."

"But I caught his vanity plate, Dad," Joe said proudly. "It's Awesome Dude!"

"Awesome?" Dad asked with a smirk. "Are you sure it wasn't Awful?"

"What we need now is his real name," I said. "That's where you come in."

"Me?" Dad asked, raising a brow.

"Could you please do a search and tell us who this Awesome Dude is, Dad?" Joe asked, jumping off the sofa. "I'm sure you private-eye guys have ways of finding out that stuff."

Dad immediately shook his head. "Sorry," he said. "But no can do."

"Why not?" Joe asked.

"Because license plates are federally protected information," Dad explained. "I never use those tracking methods unless it's an absolute emergency or I have a reason to."

"But it is an emergency, Dad," I said.

I was just about to explain why when another detective, Felix Cruz, strolled into the office.

"Fenton, old man!" Felix boomed. "I hear you're writing your memoirs."

"Trying to," Dad said with a grin.

"Well, don't forget to mention me!" Felix said, winking at Joe and me.

"You bet, Felix," Dad said. "You remember my boys, Frank and Joe?"

"Sure I do," Felix declared. He reached into his pocket and pulled out his phone. "Let me show you some recent pictures of my kids, Fenton. You won't believe how big they've gotten."

Dad smiled politely as Felix flashed pictures of his five kids.

"I have a feeling this is going to take a while," I whispered to Joe. "We'd better go."

We left just as Felix was describing his son's birthday party at Charlie Cheese. Once in the hall, Joe turned to me. "Why did Dad give us such a hard time about the vanity plate?" he asked.

"He may be retired, but when it comes to detective work, he still goes by the book," I said.

"Some things never change." I sighed.

Suddenly we heard a voice hiss, "Psst. Psst."

Turning, I saw a woman with short, curly black hair waving us into her office. It was Connie Fleishman, another detective. Joe and I smiled. Out of all of Dad's coworkers, Connie was the coolest—always showing off her state-of-the-art spy gadgets and gizmos.

"Hi, Connie!" I said.

"What's up?" Joe asked.

"I've got something for you guys," Connie said. She grinned as she held up something that looked like an earbud for an MP3 player. "Guess what this is? Take a wild guess."

"Um . . . can I listen to music with it?" Joe guessed.

"It does a lot more than that, Joey," Connie said. "Pop this in your ear and you'll be able to hear conversations up to one hundred feet away. Even whispers."

"Cool," I said.

"Way cool!" Joe said.

"Here. Consider it a gift," Connie said, slipping it into Joe's hand. "So what are you guys doing here today? Visiting the old man?"

"Sort of," I said. "We were hoping Dad would give us the name of the owner of a vanity plate we saw."

"But according to Dad, that information is top secret," Joe added.

Connie snorted and flapped her hand. "Your dad's retired," she said. "I'm the big cheese here now."

Connie waved us to her computer. After about five minutes

of searching files, she was able to give us the full name of Awesome Dude.

"Colin Sylvester," Connie reported. "Name ring a bell?"

"I think so," I said slowly. "Don't his parents own a line of cruise ships or something?"

"Whatever they do, they're superrich," Joe said. "I think they have a house by the bay that makes the Peytons' look like a shack."

"Is there anything else you want me to look up while I'm here?" Connie asked.

I thought about the YouTube clip and slickbro13, but shook my head. "You've done plenty for us already, Connie," I said. "And if Dad finds out—"

"Tell him whatever you want," Connie said with a grin. "If he doesn't like it, I'll probably read about it in that book of his."

We left Dad's office building with the best clue we'd gotten all day—the name of the guy in the black Benz.

"Now we know that it was Colin Sylvester outside our school today," I said when we were halfway home. "But we still don't know why he was there."

Joe shrugged and said, "Maybe it's no big deal. Maybe he saw the commotion and stopped his car to be nosy."

"With that look he gave us?" I said, remembering the icy glare. "I don't think so."

We were walking up Foley Street when Joe's tablet beeped.

"What was that?" I asked.

"I got a text or an e-mail," he said, pulling it out.

"That thing gets e-mails too?" I said, impressed. "It really can do everything."

Joe stopped to check out the e-mail. He wrinkled his brow and said, "I don't recognize the sender. There's an attachment, too."

"Then delete!" I declared. "Never open an attachment you don't recognize."

"Too late," Joe said. "I already did."

I peered over Joe's shoulder as a video appeared on the small screen. As he and I watched the clip, our eyes popped wide open. It showed some guy hurling a rock through the window of Bayport's only flower shop. His back was to the camera as he jumped up and down, cheering.

"Another Scaredevil," I said through gritted teeth. "But why was it sent to you? That's what I want to know."

"Yeah, me too," Joe said. "And how did those lowlifes get my e-mail?"

Joe was about to replay the clip when I heard what sounded like heavy footsteps behind us. Spinning around, I saw two tall, beefy guys coming our way. I blinked hard when I saw what they wore: steel breastplates, leather sandals—and heavy, glistening swords!

"Um . . . Frank?" Joe said when he saw them too. "Who are those guys?"

"I don't know," I said. "All I do know is that they're armed—and dangerous."

INVITE ONLY

6

JOE

FRANK AND I STOOD FROZEN LIKE STATUES. The armored guys' eyes were on us as they came closer and closer. My own eyes stayed fixed on those swords!

"Either we're in a time warp," I murmured, "or I'm seeing ancient warriors."

"In case they attack," Frank said out of the corner of his mouth, "do we fight them off?"

"With what?" I whispered. "Our backpacks?"

The steel-plated giants came within inches of Frank and me. Before I could ask what they wanted, they made a sharp right turn. We watched as they headed straight up the front walkway of a large Colonial-style home.

"Who are those guys?" Frank asked.

One warrior rang the doorbell with the handle of his sword. While the two stood facing the door, Frank and I inched closer to the house and hid behind a shrub. We peeked out and watched as a woman wearing a white uniform opened the door.

"Hello, ma'am," one warrior said. "Is Stacy Chung here?"

The woman looked super nervous as she stepped away. In a matter of seconds a girl of about sixteen came to the door.

"Does she go to our school?" Frank whispered.

"I don't think so," I whispered back.

We watched as the other warrior held up what looked like a large square envelope. "Stacy Chung, lend us your ears!" he boomed. "By orders of the royal empire, you are hereby invited to the Sweet Sixteen of Empress Lindsay Peyton!"

The two then beat their chests and declared, "Veni, vidi, Versace!"

Stacy stood with her mouth open. Then, without warning, she let out an earsplitting shriek.

"Lindsay Peyton's Sweet Sixteen—no way!" Stacy screamed happily, jumping up and down. "No way! No way!"

I leaned over to Frank and said, "I get it. Those guys are the gladiators Lindsay was talking about at our interview."

"Yeah, but why is she getting an invitation today?" Frank said. "The party is this weekend."

We ducked behind the tree trunk as the gladiators

stomped by. I could hear one of them saying, "Was she the last on the B-list?"

"Yeah." The other one sighed. "Let's ditch these tin cans and get some pizza."

Stacy was still shrieking as the gladiators walked up the street.

"B-list," Frank scoffed, shaking his head. "No wonder her invitation's late."

"Let's go," I said. "Before Stacy detonates my eardrums."

"Not yet, Joe," Frank said. "If Stacy goes to Bay Academy, she might have some info on Colin."

Frank slipped out from behind the tree. I raced to catch up with him as he approached the house.

"Um—Stacy?" Frank called as she began to shut the door. "Can we ask you something?"

Stacy was still smiling from ear to ear as she said, "I think I've seen you guys around."

"I'm Frank Hardy, and this is my brother, Joe," Frank said. "You go to Bay Academy, right?"

"Right," Stacy said. She wrinkled her nose impatiently. "Um . . . is that all you want to know? I've got to text my friends and tell them the awesome news."

"Real quick," Frank promised. "Do you know a guy at your school named Colin Sylvester?"

Stacy rolled her eyes. "Unfortunately," she groaned, before holding up the invitation. "He won't be going to this party—that's for sure."

"How come?" I asked.

"Du-uh!" Stacy said. "Everybody knows Lindsay can't stand Colin."

"Why doesn't she like him?" Frank asked.

"It's complicated," Stacy said. "Look, I can't hang around and talk right now. I've got a gazillion things to do!"

"But—" Frank started to say.

"I've got to call Elise, Lily, and Beth, make a hair appointment, shop for a new dress and shoes. . . ."

Stacy's voice trailed off as she shut the door in our faces. We stood staring at the door before Frank said, "So Lindsay can't stand Colin."

"Can you blame her?" I said, walking away from the door. "Now can we forget about Colin for a minute and try to figure something out?"

"Like what?" Frank asked.

I turned to my brother and said, "Like—how did the Scaredevils get my e-mail address?"

"See?" I said, holding out my tablet. "More and more videos are going viral, and they're coming straight to me."

Frank, Chet, Iola, and I were holding court in our usual favorite booth at the Chomp and Chew. But no one was looking out the window or at the game on the TV. We were too busy checking out the latest viral video starring the Scaredevils. This one showed the same bunch of bandanna-sporting thugs setting a Dumpster on fire.

"That's enough to make anyone's skin crawl," Chet declared. His eyes then darted around the Chomp and Chew, busy with the dinner crowd. "Should we even be watching these videos out in the open like this?"

"Why not?" Iola asked.

"What if the Scaredevils are here?" Chet whispered. "They could like burgers too, you know."

Frank and I glanced around. The booths and tables were packed, probably because of the free dessert special they had that night.

"Doubtful," Frank said. "The Scaredevils strike mostly at night."

"Yeah, they're too busy being evil to stop for hot fudge sundaes," I scoffed.

"Speaking of," Chet said. "Where's our food? I'm starving."

"Eat a pickle chip," Iola said, pushing a dish of pickles and olives toward her brother. She then turned to Frank and me. "If the Scaredevils are a gang, how will you catch them? There could be dozens of members running around Bayport!"

"Every gang has a ringleader," Frank explained. "If we get him, we get the whole gang."

I was about to grab a pickle myself when my tablet began beeping. "Here we go again," I sighed.

"Is it from slickbro13?" Frank asked.

I glanced down at the user name. "Who else?" I said. "But this time he sent me a little message."

"What does it say?" Iola asked.

"Special delivery," I read out loud.

Everyone huddled around my tablet as I opened the attachment. The latest video was different from the others. Instead of showing vandalism, it showed two Scaredevils rolling on the ground in a fight. I turned up the volume to hear voices in the background, cheering them on.

"Why do you think they sent me a fight video?" I asked.

"Could be a warning," Chet said. "That next they're coming after you and Frank!"

"Thanks, pal," Frank said.

Chet shrugged and said, "Just saying."

But as I watched the fight clip, something about one of the guys looked familiar.

"I know this sounds crazy," I said. "But I think I know one of those guys."

"But you can't see their faces," Iola said, squinting to get a better look. "Can you?"

"It's not his face," I said, studying the video. "It's those long, skinny legs—"

"Okay, who gets the chunky chili burger with the sweet potato fries?" a voice asked, interrupting my thoughts.

I looked up to see a waiter holding a tray filled with our long-awaited burgers.

"Sweet potato fries, baby!" Chet said, hungrily rubbing his hands together. "Bring it!"

The last thing I wanted was pizza burger sauce all over my tablet. But just as I was about to put it away, Frank gave me a kick under the table.

"What?" I asked.

"Tony Riley's here," Frank said.

"So?" I said. "He works here."

Frank shook his head. "He's not bussing tables," he said. "He's sitting at that booth over there."

I followed Frank's gaze. Sure enough, Tony was in the house—sharing a booth with a cute red-haired girl. Tony was smiling coolly at her as he stretched his lanky leg into the aisle.

"I know her," Iola said as she shook a clogged ketchup bottle upside down. "That's Carolyn Meyer from school. She's in my gym class."

"Looks like Tony's on a date," I said. "It's probably his night off."

Frank furrowed his brow as if he didn't get it. "Why would Tony spend his night off in a place he hated?" he asked.

"Unless the guy quit," Chet said through a full mouth.

"Yeah, but he said he needed the money," Frank said. "To buy that phone he wanted."

"For a guy with no money, he sure ordered a ton of food," Iola pointed out.

"And if I'm not mistaken," Chet said, glancing over his shoulder, "that's the lobster burger Tony's eating—the most expensive thing on the menu."

Frank and I traded grins. If anyone was an authority on the Chomp and Chew menu, it was Chet.

"So the guy could have saved up," I said, glancing back at Tony. It was then that I noticed something other than his date and lobster burger.

Tony had what looked like a deep scratch under his left eye. When I quietly pointed it out, Chet said, "Tony works in a restaurant. Maybe it was some kind of kitchen accident."

"That," I said, "or some kind of fight."

"Tony in a fight?" Iola said unbelievingly. "He's so nice one of the teachers calls him Gentleman Riley."

Tony was a nice guy. Even if somebody did beat on him, he probably wouldn't fight back.

"I guess you're right," I decided.

I was about to turn away from Tony when I spotted his jacket hanging from a hook over his booth. Sticking out of a pocket was something dark blue with some kind of white paisley design.

"Whoa!" I gasped, realizing what it was.

It was a bandanna—a dark-blue bandanna!

SECRETS

7

FRANK

THIS TIME JOE KICKED ME UNDER THE table. I stared at my brother as if to say, *What?*

"Tony's jean jacket is hanging next to his booth," Joe said.

"And?" I asked.

"And take a look at what's sticking out of the pocket," he whispered.

I glanced over to Tony's booth and his jacket. Some kind of dark blue material with a white design was sticking out.

"Rhymes with . . . banana?" Joe hinted.

"Bandanna!" I said. "Tony's got a dark-blue bandanna in his pocket."

"You're kidding me, right?" Iola said, stretching her neck to see.

"It's a blue bandanna, all right," Chet confirmed. "Good catch, Joe."

"Thanks," Joe said. "But you know what this means, don't you?"

"Hard to believe," I said. "Tony Riley, a Scaredevil?"

Joe leaned forward, lowered his voice, and said, "No wonder the fighter in the video looked familiar. He had the same long, skinny legs as Tony's."

"So that was Tony fighting?" Iola said, scrunching up her nose. "The guy doesn't even arm wrestle in the school lunchroom for fun!"

Trying not to look obvious, I watched Tony eating his lobster burger. Sure, the scratch and the bandanna made him look guilty. But I wasn't going to accuse the guy until we got more facts. At least, that's the way Dad taught us.

"We've got to go over to Tony and ask him a bunch of questions," I told Joe. "Before he finishes his food and leaves the place."

"Okay," Joe said.

But Chet shook his head and said, "Nuh-uh. Not okay."

"Why not?" I asked.

"Because Tony is out with Carolyn," Chet explained. "And the last thing he'll want to do is answer questions in front of her."

"Especially since Carolyn Meyer is the ultimate gossip girl," Iola said. "No one talks in front of her unless they're totally clueless."

My shoulders slumped as I stared at the Mortons. Since when were they such drags?

"You guys," I complained. "If Tony is in the Scare-devils, he can lead us straight to the ringleader—whoever he is."

"Frank is right," Joe said. "We have to get him to spill."

"Any suggestions?" I asked Chet and Iola.

"Nope," Chet said, going back to his burger. But Iola flashed a smile and said, "I know what to do."

"What?" Joe asked.

"I'm going to tell Carolyn I just found something out that will make her teeth curl," Iola whispered.

"You mean you're going to lure her away with gossip?" Chet said. "As if any girl would leave a date to dish with another girl."

"This girl would," Iola said as she squeezed past me out of the booth. "Watch and learn."

The three of us did watch as Iola headed to Tony and Carolyn's booth. I had a feeling she was speaking extra loud so we could all hear.

"Carolyn, you're not going to believe the dirt I just dug up on Deanna DaCosta," Iola said.

"The captain of the girls' basketball team?" Carolyn gasped excitedly. "What are you waiting for? Spill!"

"Tony doesn't want to hear this," Iola said, smiling at Tony. "Come on, Carolyn. I'll tell you the whole story in the restroom."

"I'm there," Carolyn said, already halfway out of the booth. "I'll be right back, Tony."

"Yeah, sure," Tony said. He barely looked up from his lobster burger as Carolyn followed Iola up the aisle to the back.

"I can see who has the brains in the family!" Joe teased Chet.

"But I have the good looks!" Chet joked.

"Yeah, right," I said, smirking. "Joe, let's go over to Tony's table and see what we can get."

"What about me?" Chet asked.

"Stay here and make sure nobody eats our burgers," I said.

"Just let 'em try!" Chet chuckled.

Tony looked surprised as we slipped into his booth. "Hey. What's up?" he asked.

"I'll cut to the chase," I said quietly. "It's about the bandanna in your jacket pocket."

Tony's eyes darted over to his jacket. "Wh-what bandanna?" he asked with a stammer. "It must be one of my gloves."

Joe shook his head and said, "Bandannas have looked the same since the Wild West."

"Come on, Tony," I said. "Are you one of those Scaredevils?"

Tony's eyes flew wide open. He leaned across the table and whispered, "I don't belong to any gang, if that's what you're saying."

I pointed at the scratch under Tony's eye. "Then how did you get that?" I asked.

Joe was already running the fight video as he held the tablet in Tony's face. "Is this how?" he asked.

Tony stared straight at the video. "How did you find that?" he asked.

"Special delivery," Joe replied. "Were you the sender, Tony?"

Shaking his head, Tony said, "No, it must have been—"

Tony stopped midsentence.

"It must have been who?" I asked.

"Um . . . it must have been . . . someone else," Tony finished lamely.

"Come on, Tony, throw us a bone," Joe groaned. "Can't you give us a name?"

Tony hunched forward. "No, I can't."

"But you are in the Scaredevils?" Joe said.

Tony groaned as if to say, *Give me a break*. Then he whispered, "Yeah, I'm in the Scaredevils, but not because I want to trash Bayport."

Joe and I exchanged confused looks. Why else would someone join that gang unless they wanted to make trouble?

"I'm in it for the money," Tony said.

"Money?" I repeated.

"You're getting paid to do all that stuff?" Joe asked, just as surprised as I was.

"We all are," Tony explained. "Look, I am sick of wiping down dirty tables five days a week. The other day someone barfed up a whole—"

"Spare me the gross details," Joe said.

"And now I can finally get out," Tony said. "Why do you think I asked Carolyn here? For once I wanted to be able to sit back, relax, and order the most expensive stuff on the menu, like I always saw everybody else do."

Tony reached into his pocket. He pulled out a shiny silver phone and held it up. "And check out the sweet phone I was able to buy after the fight. With my busboy job it would have taken me weeks to be able to afford this," he continued.

"Yeah, okay, nice phone," Joe said. "Question is—who's been paying you and the other Scaredevils to trash Bayport?"

Tony placed his phone on the table. He leaned back and shook his head. "Sorry, guys," he said. "Can't tell."

"Why not?" I asked.

"The guy said he'd wipe tables with my face if I did," Tony said nervously. "Not worth it!"

I looked sideways at Joe, who was gazing out the window. He had to be as frustrated as I was. We'd finally pinned down a member of the Scaredevils—but he was too scared to rat on his leader.

"Uh-oh," Joe said, interrupting my thoughts. "Hey, Tony."

"What?" Tony asked.

Joe pointed at the window. "Is that your car out there getting keyed?" he asked.

"Someone's keying my car?" Tony cried.

In a flash, Tony was running up the aisle and out of the Chomp and Chew.

"Come on, Joe," I said, starting to stand. "We'd better help Tony—"

"Sit down," Joe said, picking up Tony's phone. "Now, how do you read texts on this thing?"

Texts?

"Oh, so that's your plan," I said with a grin. I turned to Chet and called, "Look out the window and let us know when Tony's coming back!"

Chet didn't ask why. He just nodded, a sweet potato fry dangling from his mouth.

"This is kind of like my tablet," Joe said as his fingers worked Tony's phone. "Got the texts. Now let's play Find the Ringleader."

"How will we know who he is?" I asked.

Joe leaned forward so I could see the phone too.

"We'll know him when we see him," Joe said. He scrolled down the texts until he reached one that read: GJ!! PU $$. "This is it!"

"Whaaaa?" I said.

I wasn't totally clueless when it came to texting—but this one was about as clear as ancient hieroglyphics.

"Allow me to translate," Joe said. "It says, 'Good job! Pick up cash.'"

"That's got to be the guy who's paying off the Scaredevils," I said. "Does it say who sent it?"

"Someone called Sylvester, C," Joe read. He looked at me questionably. "Sylvester, C . . . Sylvester, C—"

"Colin!" I blurted out as it hit me. "Joe, the text was sent by Colin Sylvester."

8 THE WARNING

JOE

"COLIN SYLVESTER?" I SAID, STARING AT the phone. "He's the ringleader of the Scaredevils?"

"He was creeping around our school right after the Scaredevils hit," Frank said. "And if anyone has the cash to pay up, it's Colin."

"Heads up, you guys," Chet hissed. "Tony's coming back."

"Drop the phone, Joe," Frank said.

"Wait," I said, my fingers fumbling on the keypad. "I have to close the texts."

After I did, I placed Tony's new phone on the table exactly where he'd left it. It was a cool phone—until we found out how he got it!

"Remember," Frank said. "Pretend to act concerned about his car."

Leaning forward and scrunching my eyebrows, I put on my best "worried" face. "So?" I asked as Tony slipped back into the booth. "How's the car?"

"Nobody keyed it," Tony said with a relieved smile. "You must have been seeing things, Hardy."

"Hey," Frank said. "Better safe than sorry."

"Especially with those Scaredevils around town," I said with a hint of sarcasm.

"Okay, are you finished asking me about the Scaredevils and the ringleader?" Tony asked. "Because I told you, I'm not spilling."

He didn't have to. After opening his texts, we had all the stuff we needed. At least for now.

"No more questions," Frank said.

"Good," Tony said, glancing over his shoulder. "Now, can you guys go back to your table? Carolyn's coming back!"

"The Scaredevils aren't your style, Tony," Frank said as we stood up. "You really ought to ditch them."

"And go back to wiping tables?" Tony said. "You think Carolyn would date a busboy?"

I wanted to say sure, but Carolyn was already at the booth. She wasn't smiling anymore, which made me wonder what Iola had told her.

Frank and I slipped back into our booth, where Iola was sipping her root beer float.

"What did you tell Carolyn about the captain of the basketball team?" I asked.

"That she got all As on her last report card," Iola said, twirling her straw in her shake. "Carolyn was totally bored, but I gave her an earful to kill time."

"Hey, it worked," Frank said. "Joe and I got some good stuff from Tony."

"You mean Tony's phone," I said, going back to my burger, which was already cold. "The Scaredevils are trashing Bayport for the money."

"And their ringleader and benefactor is Colin Sylvester," Frank added.

"You mean the rich kid?" Iola said. She shrugged. "If he's got deep pockets, then I guess it makes sense."

"Makes sense to me, too," Chet said. "Colin meant business when he hurled that soda can at me. That's one mean dude."

"Don't you think you should tell the cops about Colin?" Iola asked.

I frowned. "If only we could," I said. "But Chief Olaf doesn't listen to 'so-called detectives.'"

"Plus, we don't have any hard evidence on Colin other than that text on Tony's phone," Frank said. "And we can't get our hands on that anymore."

It made sense to me too that Colin was the Scaredevils'

ringleader. Who else would have all that money to burn? But there was still something I didn't get. . . .

"What do you think is in it for Colin?" I asked. "I mean, why would a guy who has everything want to spend his money on a bunch of stupid pranks?"

"And hang out with a bunch of Bayport High guys," Frank said. "That's what I don't get."

I watched Tony from the corner of my eye as we finished our burgers and drinks. He was smiling as he chatted up Carolyn, but every now and then his eyes would dart over to our table. When he caught me watching, he'd quickly glance away.

The guy was obviously nervous about us knowing his secret. Little did Tony know we knew more than he thought!

"Done," Frank said, pushing away his plate.

"Me too," I said. "Let's figure out the check and go."

"Why don't we just split it?" Chet said.

"Wait a minute!" I said, leaning over to read the check. "You ordered twice as much as we did, Morton—no way are we splitting it."

"But you guys ate my sweet potato fries!" Chet argued.

"Yeah, like one!" Iola said.

"Problem solved, you guys," I said, reaching for my tablet. "This thing has a calculator on it—"

CRASH!!!

My hands flew over my head as glass from the window exploded across our table. For the next few seconds, everything was a blur. People were screaming and diving under tables.

When the sound of falling glass and screams died down, I slowly and carefully looked up. Iola's hands still covered her head, while Chet crouched halfway under the table. Frank looked about as shaken up as I felt.

We weren't the only ones. I glanced around to see parents with their arms wrapped around crying kids. Customers were frantically leaving the place, forgetting to pay their bills. Others just sat frozen in stunned silence.

"Wh-what was that?" I asked, my voice shaky.

Careful not to touch the broken glass, Frank reached out and picked up the culprit. It was a medium-size rock with the word "Scaredevils" painted across it.

It was bad enough that I was getting the Scaredevil viral videos by special delivery. Now we were getting rocks hurled through nearby windows!

"Something tells me this is getting personal," I said.

"Jeez!" Chet cried, coming out from under the table. "We're not even safe at the Chomp and Chew. It's the end of civilization as we know it!"

Worried customers and waitstaff hurried over to see if we were okay. But not everyone stuck around. Tony and Carolyn were squeezing through the crowd toward the back door. Carolyn looked confused, while Tony kept glancing back nervously.

"Are you kids all right?" a worried voice asked.

I turned to see the owner of the place, Marty Rios, standing over our booth.

"We're okay," Frank said, forcing a smile.

"Two of my biggest waiters are outside trying to catch the punks," Marty said. "Whoever they are."

"Thanks, Marty," Frank said. "But I have a feeling they ran away right after they threw the rock."

"Who's they?" Marty demanded.

"The Scaredevils," Frank said, showing him the rock. "It's a gang that's pulling pranks around Bayport."

"Tell that to the police as soon as they get here," Marty suggested. "My cashier just put a call in to the station."

Marty cleared out the Chomp and Chew except for Frank and me. As we sat in another booth, waiting for the police, we talked about the case.

"Do you think Tony knew about the Scaredevils' plans?" I asked.

Frank shook his head. "He wouldn't bring Carolyn here if he did," he said. "Not exactly an awesome first date."

After a beat I turned to Frank. "So, what do you think?" I asked. "Do we tell the police what we know about Colin? Even if we don't have any proof to show them?"

"Definitely," Frank said. "One of us could have gotten seriously hurt just now . . . or even killed."

Two police officers were already at the Chomp and Chew, talking to Marty. But then the door opened wide and another walked in. My heart sank when I saw who it was.

"Olaf's in the house," I muttered.

"Great," Frank groaned.

Frank and I watched as Chief Olaf walked toward us, followed by the two officers. He was wearing his big shiny badge and his usual cynical smirk.

"Boys," Chief Olaf said with a nod. "So, tell me what you saw."

"This!" I said, showing him the rock. "It was hurled through the window we were sitting next to."

"The word 'Scaredevils' is painted on it," Frank pointed out. "It's the same gang that tagged our basketball court."

The chief took the rock from me. He turned it over in his hand before saying, "Tell me something I don't already know."

"Okay," Frank said. "We know who the ringleader of the gang is."

"How do you know?" Chief Olaf asked.

"We read it in a text," I said.

The chief held out his hand. "Can I see the text, please?" he said.

"Um . . . we don't have it," I said.

"It was on someone else's phone," Frank explained.

"Well," Chief Olaf said. "Then it won't do us much good, will it?"

"We can tell you what we found out," Frank said quickly. "For one, there's a guy paying the Scaredevils to pull the pranks."

"Paying them?" one of the officers piped up.

"Yeah!" I said. "And that person is Colin Sylvester!"

The chief's eyebrows flew up so high and fast I thought they'd hit the ceiling. Had we finally told him something he wanted to hear?

But then Chief Olaf shook his head. "It can't be Colin," he said. "Not a chance."

"Why not?" Frank asked.

"Because the Sylvesters are respected citizens of the community," Chief Olaf explained. "Their son Colin goes to Bay Academy."

"So all Bay Academy students are honest?" I asked.

I looked over at the other officers, Lasko and Fernandez, for help. They were usually friendly guys, but now they stood behind Chief Olaf, as motionless as Mount Rushmore.

"Look, boys." Chief Olaf sighed. "I am not going to bring in Colin Sylvester based on a text that I can't even read."

"But—" I started to say.

"Kids these days and their texts," Chief Olaf said to the other officers with a chuckle. "Maybe if they'd all interact more on a personal level, we wouldn't have all this trouble!"

I couldn't take it anymore. If Chief Olaf wouldn't listen to Frank and me, maybe he'd listen to Tony Riley.

"It wasn't our text, Chief Olaf," I blurted. "It was—"

"It was something we heard about," Frank cut in.

I glanced sideways at Frank. Why was he protecting Tony? If Tony knew that rock was coming, he sure did nothing to protect us!

"All we know is that the Scaredevils are starting to target Joe and me," Frank told the chief. He turned to me. "Show him the videos, Joe."

I was about to pull out my tablet when the chief held up his hand.

"Those punks are targeting the entire town of Bayport," Chief Olaf said. "So don't think you're so special, Detectives Hardy and Hardy."

"Can you at least question Colin and see what he has to say?" Frank asked.

"Absolutely not," Chief Olaf said. "There is no way I am going to embarrass good people like the Sylvesters when there's no evidence on their son."

The chief then turned to the officers and said, "Lasko, write up what the kids told us, but leave out the garbage about Colin."

"Garbage?" I gasped.

All three officers turned away from us. As they started up the aisle, Officer Fernandez glanced back and smiled. Maybe he believed us. But with Olaf as chief, did it even matter?

"Can't say we didn't try," Frank said with a sigh as we pulled on our jackets.

"Yeah," I said, giving the broken window one last look. "I guess it's up to us 'so-called detectives' to investigate Colin."

CLOSER 9

FRANK

THE LAST THING JOE AND I WANTED TO do was get up extra early the next morning—especially after that intense night at the Chomp and Chew. But if we were going to make a pit stop at Bay Academy on the way to school, we'd have to get going.

"What if we don't see Colin?" Joe asked me as I drove up Bay Academy's block.

"Maybe some of the other kids can help us out," I said.

"Other kids as in Sierra Mitchell?" Joe teased.

"I never said that," I insisted, although the thought of running into Sierra had definitely crossed my mind.

I pulled up to the curb across the street from Bay Academy.

With the other expensive student cars parked on the block, mine stuck out like a sore thumb.

As I did my best to parallel park, I caught Joe eyeing his tablet.

"What are you looking at?" I grunted as I turned the wheel. "Anything new go viral?"

Joe shook his head. "I did a search on the Sylvesters," he said. "No wonder the chief didn't want to go after them."

"What did you find?" I asked.

"The Sylvesters donated a whole chunk of money to a Bayport Police charity," Joe said.

"Money talks . . . Colin walks." I sighed.

"Speaking of Colin, I don't think we have to worry about not finding him," Joe said, pointing out the window. "Because there he goes!"

I leaned over to look out Joe's window. It didn't take long to find Colin. He was strutting confidently across the school grounds toward a group of other guys.

"Those are the guys from the Chomp and Chew," I said.

Colin and his buds fist-bumped, then exchanged words. He seemed distracted, looking past his friends to something in the school yard. I followed Colin's gaze to a bunch of girls standing a few feet away. One of those girls was Lindsay Peyton.

Joe and I watched as Colin broke away from his crew and began moving toward Lindsay. As far away as we were, I could still see Lindsay's look of disgust as he approached.

Lindsay jutted her chin in the air. She appeared to say a few angry words to Colin before huffing off with her friends.

"That girl Stacy was right," Joe said. "Lindsay can't stand Colin."

Colin glared icily at Lindsay until a slow smile spread across his face. Aunt Trudy would call it a "cat who swallowed the canary" type of smile. What was going on inside Colin's head to make him grin like that?

"We still don't know why Lindsay hates Colin," I said.

"Frank, isn't it a no-brainer?" Joe said. "The guy's a creep."

"It might be more than that," I said.

"Okay, then," Joe said. "He's a major creep!"

He reached over and blared the car horn. It caught the attention of Colin and practically all the other students.

"What are you doing?" I asked Joe.

"We came here to talk to Colin, remember?" Joe said. He then leaned out the window and shouted, "Hey, Sylvester! Can we ask you something?"

Colin grinned nastily, then yelled back, "The answer is no! You cannot switch lives with me, even for a second!"

Joe muttered something under his breath as he pushed open his door. I opened mine and stepped out too.

As we headed toward the school, we could see Colin talking to a guard. Colin turned to leave, but the guard held up his hand and called, "Excuse me. Are you Bay Academy students?"

"No, sir," I said.

"Then you can't be here," the guard said.

"If we need visitors' passes, we'd be happy to get some in the office," I said quickly.

The guard shook his head. "Sorry, boys," he said firmly. "You'll have to leave now."

Colin was back with his friends, this time smiling slyly at us. Joe was right. Colin wasn't just a creep—he was a major creep!

"You know something, Frank?" Joe said as we trudged back to our car. "I have a feeling this is going to be a bummer of a day."

I thought so too—until my phone beeped with the text that changed everything. . . .

"Okay, what's her name?" Joe teased as I smiled at my phone.

"Sierra just texted me," I said.

"She might have seen you here," Joe said. "What does she want?"

"She wants to meet me at the Meet Locker tonight," I said, still smiling as I read the text.

"You mean the coffee place?" Joe said. "I thought she didn't drink coffee."

"They serve tea, too," I said, texting back. "Twenty different kinds, as a matter of fact."

"Well, what did you tell her?" Joe asked.

"What do you think?" I said. "I said sure."

I pretended to be cool on the outside, but on the inside—cartwheels. As we stepped out of the car, Joe didn't seem so stoked anymore. In fact, he looked pretty bummed out.

"What's up?" I asked. "Don't tell me you're jealous!"

"No!" he insisted.

"Then what?" I asked.

"How did Sierra get your number?" Joe asked. "If I remember, she wrote hers on your hand. Not the other way around."

Joe had a point. How had she gotten my number? But after I thought about it, it clicked.

"We filled out those job applications at the Peytons'," I said. "We had to write our telephone and e-mail addresses on them, remember?"

"Oh yeah," Joe said, slapping his forehead.

As I adjusted the rearview mirror, I thought about my date with Sierra. First dates usually meant small talk. But this date didn't have to go that way.

"I'm going to ask Sierra about Colin tonight," I told Joe. "If she knows him from school, maybe she can give us some information."

"So this will be a working date?" Joe declared. He then smirked and said, "Yeah, right."

As I drove slowly away from Bay Academy, I took one last look at the school. Most of the kids were filing into the building, but Colin was still hanging with his friends. This time a dark-haired girl stood with them. Her back was to the street, so I couldn't see her face. I just knew it wasn't Lindsay.

"Hey, Frank," Joe said as I turned onto the highway. "I'm going to Chet's house tonight, but I want a full report after the date."

"About Colin?" I asked.

"About Sierra!" he said with a grin.

It wasn't easy focusing on school or our case the rest of the day. All I could think about was my date with Sierra. Maybe "date" was too strong a word. Maybe Sierra wanted to meet because she felt bad about what had happened at the Peytons' . . . or maybe I was overthinking the whole thing!

I got to the Meet Locker at seven forty-five and waited inside my car until four minutes past eight. Didn't want Sierra to think I was too eager—even though I was.

By the time I walked into the Meet Locker, Sierra was already there, sitting in a cushy chair and drinking a cup of tea.

"Sorry I'm late!" I blurted out as I sank into the opposite chair.

Sierra's eyes sparkled over her cup as she said, "You're not late—I'm early."

I ordered my usual iced caramel chiller. Sierra's tea smelled like vanilla. Or was that her perfume?

"This place is packed," I said.

"It usually is on a Friday night," Sierra said.

Glancing around, I wondered if there were any Scare-devils in the place. Probably not. They'd be out trashing Bayport, not sitting around sipping tea and coffee.

I turned back to Sierra. She seemed relaxed for someone working on the biggest Sweet Sixteen of the decade in just two days.

"I'm surprised you're not running around for Lindsay tonight," I said.

"Who says I'm not?" Sierra asked with a smile. "Lindsay wanted me to order a ton of coffee for her party. That's the reason I was here early."

She took another sip, then said, "So you and your brother are detectives? How did that start?"

"Our dad is a private investigator," I explained. "When Joe and I were kids, we asked a lot of questions about his cases. When he got sick of answering us, we decided to work on our own. We were only about eight and nine."

"Kid detectives?" Sierra smiled. "How sweet!"

She called me sweet! As we talked about other stuff like movies, school, and favorite foods, I started loosening up. Turns out Sierra loved mac and cheese just like me. But by the time I was on my second chiller, I decided to switch from small talk to spy talk.

"Do you know a guy at Bay Academy named Colin?" I asked.

"Colin?" Sierra said with a shrug. "There are a few guys at school named Colin."

"Colin Sylvester," I said.

Sierra put her teacup down on a side table. "Yeah, I know that Colin," she said. "He sits near me in math."

"So . . . is he bad news or what?" I asked.

Sierra blinked in surprise. "Bad news?" She chuckled. "What makes you ask that?"

I'd been hoping she wouldn't ask me that.

The friend part of me wanted to tell Sierra everything about our case—the viral videos, the vandalism. But the detective part knew not to share too much.

"Joe and I think he might be up to something," I said. "But that's all I can say for now."

"Ooh," Sierra said, her eyes flashing. "A man of mystery!"

Man of mystery. I liked that.

"Actually, Colin can be a jerk sometimes," Sierra offered. "Truth is, I think his bark is worse than his bite."

"I doubt it," I murmured, remembering the hurled soda can.

"What?" Sierra asked.

"Nothing," I said.

"By the way," Sierra chuckled, "you'll be happy to know that Mr. Peyton found a solution to Lindsay's keyed car. He bought her a new one!"

"Surprise, surprise," I laughed.

"Mr. Peyton was going to give Lindsay a new car for her sixteenth birthday anyway," Sierra said. "And speaking of the Sweet Sixteen, I'd better call it a night. I'm going to be crazy busy tomorrow with last-minute prep."

"Sure," I agreed as we stood up. "Um . . . can I call you again?"

Sierra tilted her head at me and smiled. "If I may remind you," she said, "I was the one who called you . . . so the next move is yours."

I offered to follow Sierra's car home, but she refused. She didn't seem worried about the pranks going on around Bayport. I guessed she was too busy with the party to worry about anything.

"Okay," Joe said after I picked him up at Chet's house. "So how'd it go?"

"Great!" I said as I drove the two of us home. "We talked about a lot of stuff."

"About Colin?" Joe teased. "Or about your future together?"

"Will you quit it?" I said. "I did ask Sierra about Colin, but she didn't have a lot on him. Just that he's an idiot and not dangerous."

"Glad she thinks so," Joe said. "And I'm glad you have a new girlfriend."

"Joe!" I sighed as I turned onto our block. "She's not my girl."

Yet.

As I drove up our street, I saw flashing lights in the distance.

"What's that?" I wondered.

I drove a few more feet, and then Joe said, "Frank, there's a fire truck in front of our house!"

"Fire?" I exclaimed. "No way!"

My heart pounded as I stopped behind the fire truck. Jumping out of the car, Joe and I raced toward our house. The house wasn't on fire—but our garage was.

My first feeling was relief—at least our house wasn't burning down. And since I had the car, there was nothing in the garage but some stored patio furniture and a lawn mower. But then I remembered the apartment above the garage—the apartment occupied by our aunt.

"Oh no!" I shouted. "Aunt Trudy!"

FIRED UP 10

JOE

FRANK AND I CHARGED TOWARD THE BURN-ing garage. Mom and Dad watched silently, looking very worried as the firefighters worked on the blaze.

"Mom, Dad," I said, my voice cracking. "Is Aunt Trudy up there?"

"We don't know yet," Mom said quietly. "One of the firefighters is climbing up to see."

Frank turned to me, his mouth a grim line. I didn't have to read his mind to know he was thinking the same as me: Was this the work of the Scaredevils? Were they such evil psycho creeps they would target not only Frank and me, but our family, too?

"I knew it," Dad groaned, cutting into my thoughts. "All

those smelly candles Trudy loves to burn. I warned her several times!"

"Warned me about what?" came a voice.

The four of us spun around. Standing right behind us was—

"Aunt Trudy!" Frank exclaimed.

"Where were you?" Dad asked, looking relieved.

"At the movies, seeing that new action flick," Aunt Trudy said. She stared at the now-smoldering garage. "But I guess there's more action going on here!"

Frank and I traded relieved smiles. Leave it to Aunt Trudy to crack a joke—even when her apartment was about to go up in flames. Luckily, the firefighters were getting the blaze out before it could spread that far.

Chief Madison, the fire chief, came over to us with the report.

"The garage has considerable damage," he told us. "But the apartment upstairs is unscathed."

"Great," Aunt Trudy said, walking toward the garage. "I'm going to catch up on my *Dancing with the Stars*—"

"You can watch it in the house, Trudy," Mom insisted. "Which is where you'll be staying until we know your apartment is safe."

"And no more candles," Dad said. "Please!"

Aunt Trudy flapped her hand dismissively.

"For your info, Fenton, I didn't burn any candles today," she insisted. "And if I did, I'd certainly have the brains to snuff it out before going to the movies."

"The fire couldn't have started in Aunt Trudy's apartment if there was no damage up there," I said, turning to the fire chief. "Right?"

"Right," Chief Madison agreed. "The fire started in the garage, which isn't uncommon. Lots of oily rags, clutter—"

"Sabotage," Frank cut in.

Chief Madison stared at Frank. "Excuse me?" he asked. "Did you say sabotage?"

"Someone could have set the fire as a prank," Frank said.

"Someone or someones," I agreed.

"Do you mean those kids who've been pulling pranks all over Bayport?" Mom asked. "You think they set fire to our garage?"

"They're not just any kids, Mom," I said. "They're a gang who call themselves the Scaredevils."

"We've heard about them," Chief Madison said with a frown. "But setting a fire is a lot more serious than throwing eggs down a book drop."

"Whoa," Aunt Trudy said. "Maybe I will stay in the house after all."

"We have tests to see where the fire started and how," Chief Madison said. "But it might take a few days."

He walked away to join his ladder company.

The damage wasn't too bad, but it was enough to leave the garage unusable.

"This is serious, guys," Dad said. "I think you should go to the police first thing tomorrow and tell them what you know."

"You mean talk to Chief Olaf?" I grimaced. "I'd rather get a tooth filled."

"Dad, we just told Chief Olaf we thought the Scaredevils were targeting us," Frank complained.

"We told Olaf who the ringleader was," I said. "But he didn't even listen."

Mom turned to Dad, a worried look on her face. "Maybe you should go talk to the chief, Fenton," she said. "Better yet, we both should."

"Good idea, Laura," Dad said.

Frank and I exchanged frantic looks. If Chief Olaf didn't take us seriously now, he sure wouldn't with our mommy and daddy speaking for us.

"Mom, Dad—no," I said.

"No what?" Dad asked.

"No thanks," Frank said. "Joe and I will talk to the chief tomorrow."

"But you said he won't listen to you!" Mom said.

"Oh, let them go, Laura," Aunt Trudy said, smiling in our direction. "If at first you don't succeed—try, try again!"

After the fire truck left, Frank and I climbed the stairs to our rooms. The smoke smell from the garage had wafted all the way into the house.

"Of all nights for us to be out," Frank said. "If I hadn't gone to meet Sierra, I might have caught the Scaredevils in the act."

I remembered my tablet and pulled it out. "Maybe we still can," I said. "Catch them in the act, I mean."

In Frank's room I searched YouTube for slickbro13's latest "hit." It didn't take long to find the clip I was looking for—a bunch of bandanna-wearing punks running away from our garage as the bottom edge of the door began to smolder.

"No cheering in the background this time," I pointed out. "They probably didn't want to attract Mom's and Dad's attention."

Frank moved closer to the tablet. "I did hear something on there," he said. "It sounded like someone's voice."

I replayed the clip and listened. "I don't hear anything," I admitted.

"Wait, here it comes," Frank cut in.

Quickly I turned up the volume. That's when I heard someone snicker and say, "Hah! This ought to keep the cops busy!"

That was a voice I'd know anywhere. It belonged to the gang's now infamous ringleader, Colin Sylvester!

"That's Colin on the tape, Frank," I declared. "What do you think he means about keeping the cops busy?"

"Who knows?" Frank said. "But at least we have some proof for Olaf that Colin was in on this."

"And this time," I said, smiling as I held up my tablet, "we'll convince the chief to watch the clip!"

• • • •

We usually slept in on Saturdays, but this morning Frank and I were up at the crack of dawn. With Aunt Trudy now in the house, we were treated to an awesome breakfast of buckwheat pancakes and banana smoothies.

"Where'd you get these ingredients, Aunt Trudy?" Frank asked.

"I climbed the ladder up to my apartment," Aunt Trudy pretended to whisper. "Don't tell your mom and dad."

Mom and Dad came into the kitchen. When they wished Frank and me luck with Chief Olaf, I had a feeling we were going to need it—even with the clip we had of Colin at the scene of the crime.

When Frank and I arrived at the station, we walked straight to the front desk. An officer was drinking from a goofy coffee cup. On it was a pair of handcuffs and the words ONE SIZE FITS ALL.

"Good morning," Frank said. "We're here to see Chief Olaf."

Before the officer could look up from his cup, the chief himself marched right past us, followed by an angry Sanford Peyton!

"What else do you want me to do, Mr. Peyton?" Chief Olaf asked.

"Plenty!" Sanford replied. "My daughter's party is tomorrow night. You can schedule the number of officers you assured us a month ago."

"That was before all the pranks started happening around

here," Chief Olaf said. "I can't afford to put my force in one place when stores and cars are being trashed on a daily basis."

"I understand," Sanford said. "But all we have now is one officer for the whole party."

"And a good number of private security guards, I'm sure," Chief Olaf said. He gave a chuckle. "It's a Sweet Sixteen, Mr. Peyton. What's the worst that could happen—someone tries to melt the ice sculpture?"

"Funny, Olaf," Sanford said gruffly. "If this is what I pay my taxes for, I can easily retract my donation to the Bayport Police Department."

I could see the chief's face pale. He seemed to force a quick smile before saying, "Mr. Peyton, why don't we discuss this further in my office? How do you like your coffee?"

"In a French press," Sanford replied as he followed the chief through his office door. "With steamed milk, no sugar."

Frank and I watched the door slam shut. The officer looked up from his goofy cup and said, "Still want to speak to the chief?"

"Um . . . could you excuse us?" Frank said politely.

As we stepped away from the desk, I could still hear the sound of Sanford Peyton's voice arguing with the chief behind closed doors.

"Something tells me this is going to take a while," Frank said.

"Yeah." I sighed. "And who knows if the chief will even speak to us after dealing with that?"

Frank shrugged. "Maybe Mom and Dad ought to speak to the chief after all," he said. "Maybe they would have more luck."

I shook my head. "I'm not ready to go there yet," I said.

"Then what?" Frank asked, trying to keep his voice down.

"Let's find Colin and get in his face," I suggested. "We know where the Sylvesters live."

"Yeah, but how do we know Colin will be home?" Frank asked.

"It's Saturday morning, so he's probably sleeping in," I said. "Especially after a busy night of setting fires."

The chief and Sanford Peyton were still going at it when Frank and I left the police station.

"Aren't you glad we're not working that party?" Frank said to me as he drove off.

"That's for sure." I smiled. "I knew those togas were a bad sign!"

The road leading to the Sylvester house was a steep one. It wound through a wooded area until reaching a three-story glass-walled house overlooking the bay. The place looked more like a dream getaway than a family home.

"Glass walls," I observed. "Doesn't leave much to the imagination."

Frank parked at a safe distance.

As we quietly walked toward the house, I couldn't help

244

but wonder what Colin was dreaming about as he slept in. More fires? A detonation somewhere? The possibilities were endless in a sick mind like his!

Once at the house, Frank and I got nosy. We peered through the glass into what looked like the Sylvesters' den. But unlike most dens, the walls weren't lined with bookshelves or entertainment equipment. These walls were covered with guns and rifles!

"Will you look at that?" I whispered.

"There must be two dozen guns in there," Frank whispered back. "Some look like antiques. One looks as old as the Civil War."

"That's a lot of coinage," I said.

"Whatever they're worth, it's probably lunch money for the Sylvesters," Frank scoffed.

I couldn't take my eyes off the guns. Why did the Sylvesters have them hanging in plain sight like that? As a warning to home invaders? Or to snoopers like Frank and me?

"Joe!"

"What?" I said, turning to Frank.

"Colin is out on his deck," he said. "I can see him through the glass."

"That's what we're here for," I said. "Let's go over to him and—"

"He's with his friends," Frank finished.

"Oh," I said.

I peered through the glass all the way out to the deck.

There was Colin, leaning back in an Adirondack chair and eating what looked like a muffin. Standing around him and drinking coffee were the same guys from his school.

"Five against two?" I said with a sigh. "I think this calls for a change of plans."

"Let's go around the house," Frank said. "Maybe we can hear what they're talking about."

Sticking close to the wall, we moved toward the back where the deck stood. When we got to the end of the wall, we stopped and strained our ears to listen. We heard a few words thrown around but couldn't make out the conversation.

"This isn't going to work," Frank murmured.

I was about to agree until I remembered something inside my jacket pocket—the ear amplifier Connie had given me at Dad's office.

"Let's see if this thing works," I whispered. After untangling the wire, I stuck the bud in my right ear. Yes! The voices of Colin Sylvester and his peeps were coming in loud and clear!

I gave Frank a thumbs-up, then listened closely.

"I wish you could taste how awesome this muffin is," Colin was saying. "The blueberries are, like, the size of my fist."

I rolled my eyes. Colin's breakfast? Was this how good it was going to get?

"What?" Frank hissed, dying to know what I heard.

Suddenly I heard a girl's voice speak up. It sounded scratchy, as if it was coming through a speakerphone. It also sounded familiar.

"So tell me about the plan," she said. "How's it coming along?"

"The plan is going according to plan!" Colin chuckled. "Trust me, babe. Soon it'll all be worth it."

"Yeah!" one of his friends said. "This is going to be huge!"

Frank must have seen my eyes pop wide open. "What?" he whispered. "What are you hearing?"

I shook my head as if to say, *Wait*. It was the girl's voice I heard next.

"Colin, you are soooo bad," she said. "But that's why you're my guy."

I yanked out the earbud and turned to Frank. "Colin is planning something big," I whispered. "And it's going down soon."

"A plan?" Frank whispered. "What kind of plan?"

"Don't know." I shrugged.

"That's it," Frank said, no longer whispering. "I don't care that he's with his friends. We're questioning him right now—"

"Hello," a voice said.

Frank and I spun around. A tanned, middle-aged woman wearing a white tennis outfit was standing a few feet away.

"G-good morning!" Frank stammered.

"Um . . . Mrs. Sylvester?" I asked.

"Mrs. Sylvester?" She laughed. "All of Colin's friends call me Barbara."

"I meant . . . Barbara!" I said, laughing too. All the time my heart was pounding inside my chest. Had Colin's mom seen us snooping around? Had she caught the listening device in my ear?

"Why don't I tell Colin you're here?" Barbara Sylvester said, heading toward the deck. "I can get Helga to bring out more muffins."

"No!" Frank said quickly. "I mean, thanks, but we were just leaving."

"The muffins were great, by the way," I said. "Blueberries the size of my fist!"

I felt Barbara's eyes on us as we hurried back to our car.

"That was close," Frank said.

"Yeah, but what happened to questioning Colin?" I asked.

"I'm not questioning anyone in front of his mom," Frank said as we climbed back into the car. "So how soon is this plan going down? Did anyone say?"

"No, but I found out something else," I said.

"What?" Frank asked.

"It sounded like Colin Sylvester has a girlfriend," I said. "He was talking to her on speakerphone."

"A girlfriend?" Frank scoffed as he turned the key. "Anyone interested in that guy has got to be bad news too."

"That's for sure," I agreed. "What do you think this 'huge' plan of his is, Frank?"

Frank sighed as he turned the car around. "I don't know," he said. "But whatever it is—it can't be good."

CHANGE OF PLANS

11

FRANK

AS I DROVE FARTHER AWAY FROM THE Sylvester house, I couldn't stop thinking about this plan Joe had heard about.

How would we stop it when we didn't know what it was?

"Frank," Joe interrupted my thoughts. "That girl on the speakerphone . . ."

"What about her?" I asked.

"Her voice sounded familiar," Joe said.

I shot him a sideways glance. He was staring out the passenger window, deep in thought.

"You mean like someone from school?" I asked. "If she's Colin's girl, chances are she goes to Bay Academy."

"Then I wouldn't know her," Joe said, shrugging it off.

"It's eleven o'clock. Do you think it's too early for pizza?"

"For you, no," I said. "For me, yes."

"Think of it as a power lunch," Joe said. "While we feast on pepperoni and mushrooms, we can talk about the case."

We had a lot to talk about, especially after what we'd heard at Colin's.

"You win," I said, turning the car onto Bay Street. "Pizza, here we come."

Saturday was the busiest shopping day of the week, so I was lucky to find a parking spot right away.

"Let's go to Pie Squared, the place that makes those square-shaped pizzas," Joe suggested.

"Are the pepperoni square too?" I joked.

Joe was too busy staring up the street to get my joke.

"What is it?" I asked.

"Check out who's coming," Joe said.

Turning my head, I saw who Joe was talking about. Strutting toward us and swinging shopping bags from both hands was Lindsay Peyton. She was walking next to another girl, also armed with bags.

"Good timing," I said. "Let's see what she knows about Colin."

It wasn't sunny, but the two girls were wearing huge dark sunglasses. One of Lindsay's bags smacked into my leg as the two breezed by.

"Hey!" Joe called after them. "Remember us?"

Lindsay peered over her shoulder. "Oh, it's you two," she said in a voice as cold as ice.

"I've heard friendlier greetings at the Haunted Mansion," Joe said as we walked over.

"It happened to be an appropriate one," Lindsay said, raising her chin. "You know, my dad had to get me a new car."

She turned to her friend and said, "Not that that was a bad thing, right, Grace?"

"Right!" Grace laughed.

The friends readied to high-five, only to realize their hands were full.

"If you're still saying we keyed your car, you're wrong," I said. "It was already keyed when we got to the parking lot."

"Whatever," Lindsay said with a shrug.

"You heard about all that gang stuff going around, didn't you?" Joe asked.

Lindsay stared at him. "Are you serious?" she said. "Do you know what tomorrow is?"

"Sunday?" Joe said.

"Omigosh, tomorrow is Lindsay's Sweet Sixteen!" Grace said as if we'd just touched down from another planet.

"Who has time to think about anything else?" Lindsay asked. She tilted her head and said, "So are you kicking yourself for not working my party?"

Joe shook his head. "Togas aren't my style."

Lindsay clicked her tongue in disgust. She and Grace were about to turn when I said, "Wait!"

I couldn't let Lindsay leave before asking her about Colin.

"I heard you didn't invite Colin Sylvester to your party," I said quickly.

Lindsay's shoulders drooped at the mention of Colin. "Did he tell you that?" she asked.

"No," I said. "We must have overheard it somewhere. Can't remember where or when—"

"We just want to know why he's not invited," Joe cut in. "That's all."

Lindsay pushed her sunglasses up on her head. She narrowed her eyes and said, "Because Colin Sylvester is a psycho creep—that's why!"

"Colin's been trying to ask Lindsay out since middle school," Grace said. "He even tried to get into our clique at school."

"And you kept turning him down?" I asked Lindsay.

"I wouldn't go out with Colin if he looked like an Abercrombie model," Lindsay snapped. "I'm just glad he has a girlfriend now—maybe he'll leave me alone."

"Who is she?" Joe asked.

"Who?" Lindsay repeated.

"Colin's girlfriend," Joe urged.

"Is she bad news like him?" I asked.

Lindsay wrinkled her nose and said, "What are you guys—some kind of investigative reporters?"

"Sort of," Joe said.

"Whatever, I can't talk now," Lindsay said impatiently,

dropping her sunglasses over her eyes. "I have a ton of stuff to do before my party tomorrow."

"Like having your eyebrows waxed in ten minutes!" Grace reminded her.

"Gracie!" Lindsay complained as the two hurried away. "Like, thanks for letting them think I have a unibrow!"

When the girls were out of earshot, I said, "Well, I guess it's true that Lindsay hates Colin—he sounds like a creep."

We continued up the block, and Joe said, "Frank, do you think Colin's big plan includes the Scaredevils?"

"Probably," I said. "The Scaredevils seem to be Colin's sock puppets. They'll do anything for his money."

"And I'll do anything for pizza right now," Joe said. "You know I can't talk about a case on an empty stomach."

"Okay, okay," I said, smiling. "We're almost there."

Joe and I made our way to Pie Squared, where we shared a pepperoni pizza with olives and mushrooms.

"So," Joe said, popping a mushroom into his mouth. "What's next on the agenda?"

I wanted to answer him, but not with a big piece of mozzarella cheese hanging from my mouth over my chin. I must have looked pretty pathetic, especially when the door opened and in walked—of all people—Sierra Mitchell!

I yanked the cheese from my mouth—only to get it tangled around my hand.

"Hey, guys!" Sierra called with a wave.

"Smooth, bro, real smooth," Joe teased.

When my hand was finally cheese free, I smiled coolly and said, "Hey."

"Don't tell me you eat pizza for breakfast too," Joe said to Sierra.

"No," Sierra said. "I'm actually here on a work mission. The party planners are toiling around the clock for Lindsay's Sweet Sixteen tomorrow, so we all need lunch."

"We're working today too," I said. "Those pranks around Bayport are keeping us busy."

"Oh, that's right, you're detectives," Sierra said. She then planted her hands on her hips and added, "Well, if you ask me, I think we're all working a little too hard for a Saturday."

"It is what it is," Joe said with a shrug.

"We can still take a break," Sierra said. Her eyes lit up. "Why don't you come over to the Peytons', Frank, and we'll take one of their boats out for a spin?"

"So Mr. Peyton can accuse us of trying to steal his boat?" I scoffed. "Thanks—but no thanks."

"Borrowing the boat is one of my job perks," Sierra explained. "I get to use the small powerboat during my breaks."

"Not the yacht?" I joked.

"Maybe when I become head event planner," Sierra joked back. "But for now the small boat is cool. I took it out yesterday afternoon and had a blast."

I smiled at the thought of boating with Sierra—until I felt Joe kick me under the table and give me a look. Now what?

"I know," Sierra said excitedly. "Why don't you come with us, Joe?"

"Me?" Joe asked, surprised.

"Him?" I asked, even more surprised.

"The more the merrier," Sierra said cheerily.

"In that case," Joe said, "thanks!"

"Yeah, thanks," I muttered to Joe. Better than nothing, I guess.

"Super!" Sierra said as she glanced at her watch. "Meet me at the Peytons' docks at two o'clock. Just go around the house to the back and I'll be there."

Sierra then did something totally unexpected. She threw me a kiss before walking to the take-out counter. Me—not Joe!

"I saw that," Joe teased again. "She's got it bad for you, big brother."

We finished our pizza, then got ready to go boating. I changed into khaki shorts, a polo shirt, and flip-flops. Joe pulled on a pair of cleaner jeans, sneakers, and a T-shirt sporting a soft-drink logo.

"You look like you go to Bay Academy!" Joe joked when we reached the Peyton house.

"And you look like you're in kindergarten!" I complained.

There was no Peyton sighting as we headed around the house to the two docks.

"Can you imagine what Sanford would do if he saw us trespassing like this?" Joe asked as we walked down a hill toward the bay.

"We're not trespassing," I reminded him. "Taking out the boat is one of Sierra's job perks. She told us herself."

"So where is Sierra?" Joe asked, looking around. "She told us she'd meet us here."

I didn't see Sierra either. Were we about to get stood up?

Joe whistled through his teeth as he moved up the docks. "Hey—check out Sanford's awesome toys," he said.

There were three boats roped along the two docks—two luxury cabin cruisers and a smaller powerboat with a sleek V-shaped hull. Not too shabby, to say the least.

"Frank, Joe," Sierra's voice called.

I smiled when I saw Sierra at the top of the hill, but my good mood quickly faded. She looked upset.

"What's up?" I called up to her.

"My supervisor just called," Sierra said, her shoulders drooping. "She wants me to order a limo for the band."

"So you can't go boating?" Joe asked.

"Not right now," Sierra said. "Why don't you take the powerboat out in the meantime? I'll meet you back on the dock in twenty minutes."

"It's okay," I said. "We'll wait for you—"

"No!" Sierra said kind of quickly. "Take the boat out, so I won't feel so guilty. When was the last time you drove a boat?"

"Last summer," I said. "I have my license and everything."

"Great," Sierra said, tossing me the key. "See you in twenty minutes, okay?"

"Okay!" I called back.

Sierra ran back to the house.

"I guess we're on our own," I said as I walked up the dock to Joe. "At least for now."

Joe was already untying the powerboat. "All right!" he exclaimed. "Joy ride, baby!"

As I walked up to the boat, I felt a little uneasy. Sure, it was pretty cool to take it for a spin, but I didn't think Mr. Peyton would feel the same way. When I told Joe my thoughts, he waved me off.

"He'll never know," he assured me as he stepped in.

Let's hope he doesn't, I thought.

It took us a few minutes to untie the boat. Once it was freed from the dock, we climbed inside.

"I'll drive," I said, taking my place behind the wheel. Joe sat next to me, slipping on a pair of shades.

Before I started the engine, I did a few safety checks. There was plenty of fuel. Check. Life jackets. Check.

After a few more checks, I turned on the ignition switch. When I pulled back on the throttle, it felt loose, but it didn't seem to be an issue as I cast the boat off from the dock. After turning the craft around, I pushed the throttle forward.

"Full speed ahead!" I exclaimed as the boat cut across the water at an exhilarating pace.

"Woo-hooo!" Joe cheered.

I had forgotten what a blast boating could be—especially knowing we'd have another pretty passenger joining us soon.

But my thoughts were interrupted by the roar of a Jet Ski engine.

Turning my head, I saw the Jet Ski in the distance, heading right into our path.

"Slow down so you don't hit her," Joe said.

"Duh!" I responded as I grabbed the throttle. But as I pulled back on the throttle, something happened that turned my blood to ice.

The handle came off in my hand!

"Frank, slow down!" Joe cried, his eyes still on the Jet Ski. "We're going to crash!"

"I can't, Joe!" I shouted, staring at the handle in my hand. "I can't!"

12

ROUGH SEAS

JOE

I N A PANIC, FRANK FUMBLED TO POP THE THROTTLE
back in, only to watch it pop out again.

"Turn around!" I started yelling at the jet skier.
"Turn around!"

By now I was standing up in the boat, my head spinning. We were either going to crash into the Jet Ski or
into some trees on the opposite bank. Just as I was about
to brace for the worst, I remembered another way to stop.

"The key!" I shouted.

My hand jutted out and turned the ignition key. The
boat sputtering to a stop was like music to my ears. I could
hear Frank heave a sigh as he slumped back on the seat.

The jet skier zoomed past us, just a few feet away. "When

are you going to learn how to drive?" she shouted above the whirring engine.

"When you learn how to turn that thing around!" I shouted back angrily.

"I think I'm going to barf," Frank groaned slowly.

Picking up the fallen throttle, I shook my head. "I hope the Peytons get a refund on this hunk of junk."

"I don't get it," Frank said. "How could a boat that must have cost hundreds of thousands of dollars fall apart like some kid's toy?"

"Whatever happened, we'd better find a way to put this thing back where it belongs so we can get back to the dock!" I said.

As I leaned over to check the throttle, something caught my eye. On the floor of the boat, tucked deep under the dashboard, were a bunch of loose screws and a screwdriver.

Picking up one of the screws, I sized it up with the throttle. A perfect fit!

"Something tells me this wasn't an accident, Frank," I said.

"Wait a minute," he said. "Are you saying someone unscrewed the throttle before we got into the boat?"

"It's possible," I said.

"But I used the throttle to cast off," Frank said.

We studied the throttle. The most likely explanation was that only part of it had been unscrewed before we got into the boat. It would have been just a matter of time before the whole thing would pop off—which it had.

"Looks like somebody was trying to hurt the Peytons," I said. "Or us."

"Us?" Frank repeated.

"The Scaredevils already got to us," I said. "The fire, the rock through the window . . ."

"How would they know we were going boating?" Frank asked. "The only one who knew was Sierra, and we know she isn't a Scaredevil."

Maybe not. But something about Sierra was starting to feel sketchy to me. Like, why had she invited Frank out at the last minute the night of the fire? And why had she invited both of us boating when the boat was unsafe?

Frank must have noticed me deep in thought, because he raised his eyebrow and said, "What?"

"Nothing," I said. "Let's just fix this thing so we can get back."

"Yeah," Frank said. "Sierra's probably wondering where we are."

We used the screwdriver to reattach the throttle handle. When we were sure it was safe, Frank turned the boat around and drove toward the dock—slowly this time!

"I think I know how this happened," Frank said as the boat bounced over the rippling currents.

"How?" I asked.

"The Peytons could have had someone working on the boat before we took it out," Frank explained. "Sierra might not have even known it."

"Didn't she say she took the boat out yesterday afternoon?" I reminded. "She didn't mention anything being wrong with it then."

Frank rolled his eyes. "Someone could have noticed the problem this morning," he said.

"Right," I murmured, but I didn't buy it. The whole thing smelled of sabotage to me, but Frank was way too in love to get a whiff.

As the boat approached shore I could see Sierra, waving both hands in the air.

"Are you guys okay?" Sierra called out. "It looked like you were fixing something on the boat!"

Frank nodded as we climbed out onto the dock. "We're fine," he said. "We just had a little . . . mechanical difficulty."

"Mechanical difficulty," I muttered. "Yeah, you could say that."

I got a hard glare from Frank, telling me to shut up. He then smiled at Sierra and said, "Did you finish your work? That order you had to call in?"

She nodded and said, "I got the extra flowers we needed."

"Flowers?" I said, tilting my head. "I thought you had to order a limo for the band."

Sierra blinked fast before saying, "I did. Then I got a text from my boss telling me to order more flowers."

I frowned. Was she lying to us?

"Where's Mr. Peyton?" I asked.

"Why do you want to know?" Sierra asked.

"I want to tell him somebody messed with his boat, that's why," I said.

"You don't have to tell Mr. Peyton," Sierra blurted out.

"Why not?" I asked.

"Joe . . . ," Frank started to say.

"Because while I was inside, I found out there was a problem with the boat," Sierra said. "I tried to stop you from going out, but it was too late."

"Who told you about the boat?" I asked.

"Joe, will you quit it?" Frank snapped. "She's trying to explain what happened."

Sierra glared at me. "Why does it matter who told me?" she demanded. "You wouldn't know him anyway."

"So introduce us!" I said with a shrug.

"You don't believe me, do you?" Sierra demanded. "What do you think—that I messed with the boat?"

"Forget it, Sierra," Frank said gently. "Joe is just shaken up from the whole thing."

"Shaken up?" I cried.

"This boating idea was a bad one, Frank," Sierra said. "I'm sorry I suggested it."

"No, it was a great idea!" Frank said. "Maybe we can do it another time?"

"Yeah, like when the boat's safe?" I added, before Frank gave me a shove.

"We'll definitely do it another time," Sierra said directly to Frank. "But just the two of us, okay?"

Without looking at me, Sierra turned to walk back to the house.

"Okay, what was that all about?" Frank demanded.

I waited until Sierra was back inside before saying, "You tell me, Frank. Are you so into Sierra you refuse to call her out on her stuff?"

"What stuff?" Frank cried. "She told us the boat was busted before we got in."

"I'm not sure I buy it," I admitted. "And I'm starting to have bad feelings about Sierra, Frank. Sorry, but I do."

"Yeah, well, I have feelings for her too," Frank said. "And FYI, they're all good."

"Does that mean you're not buying my sabotage theory?" I asked. "Any of it?"

"Only if the Scaredevils knew we were going boating," Frank said. "And I can't imagine how they would."

"That's why we're going to track down Colin," I insisted. "I don't care if he's with his friends or his great-grandmother—we're going to question him until he's blue in the face."

I could see Frank was disappointed as we walked back to the car. But just as he started unlocking the car door, he got a text.

"Who's it from?" I asked.

Frank's eyes widened as he read the message. "It's from Chet," he said. "He wants us to come over ASAP."

"Did he say why?" I asked.

"It's the Scaredevils," Frank said, looking up from the phone. "They got to Iola."

TWISTS AND TURNS

13

FRANK

I T WAS HARD NOT TO GO OVER THE SPEED LIMIT as Joe and I drove to Chet's house. The text hadn't explained what had happened to Iola, so we could only think the worst.

"Why would the Scaredevils want to do something to Iola?" Joe asked as I careened into the Mortons' driveway.

"Because she's our friend?" was all I could guess. "And any friend of ours is probably an enemy of theirs."

Chet was already at the door as we raced up to the house. "Hey," he said.

"How's Iola?" I asked.

"She's in the living room," Chet said, opening the door wider to let us inside. "See for yourselves."

Joe and I headed down the hallway. We turned into the

living room to see Iola sitting on the sofa. She looked okay, but was she really?

"Hi," Iola said, looking up from a magazine she was reading.

"Just hi?" Joe asked. "What happened?"

"Nothing." Iola sighed. "I'm fine."

"She thinks it's nothing," Chet said. "But Iola was in a fight."

Iola rolled her eyes. "Almost a fight, Chet," she said. "Will you stop being the overprotective big brother and give me some space?"

"Tell us what happened!" I urged Chet.

Chet turned to us, his face grim. "Some girls wearing blue bandannas over their faces started picking on Iola as she was walking home from her friend's house," he explained.

"What did they do to you?" I asked Iola.

"It didn't go anywhere," Iola explained. "Even though half their faces were covered, I recognized two of them from school. When I called them out, they turned and ran away."

"Good thing," Chet said.

"Do you know where they went?" Joe asked.

Iola shrugged and said, "Up the block, then around the corner."

I was still trying to process the whole thing. "I didn't know girls were in the Scaredevils," I said.

"I guess they need the money too," Joe said. He shook his head. "Man, whatever happened to flipping burgers and babysitting?"

The money made me think of the Scaredevils' benefactor—Colin Sylvester.

"Was anyone else there?" I asked Iola. "Any guys?"

"No," Iola said, but quickly added, "Yes . . . well, maybe."

"Jeez, Iola!" Chet complained. "Is it yes, no, or maybe so?"

"I'm not sure," Iola said. "There was a black car parked on the block. After the girls ran off, the car took off too, practically speeding."

"Could you see who was inside?" Joe asked.

"No, but I remember his plate," Iola said. "It said something like Awesome . . ."

"Awesome Dude!" I declared. "Better known as Colin Sylvester."

"Him?" Iola wrinkled her nose. "That creep was in the car watching us all that time? Eww."

"I'll bet he taped the whole thing too," Joe said. "It's probably gone viral by now."

"But nothing happened," Iola said.

Chet was already on the computer, browsing YouTube. He held it up and said, "Here it is. Slickbro13's latest viral venture."

"Slickbro13 . . . Awesome Dude?" Iola scoffed. "The guy obviously has no self-esteem issues."

We huddled around the computer to check out the video. Colin's shaky camera caught the Scaredevils approaching Iola, but ended right before they bolted.

"There's no audio on this one," Joe pointed out.

"No surprise," Iola said. "I said the girls' names—Amy and Desiree."

"It's a good thing you did," Chet said. "Who knows what could have happened if you didn't recognize them?"

Iola patted Chet's shoulder. "Thank you for your concern, big brother," she said. "But I'm okay. Really."

We were all glad Iola was okay. But the thought of Colin pitting his gang against our friends made me want to hunt him down even more. How could we even think of going boating when he was still on the loose?

"Tonight we find Mr. Awesome Dude," I told Joe. "Once and for all."

"Tonight?" Joe exclaimed. "Why don't we go to his house right now?"

"Because we promised Dad we'd help him fix up the garage for a bit, remember?" I reminded him. "And tonight is Saturday night. Everyone will be out, especially the Scaredevils. And where there're Scaredevils, there's Colin."

Joe nodded thoughtfully. "Tonight could be the night Colin carries out his big plan," he said.

"Yeah, well, we have a plan too," I said, glaring at the YouTube clip on Chet's computer.

Fixing up our fire-wrecked garage was grueling work, and it would take more than a few hours to finish the job. By the time we stopped for the day, Joe and I were ready to take on another wreck—Colin Sylvester!

But first . . . we had to be excused from dinner.

"What do you mean, you won't be home for dinner?" Mom asked. "Your dad is grilling some steaks."

"Save us some leftovers, please," Joe said. "We'll be hungry when we get back."

The last thing we wanted to do was worry Mom or Dad with the details. All we wanted to do was wait outside the Sylvester home for Colin. As soon as his car left the house, we wouldn't be too far behind.

"I'm getting hungry," Joe said after about an hour of watching for Colin. "Maybe we should have taken some food for the road. Steak for a stakeout . . . get it?"

"Got it," I groaned as I slumped back on the seat. My eyes burned from looking for Colin in the dark. "Maybe this wasn't such a great idea."

My phone beeped. Another text from Chet. Had the Scaredevils come back for Iola? Or for him? But when I read his message, it was good news, or at least helpful.

"Chet said he just spotted Colin's car parked at the Cineplex," I said, sitting up straight again. "The Awesome Dude plate gave it away."

"Perfect!" Joe said with a grin. "I'd rather stake him out at the movies than here."

"What's the difference?" I asked.

"Three words," Joe said. "Take-out food!"

Awesome Dude's black Benz was still parked at the Cineplex when we arrived. We were able to find a spot close to Colin's car but not close enough for him to see us waiting.

"I wonder what movie Colin is seeing," I said.

"Probably one that makes him laugh," Joe said with a smirk. "Like a slasher movie."

Joe browsed his tablet for movie times. "The next movie ends in forty-five minutes," he said. "Plenty of time to grab some grub."

My stomach was starting to growl too, so we left the car for the Stop and Snack. The convenience store did a good business, being right next to the Cineplex. It was owned by Bruce and Sheila Davis, a cool couple who were there most of the twenty-four hours it was open.

But as Joe and I walked inside, something felt and looked different. The place wasn't packed with the usual movie-goers. It was just Bruce, Sheila, and two police officers.

Sheila saw us and waved. "Come on in, guys," she called. "Everything's back on the shelves now. We're taking customers again."

"Back on the shelves?" Joe murmured as we stepped inside. "That doesn't sound good."

The police officers walked past Joe and me on their way out of the store.

"What do you mean, you're taking customers again?" I asked the Davises. "What happened?"

"Ah, some crazy kids were in here a couple of hours ago," Bruce said. "They were running up and down the aisles and knocking stuff off the shelves."

"No way!" I gasped. A few hours ago it was still light out. If it was the Scaredevils, they were getting bold.

"Were they wearing blue bandannas?" Joe asked. "Over their faces?"

"Yeah," Bruce said. He raised an eyebrow. "How did you guys know?"

"It's the same gang that's been trashing Bayport the last few weeks," I explained.

"I know all about those pranks," Sheila said, shaking her head. "I'm sure the cops are working hard, but when are they going to catch those punks?"

"Probably when they catch the ringleader," I replied.

As we walked over to the pretzels and chips Joe whispered, "You mean when *we* catch the ringleader."

We bought a medium-size bag of honey-mustard pretzels and two cold lemonades. As we walked back to the parking lot, Joe suddenly said, "Frank—over there!"

Joe's hands were full, so he pointed with his elbow. I turned to see Colin walking away from the Cineplex, his arm around a girl.

"I guess he didn't stay for the credits," I said, narrowing my eyes. "Come on. Let's let him know we're here."

Colin was already in the car as we got near.

"Spare me," I groaned. "Colin and his girl are kissing."

Joe's eyes suddenly grew wide.

"What?" I asked.

"Get back here," Joe said. He darted behind a Dumpster

directly in front of Colin's car. I joined him there as he placed our snacks on the ground.

"So what are we doing?" I asked.

"This is the perfect place to spy on them," Joe said, his voice low.

"You mean spy on them kissing?" I cried. "What are we, in grade school? We should be pinning Colin against his car, demanding answers!"

"We will," Joe said as he peeked out from behind the Dumpster. "First I want to see who the girl is."

"It's too dark to see anything, Joe," I said. "And who cares who she is?"

Another car drove by. Its headlights illuminated the area, including Colin's car. For a split second I was able to see the girl as she leaned back against the car seat and smiled. My heart sank like a stone when I suddenly realized who she was. It was Sierra!

DECEPTION 14

JOE

"OH, MAN, FRANK," I SAID WITH A SIGH. "Sorry."

Frank seemed too stunned to say a word. It was then that I realized why the voice on Colin's phone had sounded so familiar. I also realized why I'd had those weird feelings about Sierra. Not only was she Colin's girlfriend, she was probably his spy!

"Frank?" I said, looking over at him. He wasn't peering out from behind the Dumpster anymore. He was sitting on the ground, slumped against it. "Frank, are you okay?"

Frank stared straight ahead. "Looks like your bad feelings about Sierra were right," he muttered.

"Hey," I said with a shrug. "A lucky guess."

I turned back to the car. Colin and Sierra were kissing

273

again—the perfect time to catch them by surprise.

"Come on, Frank!" I said. "Let's surprise them."

He shook his head. "Colin's in his car. He'll either take off—or knowing him, run us over."

"But we have enough time to get our car," I said. "As long as they're still kissing—"

Frank glared at me.

Oops.

"Okay, I'll shut up," I said. "But we're wasting precious time here!"

I turned back toward the car. Colin and Sierra had stopped kissing and were talking now. After sharing a laugh, they high-fived. Were they talking about the plan? The car windows were open, but they were too far away for us to hear a thing.

. . . Or were they?

I reached for the amplifier, still in my jacket pocket. I stuck it in my ear, but this time heard nothing.

"Arrrgh!" I said. "The battery must have died."

The sudden sound of an engine made me jump. I yanked out the earbud just as Colin's headlights flashed, illuminating the Dumpster and us. I ducked behind the Dumpster. Was it too late? Had Colin or Sierra seen us?

With a loud screech, the car backed out of the parking lot. It turned, then roared off.

"Frank, let's chase them," I said. "If we get to our car in time, we might have a chance—"

"Forget it, Joe," Frank said. "They're already out of the lot."

"So, what, we're not even going to try?" I cried.

"Not with Sierra in the car," Frank said. He then shook his head and murmured, "Sierra and Colin. Unbelievable."

I sank down next to Frank. I took a noisy slurp of my lemonade and said, "I kind of believe it. Remember how she invited you out last night, the night of the fire?"

"What are you saying?" Frank asked. "That she wanted to get me out of the way so the Scaredevils could burn our garage?"

"That—or get information from you," I said. "Maybe Colin wanted to know how much we knew about him and the gang."

"Great," Frank grumbled.

"I'll bet that's how the Scaredevils got my e-mail address," I figured. "Sierra took it from the job application I filled out."

I knew Frank didn't want to hear it, but I had to go on about Sierra.

"Sierra invited us on that boat," I said. "Probably knowing that it was rigged by Colin—or maybe herself."

"It's my fault," Frank said, standing up. "I told Sierra about the case we were working on, so the Scaredevils came after us."

"It wasn't your fault, Frank," I said.

"Sure it was," he said angrily. "Sierra played me, and I fell for it."

We carried our drinks and pretzels back to our car. Frank didn't say a word.

"Frank," I said, "how do you think someone like Sierra got a job working for the Peytons?"

"Sierra's obviously good at deceiving people," Frank said bitterly. "She could be playing the Peytons too."

Playing the Peytons?

The idea made me stop in my tracks.

"Maybe Sierra isn't there to help plan Lindsay's Sweet Sixteen," I told Frank. "Maybe she's there to help Colin bring down Lindsay's Sweet Sixteen!"

Frank shot me a puzzled look.

"Think about it, Frank," I continued. "Colin wasn't invited to the party of the decade. A guy like him wouldn't take that lightly."

"Especially since Lindsay's been rejecting him since middle school," Frank agreed.

"Not only did she reject him," I said, "she kept him from being a part of her clique."

"So trashing Lindsay's Sweet Sixteen makes sense to him," Frank said.

"I just can't figure out what the Scaredevils have to do with the party," I said slowly. "You know, all those pranks that went viral."

Frank took a long sip of his lemonade. I could tell he was thinking hard from the way his eyes darted back and forth. Suddenly both eyes snapped wide open. He turned to me and said, "Joe, do you remember what Colin said in that video?"

"Which one?" I asked.

"The one where we heard his voice in the background," Frank said. "He said, 'This ought to keep the cops busy.'"

"Yeah . . . so?" I asked.

"Remember when Sanford Peyton came to the police station?" Frank said. "He was complaining that there weren't enough cops scheduled for Lindsay's party."

"Yeah!" I said, the pieces starting to come together. "Colin was keeping the cops busy with the Scaredevils' pranks so they'd be too busy to cover Lindsay's Sweet Sixteen."

"And if Colin is planning on trashing it," Frank said, "the fewer cops, the more trouble!"

It made total sense to me now. Trashing Lindsay's Sweet Sixteen was the perfect act of revenge. And if anyone seemed the vengeful type, it was Colin Sylvester.

"Okay," I said. "Now that we've figured out Colin's plan—what's ours?"

Frank took another long sip of his lemonade. He then looked me straight in the eye.

"If Colin is planning to trash the party," he said, "then we're going to crash the party."

"I thought you wanted to work this Sweet Sixteen, Chet," I said.

"Not wrapped in a sheet, dudes," Chet groaned. "I feel like a pig in a blanket without the mustard!"

277

It was early Sunday night. Frank, Chet, and I had parked all the way down the hill from the Bayport Bijou, the hall where Lindsay's Sweet Sixteen was about to rock. We spent the whole day mapping out our plan and suiting up for the party we were about to crash. And that meant togas.

"We told you a million times, Chet," Frank said as we trudged up the hill. "These costumes are the best way to sneak into the party. It's what all the waiters will be wearing."

"I doubt they got theirs on sale at Sid's Novelty Shop," I said. Then, striking my best ancient-Roman-senator pose, I added, "So, do I look like Caesar?"

"With those leaves around your head?" Chet snorted. "More like Caesar salad."

I gazed upward. Besides the head wreath, the costume came with fake leather sandals, a white tunic, and a gold sash. Sid threw in some freebies—fake gold wrist and ankle cuffs.

"I just wish these things had pockets," I complained. "Where am I going to keep my tablet?"

Chet tugged at his waist pouch. "I'll carry it for you in here, Joe," he said. "I brought it for leftover party food."

We reached the top of the hill to look out at the Bayport Bijou. Valets were busy parking classy cars as they drove up to the entrance one by one. Blinged-out guests strutted up the lantern-lit path like celebs on the red carpet.

"Serious bling going in there, dudes," Chet said. "If crazy Colin is planning a heist, he's coming to the right place."

I hoped Colin would show up. Frank and I were going on

a hunch, and as good as it was, it was still just a hunch.

"It looks like the staff is entering through the side," Frank said, pointing to some other toga-sporting guys. "Let's give it a shot."

We walked toward the building, trying our best to look like we belonged.

"I just had a bad thought," Frank murmured. "What do we do if Sierra sees us? She knows we're not working the party."

I shook my head. "There are over two hundred people in there, Frank," I said. "It'll be dark, and we're in costume. We'll blend right in. Besides, no one will be paying close attention to the help."

"Okay," Frank whispered as we approached the door. "Let's do this."

A guy dressed in head-to-toe black stood planted at the door, checking names on a clipboard.

"Waiters?" he asked us, not looking up.

"At your service!" I said with a smile.

"Names?" he said.

I shot Frank a sideways glance. We had planned everything else except this part.

"Um—we're from the temp agency!" I blurted.

The guy finally looked up. "Temp agency?" he said.

"More like a catering and waitstaff agency," Frank explained quickly.

"Yeah!" Chet said. "It's called . . . Foods and Dudes."

"Who called your agency and asked for you?" the guy demanded.

Uh-oh.

"Um—it was Sierra!" I blurted. "Some girl named Sierra, I think. I'd have brought the job voucher, but I don't have pockets."

I held my breath. What if the guy went to get Sierra to confirm our story? But to my total relief he nodded and said, "Sierra does work for us. I can't be too careful, you realize. Everybody within twenty miles of Bayport wants to crash this party."

"We hear ya!" I told the guy as we filed past him into the kitchen.

"Look at this place!" Frank said as waiters and waitresses brushed past us, grabbing platters from long wooden tables.

"Look at the food!" Chet exclaimed.

A woman dressed in black hurried over to us. "Go ahead, guys," she said. "Grab some platters and make your rounds!"

Chet, Frank, and I darted to the food-filled table. As we took hold of the platters, we whispered our plans.

"Stay as close to each other as possible," Frank said. "Keep your eyes peeled for Colin without looking obvious."

"Check!" I said, lifting a round tray filled with mini pizzas.

Platters in hand, we followed the other waiters into the party hall. Our jaws must have hit the floor as we checked out the place.

"Whoa!" I cried. "What is this—a movie set?"

The huge hall was designed to look like an ancient Roman villa. There were tiled fountains, flaming torches, fake cedar trees, and—last but not least—mosaics on the wall and floor depicting Lindsay at different stages of her life.

"Sierra never told us about this," Frank said.

"There's a lot she didn't tell us," I said with a frown. "Now let's get to work before we get fired."

I'd taken about three steps forward when about a hundred hands reached for my tray.

"Is that cheese on the pizza soy or skim?" a girl with chandelier-size earrings asked.

"Can you bring out some oregano, dude?" a guy asked me. "The fresh kind, not the stuff in the jar."

"Will some mini quiche be coming out?" another girl asked. "Lindsay said there would be some."

I didn't know squat about mini quiche or the pizzas I was passing around, so I tried my best to wing some answers.

"I'll be back with the oregano," I told the guy, knowing full well I wouldn't.

The place pulsated with music as I continued on with my tray. I couldn't believe Lindsay had gotten the group Paradise Six to play her party—their latest song was number three on the charts!

"Excuse me, pardon me, excuse me," I kept saying as I squeezed through the mob of dancing and snacking guests. I spotted a few security guards, but they were busy eating and chatting at the buffet table.

Frank stopped next to me, holding a tray of barbecue wings. He saw me eyeing the guards and said, "Some security. Looks like Colin's plans to keep the police busy worked."

"Yeah, but where is Colin?" I asked.

Frank didn't answer. He was too busy staring ahead at something, his eyes wide.

When I saw who Frank was looking at, I gulped. Standing near the stage where the band was just finishing their tune was—

"Sierra," I muttered.

Sierra was staring too—at Frank, then at me. It wasn't long before her stare became an angry glare when she finally realized who we were.

"She probably figures we crashed the party," Frank murmured.

"What do we tell her if she comes over?" I asked.

Frank was about to say something when—*SMASH!!*

Screams filled the hall as something came crashing through a stained-glass window. The band stopped playing. Guests stared, stunned, at the shattered glass and what had caused it. It was a car tire!

The lights went up as Chet pushed his way over to Frank and me. The three of us watched as the tire rolled a few feet, then tipped on its side with a loud thump.

Frank, Chet, and I moved toward the tire. There, painted across the tire in red paint, was the word "Scaredevils"!

"Out of my way," a voice called out. "Out of my way, kids, please!"

I turned to see Sanford Peyton squeezing through the crowd. After staring at the tire, he shouted, "Is anybody hurt?"

When no one answered, he marched over to the security guards. "Don't just stand there," he said. "Go outside and get the criminals who did this!"

The guards and Sanford raced for the door. A half dozen Bayport Bijou employees raced to the broken glass with brooms and dustpans.

"We'd better go outside too," Frank said. "If this was Colin's doing, he's probably out there somewhere."

We were about to turn toward the door when the lights dimmed.

"Hail, good citizens!" Sierra's voice shouted.

I turned to see Sierra on the stage, a mike in her hand. The once-stunned guests were smiling again as they moved from the hurled tire to the stage.

The band struck a chord. All eyes were on Sierra as she said, "Please give it up for the most epic empress since Cleopatra—our Sweet Sixteen, Empress Lindsay!"

Guests seemed to forget about the broken window as they waved their arms in the air and chanted, "Lind-say! Lind-say! Lind-say!"

A pair of double doors burst wide open. Everyone went wild as four gladiators in full armor marched into the hall, carrying a throne balanced on two poles. Seated on the throne and waving to her adoring crowd was Lindsay—or should I say, Empress Lindsay.

The band struck up "Hotter Than Vesuvius" as the gladiators marched in a circle around the hall. The guys looked pretty authentic in their steel breastplates and heavy helmets, which covered three-quarters of their faces.

"Shouldn't we be outside looking for Colin?" Frank asked over the music.

Frank was right. But then I noticed something about the gladiators' costumes that didn't seem authentic at all.

"Hey, Frank?" I said slowly. "Since when do gladiators carry guns?"

SWEET SIXTEEN

15

FRANK

UNS?" I ASKED, TRYING TO YELL OVER the music. "What guns?"

Joe gestured at the gladiators' sheaths as they marched by with Lindsay's throne. I saw what Joe was talking about. Instead of fake swords, these gladiators were packing heat!

"See what I mean?" Joe said to me.

I nodded slowly.

All I could see of the guns were the handles. The carved ivory told me they were antique.

"Joe," I whispered urgently. "Those are the kind of guns we saw at the Sylvesters'."

Chet was right behind us, listening in. "So what are you saying?" he asked.

"I'm saying one of those gladiators is Colin," I said, narrowing my eyes at the procession. "And he didn't come alone."

The parade of gladiators came to a sudden stop. Lindsay gasped as her throne jerked. Without warning, the gladiators released their grips on the throne, sending it to the floor with a heavy thud. Many of the guests gasped as Lindsay tumbled off the throne onto the floor.

"Hey!" she shrieked.

All four gladiators drew their guns. One pulled out a rifle, which he turned toward the band. "Shut up!" he shouted. "All of you!"

I didn't have to see beyond the heavy helmet to know it was Colin.

"Okay, what's going on?" a Bijou manager said as she squeezed through the crowd of guests. She took one look at the gun and paled. "I see."

Guests and staff stood frozen, too stunned to speak. The only one in the crowd who seemed cool was Sierra. With a small smile on her face, she joined the gladiators.

"Friends, Romans, countrymen, lend me your ears!" Colin shouted through his helmet. "Or better—lend me your bling-bling, watches, and phones!"

I glanced around for the guards, but they had gone outside to investigate the hurled tire. The smashed window must have been Colin's idea to get them out of the way.

"Frank, we've got to do something!" Joe said.

"Do what?" I shot back. "Those guns weren't part of our game plan!"

Two of the gladiators waved their weapons at the guests. One by one, they dropped their jewelry and electronics onto a third gladiator's shield, held out like a tray. The clinking sound of each item hitting the metal was chilling and infuriating.

Joe was right. We had to do something. And fast.

"Here's what I think we should do," I whispered to Joe and Chet. "It's not foolproof, but it's worth a shot."

"Shot?" Chet murmured. "Bad word choice, dude."

"Go on!" Joe urged me.

With one eye on the gladiators, I whispered my plan. "We wait until they come over to us. Chet, you knee the shield up into the guy's face. While that's going down, Joe and I will go for the guns."

"What about Colin over there?" Joe whispered. "He's got a gun too."

"Uh, like, a big gun!" Chet added.

A commotion broke out across the room. One guy was refusing to hand over his expensive-looking phone.

"Come on," Sierra shouted at him. "Hand it over!"

Lindsay pulled herself up off the floor and stared open-mouthed at Sierra.

"Wait a minute, Sierra," Lindsay said angrily. "You're in on this? Who are these guys?"

"Shut your mouth, birthday girl!" Colin shouted at Lindsay.

Lindsay planted her hands on her hips.

"Look, jerk," Lindsay shouted back. "I don't know who you are, but you're ruining my Sweet Sixteen!"

Colin threw back his helmeted head. "That's the idea, Linny," he said with a laugh.

"Wait a minute, I know that voice!" Lindsay said through gritted teeth. She ran up to him so they were inches apart, face to face. Colin threw off his helmet. "I knew it!" Lindsay exclaimed. "You guys, it's Colin Sylvester!"

Groans rose up from the crowd—until Colin pointed his rifle straight at Lindsay's head.

The crowd fell silent. A few guests sobbed softly while Lindsay froze with fear. Without moving a muscle, she uttered, "Don't shoot . . . please."

I knew we couldn't wait. We had to stop Colin now!

I saw Joe grab one of the flaming torches from its stand. I grabbed one too. Together we marched toward Colin and his menacing rifle.

"Drop the gun, Colin!" I demanded.

Colin turned away from Lindsay. When he saw us, he chuckled. "Well, if it isn't the boy detectives," he said. "I suppose you can fight with fire. Although I prefer firepower!"

Gasps filled the room as Colin aimed the rifle at Joe and me. I thrust my flaming torch at Colin. It didn't touch him, but he jumped, letting the gun drop from his hands.

Joe and I lunged for the rifle. We didn't get very far. . . .

"You guys, look out!" Lindsay shouted.

I glanced over my shoulder to see the other three gladia-tors moving toward us. Joe and I traded worried looks. Our torches might have been effective with Colin, but they were no match for three powerful guns coming our way!

I thought it was over, until I heard a loud, long creak. Looking up, I saw a fake tree beginning to tip over. I watched in shock as the tree came crashing down on the three gladiators, pinning them to the ground and knocking their guns from their hands.

"How did that happen?" Joe exclaimed.

We turned to see Chet at the base of the tree. Grinning triumphantly, he ran to grab the guns scattered on the floor. He was about to go for the last one when Sierra grabbed it first.

"Heads up!" Sierra shouted as she tossed the gun to Colin. He caught it with one hand, then turned it on us.

"Nice try, Hardys," Colin snapped. "But I win."

"Game's not over, Sylvester!" Joe shouted as he karate-kicked the gun out of Colin's hand. Colin stood stunned long enough for me to run around and grab him in a choke hold.

"Now game over!" I shouted.

But was it? From the corner of my eye, I saw one of the gladiators dragging himself out from under the tree. His eyes burned through his helmet as he slowly stood up. But before he could come after us . . .

"Stop right there!" a gruff voice boomed.

Joe and I whirled around to see Chief Olaf and his officers pushing through the crowd. Behind them, looking horrified, was Sanford Peyton.

I loosened my grip on Colin as the chief took hold of his arm.

"Nice work, boys," Chief Olaf grunted.

"Um . . . thanks," I said, surprised to hear the words coming out of the chief's mouth. "How did you know to come?"

"Are you kidding me?" Chief Olaf said. "Our station must have gotten a dozen calls and texts within the last fifteen minutes!"

I smiled as a slew of guests raised their cell phones triumphantly.

"Hey, Colin," Joe said with a laugh. "I guess not everybody handed over their fancy phones!"

Sanford had his arm draped around Lindsay's shoulder. "If only I'd been here to stop this," he said. "Why did I have to go outside?"

"You did fine, Mr. Peyton," Chief Olaf said. "You and the guards tracked down those Scaredevil punks. They're on their way to the station now."

Colin stared at the chief. "What did they tell you?" he demanded. "If they told you I robbed the party, they lied."

He pointed at Joe, Chet, then me. "Those are the guys who came with the guns. They're the ones you should be taking in!"

"Oh, blah, blah, blah, Colin," Lindsay said with a sigh.

She turned to Chief Olaf. "Colin and his friends snuck in here dressed as gladiators, with the help of Sierra, may I add. They're the ones who tried to rob us."

Colin's face glowed red as guests called out in agreement. I glanced at Sierra. She appeared to be muttering something to Lindsay through gritted teeth. I had a feeling it wasn't "Happy birthday!"

"Thank you, Miss Peyton," Chief Olaf said. "I'm sure we've got some Scaredevils at the station attesting to everything you said."

"Call my father!" Colin demanded as cuffs were put around his wrists. "I'm sure you can both work something out."

The chief shook his head. "Your dad's money won't help you this time, Colin," he said. "And I'm sure your dad won't be thrilled to know you were playing with his guns."

"Which were not loaded, by the way!" an officer holding the guns called over.

Colin really turned red now. No wonder the vintage guns hadn't gone off when they'd hit the floor.

"Let's hope your dad can afford the bail," Chief Olaf told Colin. "And I'd be interested in seeing some of those videos you and your friends starred in."

Joe folded his arms across his chest as he eyed Colin.

"Did you do it, Colin?" he asked. "Did you pay off those kids to keep the police away from the party?"

"What if I did?" Colin snapped. He turned his glare

toward Lindsay. "After the way she treated me, it's a small price to pay for revenge."

Lindsay stared at Colin as the chief led him out of the hall. I turned to see Sierra being led out too, along with the other gladiators, their helmets removed to reveal their faces.

"Sierra must have canceled the real gladiators and replaced them with Colin's friends," Joe figured.

"Man," I sighed, "did she have me fooled."

"She had us all fooled, Frank," Joe said. "But now the joke's on her."

"And on her psycho boyfriend," Chet added.

Sanford Peyton smiled at Joe, then at me. It was the first smile I'd seen from him yet.

"I'd like to thank you guys for your help," he said. "I'm just learning that you're quite the detectives."

"Don't forget our friend Chet," Joe said. "If he hadn't brought down that tree, who knows what would have happened?"

"Hey," Chet joked, wiggling his hand. "It's all in the wrist!"

This time Lindsay smiled. "I guess all three of you guys are gladiator material after all," she said. "Why don't you stay and hang with us?"

"Why?" Joe teased. "So we can serve mini quiche and hot wings?"

"No!" Lindsay laughed. "So you can party!"

She spun around, calling out to her friends, "Bayport High guys really rock—am I right?"

Their answer came in an earsplitting cheer. Chet shrugged and said, "Cool."

Paradise Six struck a chord as Lindsay jumped back on her throne. Waving both arms in the air, she shouted, "By order of your divine empress, let's get this party started . . . again!"

Some of the cops stuck around to return the stolen goods and make sure everybody was okay. As for Joe, Chet, and me—our job was done.

Joe grinned at me as we made a beeline for the dessert table. "You know, Frank," he said. "Those Bay Academy kids aren't so bad."

"With the exception of a few," I said. "Like maybe four or five?"

"What about those Scaredevils who go to our school?" Chet asked. "What do you think is going to happen to them?"

I shrugged. "They trashed Bayport for the money," I said. "Hopefully they'll fix it up. But that'll be up to the judge."

We stood in line for the designer birthday cake, sculpted to look like an ancient Roman temple. A model of Empress Lindsay chiseled from Rice Krispies treats waved from the top.

"You got to see it to believe it," Joe said, chuckling.

"Speaking of believing," I said, "do you think the kids at school will believe we just battled an army of gladiators with nothing but torches and karate kicks?"

"Sure they will!" Chet said. He pulled Joe's tablet from his waist pouch and held it high. "And if they don't, I've got it all on tape!"

THE VANISHING GAME

G-FORCED

FRANK

DID YOU KNOW THAT COTTON CANDY depends heavily on the molecular construction of sugar?" I asked brightly, grabbing a hunk of my brother Joe's fluffy pink confection and popping it into my mouth. "The cotton candy machine uses centrifugal force to spin hot sugar so quickly and cool it so rapidly, the sugar doesn't have time to recrystallize!"

My date—or so I'd been told, because she didn't seem super attached to me—Penelope Chung, rolled her eyes. "That's fascinating, Frank," she said, shooting a glare at her best friend, Daisy Rodriguez, who was Joe's date and the glue barely holding our foursome together. "Please tell me more about molecules. Or force times acceleration. Or the atomic properties of *fun*."

297

Joe coughed loudly, grabbing my shoulder and pulling me close enough to hear him mutter, "Ixnay on the ience-scay."

I couldn't help it. Joe is always telling me science isn't romantic, but *come on*. Isn't "romance" itself a scientific concept? Attraction, biology, all that stuff?

Daisy smiled, a little too enthusiastically. "Shall we head over to the G-Force?" she asked, looking hopefully from Penelope and me to Joe. "My dad said the first ride would be at eight o'clock. And it's just about quarter of."

"Yes!" Penelope cried before Joe or I could respond, grabbing Daisy's arm and pulling her ahead of us toward Funspot's new ride, G-Force. Penelope leaned close to Daisy's ear, and while I couldn't hear what she was saying, her tone did not sound warm.

Joe met my eye and sighed.

"I don't think she likes me," I told him.

Joe just shook his head and patted my back. "I think your powers of detection are dead-on true."

We started walking. "Sorry," I said. "I know you're really into Daisy."

Joe nodded. "It's okay, man," he said, holding out his cotton candy for me to take another hunk. "I just don't think you're Penelope's type."

I nodded. "But it's pretty cool that we get to be some of the first people to check out G-Force, right?"

"*Very* cool," Joe agreed.

G-Force was the new, premiere attraction at Funspot,

a small amusement park that had been a staple of Bayport summers for generations, but had been getting more and more run-down over the years. Last fall, Daisy's dad, Hector, had used their entire family's savings to buy the park from its longtime owner, Doug Spencer, who had fallen on hard times. Hector wanted to build Funspot into a top-tier amusement park—the kind of place people would drive hours to visit. His first step toward making that happen had been to install G-Force.

The ride was a new creation of Greg and Derek Piperato, better known as the Piperato Brothers—*the* hip new architects of premiere amusement rides all over the world. They built the HoverCoaster for Holiday Gardens in Copenhagen, the Loop-de-Loco for Ciudad de Jugar in Barcelona, and the ChillTaser for Bingo Village in Orlando, right here in the USA. These guys are seriously awesome at what they do. They know their physics, they know their architecture, and they keep coming up with new ideas to revolutionize the amusement industry.

They don't work cheap, though. According to Daisy, Hector had to take out a major loan to afford G-Force. And unfortunately, right after Hector signed the contracts—Funspot had exclusive rights to the ride for five years—Daisy's mom had been laid off from her job as a manager at some big bank in New York City. If Daisy and her family had hoped Funspot would be successful before, now their whole future was riding on the park's success.

"Wow," Joe breathed as we turned a corner, and there it was: G-Force!

For weeks, Hector had paid for advertisements on all the local radio stations: "Come to Funspot to ride G-Force! What does it do? You'll have to ride it to find out . . . but one thing's for sure"—here the voice got deep and creepy—*"you'll never be the same!"*

I had been sure that seeing the attraction would be a disappointment. I mean, how could you live up to that ad? Put aside the basic scientific impossibilities of its promises (*Never be the same?* What, would it change your molecular structure?); it was hard to imagine a ride so impressive that it could stand up to weeks of wondering what it might look like. But the structure in front of me was, in a word, *awesome*. It was sleek and silver and had the curved, aerodynamic shape of a spaceship.

"Wow," I echoed pointing at it like a kindergartner. "That thing is cool!"

Joe looked confused, then followed my gaze and nodded. "Oh, sure. It does look cool. But I was talking about the crowd—check it out!"

I looked around. Joe was right. The line coiled around several times before stretching all the way from the ride, through the "kiddie park" (where Joe and I had spent countless hours on the helicopter ride as kids), down the row of food stands, and nearly to the parking lot. When we'd arrived at the park hours earlier, it hadn't been nearly as long. But it looked like all those radio advertisements worked!

"Looks like a lot of people want to be g-forced!" I said, smiling, as Daisy and Penelope slowed their pace and we caught up to them.

Daisy looked thrilled. "I guess so!" she said, looking around at the crowd like she couldn't believe it. "It looks like the whole student body of Bayport High is here!"

Joe nodded, surveying the huge line. "We—uh—don't have to wait in that, do we?"

"Of course not." Daisy smiled and shook her head, gallantly taking Joe by the arm. "Follow me, mister. The four of us are skipping this line. It pays to have friends in high places!"

Penelope glanced at me warily, but we both fell into step behind Joe and Daisy. She'd been right: The line was crowded with our classmates from Bayport High. Some smiled and waved at Daisy as we passed, or called out their congratulations. But as we walked by one sullen-looking group of boys, a dark-haired kid stepped out and blocked Daisy's path.

"Well, well, well," he said, giving the four of us a not-very-friendly once-over. "What have we here? The kings and queens of Funspot?"

As Joe shot her a questioning glance, Daisy frowned at the kid. "Let us by, Luke."

He didn't move, but met her gaze without a smile. "Is this your new *boyfriend*?" He scowled at Joe.

Joe stepped forward, holding out his hand. "Hey, man . . ."

But Daisy just shook her head. "What do you care?" she asked, looking from the boy to his chuckling friends in line. "Joe, Frank, this is my *ex*-boyfriend, Luke."

"Emphasis on *ex*," Penelope piped up, stepping forward to give Luke a withering stare.

Luke glared at Penelope for a moment, but her words seemed to wound him, and he quickly looked down before stepping aside. Daisy hesitated for a moment, then turned around and walked briskly past. Penelope followed, her head held high, and Joe and I and began to follow.

"Hey!" Luke called after us when we were a few feet away, and Daisy was almost at the ride. "Congrats on the turnout tonight!"

Daisy paused, turning slowly to look back at him.

Luke's expression turned to an ugly smirk. "Guess you can go to college after all!" he shouted, loud enough for the crowd to hear. His group of friends erupted into loud chuckles. Daisy cringed.

Joe was furious. I could tell he was upset on Daisy's behalf and would have loved to teach Luke a lesson. But instead he pulled out his smartphone. "Smile," he said to Luke, snapping a picture.

Luke was taken aback. "What did you do that for?" he demanded angrily.

Joe just smiled. "When we go to security and tell them a

group is being rowdy and disruptive, this way they'll know who to look for."

Luke glared at Joe. I had to smile. I seriously doubted Joe had any intention of going to security—but the look on Luke's face made it clear he didn't know that.

Joe touched Daisy's arm. "Shall we?" he asked, gesturing to the ride.

Daisy looked like she wasn't sure what to do. Penelope shot Luke another icy look, then moved toward Daisy. "Let's go, Daze," she said, pushing her forward. "He's such a jerk."

After a moment, Daisy moved on, and the three of us followed close behind.

At the head of the line, an older, gruff-looking guy with ruddy skin and dark hair and beard stood behind a narrow metal gate. He looked at Daisy and nodded. "Miss." Without another word, he opened the gate, and the four of us walked through.

"Thanks, Cal," Daisy said, smiling brightly. "Do I have time to quickly show my friends the ride before it starts?"

Cal nodded, not making eye contact. He locked the gate, then led the four of us up a metal gangplank toward the shining, brushed-chrome ride. A small rectangular door was embedded in the side, and Cal easily pulled it open, gesturing for us to enter. Behind us, people were hooting and hollering, clearly eager to get onto the ride themselves.

Inside, small purple lights recessed into the ceiling and walls provided just enough light to make out a circle of huge, cushy seats, each with a sturdy restraining bar, surrounding an open center. I strained to see the ceiling, the floor, anything that would give a hint to what the ride actually *did*—but it was too dark.

"So . . . what does it do?" I asked Cal, who had paused in front of a bank of seats.

He turned to me and smiled. In the low purple light I could just make out that he was missing several teeth. He laughed, a low, raspy sound.

"I guess you'll just have to ride it and find out, won't you?" he asked. Then he nodded at the door. "Let's get you strapped in."

Daisy and Penelope smiled and eagerly chose seats next to each other. As Cal was securing the restraints around each of them, I glanced at my brother. I thought he looked pale.

"Are you okay?" I whispered. His eyes were darting around the ride nervously.

He bit his lip. "What do you think the ads meant," he whispered, "when they said, 'You'll never be the same'?"

I opened my mouth to answer, but Joe immediately held up his hand to shush me. "Never mind," he whispered. "I don't want Daisy to hear."

At that moment, Cal finished strapping in Penelope and looked back at us. Joe smiled eagerly—I mean, I guess it was supposed to look eager, but to me it looked kind of insane—and walked over to the seat next to Daisy. As he got strapped in, I settled into the seat next to Penelope.

She looked at me warily. "Great," she said tonelessly, "we get to ride together."

I nodded. "There was a rumor on amusementgeeks.com that this ride will send you into another dimension," I told her, "but of course that's scientifically impossible."

"Good to know," she said, and turned back to Daisy.

Cal came over and quickly strapped me in, placing two restraining belts over my shoulders and clicking a wide metal bar into place just inches from my stomach. He jiggled the bar a little to make sure it was tight, then, apparently satisfied, turned and exited the ride without a word.

"So, have you test-driven the ride?" Joe asked Daisy, breaking the silence.

She shook her head. "I wish," she said with a sigh. "But my dad's agreement with the Piperato Brothers was very specific. *No one*—except the test subjects they used when they were designing the ride, I guess—gets to ride G-Force before its official opening." She checked her watch. "Which happens—wow—in about three minutes!"

Before any of us could reply, the door opened again, and eager riders from the line began filing in, oohing and aahing, straining to get a good look at the ride's interior. They milled around and selected seats, and after a minute or so, Cal entered and began to strap all the riders in.

"So, Daisy," Brian Mullin, one of the football players,

spoke up. "Is this ride going to change my life, or what?"

Daisy chuckled. "You know what the ads say, Brian," she replied, deepening her voice. *"You'll never be the same."*

Brian snickered. "Well, I hope I come out taller."

Cal was just finishing strapping in the last rider, and as we all laughed at Brian's joke, he glanced around at all of us, then nodded. "Enjoy the ride," he said, not smiling, and then exited through the tiny door. It closed behind him, and the inside of the ride darkened even further.

Everyone grew quiet as we waited for the ride to begin. In the quiet, I picked up a weird clicking sound—like someone tapping their fingernails against a hard surface. I looked to my right, where the sound was coming from. Penelope was looking around too, seeming to hear it, and Daisy glanced at her and frowned, then turned to Joe.

"Are your *teeth chattering*?" she asked.

But Joe didn't get a chance to answer—at that very moment, the purple lights clicked off and we were immersed in darkness. A huge *whoosh* emanated from the floor—probably the ride's engine cranking up. Then a loud guitar chord sounded: I recognized it as the beginning of "Beautiful," a rock song that was climbing the charts. The song started up, and then suddenly we were moving—suddenly we were moving *really fast*! The circle of seats orbited faster and faster around the center, and I could feel the centrifugal force pushing me against the back of the seat. My head slammed back into the headrest, and it felt like the skin of my face was tightening, being pulled back by the force of the revolutions.

People began screaming, and suddenly the darkness was cut by a bright white light. I could make out the riders on the other side of the circle grimacing and beaming, screaming in fear and pleasure. Then the light cut out, then on again—a strobe light, making the whole ride look like it was in stop-motion.

The ride seemed to slow, and then suddenly the seats rose into the air. I gasped, exhilarated by the sudden motion. Just as quickly as they'd risen, though, they plunged down, farther, I think, than we'd been when the ride started. The strobe lights changed, suddenly, so that instead of bright white light, we saw neon images projected on the riders across from us—symbols, photographs of beautiful nature scenes, crying babies, an old woman smiling. The ride kept spinning, ascending, descending, but as hard as I tried, I couldn't keep track of all its motions. The scientist in me had wanted to break down exactly what G-Force did, but in the end, I just couldn't. The experience of the ride took over, and I screamed and laughed with everyone else, feeling totally exhilarated.

After some time—it could have been seconds or it could have been hours—the ride spun around again, gluing us all back in our seats. I closed my eyes as the revolutions slowed, and the music began to fade. Slower, slower, slower still we circled, until finally I felt the ride click into its resting position. I opened my eyes as the purple lights kicked on again, illuminating the ride with dim light.

Everyone looked like they'd been tumble dried. Hair stuck out in all directions, clothes were rumpled, expressions dazed. But as we all looked at one another, not sure how to capture the experience, suddenly Brian Mullin began to clap slowly. The girl on his right joined in, and after a few seconds, so did everyone else on the ride.

"That was AWESOME!" Brian shouted.

His words seemed to give everyone else permission to speak too.

"That was AMAZING. . . ."

". . . unreal . . ."

"I've never felt anything like that."

"Omigosh, I want to ride that, like, *ten* more times!"

I looked over at Daisy, who looked a little dazed herself, but a smile was creeping slowly to her lips. Joe (who looked less pale now) smiled at her and took her hand, giving it a little squeeze.

"Looks like Funspot's new main attraction is a hit," I heard him whisper to her.

But as everyone seemed to be giving their personal review of the ride, an increasingly concerned voice broke through the din.

"Kelly?"

Penelope sat up, grinning, and patted Daisy's shoulder. "Good job, Hector," she said. "I think he bought a winner!"

"Kelly?"

I looked across the ride, where the voice was coming from. People were gradually stopping their own conversations, turning their attention to the spot where a girl about our age struggled against the restraints, stretching her neck to look around.

"Kelly? KELLY!"

The girl let out a sob.

"Oh no!" she cried. "No, no, no! Where is she?"

That's when I caught sight of the seat next to her.

"My sister *disappeared*!"

It was empty. And the restraints that should have held Kelly in place had been cut.

THE DEATH RIDE

2

JOE

"COMING UP AT NOON," THE SMALL television on our kitchen counter blared, "the owner of Funspot responds to allegations that his newest attraction is a *death ride*." The image cut to grainy footage of Hector Rodriguez walking to his car in the Funspot parking lot, trailed by a crew of reporters and cameramen.

"Mr. Rodriguez," one woman trilled, shoving a microphone at him, "did you know G-Force was this dangerous?"

Across the table, Frank groaned. "She's not *dead*," he said with a sigh; "she's *missing*."

"Missing with no trace," I added, pushing my eggs around my plate. It was the following Friday, six days since Kelly Keohane went missing, and somehow, whenever the incident was mentioned, I lost my appetite. "No footprints, no finger-prints, no cell phone records, no witnesses reporting any sign of her." I sighed. "It's like she just disappeared into thin air!"

Frank nodded and shot me a concerned look. "Have you talked to Daisy?"

I frowned. "I keep trying," I replied, shrugging. "She doesn't return my calls. I talked to her really quick between classes yesterday, and she said she's not mad at me—just stressed out."

"They must have a lot on their minds," Frank agreed.

I could imagine. Funspot had been the talk of the town since G-Force opened—and not in a good way. I was sure Daisy's father was regretting his decision to invest in the new, expensive ride.

Frank stood and clapped me on the back. "Come on," he said, grabbing his book bag. "Let's get going. Maybe we'll find something new out at school."

I put down my fork and got my stuff together without answering. I knew Frank was trying to be positive, but any news we'd gotten about Funspot hadn't been good.

"Aaaaaanyway," Jamie King was saying, flicking a high-lighted blond lock behind her shoulder with a long purple fingernail, "I was like, 'Are you serious?' I mean, do you really think I'd ever go out with you?"

She smiled at all of us who surrounded her at a lunch table. Daisy had grabbed me after history class and apologized for being so distant lately; she'd invited Frank and me to sit with her friends at lunch. So far, sitting at a girls' lunch table was not so exciting.

"You know?" Jamie went on, looking around at her girlfriends, not satisfied with their reaction. "Daisy? Am I right?"

Daisy didn't respond. She was staring into her vegetarian chili like it held the secrets of the universe. I didn't think she'd even heard Jamie.

I was sitting next to her, so I gave her a nudge. "Daisy? You okay?"

She looked up, startled. "Sorry—did you say something, Joe?"

"No, but *I* did," Jamie said, pointing to herself. "I was talking about this guy who came up to me while I was working at Funspot last night. I swear, people just love entertainers."

Over lunch, Frank and I had learned that Daisy had gotten Jamie a job singing and dancing in the Funspot Revue at the park. They had wanted her to wear a big Fannie the Funspot Falcon costume, but she convinced them to let her be Princess Funfara instead.

Daisy sighed. "I guess we should be happy that there was even anybody *in* the park to approach you," she said, poking her chili with a spoon. "Attendance has been down ever since the G-Force opening. *Way* down."

Penelope, who was sitting across from us next to Frank, shot Daisy a look of concern. "When can you open it again?" she asked.

"Tonight," Daisy said without excitement, "but I can't imagine that many people are going to show up to go on a ride that was involved in a girl's disappearance. The inspectors didn't find anything wrong with it, but everyone's still calling G-Force 'the Death Ride.'" She spooned a bite of chili into her mouth, then grimaced.

Jamie looked thoughtful. "I bet that girl ran off on her own," she said, pointing a carrot stick at us. "She could have had trouble at home. You don't know."

Daisy just shook her head.

Jamie bit into her carrot stick with a loud *crunch* and chewed. "What you need," she said after a minute, "is someone to look into it. Someone besides the police." She looked up at Frank and me. "Someone like these two!"

Penelope looked at her like she was nuts. "These two?"

Jamie nodded, giving me a frankly appraising look. "They investigate things for people. You didn't know that?"

Frank blushed and coughed on his tuna sandwich.

Jamie chomped on another carrot stick and turned away with a mysterious expression.

I was beginning to think Jamie knew everything about everybody at Bayport High.

Daisy seemed to be coming out of her fog a little bit. She looked at me thoughtfully. "*Would* you guys look into it for us?" she asked. "I know you're both smart. We could really use someone to help us get to the bottom of this. I don't know what we could pay you, but . . ."

Frank waved his hand dismissively. "We don't need any money," he said. "We just help out friends."

Daisy smiled. It was the first time since G-Force opened that I'd seen anything like hope on her face. "Am I a friend?" she asked.

"You," I said, putting my hand on her shoulder, "are such a good friend, we'll get started on this today."

Julie Keohane was in gym class with me. In fact, she had once knocked me to the ground in a particularly heated basketball game. She was Kelly's sister—now the missing Kelly. A crowd of students surrounded her after our daily run to give her their condolences. After gym class today—a particularly embarrassing lesson called Dances of the World—I ran up to Julie to offer my sympathies and see if I could ask her a few questions.

We sat on a bench outside the locker rooms. "Are you and Kelly close?" I asked gently.

Julie nodded. "Very close," she said, and sniffled. "She's fourteen, only two years younger than me. We tell each other everything."

I nodded. "Has anything been going on with Kelly that's out of the ordinary?" I asked. "A new boyfriend, or an argument with someone?"

Julie looked up from the spot on the ground she'd been staring at. "No," she said, a little forcefully.

Hmm. "Does Kelly get along well with your parents?" I asked. "Do you guys ever fight?"

Julie sighed. "She gets along with everyone," she said, sounding exasperated. "Look, I know where you're going with this. I know you want me to say someone was mad at her, so you can tell the police or whoever that she ran away or something."

I paused. "I wasn't trying to get you to say that," I said, although I'd kind of been hoping she would. I really wanted to find out what had happened to Kelly. If she could give me a reason Kelly might have run away, at least that would make sense. Right now nothing about this made sense. "I just want you to tell me the truth, so I can help figure out what happened to her."

Julie widened her eyes. "She *disappeared* on that *ride*," she said, then shrugged in frustration. "I don't get it either. I know it's weird. But when the ride started, she was strapped in right next to me, and I could hear her screaming with everyone else. When the ride was over, I looked and she was gone. The restraints were cut. She didn't *run away*. She didn't go with someone. Kelly was a good kid. She always told me or my parents what she was doing."

She stood, then stopped and leaned down, saying these next words right into my face. "*Someone took her*," she hissed. "And that scares me more than anything."

I was a little shaken by my conversation with Julie, so I didn't try to talk to anyone else for the next two periods until school ended. When I went outside to meet Frank at our usual meeting spot, though, I saw him talking to a group of boys who had been waiting to ride G-Force that night.

"It was a guy I'd never seen before," one of them was saying. "He got *out* of line, which I thought was weird."

"He was pretty close to the front, too," one of the other guys said.

"Yeah," said the first guy. "And I saw him on one side of the ride, then the other, like he was circling it."

Frank glanced at me and nodded. "Thanks, guys. Joe, this is Dave and Eli. Guys, this is my brother, Joe. What did the guy look like again?"

The first guy, Dave, didn't hesitate. "He had dark hair and blue eyes, and he had freckles. He was about this tall." He gestured a few inches above his own head.

That description sounded very familiar. Unpleasantly familiar. It suited Daisy's ex-boyfriend, Luke Costigan, to a T. I took out my phone and showed them the picture I had taken of Luke. They nodded—that was Luke, all right.

Frank thanked the boys and sent them on their way as I mulled this over. Finally he turned to me.

"Sounds like Luke, right?"

I nodded. "The one and only."

Frank looked thoughtful. "We know he's a jerk," he said. "Is he enough of a jerk to sabotage a ride opening to get back at Daisy for breaking his heart?"

ARE YOU READY?

3

FRANK

THE NEXT MORNING WAS A SATURDAY, but no sleeping in for Joe or me. No, we were up at the crack of dawn to get to Funspot before it opened. The security guard told us that Daisy had warned him we were coming, and ushered us into the employee entrance. As elephants, giraffes, and pirates struggled to get their huge stuffed heads situated *just right*, a mustached man who had to be Hector Rodriguez walked up to us and held out his hand.

"You must be the Hardy Boys," he said, offering a mega-watt smile that showed off a row of perfect white teeth. "Thank you so much for looking into this for my family. We are very grateful."

Joe held up a finger. "We're happy to help out our friends.

But if you could keep the fact that we're doing this under your hat . . ."

"Yes," I chimed in. "We've found that working under-cover makes it easier to look around and get information."

Hector looked from my brother to me. "Of course. I won't tell anyone you're working here, if that's what you mean."

"Excellent," I said. "Okay, can you show us the ride?"

Hector nodded and turned to lead us out of the employees-only area, through the food stalls, and past the kiddie park. And then there it was, in front of us: G-Force, the sleek, enigmatic ride that had blown me away.

I assumed the park was still pretty empty, so I started when I saw someone moving in the glass-paneled control booth that jutted out from the side. On further inspection, I realized that it was Cal, the ride operator from the week before. He opened the door to the booth and shuffled down the steps, not making eye contact.

"I know you boys both were on the ride on Saturday night, so you know the basics," Hector said.

"We did," I agreed, "and it really is an amazing ride, Mr. Rodriguez."

He shook his head. "Please, call me Hector," he said. "And thank you. I really thought we had a winner here . . . until, well, all this happened."

Joe nodded sympathetically. "Hector, do you have any

idea what happened to the girl?" he asked. "Any idea at all?"

Hector sighed and shook his head. "I'm as stumped as everyone else," he replied. "We searched the ride, the whole park. Nobody has seen anybody matching Kelly's description in a twenty-mile radius. It's like she just vanished."

He stopped, sighing again and looking down at the ground, then raised his eyes to meet Cal's. "Boys, this is Cal Nevins," he said, "G-Force's first and only ride operator. I'd bet he knows this ride almost as well as the brothers who designed it. He can take you inside and answer any questions you have."

"Great, thanks," I said, nodding at Cal. He nodded back at me, making eye contact for only a second, and then turned back toward the ride.

"Should we go in?" he asked.

Joe caught my eye. I could tell from the tiny bit of fear in his eyes—invisible to anybody except his brother, I'm sure—that he wasn't exactly looking forward to riding this thing again.

"We should," I said. "And hopefully we'll find something that will tell us what happened to Kelly."

"So how does it work, exactly?" Joe asked for what seemed like the hundredth time, running his hand along the sleek silver walls of the inside of G-Force.

"I keep telling you," Cal replied gruffly—and accurately, "it's a mixture of a few things. Shifting perspective, strobe lights, and centrifugal force." He sounded as though he were quoting directly from the ride's manual.

"And there's absolutely nowhere for anyone to hide in here?" I asked, looking around the ride with a careful eye. Cal had turned on all the interior lights, making it much brighter than it had been on the night of its opening. But I still couldn't find anything suspicious. Inside, the ride was just as sleek as it was outside, with brushed silver metal forming the sharply curved walls. Aside from the main door, there didn't seem to be any way to get in or out, or anywhere to stay out of sight.

Cal sighed. "Not that I'm aware of." He paused, looking around the ride with a faraway expression. "I've racked my brain trying to figure out what happened to that poor girl," he added. "But I've got nothin'."

I nodded, frowning. "I think," I said, "we're just going to have to ride it again."

Joe paled a little. But he seemed to push past his fear as he sat down in one of the cushy purple seats and put his game face on.

"Let's do this," he said, clutching the restraint bar. "For Kelly!"

Cal strapped us both in and walked out to the control booth, shutting the door behind him. The lights went down, then out entirely. I heard the same *whoosh* sound as we had the previous Saturday.

"Joe?" I asked as the first guitar chord of "Beautiful" played, because his silence was starting to freak me out.

"Frank, was this a mistake?" Joe asked, but before I could answer him, the music crescendoed and the strobe lights started up and we started moving, and pretty soon I couldn't think about anything but how awesome this ride was. Every so often I would catch myself and try to focus: *Look around! Observe! Listen for strange noises! Check the strength of my harness!* But I could barely see anything through the flashing lights, fog, and random images. I couldn't even see Joe anymore.

Wait.

"Joe?" I yelled.

No answer. The music wailed, a flower wilted, a sad-looking toddler pointed her finger at me accusingly. Then the strobe lights started up again.

"JOE?"

The ride started slowing down. I could feel the seats returning to their original orbit, and the music was quieting, reaching the end of the song. I blinked, shaking my head and trying to squint through the darkness for my brother. He'd been right across from me . . . right? Or was he next to me? Or . . .

The images faded and the lights cut out. We were

plunged into darkness. I closed my eyes and reached up to touch my head, almost wondering if it was still there. My brain felt like it was bouncing around in my skull, after being flung this way and that for however long the ride lasted (I honestly had no idea).

"Joe?" I asked again, rubbing my temples and opening my eyes. The weak purple lights flickered back on.

Joe sat across from me, looking like he'd just stumbled in from a hurricane. His straw-colored hair poked out in random directions. His clothes were mussed. He looked like he was sweating.

He blinked and looked over at me. "Yeah?"

I glared at him. "Why didn't you *answer* me during the *ride*?"

He blinked again. "You said something?"

Before I could reply, the small door was pushed open, letting in a ray of sunlight, and the dark profile of Cal appeared. "You boys see anything suspicious?" he asked curiously.

I sighed.

"No," I said. "I think we're going to have to ride it again."

And again. And again.

Joe looked awful. After the fifth ride, he asked Cal to unharness him, stood up, ran out of the ride, and returned a few minutes later.

"All right," he said, settling back into his seat. "Strap me in and fire this baby up again."

Cal looked impressed despite himself. "Okay." He did

as Joe asked, then walked out of the ride, closing the door behind him.

"Joe," I said, "are you okay?"

Joe coughed. "I am not okay," he replied, "but at least Aunt Trudy didn't make us a huge breakfast today."

I groaned. My own head was pounding, and the ride was beginning to hurt, not feel awesome.

"Maybe we should take a break," I suggested. "This is going nowhere. We're five rides in and I still haven't noticed anything that might explain what happened to Kelly. Have you?"

Joe winced and shook his head. "I have noticed the contents of my stomach," he replied. "That's it."

I tried to sit up. "Those boys I talked to yesterday—they said they saw Luke getting out of line. Remember?"

"And he circled the ride," Joe added, life coming back to his eyes.

"Maybe we could get out and walk around the ride?" I suggested. "See if we notice anything unusual?"

Joe nodded. "Yes. Yes, please!"

I looked at my brother. We both seemed to reach the same realization at the same time.

"CAL!!!" we screamed.

But it was too late. The lights went off, and the *whoosh* of the motor started up again.

I would say that our last, unnecessary ride on G-Force that morning wasn't so bad, but really? It was. Joe barfed again afterward. I was pretty sure my brain had become permanently unstuck from my skull and would just rattle around in there for the rest of my life.

But the good news? I don't think I had ever appreciated solid ground as much as I did when we got off the ride. I walked around, stamping my feet into the ground, enjoying the pleasant, solid resistance. It was like slipping between the sheets of the world's most comfortable bed after sleeping on the floor for a week.

"You see anything?" Cal asked, following Joe and me down onto the ground. "In the ride, I mean? Did it help?"

"We didn't see anything, but it did help," I told him. "I guess we just need to think about it a little more. In the meantime, we're going to look around outside. Is that okay?"

Cal looked surprised, but he quickly nodded. "Sure. Sure, whatever you think will help."

He backed off, and Joe and I took another minute or two for the world to stop spinning before we walked over to the smooth metal side of G-Force. Apart from the one entrance, there were no hinges or doors; not even a seam so you could clearly see where the sheets of metal had been hammered together. It simply looked like it had dropped out of the sky, sleek, shiny, and fully formed.

"See anything?" I asked Joe after a minute or two.

"No," he said with a sigh, "but let's take our time here. Maybe Luke dropped something in the grass. Or maybe we'll spot something of Kelly's."

I agreed, and we slowed our progress, making sure to take in everything we possibly could. It was about half an hour before we reached its far side, and the ride cut us off from the early-morning sun, plunging us in shadow.

I was running my hand along the ride's outer surface when I heard a nightmarish cackle behind me, followed by a creepy voice:

"Are you ready to ride . . . THE DEATH RIDE?"

PUBLIC RELATIONS

4

JOE

JUMPED ABOUT TEN FEET IN THE AIR. OR THAT'S how it felt. I'm not ashamed. You have to remember that I was in a delicate state, with my brains all scrambled into a gray-matter omelet, and that I had recently vomited not once, but twice. Truly, I was operating on a nutritional loss. Plus, that voice was just *creepy*.

So imagine how foolish I felt when I turned around and saw not the terrifying bat-demon of my nightmares (I mean, some of them), but two hipsterish dudes, wearing matching fedoras and laughing hysterically.

"We got you!" one of them, a redhead, yelled, pointing at us.

"You got us, all right," Frank replied, deadpan, straightening up. "You sure got us!"

I should mention here that, once the shock wore off

and I was able to be more observant, it became apparent that both of these guys were dressed like gangsters from the 1920s or something. Fedoras, striped trousers, vests, oxfords, funny little bow ties, the works. And they each had mustaches that had been waxed—yeah, waxed—into different shapes.

"Who are you?" I asked, seriously curious now.

The redhead was still too busy cackling to reply. But his friend, a blond with sausage curls, stood up straight and then gave me a formal bow. "Pleased to meet you, good sir," he said. "*We* . . . are the Piperato Brothers!"

"*The* Piperato Brothers?" Frank asked, his jaw suddenly on the ground. "The guys who designed G-Force—and, like, a million other rides?"

Frank never says "like," so I figured I was on my own as far as getting useful information out of these weirdos.

"I'm Joe Hardy, and this is my brother, Frank," I said. Then I asked, "What are you two doing here? We heard you were at the opening of a HoverCoaster in New Zealand or something."

"Correction," said the redhead, holding up a finger, "we *were* at the opening of the PhantomRider in Christchurch. But at about seven o'clock last night, we arrived at the airport."

Frank seemed to be returning to earth. "Did you come because of the disappearance?" he asked.

The blond one cut his eyes at Frank. "If you mean the

incident last Saturday night, then yes, that is why we're here." He straightened up and suddenly put on a serious face. "When something like this happens, you only get a brief window to add your spin to the story. That's what Greg and I are here to do."

I raised my eyebrows. "You have a theory about what happened to Kelly?" I asked.

The redhead—Greg, I guessed—shook his head. "Not exactly," he said. "But Derek and I do have theories about how to handle the press."

I glanced at Frank. Hmm. "It sounds like you guys need to talk to Hector," I said. "You know, the owner of Funspot?"

Derek nodded, pulling the latest iPhone out of his pocket and jabbing at it with his narrow fingers. "That's right," he said, squinting at the screen. "One . . . Hector Rodriguez. Would you know where we can find him?"

"Sure," I said, shooting a quick *Go along with me* look at my brother. I had the feeling we were going to want to hear what these guys had to say. "We can take you back to his office. I'm sure he'll be there."

We started walking back toward the entrance we'd come in that morning, where the administration building stood. I knew from Daisy that Hector's office was inside on the second floor. As we walked, Frank peppered the brothers with questions about their most recent roller coasters and thrill rides, and the brothers seemed to lap up his attention like two cats licking up cream.

Back at the administration building, employees were gathering in the lobby, fixing up their character costumes and strapping on their change belts. It was almost time for the park to open, and the place was starting to buzz with activity. A quick glance at the parking lot confirmed my fears: There didn't seem to be any customers waiting to get in. It was another reminder that Frank and I needed to get to the bottom of this—for Daisy.

"Hector's office is in here," I said, leading the Piperato Brothers through the glass doors of the administration building.

"You've really never been here before?" Frank asked the brothers as we led everyone up a flight of stairs.

"Indeed no," Greg replied. "Actually, it's rare that we get a chance to come out to a park and see our rides in action."

"But you said you just got in from doing that in New Zealand," I pointed out.

Derek chuckled. "Yeah, but that was *New Zealand*," he said. "The park owners were nice enough to pay for our flights and hotel. No offense, but Baytown just doesn't hold the same appeal."

I raised an eyebrow. "It's Bay*port*," I said.

"What Derek means," Greg cut in, with a conciliatory smile (I was getting that Greg was perhaps the nicer of the two), "is that we're usually very busy in our lab designing the rides of the future. Sadly, we just don't get a lot of time to travel."

We were outside Hector's office now, so I just smiled

and knocked on the door before we entered "How lucky for us to get to meet you."

Inside, the office wasn't glamorous. Faux wood paneling that looked at least thirty years old covered the walls, and wrinkled, framed maps of Funspot during different times in its history were the only decoration. The office was really a glorified closet—there was barely room for Frank, the Piperato Brothers, and me to stand facing Hector's old wooden desk.

Hector looked surprised. "Hello?" he asked, looking from me to Frank. Then his eyes settled on the fedora'ed faces of the duo who'd been expected to save Funspot. "It can't be . . . Derek and Greg Piperato?" He stood.

"None other, good sir," Derek replied, firing out a hand for Hector to shake. Hector did, slowly, staring at the brothers like they were some kind of apparition. "And you must be Mr. Rodriguez, the forward-thinking gentleman who purchased G-Force."

Hector nodded, dropping Derek's hand and reaching out to shake Greg's. "That would be me. Although you might have heard we've been having some, er . . ."

Derek smiled, his teeth flashing straight and white beneath his shiny waxed mustache. "We are well aware of your difficulties, sir," he said with a nod. "In fact . . ." He looked expectantly at his brother.

Greg took the bait and nodded, turning to Hector with a grin. "That's sort of why we're here."

A wave of relief washed over Hector's face. "Does that mean you know where the girl could be?" he asked, gesturing to a pile of papers on his desk. I looked down and realized that he had been studying what looked like blueprints for the ride. "We've looked and looked and found nowhere for the girl to hide, but I noted that there might be space for a chamber here, or here, or here . . ." He pushed the papers toward us, pointing at several *X*s he'd marked in with red pencil.

But the Piperatos barely looked down. "There's no space inside G-Force for someone to hide," Derek said brusquely. "We designed a thrill ride, not a place to store knickknacks."

Hector looked confused, but his confusion quickly turned to anger. "But the girl—"

Derek held up his hand as if to say *stop*. "We came here to discuss how to handle public relations moving forward," he said, reaching inside his jacket and pulling the smallest, thinnest laptop computer I'd ever seen from some inner pocket.

Hector turned to look at my brother and me with an expression of befuddlement, as if to say, *Are you guys seeing this?* I just nodded and watched Derek Piperato open up his tiny computer. He made a few clicks, then brought up a video. It was frozen on a photograph of two teenage girls riding a roller coaster, shrieking with delight.

"Public relations?" Hector asked finally, as if it had taken some effort to find his voice.

Greg nodded, flashing a bright white smile. "We couldn't help but notice that you're in a bit of a public relations jam," he explained. "The stories in the press are not . . . kind."

Hector widened his eyes. "No," he said, "because a young girl disappeared on your ride."

Derek waved his hand dismissively. *"Allegedly,"* he insisted. "She allegedly disappeared on our ride. How does everyone know she didn't sneak out before the lights came up? Maybe she had a boyfriend the parents disapproved of. Maybe she went *shopping*."

Frank cleared his throat. "Um, that seems extremely unlike—"

But Derek cut him off. "Let's not speculate," he said. "The truth is, only the girl herself knows what happened. And the only thing we can control is how we react to our ride being attacked. Yes?"

He didn't wait for an answer before reaching down to the laptop and clicking on the video.

A deep, scary voice played over stock footage of young people screaming on amusement rides.

"You've heard about it on the news."

A quick shot of G-Force was shown, but too fast for the viewer to really make out what it was. The effect was a little disturbing.

"You've heard about it from your friends."

A shot of a teenage girl in the dark, a tear rolling down her face. Then three girls, whispering eagerly into one another's ears. Then a shot of a boy texting. Then . . .

"But are you brave enough to find out what really happened?"

A shot of the entrance to G-Force, with the line to get in snaking around the whole park. A grainy video of kids screaming, waving their I WAS FIRST TO RIDE G-FORCE T-shirts. A super-quick shot of one of its seats, restraints undone, sitting in the dark. The effect was weird and creepy—it looked almost like an electric chair.

"Are you brave enough to ride . . . the DEATH RIDE?"

The voice dissolved into a maniacal cackle as the camera jutted farther into G-Force, and the picture gave way to static, like a video feed cutting out.

There were a few seconds of creepy cackling over a black screen, then Funspot's logo and directions came up.

Greg and Derek turned to us eagerly. Frank, Hector, and I looked at one another in surprise. I don't think any of us knew what to say.

It was Hector who finally spoke. "What was *that*?" he demanded.

Derek, seemingly mistaking Hector's anger for enthusiasm, rubbed his hands together in excitement. "Isn't it magnificent? This was put together for us by Viral Genius, one of the foremost advertising firms in—"

Hector slammed his fist down onto his desk, and the room fell silent. "What do you think this is?" he demanded, glaring at the Piperato Brothers. "Is this a *joke* to you?"

Greg smoothed his mustache, looking offended. "Not at all," he said with a frown. "This is our livelihood and reputation on the line, as well as yours."

Derek looked angry now. "We *have* to control the conversation about what happened here last Saturday, or we're going to be the losers," he said, jabbing his finger at Hector for emphasis. "Really, Hector, it's Public Relations 101: Get ahead of the story."

Get ahead of the story. I'd heard that before, and I was pretty sure Derek was right: It was a big rule in public relations. But I was also pretty sure Hector was disgusted by the ad.

He gestured at the laptop. "What do you mean to do with that?" he asked. "Do you expect me to put it on TV? Because I won't."

Greg shook his head, smiling again. "You don't have to do anything, Hector. That's the beauty of our plan. You just sit back and watch the kids return. We've taken the liberty of placing this viral trailer on the Internet, where the kids are *already*—"

"What?" Hector asked, his eyebrows making angry points on his forehead. "You posted this somewhere without telling me?"

Greg gave a rueful smile. "Per our contract, when the park owner disagrees with us about the marketing of our creation, we have final say."

Hector groaned and closed his eyes. I could tell he remembered that part of the contract, and I could also tell he'd never thought such a situation would arise. In the silence that ensued, I moved forward, gesturing to the laptop.

"Can you play that again?" I asked the nearest Piperato brother—Derek.

"Gladly," he said, with the happy expression of someone who thought his brilliance was finally being appreciated. He clicked on the ad again, and it started up.

"You've heard about it on the news."

Stock footage. Creepy shot of the ride. Stock footage. Creepy shot . . .

I pointed at the shot of the ride with a line snaking around all of Funspot. "There—that had to be taken on Saturday night, right?"

That was the only time the line had been that long—or the people in it had looked so excited.

Derek nodded. "That's right."

Frank moved forward, his interest piqued. "Did you buy cell phone footage off someone in line or something?" he asked, squinting at the screen to get a better look.

Derek looked pleased. "It does look like that, doesn't it?" he asked proudly. "But actually, no, that's professional footage that's been given a filter to look more 'gritty' and 'immediate.' Studies show that modern teenagers respond more strongly—"

"Professional footage?" I asked, clicking on the touch pad to stop the trailer. "Does that mean you had someone shooting footage of the opening Saturday night?"

Greg stepped forward. "Sure," he said. "It's standard procedure to send a videographer to shoot the opening. You never know when a promotional opportunity might—"

Frank cut him off. "Do you have that footage with you?" he asked. "All of it?"

Greg and Derek glanced at each other, as if deciding how much they trusted us. Greg gave a slight nod, and Derek pursed his lips. Finally Derek turned back to us and spoke.

"We have a full DVD of footage," he said. "Probably an hour or more."

I practically jumped. *"Can we see it?"* I shouted, and at the brothers' perplexed expressions, tried to get ahold of myself. "Sorry. Can we see it? My brother and I are, ah . . ."

Hector spoke up in a calm, quiet voice. "The Hardy brothers are studying thrill ride design," he said smoothly, catching my eye and winking. That's when I remembered: We'd asked Hector not to tell anyone we were investigating this for him. I'd almost blown our cover.

Derek looked perplexed. "Well, that explains the third degree earlier," he said, nodding at Frank.

"I suppose we could let you borrow the footage," Greg went on, folding his arms in front of him. Then he cracked a small smile. "The Piperato Brothers of the future."

I had a sudden vision of Frank and me ten years from now, dressed in bow ties and fedoras, carrying computers the size of a deck of cards. I had to bite my lip to keep from laughing.

"Thanks. We really appreciate it," Frank was saying.

Hector stood. "I think this meeting is over," he said,

looking at the Piperatos. "In the future, I would appreciate it if you contacted me before placing any communication from Funspot anywhere."

"But we have the contract—" Greg tried to put in, but Hector cut him off, holding up his hand.

"A young girl disappeared here on Saturday night," he went on, in that same calm, quiet voice. "Do you have children, gentlemen?"

Derek and Greg looked at each other, confused. "We don't," Greg confirmed.

Hector frowned. "Well, I have a daughter," he said. "And I can tell you that if anything ever happened to her—if she ever disappeared and I didn't know where she was—I don't know how I would survive it. I can't imagine what that poor girl's parents are going through right now. And the idea that they might see this viral whatever you put up, this—" He gestured to the laptop as though it were the most disgusting thing he'd ever seen. "This trailer. It disgusts me."

Greg and Derek exchanged a glance. Derek waited a moment before saying, "I'm sorry we disagree. But I think the trailer is brilliant. And once kids start crowding back into Funspot, I think you will too."

Hector sighed. "I think you should go."

Greg gave a quick nod, then folded up the laptop, turned to his brother, and gestured toward the door. "Here, kids," he said, slipping a small hard drive out of his pocket and handing it to me. "This has all the footage from the ride opening in a folder called 'G-Force.' I hope you learn from it."

I smiled. "Me too. Thanks."

The Piperato Brothers exited, and I turned to Hector. "Can we use your computer to—?"

He held up his hands. "Of course, of course." He sighed. "I think I'm going to take a coffee break. Will you boys be okay in here?"

"I think so," Frank said. I could tell by the way he was eyeing the hard drive that he was eager to get started.

"Good luck," Hector said as he walked out the door. From outside, I heard him add under his breath, "We all need it."

"That's Luke!" I cried a few minutes later, pointing at the screen as a black-shirted kid got out of line and walked out of the frame of the video.

Frank shook his head. "Sure enough," he said. We were watching footage of G-Force, right after the first ride had been boarded.

"Don't you think it's weird to get out of line when you're so close to the front?" I asked.

Frank nodded, his eyes still on the screen. The footage cut to a later scene, kids exiting the ride looking shaken. "It's definitely weird," he said, crossing his arms over his chest. The footage cut to Cal looking worried, then the police showing up. Then the camera panned back to the line, where kids looked both scared and disappointed.

Luke wasn't there, but the friends we'd seen him with last Saturday night were still in line.

"Maybe he got scared," I suggested. "You know, once Kelly's disappearance got out. Maybe he didn't want to risk going on a ride where someone went missing."

Frank shook his head. "No, that's not possible," he said, clicking the mouse to go back to the place where Luke stepped out of line. "See Cal closing up the ride there? Luke steps out before the ride even starts. It was way too early for him to know about Kelly."

I frowned. "Unless he knew about her . . . because he helped make her disappear."

FRANK

NLESS WHO HELPED MAKE HER DIS-
appear?"

A female voice from the doorway made my
head snap up. Joe and I had been so involved
in watching the video that we hadn't even
noticed Daisy walk in. She was watching us study the computer monitor, eyebrows furrowed.

Joe put on a goofy smile. "Oh . . . nothing," he said with
a shrug. I shot my brother a look that said, *We're not telling
her?* And he gave me a particular look back that I took to
mean *Not yet*.

"We were just watching some footage of the ride, throwing out crazy theories," I said with a smile of my own. "We
were just talking about . . . uh . . ." I tried to think of the

least likely person to be involved in Kelly's disappearance. "Chief Olaf."

Chief Olaf is the new head of the Bayport PD. As far as his view of Joe's and my detective work goes . . . Well, let's just say that it ranges from just barely tolerant to grudging admiration, depending on what day of the week it is and exactly what Joe and I have been up to.

Daisy looked utterly confused. "That's interesting," she said, "because he just so happens to be here."

Joe turned bright red. "Now?" he asked.

Daisy smiled, noting his panicked expression. "Not right here," she said. "He and a few officers are waiting outside for Dad. They're taking a look at G-Force again, along with some inspectors."

"Oh." Joe's face took on its normal color again.

Daisy looked curious. "You didn't think he could really—?"

"No," I put in quickly, shaking my head. "Not at all. Just spouting crazy theories, like I said."

Daisy looked from me to Joe, not entirely sold. "You two have a very interesting way of working," she said. "Anyway— would you happen to know where my dad is?"

"He said he was getting coffee," I said.

"Ahhh." Daisy nodded. "Okay. I'll check the kitchen. Thanks."

She started to leave, but Joe called out, "Daisy?"

She turned. "Yes?"

Joe put on a very sweet smile. "Will you come back after you find him? We could hang out."

Daisy looked touched. "Okay, Joe. Sure. Be right back."

She walked out and back down the hallway, and I turned to my brother. "Should I go?" I asked, only half joking. "Am I a third wheel here?"

But Joe just shut down the video program and disconnected the hard drive, shaking his head. "Not that I wouldn't enjoy just hanging out with Daisy," he said, "but I thought we could ask her more about Luke."

That seemed like a good idea. It was only a few minutes until Daisy returned, pink-cheeked from running. "Hey, guys," she said, walking in and casually slinging herself into Hector's chair. "Man, I hope they find something. I haven't been sleeping much, I'm so worried about Kelly. . . ."

"Us too," I said. It was the truth. It had now been a full week since Kelly had disappeared, with no evidence, and no sign of her anywhere. Each day that passed made it less likely that a missing teenager would be found; Joe and I had been involved in crime fighting long enough to know that. And each day that passed made it harder to believe that there was a benign explanation for all this.

Daisy leaned back and closed her eyes. "I've been so stressed out," she said quietly. "Between what happened with Kelly and what it's doing to the park. This is so crazy."

Joe shot me an awkward sideways glance and cleared his throat. "Was it stressful seeing Luke again?" he asked, in a faux-casual voice.

Daisy opened her eyes and angled her head up to look at him. "Huh?"

Joe coughed. "Um, you know that guy Luke? He seemed kind of nasty."

Daisy looked from Joe to me, as if I held the explanation for Joe's strange questions.

I tried not to respond.

"Um," Daisy said, turning back to Joe, "I guess it was kind of stressful seeing Luke. He wasn't very nice to me, as you saw."

I tried to look sympathetic. "Why did you two break up? I mean, if you don't mind my asking."

Daisy looked surprised, but she didn't hesitate in her answer. "Actually, *I* broke it off with him."

I had to stop myself from shooting a look at Joe. *Motive!*

"Luke had been hoping that I'd get to attend Dalton Academy with him this fall—I mean, I had too." Daisy sighed.

Dalton Academy was a ritzy private school right on the outskirts of Bayport. Its students were regarded with a mixture of wonder and jealousy from us poor slobs at Bayport High. There were rumors of an indoor swimming pool beneath a retractable basketball court, kids who were helicoptered to school, and lobster Newburg in the cafeteria.

How much of that was true was anyone's guess.

"What happened?" asked Joe.

Daisy's expression soured for just a second, then quickly recovered. "My dad bought Funspot," she said in a resigned voice. "And then my mom got laid off. Suddenly we couldn't afford ice cream anymore—let alone some fancy private school."

She paused.

"It just got too hard with Luke after that," she said, shaking her head. "Going to different schools, and me trying to help my dad out with Funspot after school and on weekends. He wasn't, well—he wasn't very understanding."

"Luke wasn't?" I asked.

Daisy nodded. "He sent me a text right after we broke up saying that he hoped Funspot failed. He thought it was a stupid idea for my father to buy it. A lot of people did, actually." She sighed. "Maybe they were right."

Joe looked thoughtful. "Why was he at the opening, then?" he asked. "If he hates Funspot so much?"

Daisy shrugged. "I figured he was just being hotheaded and stupid when he sent me that text," she said. "He might think buying Funspot wasn't the best idea, but deep down he wants the best for me. Or so I'd like to think."

I looked at Joe. I could tell from his expression that we were thinking the same thing: *Or he showed up to sabotage G-Force—and Funspot.*

Suddenly we could hear voices arguing outside the administration building.

"How do you expect me to pay you early?"

Hector.

"I barely have enough cash to keep the park running on a day-to-day basis. Pay advances are off the table!"

"I'm in a real bind, or I wouldn't ask."

It took me a minute to identify the second voice—Cal.

"I just thought, under the circumstances—"

"Forget it." Hector cut Cal off. "I'm sorry, I would like to, but I can't. Don't ask again."

I couldn't help looking at Daisy, judging her reaction. If Hector was having difficulty meeting day-to-day expenses, then Funspot was in even worse trouble than we thought. A dark look flittered across Daisy's face, but she quickly stood up, putting on a neutral expression. "I'd better go help Dad," she said quietly.

Joe stood, and I followed his lead.

"We should go too," Joe said. "After about fifty rides on G-Force, I'm finally recovering my appetite."

Daisy looked amused. "You rode G-Force?"

Joe nodded. "About fifty times," he repeated. "At least, it felt like fifty times. How many times does it take to lose your ability to feel anything but pain?"

Daisy smiled. "For you? Maybe two? Three?"

Joe chuckled. "Well, I'll do anything to solve the case, my dear."

Daisy suddenly looked serious. "Did you find anything?" She looked hopefully from Joe to me.

I slowly shook my head.

"No," Joe said, putting his hand on Daisy's shoulder. "But we will. I promise. Okay?"

Daisy looked up at him and, after a moment, nodded. "Okay. Maybe we can hang out tomorrow night? I could use some time away from this park."

Joe smiled. "That sounds great. I'll text you."

We gathered our things, and Daisy led us out of the office and back out through the lobby to the park. Outside the building, Hector stood off to the left, talking on his cell phone, and Cal stood a few yards to the right, leaning against a tree and smoking a cigarette. He looked up when we came out; Hector seemed too involved in his phone call to notice us.

"Thanks for coming, guys," Daisy said, turning back to us with a weak smile. "Seriously, the only thing that got me out of bed this morning was the thought that you two are working on this, and with your help we might be able to reopen G-Force soon."

"It's our pleasure," I said sincerely. I tried to look away as Joe gave Daisy a hug and then my brother and I headed off toward the parking lot.

"Hey there, Miss Daisy," Cal said in his gravelly voice as we walked off. Daisy didn't respond, and after a moment, I turned back to see what she was doing.

"Did you hear me? I said hello." Cal dropped his cigarette butt and smashed it with his toe.

Daisy was standing near her father, staring off at the parking lot. Her jaw was clenched, and I could tell by her posture that she'd heard Cal and was struggling not to react.

After a few more seconds, Cal shook his head and ambled off in the direction of G-Force.

JOE

'M NO SORT OF HACKER, BUT IT WASN'T TER-
ribly hard to get into Dalton Academy's online student
directory. Within fifteen minutes of firing up my Internet
browser, I was looking at Luke Costigan's home address.

He lived in Hampton Estates, a fancy subdivision over
on the west side of town. So the next morning Frank and I
shoveled down six of Aunt Trudy's fresh raspberry ricotta
pancakes (with peach compote!) and jumped into the car to
drive across town.

"He's not going to talk to us," Frank predicted, looking full of either pancakes or malaise (or both). "He hates
us, remember? He saw us with his ex-girlfriend. He knows
you're dating her."

I turned the car onto Easthampton Drive. "It's worth a

shot," I said. "If he resists, we can pull the old 'need to use your bathroom' routine."

Frank seemed to perk up a little. "And find his cell phone or computer?" Frank grinned and pointed out the window. "Here we go," he said; "119 Easthampton Drive."

Luke Costigan's house was your typical suburban McMansion: huge, red brick, enormous bay windows, four-car garage. In the front, four Greek columns held up a generous porch. Two cars in the driveway implied that the family was home.

"Quick game plan?" asked Frank, but I was already unbuckling my seat belt.

"Ask questions," I said, pushing open the driver's-side door. "Hope nobody hits us."

Frank nodded. "And if all else fails, beg to use the bathroom?"

"Exactly."

I climbed out and ambled toward the front door, Frank falling into step beside me. When we'd climbed the front steps, I reached out and knocked an enormous door knocker in the shape of a bald eagle. We heard footsteps approaching the door, and then a middle-aged man answered.

"Can I help you?" he asked, not unfriendly.

"Actually, we were wondering if Luke is home?" Frank asked smoothly.

The man nodded. He had dark eyes and close-cropped

hair, like Luke, but unlike his son, his hair had gone mostly gray. "You two classmates from Dalton?" he asked.

"Um, we go to Bayport High," I replied. "But we have friends in common."

The man nodded, then stepped back into the house. "LUKE!" we heard him yell up the stairs. "You have friends at the door!"

"Who?" we heard a surly voice yell from upstairs, followed shortly (when his dad didn't answer) by footsteps on the carpeted stairs. Luke slowly became visible—first his feet, then his legs, then his shoulders—and when he was finally able to see us outside the door, he scowled.

"What are *you* doing here?" he asked as he ran up to the doorway.

"Who are they?" asked the man in a voice that sounded more curious than suspicious.

Luke narrowed his eyes at me. "This is Daisy's new boyfriend."

The man nodded. "Ahhhh," he said, not-so-slowly backing away. "Well, I'll leave you all to . . . talk?" He glanced at his son. "I'll be out in the garage if you need me."

Luke nodded, not taking his eyes off me.

Once his father had left the foyer, Luke scowled at us again. "What do you want?"

I crossed my arms in front of my chest. "We want to talk about what happened on G-Force last Saturday night."

Luke gave us a look like he thought we'd lost our minds. "How would I know?" he asked. "I didn't even ride the thing."

"But you were in line," Frank pointed out.

Luke cocked an eyebrow. "Yeeeeeah?" he asked, clearly not seeing a connection.

"And then you got *out* of line," I added. "Oddly enough, before the first ride even started."

Luke looked at Frank, then turned his glaring eyes on me. "So what?" he asked. "You guys were on the ride. Did *you* take her?"

Take her. So Luke knew what we were really accusing him of, which gave me an odd tremor in the pit of my stomach. Nobody really knew what had happened to Kelly. Did the fact that Luke used the words "take her" mean he knew more about it than he was letting on?

Frank glanced at me and said, "We didn't even know Kelly was missing until a few minutes after the ride ended." He paused. "As we were saying, though—it's kind of strange to leave the line when you're so close to the front, don't you think?"

Luke frowned. "Why?"

I sighed. I hate it when people are obstinate. "Because one would assume you were excited to ride something you'd waited hours to board, yet you suddenly walked away like you'd changed your mind. Did you?"

"Change your mind?" Frank added.

Luke sighed now, shaking his head. "Why are you guys asking? What are you, the FBI?"

I glanced at Frank. "We're people who care about finding Kelly," I said simply.

Luke frowned. There wasn't much he could say to that. Argue with us, and it would seem like he didn't care about finding the missing girl.

He looked past us, down the driveway. "My buddies sent me out," he said. "They bet me twenty bucks I couldn't figure out what the thing did. So I walked around it, but they were right, man—" He stopped and chuckled ruefully. "I couldn't figure out a thing. It looks like a spaceship, right?"

Frank nodded, relaxing his expression a little.

"And it doesn't even look like it's moving from the outside," Luke added. "I was stumped. So I finally gave up."

I nodded. "But you didn't get back in line," I pointed out.

Luke turned to me, glaring again. "How do you know all this?"

"Someone took a video," Frank said simply, not explaining further. Luke would probably think someone shot the line with their cell phone camera—which was fine.

Luke was quiet for a moment. It made me nervous. When someone you're questioning goes quiet, it usually means they're thinking. And when the person you're questioning is thinking, it means that they could, at any moment, arrive at the discovery that they really don't have to answer your questions. After all, Frank and I are just kids like Luke—not cops or the FBI.

It was time to turn up the heat.

"Daisy says you two had a pretty nasty breakup," I pointed out.

Luke looked at me again. "She said that?" he asked, sounding a little hurt.

"She said you texted her saying you wanted Funspot to fail," I added.

Luke shook his head and let out an angry chuckle. "I *did* want it to fail," he said. "That piddly, pathetic little amusement park broke us up. Her father and his stupid ideas!"

"What do you mean?" asked Frank. We knew what he meant, of course, but it's always good to keep your subject talking.

Luke turned to Frank. "Her father spent all his money on Funspot," he said. "Suddenly there's no money to send Daisy to Dalton with me, like she'd planned. Next thing I know, she breaks up with me. 'It's just too hard,' she says, 'going to different schools.'" He snorted. "You believe that?"

"It just seems like if you wanted Funspot to fail badly enough," I said, "you might do something to sabotage it."

Luke turned his eyes back to me. I could see him trying to make sense of what I'd said—and once he got it, fury burned in his eyes. "Sabotage?" he repeated. "You think I'd kidnap some girl to get back at Daisy? That's sick!"

"Maybe you didn't kidnap her," I suggested. "Maybe you made a deal with her to hide somewhere, to make it look like she disappeared on the ride. But what I'm saying—"

Luke held up his hand, cutting me off. "I don't care what you're saying!" he shouted. "I wouldn't hurt some kid to get back at Daisy, okay?" He glared at me one last time, then turned away, like he was trying to cool off.

"So why didn't you get back in line?" Frank asked neutrally.

Luke groaned and turned back around. "I got scared, okay? When those doors opened, I realized I didn't want to get on. So I told my buddies I had to use the bathroom, and I took off."

I looked at Frank. *Scared? This guy?* "Really?" I asked.

Luke scowled. "Yes, really!"

I turned back to Luke and just stared at him for a moment. He seemed tense. Not necessarily lying-tense, but . . . "No offense," I said, "but why should I believe you?"

Luke groaned again. He looked at the ceiling. "I hate it when people say 'no offense' when they're about to insult you," he muttered.

"No offense," I said again. I knew it sounded like a line. But I meant it.

Luke closed his eyes, then looked back at me. "I actually have someone who can back me up," he said after a few seconds. "Someone who works at the park saw me. My neighbor. You know Jamie King?"

• • •

All things being equal, Jamie King was not someone I would choose to involve in an investigation. Discretion-wise, she's kind of—how do I say this?—a nightmare. I could only imagine that Jamie, not unlike Frank and me, keeps her ear to the ground and soaks up information like a sponge. But while Frank and I like to then hang out on the side of the sink, quietly absorbing all our spongy information, Jamie likes to squeeze herself out all over the nearest classmate.

I guess what I'm trying to say is that Jamie King is a gossip queen.

But we needed her to back up Luke's alibi. If he really had left the G-Force line because he got scared, then he wasn't much of a suspect. And that meant we had to look in another direction.

"Oh, heeeeyyy!" Jamie greeted us with a smile when she opened the door, not looking surprised at all. I wondered if classmates just dropped by her house every Sunday. "It's the Hardy Boys! What's up, dudes?"

Before we could respond, her expression turned serious, and she leaned toward us like she was asking us something personal. "Have you guys talked to Daisy?" she asked. "Is she, like, all right?"

Frank started up, "Well, she's—"

But I cut him off. "She's fine," I said curtly, shooting Frank a *Zip it!* look. I had a feeling that whatever we shared with Jamie would be all over Bayport within hours. And while she and Daisy were friendly, I wanted to let Daisy decide how much of the whole G-Force debacle she wanted to make public knowledge.

"Actually," I went on, "we have some questions for *you*."

Jamie blinked her big blue eyes at us. "*Moi?*" she asked, putting a hand to her chest.

"*Vous,*" I replied. (That's right. I didn't get a B-minus in French 101 for nothing!) "It's pretty simple, really. Did you see Luke Costigan last Saturday night, around the time of the first G-Force ride?"

Jamie's eyes widened. "Did I!" She leaned in confidentially. "You guys, he was like, *terrified*." She shook her head. "I was on my break and at the coin toss booth—just for fun, you know? And right next door is the ball toss? And those guys, like, the guys who run it, they really *insult* people to get them to play, especially guys. You know?"

My brain was working overtime trying to follow. But yes—I thought I knew. "Yes?" I said.

"So one of them called after him, 'Hey, Preppy Boy, what's wrong, you too scared to ride the big bad spaceship?' And he turned around—and I know Luke, you guys, he doesn't stand for stuff like that usually—and his face was just *white*. And he saw me and was like, 'Where's the bathroom?' And I was like, 'Are you okay?' And he goes, 'Yeah, where's the bathroom?' so I told him."

I looked at Frank. So Luke was telling the truth.

Which meant we still had no idea who was behind whatever happened to Kelly.

I saw his shoulders droop slightly and knew he had come to the same conclusion.

Jamie continued. "Listen, you guys, if I were you? I would look into that creepy carnie guy, Cam or Can or whatever his name is. . . ."

"Cal?" I asked.

She nodded emphatically. "My friend Katie? She works the nacho booth? She says he was totally weird to her one time when he ordered nachos. He was all like, 'No jalapeños!' and she was like, 'Um, they're *in the sauce*,' and he got all flustered, like he'd never heard of nacho sauce before. And she said when she gave him the nachos, he reached up and his sleeves fell down and his *arms* were, like, *covered* with track marks." She paused, gauging our reaction, and then leaned forward. "Like for *drugs*," she added.

I was silent for a moment, mentally calculating the likelihood that Cal used drugs versus the likelihood that Jamie was exaggerating the truth in order to have something to talk about. I doubted Hector would have hired Cal if he used drugs, and I recalled Daisy saying that they drug-tested all job applicants. Still, it was something we could look for the next time we saw Cal.

Seeming unsatisfied with our reaction—or lack thereof—Jamie huffed and crossed her arms. "He also takes the *bus* to work," she said. "I mean, who takes the bus?"

I knew the answer to that one, and it was: people who can't afford a car. It's pretty simple, really. But I was getting the feeling maybe Jamie just didn't like Cal, so I didn't see the point in giving her Bus 101.

"Did you actually see Cal do anything weird on the night of the incident?" Frank asked, trying to get us back on a logical track.

Jamie looked from Frank to me, and her eyes flashed with annoyance. I could tell she didn't like our reaction to her dirt on Cal. But after a moment, she nodded. "Yeah," she said. "In fact, I did."

She paused, waiting for us to ask her, and Frank finally did. "What did you see?" he asked.

Jamie straightened up. "He left his post," she said, "while the ride was running."

"Where did he go?" I asked.

Jamie shrugged. "I don't know," she said. "I just looked over at the booth while the ride was going, and he was gone."

Hmm. I wasn't sure what to make of Jamie's tip. She clearly didn't like Cal, and it was possible he'd left the booth for a totally normal reason—checking something on the ride, for example. Still, I filed it away. I remembered Daisy's strange behavior toward Cal the morning before. It wasn't like her to be rude.

"Well, thanks a lot for the information," Frank said with a nod. "We really appreciate it. I guess we'll see you at school?"

Jamie nodded slowly. Her expression implied that she wasn't sure what to make of us. I felt sure she was used to a more appreciative audience for her gossip. After a few seconds she shrugged, and the apprehension was gone from her face.

"See you guys around," she said lightly, and closed the door.

As we walked back to our car—still parked in front of Luke's house—my phone beeped with an incoming text.

I pulled it out and held the screen so Frank could see. It was from Daisy.

GOOD NEWS . . . THE INSPECTORS & POLICE STILL CAN'T FIND ANYTHING WRONG WITH THE RIDE, SO G-FORCE REOPENS TONIGHT.

TAKEN FOR A RIDE

7

FRANK

"OH . . . WOW," MY BROTHER SAID AS we pulled into the parking lot for Funspot that evening. "Are you seeing this?"

Dusk was just falling, and the lights of the carnival rides blinked in an enticing rhythm. But to my surprise, we weren't going to be able to park all that close to them.

Because the parking lot was *packed*!

"Seriously?" I looked at Joe in surprise. "Why? I mean, I'm happy for Daisy, but . . ."

I drove the car down a long lane of parked cars, looking for a space. Teenagers clustered around cars and strolled toward the long lines at the ticket booths, chatting excitedly. Our windows were down, so every so often I caught a few words.

". . . don't know if I'm brave enough to ride it . . ."

". . . didn't really *die*, right?"

". . . nobody knows what happened to her . . ."

". . . have to check out the Death Ride . . ."

My mouth dropped open. I looked at Joe, who looked just as flabbergasted as I felt.

"The trailer!" we both cried at the same time.

This had to be the work of the trailer the Piperato Brothers had made, calling G-Force the "Death Ride." It had never really occurred to me that the trailer might *work*. I guess I never got past it being extremely poor taste to use the disappearance of a young girl as a marketing angle. Besides, didn't the trailer basically say, "Come to Funspot and ride G-Force and you might die"? Who saw that and thought, *Yes, please*?

Who *were* these people?

Joe caught my eye and seemed to grasp my confusion. "Well . . . according to my biology class, teenagers' brains aren't fully developed yet. The unfinished parts seem to control judgment and, um, making good decisions."

I pulled into the first open parking space I saw, at least half a mile from the ticket booths.

"Teenagers also seem to view themselves as invincible," Joe went on. "So I guess, when you challenge them with a Death Ride, the most common response would be . . . ?"

"'I gotta get on that thing,'" I replied, quoting a red-haired kid we'd just passed a few seconds ago.

Joe nodded. "Yeah," he said.

I put the car in park and took the keys out of the ignition. The engine died, and we just sat there for a minute or two, listening to the excited chatter all around us.

"You realize we're both teenagers," I said finally.

Joe nodded. "Maybe we have really quick-developing brains?" he said.

I shook my head and climbed out of the car. Joe followed, and we made the long trek to the ticket booths, where Daisy had instructed us to bypass the lines, go to the 'will call' booth, and ask for her. We did, and a few minutes later Daisy came to get us—pink-cheeked and happy-looking.

"Do you *believe* this?" she asked, gesturing to the lines.

Joe nodded. "It's crazy. Is your dad excited?"

Daisy bit her lip. "I think he doesn't know how to feel," she replied. "On the one hand, we might be able to afford groceries this week. But on the other, Kelly's still missing. . . ."

"Yeah," Joe said, looking out over the lines. "It's hard to know how to react."

"It has to be that trailer the Piperato Brothers made," I suggested. "Right?"

Daisy nodded. "Yeah. They're here, and they're super excited. I guess the video went viral and has been viewed some crazy number of times . . . a hundred thousand? Maybe even more?"

I looked back at the lines snaking back from the ticket booths almost halfway through the parking lot. I could swear I could even hear the trailer playing on people's smartphones. *"You've heard about it on the news . . ."*

"Well," I said after a moment. "I guess if we can't beat 'em . . ."

Joe smiled. "Should we head over to G-Force?"

Daisy nodded eagerly. "I think they're going to let in the first ride soon."

It was hard to know what to think as we watched Cal load the first set of riders into G-Force. (Joe, Daisy, and I were watching from the dining area off to the right—we'd decided to sit it out and observe.) Cal seemed to take extra long to strap everyone in and run the mandatory safety checks. I couldn't help glancing at his arms, which were bare in his short-sleeved motorcycle T-shirt, but I didn't see any sign of the track marks Jamie had mentioned. I wondered if Jamie had a reason to want us to suspect Cal, or whether she just flat-out didn't like him.

But more than anything, as we watched Cal fire up the controls and the ride hummed into action, I found myself thinking about Kelly Keohane. Fourteen years old is not that old. It's not old enough to drive a car, or drop out of school, or do a lot of the things that older kids do to show the adults in their lives that *they're* in control. It seemed way too young to run off with a boyfriend, or even a BFF. Besides, none of Kelly's friends claimed to have any idea where she was. She'd just disappeared. Like into thin air.

Was it really possible that this was something she'd planned—that she was somewhere safe and happy?

It was getting harder and harder to believe that, and yet life was going on right in front of us.

As the first G-Force ride came to a stop and the doors opened up, the Piperato Brothers stepped up onto the ride platform, holding a bullhorn. I could see Hector off to the side, looking pained. Cal emerged from G-Force and said something to Derek Piperato, who held the bullhorn to his lips and yelled, "Everyone present and accounted for!"

The crowd went nuts, cheering, and then, after a few seconds, a few wise guys started to boo.

"What," I asked out loud, "you *wanted* someone else to disappear?"

But Derek put the bullhorn back to his lips and announced, "The Death Ride has failed to claim a second victim. Who's brave enough to ride it next?"

The line started cheering again. The first riders streamed out, looking dazed but happy, and Cal made his way to the ride entrance and let in another twenty or so people.

Daisy let out an uneasy chuckle. "I feel like a huge boulder was just lifted off my shoulders," she said quietly. "As lame as that is. I was so nervous!"

Joe put his hand on her shoulder. "You know Frank and I rode the ride about twenty times and nothing happened," he assured her.

"Except that you puked," I pointed out.

Joe shot me an exaggerated glare. "Hey, Frank, why don't you get us all some lemonade or something?"

Daisy smiled. "Actually, that's not a bad idea. Here, show them this." She handed me a Funspot ID card with her photo on it. "Ask them to put it on my tab."

I took the card and obeyed, taking my time meandering from food stand to food stand, looking for the best lemonade. (Logic told me they were probably all made from the same mix, but I was trying to take my time.) As I wandered, G-Force took in and let out another group . . . then another . . . then another. Each time the ride ran and nothing unusual happened, Derek Piperato made a pithy little announcement and the crowd whooped. After the fifth ride, Derek announced that a new item was available in the Funspot gift shops: I SURVIVED THE DEATH RIDE T-shirts. He held one up. The front showed a caricature of a girl screaming with the slogan printed in huge, horror-movie-style letters.

"Gross," I muttered, loading the three lemonades into a cardboard carrier and making my way back to Joe and Daisy.

As I got closer, I caught sight of the two of them and wondered whether I should have tried to dawdle even more. Their heads were bent close together, and they were deep in conversation. I was getting the feeling that Joe really liked this girl. I clutched my lemonade and looked around for a distraction, but before I could find one, I heard, "Frank! Hey, awesome, you got the lemonade."

I looked up to see Daisy waving me over, a warm smile on her face. I smiled back. I knew she was trying to make me feel included, and I appreciated it.

I walked over, catching the tail end of my brother's question: ". . . on purpose, then? Do you know something about him?"

Daisy shrugged, and it occurred to me that she might actually have waved me back to avoid whatever Joe was asking her about.

As Cal let the next group in, the line moved up, and a familiar face stepped out of line toward us.

"Well, well, well," Luke smirked. "If it isn't Daisy and her new boyfriend, Sherlock Holmes."

"You came back to ride the ride," I replied flatly. "Are you feeling braver today?"

A flutter of annoyance passed across Luke's face. "You talked to Jamie, then? She told you the truth?"

Daisy was looking back and forth between Luke, Joe, and me, like she didn't understand what was going on. She pulled her dainty eyebrows together, a deep crease forming in the middle. Was she upset?

"What are you guys talking about?" she asked.

Joe turned to her. "It's nothing." Then he looked back at Luke. "Yeah, Jamie backed up your story," he said, sounding not so happy about it. "You got too scared to ride the ride, and you had to pee. Thanks for being honest with us."

Luke glared at him, but any reply he might have made

was cut off by Daisy putting up her hand and leaning forward.

"Hold on," she said, looking from me to Joe. "Did you two go question Luke about G-Force or something?"

Luke let out a caustic laugh. "Yeah, they thought I kidnapped Kelly to get back at you. Sounds totally reasonable, right?"

Daisy made a face like she smelled something terrible. "Seriously?" she asked, looking at Joe.

Joe sighed. He shrugged. I could tell he was uncomfortable. But what could we have done? We were working for Daisy, and that meant getting to the bottom of what happened with G-Force. It didn't mean asking her permission to question her ex-boyfriend or anyone else.

Joe still wasn't saying anything, and Luke took advantage of his momentary silence.

"What do you say, Daze—wanna ride with me?" He gestured toward the ride, where Cal was letting in yet another group. The line was moving forward. Luke would be on the next ride.

Daisy smiled at him, and for a moment I could see that they had been boyfriend and girlfriend. Her expression was full of fondness, with no trace of the annoyance I'd seen the week before. I got a nagging feeling in the pit of my stomach. Was this bad news for Joe?

Then Daisy bit her lip. "Oh, but we haven't been waiting in line," she said.

Luke rolled his eyes in an exaggerated way. "Daze, your father owns the park," he pointed out. "I think you could pull some strings."

Daisy smiled again and got to her feet. For a minute I thought she was just going to walk off with Luke and leave us there, but then she turned around.

"You guys wanna come too?"

I could tell that Joe was about to say no—whether from hurt feelings or a genuine desire to keep his lemonade down, I couldn't say. I nodded fiercely. "*Yes*," I said, hauling Joe up by the arm and purposely walking forward.

Luke frowned, but shrugged at Daisy, who glanced back at us briefly before leading the way up to the front of the line.

"What was that about?" Joe hissed at me as Daisy walked up to Cal and started gesturing.

"Research," I hissed back. "We need to go on this thing again. And I want to keep an eye on Luke."

Joe winced, still watching Daisy. "For me or for the case?" he asked.

"Both," I answered honestly. "Hey—what were you two talking about when I came back? It seemed a little tense for a minute."

Joe frowned, then seemed to remember. "Oh, I asked her about Cal," he whispered. Daisy had now stepped back from the ride operator, who was watching G-Force wind down. "Get this—her dad told her to stay away from him."

I raised an eyebrow. "Hector? But he had only glowing things to say about Cal the other morning."

Joe nodded. "I know; it's weird, right? I tried to press her for details, but all she would say was that it was awkward and she didn't totally understand it."

A stream of people exited the ride, all chatting excitedly and whooping. One guy turned in my direction and randomly gave me the "Rock on!" sign.

"Glad you liked it," I said, nodding.

Daisy came over and touched Joe's arm. "Come on, guys," she said. "We're skipping the line. Let's hurry so no one notices."

Cal was standing by the exit gate of G-Force, and he nodded and quickly waved us in. Then he took us around to the front of the line and gestured to the open door. Joe and I definitely knew the drill by now, so we all rushed in and chose seats in a row at the far side of the circle.

As we all buckled in, I saw Joe reach over and touch Daisy's shoulder.

"Hey," he whispered. "I'm sorry we didn't tell you. I didn't want to upset you, and it turned out to be nothing."

Daisy gave him a long look before her expression warmed a bit. "Okay," she whispered. "It's just, you're doing this as a favor to me. I thought you would keep me posted."

Joe nodded. "I will from now on. Okay?"

Other riders were streaming in through the door now, and Daisy's answer was lost in the noise from the crowd.

While the new riders got settled, I carefully pulled my smart-phone out of my jeans pocket and lifted it to look at its face.

That afternoon, in anticipation of riding G-Force again, I'd downloaded a "night vision" app and installed it. I wasn't sure how it would work with all the flashing lights and pro-jections, but I figured it was worth a shot.

I got it set up and started recording as Cal strapped in the last rider and headed out the door.

"Enjoy, kids," he called behind him.

In the seconds before the ride started up, I glanced at my brother. He looked like he was steeling himself. Then I caught a glance at Luke, two seats away on the other side of Daisy. He was staring forward, with a determined expres-sion, like he was trying to psych himself up.

Was I the only one looking forward to this?

The opening chords of "Beautiful" started up, and we were plunged into darkness. Several people screamed, clearly having their first G-Force experience. I struggled to keep my smartphone up and recording the action, but it was hard. The music, the lights, and the images took over. Soon I was totally disoriented, lost in the experience.

After a few minutes the images slowed and the ride began circling again, losing speed. The song finished up. Soon the circle of seats slid to a stop. Gradually, the purple lights dimmed on.

One of the newbies started cheering, and others soon joined in. I checked my hand—yep, I was still clutching my smartphone, camera side out. I reached up and clicked off the recording. Maybe this would give us some important information about how G-Force ran.

Suddenly I heard Daisy screaming.

"Oh my God! Oh my *God*! He was right here!"

I turned around. Joe was holding her hand, trying to comfort her, as they both leaned over . . .

An empty seat, with the restraints cut.

Luke was gone.

STRIKES AGAIN

8

JOE

O, I TOLD YOU. I DIDN'T HEAR ANYTHING,"
Daisy was telling Chief Nelson Olaf for the third
time. "The ride was way too loud. The first time
I noticed anything was wrong was when the ride
was over—I looked over and his seat was empty."

I squeezed her hand. We were sitting in hard plastic chairs
in Hector's office. After Luke's disappearance, it had taken
the cops only minutes to show up.

Almost like they'd been worried about something like this.

Chief Olaf nodded, tapping the end of his pen to his lips.

"Did they find anything in the ride?" I broke in. "Any
trace of a struggle? Did they fingerprint yet?"

Olaf frowned at me and wagged his pen in my direction.
"Pipe down, Hardy."

I wondered if he could tell Frank and me apart, or whether we mingled in his mind into one big distasteful blob labeled "Hardy." Tip #1 for Unlicensed Investigators: Law enforcement will not like you. You think you're trying to do them a favor; they think you're trying to make them look bad.

Olaf turned back to Daisy. "As I was saying before I was so rudely interrupted. Was Luke having any problems at home that you know of?"

I groaned. I couldn't help it. Olaf had asked Daisy this five times—each time, the answer was no. I was getting the uncomfortable feeling that in the absence of a real explanation, Olaf was going to paint a "the kid was troubled and ran away somehow" explanation on this case.

Which would not serve Luke any better than it was serving poor Kelly.

Daisy sighed loudly. "*No*," she said for the fifth time.

Olaf looked at me, his annoyed expression implying that I'd somehow put her up to that answer. He slapped his pen down onto the table and started rifling through his notebook. "I'll need you to step out so I can question the lady alone, Hardy," he said.

I tried not to roll my eyes. Like not having me around would make Daisy answer his questions any differently. And the cops were wasting time in here, asking the same questions over and over again when they could be out looking for clues.

But I had no legal right to stay; I knew that. I stood and shot Daisy a supportive glance. "See you soon," I said, and walked out of the office.

Downstairs, Frank and Hector were standing in the lobby, shuffling around restlessly like they couldn't relax enough to sit still. The door to another room was closed, and I could hear muffled voices within.

"Who's in there?" I asked, jabbing a thumb at the second office.

Hector looked up. "An officer is questioning Cal," he replied, then quickly averted his eyes. As I was about to turn to my brother, I caught Hector looking back at the closed door, a strange look in his eyes. Was it concern? Fear?

I remembered what Daisy had told me about Cal and nudged Frank.

"Hey, Hector," I said, "is there anywhere we can speak privately?"

Hector looked at me, then across the room to the various security guards, witnesses, and cops who were hanging around. The Piperato Brothers were draped across a few plastic chairs beneath a window, apparently snoozing while they awaited their turn to be questioned. Hector nodded and gestured to the front door. "Let's go outside. I could use some fresh air."

He led the way out the door, and Frank and I followed. Outside, it was eerily quiet; all the rides and games had been turned off when the park was closed hours ago, and most of the employees—any of them not directly involved with G-Force—had been sent home. Some of the lights on the rides still blinked silently.

There is nothing creepier than an abandoned amusement park.

Hector sighed and rubbed his eyes. It was getting late, well past midnight. But I could tell that Hector's weariness ran much deeper than the late hour. He looked like a man who literally didn't know what to do anymore. I couldn't imagine how it must feel to gamble your whole family's future on a new ride and have this happen.

Hector gestured for us to follow him down the midway, where, when the park was open, hawkers would beckon guests to try their luck on shooting games, darts, and roll-the-ball horse-race games. Now the booths were dark, and every so often I caught the white of a fake horse's or clown's eye glowing from within.

"I wanted to ask you about Cal," I said finally, when we were a good distance from the offices.

Hector looked surprised. "Cal? What do you want to know?"

I glanced at Frank, who was watching eagerly. "Do you trust him?" I asked.

Hector looked surprised, but deep in his eyes, I saw something else—recognition. He knew we were onto something. "Do I trust Cal? Well, I hired him, didn't I? Would I hire someone I didn't trust?"

Frank cocked an eyebrow. "Would you?" he asked. "Or maybe the better question is—why would you?"

Hector looked from my brother to me. "I don't understand," he said.

I sighed. "I noticed that Daisy was a little strange with him the other day," I explained. "When I asked her about it, she said you told her to stay away from him. That doesn't sound like something you'd say about a person you trust."

Hector's eyes widened, then he looked down at the ground. When he looked back up, he was wearing an expression of forced calm. "It's not a big deal," he said, with a little shrug. "I guess I'm overprotective of my little girl. At least, that's what she tells me!"

He laughed, but when neither Frank nor I smiled back, he stopped abruptly.

"Why would you need to protect her from Cal?" Frank asked quietly.

Hector looked down. "It's not a big deal. Just a dad's paranoia."

I was getting frustrated. "About *what*?" I asked.

Hector sighed and looked up at me. "Cal had a rough childhood. He has—well—he has a bit of a rap sheet."

"What's on it?" asked Frank. I was wondering too. There's a big difference between a history of misdemeanors or even burglaries and a history of violent crime. The former wouldn't make Cal all that scary. The latter . . . well . . .

But why would Hector hire a guy with a history of violent crime?

"It's all older stuff," Hector said. "Burglaries mostly, some stolen cars."

"How long ago are we talking?" I asked.

Hector shrugged. "At least ten years."

Now I was really feeling confused. "So why would you tell Daisy to avoid him? It seems like he's gotten his life back together."

Hector pressed his lips together. "Well," he said after a moment, "there was this little something that happened on his last job."

I raised my eyebrows beseechingly. *What?*

Hector went on. "He, well, he was fired from working at the big Five Pennants park for this little incident with a coworker." He shrugged again. "She said he threatened her when she made a joke about his missing teeth. Flew off the handle, told her she had no idea what kind of life he'd led and he'd show her hard times. . . ."

I looked at Frank. *Yikes!*

"And this coworker . . . was she another adult?"

Hector frowned. "No," he said. "She was a teenager."

"Did he actually attack her?" I asked.

Hector shook his head. "Other coworkers broke it up," he said. "One big guy led him away and calmed him down. Cal says it was nothing—he never would have hurt her. He was just angry, he says. He just needed to yell."

I looked at Frank. People who just need to yell usually don't make specific threats. People who make specific threats usually mean their target harm—even if only in the moment.

I remembered what Jamie had told us about Cal leaving his post when Kelly went missing. Was it possible she was telling the truth? Did Cal, in fact, have a dark side?

"Can you clear something up for me?" Frank asked, tilting his head as he looked at Hector. "I'm confused. Why would you hire a guy you don't trust around your daughter . . . to work in an *amusement park*?"

Good point. I examined Hector's face. He began sputtering, waving his hands like we were making too big a deal out of this.

"It's not that I don't *trust* him," he said, shaking his head like that was a crazy interpretation. "I never said that. I just . . . it's not just Cal, really. Daisy can be a firecracker. You probably know that as well as anybody. . . ."

He looked at me and laughed feebly. I didn't laugh back. Daisy had her moments, sure, but if Hector was implying that she might set off an otherwise harmless man into harming her somehow, I couldn't get behind that.

Hector shook his head. "Forget what I said earlier. Of course I trust Cal. Everyone deserves a second chance, and I'm glad I was able to give him that. Maybe Daisy misinterpreted what I said. I don't remember what I told her, exactly. Anyway . . ."

He looked around, as if desperately looking for a way out of this conversation.

As fate would have it, an exit door was approaching—in the form of Chief Olaf.

The chief walked toward us and sighed deeply. "I think we've got what we need. Hector, you can close up the park. Let's all go home and get some sleep."

"Did you find any leads?" Frank asked eagerly. "Any evidence of Luke in the park, after he rode G-Force?"

Chief Olaf turned to him and narrowed his eyes. "That's confidential information," he said, "and to be honest, I'm still not entirely clear on what you two boys have been doing hanging around Funspot so often. It seems you've spent quite a bit of time here since the first disappearance, according to witnesses."

Hector coughed loudly, then laughed. "Joe here has been seeing my daughter Daisy." He put his arm around my shoulders and smiled. "He seems like a nice young man, but I don't know why they need to spend so much time together! They're so young! But who can stand in the way of young love, eh?"

The chief looked skeptically from Hector to me, but then smiled. "My daughter's only eight, so I wouldn't know yet," he said. "I'll take your word for it, Hector. I will say that there are certainly much worse boys in this town that your daughter could choose to spend her time with."

Hector smiled again. "Yes, these are good boys." He

pulled his arm away and stepped back. "Shall we get our things and go, boys? I'm sure we're all tired."

I nodded. "Yeah, it's pretty late."

Chief Olaf led the way back to the administration building, and Hector, Frank, and I fell into step behind him.

"I don't think I'm going to get much sleep tonight," Frank muttered, casting a glance back in the direction of G-Force.

"Me neither," Hector said gravely.

I turned his words over and over in my mind as we said our good-byes, and then took the long walk back to our car.

Was Hector going to have trouble sleeping because two kids were still missing?

Or was he going to have trouble sleeping because deep down, he knew who'd taken them?

SECRETS 9

FRANK

I T HAD BEEN A LONG, LONG NIGHT, BUT SLEEP was not in my forecast when we got home. Instead I pulled out my smartphone and held it up to Joe.

"Secret weapon," I said, walking into my room and hooking it up to my computer.

Joe stumbled after me, looking very sleepy. "What do you mean?"

I woke up my computer and then clicked on a video-viewing program that would allow us to see the footage on the monitor. "Remember that night-vision app I downloaded? I used it to film our G-Force ride tonight."

Joe raised an eyebrow, suddenly looking more alert. "You filmed the ride where Luke disappeared?"

I nodded. "I tried to, anyway. I don't know how sharp the video will be—it was hard to hold the phone straight with the ride in motion. But it's worth a shot."

A *ding* sounded to tell us that the video had uploaded to the computer, and I double-clicked to start it.

The footage started out clear, with the other riders visible, lined up across from me in their seats. Once the ride started, though, it got pretty blurry and shaky. I could make out figures moving through the frame, carried by the ride, but just like being on G-Force, it was hard to tell exactly what I was looking at or what was moving where.

Joe groaned. "This is making me queasy."

I tried to stay focused on the figures onscreen, looking for any sudden, weird movements that might be related to Luke's disappearance. So far I didn't see anything. Then all of a sudden, the motion slowed and the figures slowly circled back into place.

Soon a full row of seats slowed to a halt across from the camera.

The lights came up, and the video ended.

"I got nothing," Joe said, sounding sleepy again.

I shrugged. "Maybe there's nothing to get," I said. "This isn't exactly a professional-quality video."

Joe yawned. "It was a good idea to take it, though. Listen, I need to get some shut-eye."

I nodded, my eyes never leaving the screen. "Go to bed, Joe. I'll see you in the morning."

My brother lingered behind me. "You're staying up?" he asked.

I shook my head. "Not for long. I just want to watch this a couple more times . . . see if anything jumps out at me."

"Okay." Joe's footsteps slowly headed out the door. "Wake me if you notice anything."

"I will." Joe shut my bedroom door and headed down the hall to his room.

The house was nearly silent. I cued the video to play again . . . then again. Then one more time. Each time, as the riders spun to a stop, I told myself I would only watch it once more. I needed sleep, after all. But somehow I couldn't tear my eyes away. I felt like this video had something to tell me—something I just couldn't make out yet.

I finally shut my eyes, but was still restless. I know I must have fallen asleep, because I had a terrifying dream: Someone had pushed me off the Funspot Ferris wheel and I was hanging on to Joe for dear life! I woke up soaked in sweat.

Soon pale light was shining through my windows, and I could hear the calls of birds waking up to search for food. In an hour or so Joe would be up. I'd given up my chance of getting any real sleep that night.

But then I saw it. A crouched shape moving just *behind* the row of seats. It seemed to come up from the floor. Just as quickly as it appeared, it vanished, darting off to the left.

I replayed that section of video. Was I just so tired I was seeing things? But no, it was real. A person—sneaking into the ride as it was in motion. It was impossible to make out features, but the figure looked too tall to be Luke himself.

It was more the size of a tall, skinny grown man.

A tall, skinny grown man like Cal Nevins.

It was Monday, and Joe and I were due at school in just an hour or so. But instead of eating Aunt Trudy's sweet potato pancakes and leisurely getting ready, we threw on clothes, grabbed a couple of granola bars, and jumped into the car.

Hector had mentioned that the ride inspectors were coming back this morning, and Joe and I wanted to be there.

Funspot was still closed, so we parked right near the service entrance and waved at the security guard, who recognized us by now. He let us into the employees-only area, which was bustling with activity. The ride inspectors had just arrived, and Hector was getting ready to lead them out to G-Force. Daisy wasn't here this morning, but as we fell into step behind Hector and the crew of three ride inspectors, Joe pointed back at the administration building.

"Look who's here," he said darkly.

Two suit-wearing figures stumbled out of the office building.

"Yoo-hoo! Wait for us, please!" Derek Piperato called. He was followed by Greg and a woman holding a large, professional-looking video camera. "Our videographer has just arrived!"

Hector sighed, glaring at the Piperatos. "I will say *again* that I don't feel that filming this inspection is appropriate."

The Piperatos just smiled and joined the group.

"We only quadrupled your business with the last video, Hector," Derek said with a smirk. "Maybe you'd better leave the marketing to us."

Hector grumbled something unintelligible, and we all followed him. Early-morning sunlight glinted off the polished silver sides of the ride, which looked infinitely more menacing than it had that first night we saw it. Cal stepped out from the operation booth and came down the steps to meet the inspectors. I watched as they each shook his hand, clearly remembering him from their previous inspection.

"Let me take you in," Cal said, gesturing to the ride. He opened it up, and in they went.

Joe and I didn't want to interfere with the official inspection, so we hung back while the inspectors did their work. From our vantage point just a few yards from the ride platform, we could watch the Piperato Brothers directing the videographer.

"I'm thinking of something along the lines of, 'Another one missing. Inspectors can't figure out what's going wrong. Are *you* brave enough to risk it?'" Greg said.

"That's good," Derek said, "but somewhere in there we need the line 'The Death Ride has claimed another victim.'

I'm convinced that branding this the Death Ride is responsible for at least half the response!"

"Good point," Greg agreed. "How about, 'The Death Ride has claimed another victim. Inspectors can't figure out what's wrong. The cops don't know where the victims are. Are *you* brave enough to risk . . . DUN DUN DUN . . .'"

"THE DEATH RIDE!" Derek joined in, and both Piperato brothers started laughing.

"Make sure you get lots of creepy footage—weird angles, odd lighting," Derek said casually to the videographer.

Suddenly Hector strode purposefully over to the brothers. He looked at Derek and held up a fist. "Do you actually want me to hit you?" he shouted.

Derek stumbled back, looking stunned. "Why would you hit me?" he asked. "I'm saving your amusement park!"

Hector took in a breath, like he was trying to calm himself down. "Two children are missing off this thing," he said, gesturing to G-Force. "We don't know where they are. *Do you understand that?*"

Derek looked puzzled. He shot an inquisitive look at his brother, who also seemed confused.

"Of course we do," said Greg. "And it's terrible. But we can't control that. We can only control how we respond."

"We designed a phenomenal ride," Derek added, "and now its legacy is being overshadowed by a crime or prank that we had nothing do with. We're trying to protect our own reputation here."

"Yeah," Greg agreed. "The ride wasn't designed to hurt anybody. You must know that. Whatever's going on here, it isn't our fault."

Hector sighed. "I do know that," he said. "But this is still a tragic event. Right?"

Greg and Derek looked at each other. After a moment, Derek shrugged. "It could be," he said. "Or it could be kids pulling a prank. Either way, why shouldn't we get as much publicity for our ride out of it as we can?" He nodded at the videographer. "When the inspectors are done in there, let's get some footage of the seat with the restraints cut. Okay?"

Something seemed to snap in Hector. He sprang forward and grabbed Greg by the arm. "I want you out," he said in a low, furious voice.

Derek jumped into action, pushing Hector off his brother. "What are you doing? Stop it! We're within our contractual rights!"

Hector let go of Greg and yelled, "GET OUT OF MY PARK!"

That seemed to get through to them. The Piperato Brothers scrambled around, gathering their belongings and their videographer, then scurried away from G-Force and along the path that led back to the service entrance and out of the park. Hector straightened up and watched them go, a thoughtful look in his eye.

I glanced at Joe, and together we gently approached Hector.

"Wow," I said quietly when we were just a few feet away.

Hector shook his head. "Buying this from those idiots was the worst decision I've ever made," he said in a low voice. "Worse than buying this park, even."

Before we could reply, he turned and disappeared into the ride.

Joe and I waited around while the inspectors completed their business, confirming that G-Force seemed to be in perfect working order and that there was nothing wrong with the ride itself.

The ride was just a crime scene. Not the criminal.

When the inspectors left, we stepped up onto the ride platform, waiting for a chance to get Cal alone. He puttered around for a few minutes, checking things, then locking up. Finally he strode toward the stairs—right into our path.

"Cal," Joe called, stepping out to block him. "Can we talk to you for a minute?"

Cal glanced at us, then at his watch. "Sure, boys," he said after a moment. "What can I help you with this morning?"

I gestured to G-Force. "The inspectors—have they found an alternate entrance to the ride, besides the front door?"

Cal glanced back where I was pointing. "No, they didn't find nothing like that," he said, shaking his head. "This is still a mystery, boys. I hope those kids are okay."

I leaned in. "And you don't know of another entrance to the ride?" I asked. "One that comes through the floor, maybe?"

Cal looked me in the eye. For a moment, I saw a flash of concern pass over his features, but it quickly dissipated. He shook his head. "No, sir," he said. "The only way in is through the front door. No hidden entrances, no hidden passages."

I looked at Joe. I didn't like where this was going. But I had no choice but to call Cal on his lie.

I pulled out my smartphone. "You sure about that?"

Tapping on the screen, I brought up the video I'd taken of our ride. I turned it on, and Cal watched it, looking mystified. At the 3:32 mark, I paused the video and pointed at the screen.

"See that figure?" I said. "Let me show you again."

I backed the video up so that it started just as the figure rose up through the floor.

Cal watched it, his eyes widening. He swallowed hard and took a step back.

"That looks an awful lot like you," Joe pointed out.

Cal was fidgeting nervously with his hands, folding them, unfolding them. He lifted his right index finger to his lips and bit down hard on the nail. The color was draining from his face.

"Ah, I don't know . . . ," he said, not making eye contact.

"I just . . . You know, I might remember something. . . ."

The impact came as fast and as hard as a bowling ball dropped on you from ten feet above. Suddenly I was grabbed by the back of the neck and shoved hard into G-Force's shiny silver side. Pain exploded in my head, and the edges of my vision blurred. Out of the corner of my eye, I saw Cal opening up the door of the ride. . . .

Before I understood what was happening, I was roughly shoved into the darkness. As I tried—and failed—to get up, Joe was pushed through the door too and landed in a heap beside me.

"I'm sorry, boys," Cal's voice came from somewhere above us. "I really am. . . ."

Then the door slammed shut, and everything went dark.

UNDER THEIR NOSES

NOSES

10

JOE

IT WAS PITCH-DARK INSIDE, WITHOUT EVEN A shaft of light entering from anywhere. It was like being inside a cave. Thankfully, since the ride had been up and running for the inspectors, the air-conditioning lingered, and it wasn't too hot.

"Now what?" said Frank, sighing deeply.

"I guess we know Cal's involved," I said to the deep blackness to my left, from which Frank's voice had come.

I could hear him nodding. "Involved enough to be scared," he agreed. He sighed again. "I guess we'd better try to get out of here."

"Right."

I stumbled in the dark until I hit what felt like a wall, then banged on the shiny metal side of G-Force as hard as

391

I could. "HELP! HELP! IS ANYONE OUT THERE?" I paused. "Is this thing soundproof? Do you remember?"

"I dunno." Frank seemed to think. "I don't remember hearing anyone screaming from inside."

I groaned. "I have a test in geometry today."

I could hear the smile in Frank's voice. "And you think 'A criminal carnie locked me inside an amusement ride' isn't an acceptable excuse?"

I started pounding the walls with my fists again. "CAL! HECTOR! DAISY! ANYONE!!"

Frank joined in. "WE'RE TRAPPED IN HERE! WE'RE INSIDE G-FORCE!"

All in all, it probably wasn't that long before Hector doubled back and found us. It felt like hours, but must have been just a few minutes before we heard a "Hello?" and the door slowly swung open. "Who's in there?"

From that point on, it was hours of explaining, telling the same story countless times to countless people.

I did end up missing my geometry test, but only because once Hector called the police, it took a long time to get everything straight. Chief Olaf came back with a whole team. Two officers were sent to Cal's apartment to look for him, and G-Force was opened up again, this time for a crew of police inspectors.

About an hour later, one of the inspectors came running out, shaking a flashlight. "We found it!"

Frank and I were sitting on a bench with Chief Olaf,

and when we looked at him pleadingly, he seemed to understand.

"All right, boys," he said under his breath. "I probably shouldn't do this, but come take a look with me."

We stood and mounted the little platform that led to the ride's door, then ducked and stepped inside. The police had brought in big floodlights, and the interior was lit up like a baseball stadium. It looked totally different from the way it did when we'd entered to go on the ride. With the bright light shining, you could see that the interior walls were cheap plastic, not metal, and that the plush purple fabric that covered the seats was not all that plush—or that clean.

The officer who'd called out, a tall man with sandy blond hair and a mustache, signaled to Chief Olaf. "It's over here," he said, pointing to an indentation in the floor that sat in the middle of the seats and was set off by a short metal railing. He reached out and grabbed a section of railing, and it came loose in his hand. A hidden gate! Then Olaf stepped down into the lowered section. Looking down, I could see that the shaggy purple carpet had been pulled up.

As we watched, the officer shone his flashlight in a small rectangle along the floor. I gasped as I realized what he was pointing out: a tiny raised lip on the floor, hidden beneath the carpet while the ride was in motion.

A trapdoor.

"There's a catch here," the officer said, pushing down with his toe on one of the short sides of the rectangle. It sprang up easily, clearly on springs, and the officer reached down to grab the raised section and swing it upward.

The trapdoor opened onto a tiny, closetlike room.

We all peered inside as the officer shone his flashlight in. The secret room was nothing more than a dark, tiny box hidden in the floor of the ride. There was nothing on the polished metal walls, nothing on the concrete floor. The officer shone his light on a tiny plastic flashlight that had been left in the corner.

The whole room was barely large enough for Frank or me to fit into, crouched down on all fours.

"So we're thinking this is where he placed them while the ride was in motion," the officer said. "It appears to be soundproof."

Chief Olaf winced, passing his hand over his face. "All right. So he sneaks in while the ride is in motion and cuts the restraints. He takes the victim and forces them down the step, opens the trapdoor, and pushes them in. How does he keep them quiet while he's doing all this?"

There was silence for a few seconds, and I cleared my throat. Chief Olaf turned to me.

"He wouldn't have to," I explained. "The ride is pretty loud, and kids are screaming the whole time. If the victim put up a fight, it would probably just blend into the background noise."

Chief Olaf grimaced and nodded. I looked into the tiny room. It was really giving me the willies to imagine Kelly and Luke trapped in there, only a flashlight to keep them company until Cal could get them out. Who knows how long they were down there? Who knows what happened to them when they were finally let out?

"So when they disappeared," Olaf said, "all the time we spent looking for them, searching a twenty-mile radius, they were right here." He sighed. "Under our noses."

I looked into the little room again and felt my stomach lurch. All at once, I realized what was happening and ran to the little door, shoving an officer or two out of the way as I went.

I got onto the platform and managed to stagger down the steps before I lost my meager breakfast on the grass just outside the ride.

Thinking about what had happened to Luke and Kelly was way worse than riding G-Force ten times in a row.

A few days later, I met Frank in the school parking lot after taking my makeup geometry test. (It turns out that teachers are pretty understanding when the cops are involved.) His expression was grim, and I could tell immediately that he was thinking about the G-Force case.

"What did you learn?" I asked.

He frowned as he pulled out and drove slowly to the parking lot exit.

"They found Cal's fingerprints all over the trapdoor," he said. "Still no sign of him, though." He pulled out of the parking lot and began the short drive home.

"No," I said, not surprised. The officers sent to find Cal when he'd run off had found an empty, ransacked apartment with no evidence of anyone being kept there. They'd been tracking Cal's activity, but nobody had used his credit cards or cell phone, and random searches set up on the roads leading out of town had turned up nothing. He'd simply disappeared.

"And I asked Chief Olaf about Cal's criminal history," Frank added. "It's just as Hector told us. Burglaries and thefts as a kid. The incident Hector mentioned at his last job isn't on his criminal history, but the police called his last employer, and that story checks out too. He did threaten a female coworker."

I was silent for a few minutes as we drove the quiet residential streets, mulling that over. So Cal had threatened a coworker. That was very different from kidnapping two teenagers off an amusement ride, for who knows what purpose. There was something about Cal that just didn't add up.

"Do you feel like we're missing a crucial part of the story?" I asked Frank.

He let out a deep sigh. "Yes," he said, sounding relieved that I felt the same way. "It's driving me crazy."

"How does Cal go from stealing cars twenty years ago to kidnapping two kids he doesn't know?" I asked. The police had tried to find connections between Cal and Kelly and Cal and Luke, but had come back with nothing. It really seemed that the two teenagers had never come in contact with Cal before they rode G-Force.

Frank was nodding. "Hector acted pretty strange when we asked him about it too. I still don't understand why he would hire Cal if he had reservations about him."

"It's like he's hiding something," I said.

We had just turned onto our street, and we were quiet as Frank pulled into the driveway, both thinking this over.

He turned off the car, still staring straight ahead.

Finally he spoke. "Just for giggles," he said, unclasping his seat belt and throwing open the door, "let's do an Internet search on Hector Rodriguez."

There was a Hector Rodriguez, apparently, who was a pretty big heartthrob on a Colombian soap opera called *La Corazón Violeta*. There was also a Hector Rodriguez based in Cushing, Maine, who sold car parts on the Internet. There was a Hector Rodriguez who'd written a very enlightening article about nesting instincts in white mice for a scientific journal in 2007.

It took us six pages of results before we got to our Hector Rodriguez.

"Hector Rodriguez, Jamaica, New York," Frank read off. "Jamaica is part of New York City, right?"

"It's part of Queens," I said, "I think."

Frank clicked on the link. It was an old article from something called the *Queens Courier*, scanned in by hand. (Clearly

this article predated the newspaperzsite.) JAMAICA BOY WINS
PRESTIGIOUS SCHOLARSHIP FOR CHANGING HIS WAYS was
the headline.

JAMAICA—High school senior Hector Rodriguez, 18, says his future looks bright. "I have the opportunity to go to college now," he tells a reporter. "My parents are so proud. And two years ago, this wouldn't have seemed possible."

Indeed. Two years ago, it might have seemed more likely that Rodriguez would end up in prison once he reached adulthood. The teenager admits that he spent his free time prowling the streets, often engaging in criminal acts like burglaries and car theft. "I was bored," he says. "I didn't know better."

But in the last year, Rodriguez cleaned up his act and rededicated himself to his studies. He now maintains a 3.2 GPA at Bayside High School, and last week he was chosen as the recipient of the Daniel J. Elliott Scholarship Award for Previously Troubled Youth.

"We are so proud of Hector," says board member Maggie Elliott. "He's completely changed his life in a short amount of time, and he deserves the best chance he can get for a successful future."

A tiny photograph was printed alongside the article. He was decades younger and had considerably more hair, but that definitely looked like Daisy's father staring back at us.

"Huh," I said, not sure what to make of this.

"So Hector had a rap sheet too," Frank said, tapping his lip. "At one point. When he was young."

"It's weird that he neglected to mention that to us," I said. "I mean, since Cal's crimes are all from his youth too."

Frank and I looked at each other.

"Search for Cal Nevins," I suggested on a whim. "Cal Nevins of Jamaica, New York."

Frank typed all that in, and this time only one article popped up.

It was from the *New York News*. STRING OF CAR THEFTS TROUBLES JAMAICA RESIDENTS.

Frank clicked on the link, and we quickly skimmed down. The article was talking about a string of four or five car thefts that had occurred in the same neighborhood about twenty years ago—right around the time Hector got his scholarship.

The last paragraph contained an intriguing bit of information.

> Cal Nevins, 18, a local teenager, has confessed to the most recent crime, the theft of a white Chevrolet Cavalier from Bayside High School teacher Peter Winewski. Although the police admit that fingerprints collected from the car do not match Nevins's or Winewski's prints, they have accepted Nevins's confession and have sentenced him to two years in prison.

I whistled. "Two years," I said, shaking my head. "That's a long time. Especially so young."

Frank pointed at the screen. "I'm more interested in this bit here," he said. "'Fingerprints collected from the car do not match Nevins's or Winewski's.' Do you think there's a chance he didn't do it?"

I frowned. "Why would he confess if he didn't do it?"

Frank turned to me with a knowing look. "Maybe he was covering for somebody?"

"Joe!"

Daisy opened her front door looking pleased to see me, and I felt a little twist in my gut. I'd been neglecting her ever since the G-Force case kicked into high gear. I really liked her, but I have a tendency to disappear into a case . . . which is not exactly great for the love life.

Now I pasted on a smile. "Hey, Daisy. I . . . missed you. I thought we could hang out."

Daisy smiled back. "That sounds great. I'm actually making brownies. Let me stick them in the oven, and maybe we could watch a DVD."

"Perfect."

Daisy led me into the small but neat living room, where she gestured to the couch. "Seriously, I just need to put them in the pan and put the pan in the oven. Shouldn't take me five minutes. You check out our DVD collection and pick out something you like."

She walked over to a bookshelf, picked up a big book-style DVD organizer, and then walked back to hand it to me.

"Oof!" I said jokingly.

Her eyes crinkled. "We like movies in this family," she said with a chuckle. "You can rule out the second half. Those are all in Spanish."

I nodded. "Thanks for the tip."

Daisy smiled again, then gestured to the kitchen. "I'll be right back," she said, and then disappeared down the hallway.

As soon as her footsteps disappeared down the hall, I set the DVD book on the couch next to me. I'd been in Daisy's house a couple of times before. When we first started dating, she'd invited me over for a family barbecue. I'd spent just enough time inside to know that Hector's home office was the next room down the hall toward the kitchen.

Stealthily, I stood up and tiptoed to the entrance to the living room. I listened, and could hear Daisy scraping the sides of a bowl in the kitchen at the end of the hall.

I sucked in a breath and walked down the hall and into Hector's office.

Hector's home office was actually nicer than his Funspot one—possibly because Daisy's mother also used this one to do Funspot's accounting. An older desktop computer sat on a neat wooden desk, and dark wooden bookshelves, all laden with books, lined the walls.

I searched the titles on the shelves as fast as I could. On the shelves behind Hector's desk, I found what I was looking for—tall, thick hardcover tomes that could only be one thing.

Yearbooks.

I scanned the spines. Some were from Ocean City, New Jersey—those must be Daisy's mom's. But next to those I found three bright orange books with blue foiled lettering on the side: BAYSIDE HIGH SCHOOL. I selected the one from the same year as Cal's confession and pulled it out.

I quickly flipped it open and started scanning the signatures on the endpapers. *Fatima Lupo, Billy Cardigan, Jamal Parker, Deanna Vanuto.* Finally I flipped open to the senior photos and scanned the names. *McMahon, Miele, Murray, Mynowski* . . . I flipped the page.

A smiling, fresh, young Cal Nevins stared back at me. He looked utterly different from the man I'd met. More innocent. Happier.

I could hear Daisy clanging a pan around in the kitchen. She must be about to put the brownies in. I had to hurry. I flipped to the back of the yearbook and began crazily searching the signatures. *No . . . no . . . no . . .*

There it was. Two pages from the back, a full-page note. But the only part that mattered to me was the salutation.

To Hector, my best friend, my brother from another mother, I'm so proud of you. . . .

"*What* are you doing?"

You would think I'd be used to getting caught snooping by now, but I still jumped about three feet in the air, dropping the yearbook to the floor. Daisy did not sound the least bit amused. When I pulled myself together enough to turn around, I saw that she wore a hurt expression, with a crease of confusion tucked between her eyebrows.

"I'm sorry," I blurted.

"Is this for the case?" she asked, moving forward. She stepped around me to pick up the yearbook, examining the cover. "This is my father's. Do you suspect my father now?"

I shook my head. I had absolutely no idea what to say. "Not exactly. I, ah . . . I was just passing your father's study and . . . I got curious . . ."

Daisy was frowning at me. I could tell she wasn't buying any of this. "Did you really come over here to spend time with me?" she asked.

You would also think I would be a really smooth liar by now. I'm not.

"Ah . . . ah . . . I . . ."

Daisy sighed and shook her head. "I don't think this is going to work out, Joe. I like you, but . . . you never tell me what's going on. I think you'd better leave."

I found my voice then. "I'm so sorry, Daisy."

And I was. But I had to admit that somewhere along the line things got turned around: Now solving the case was more important to me than getting the girl.

We Hardys are messed up that way.

Daisy took my arm and led me to the door. "Good-bye, Joe. And obviously, you don't have to work on my dad's case anymore. I think we're fine without you."

I was out on the stoop with the door slammed in my face before I could even reply.

TRUE CONFESSIONS

11

FRANK

SO SHE THREW YOU OUT," I SAID WITH sympathy as Joe and I dug into bowls of Aunt Trudy's homemade maple-cinnamon ice cream. It's better than Ben & Jerry's, I swear. Cure for whatever ails you.

Joe ate a spoonful and nodded. "She slammed the door in my face. Not that I can really blame her."

"It had to be kind of a shock to find you snooping in her dad's stuff," I said.

Joe sighed and nodded again. "I don't know how else I could have done it, though. She would never have let me in there. Remember how upset she was when we questioned Luke? Imagine if she knew we suspected her dad of hiding something."

I nodded sympathetically, eating my ice cream. It was true. Even though she'd hired us, Daisy had been a little touchy about us investigating her case—almost as though she wanted to do it with us.

"Maybe it's for the best," I said.

Joe poked at his ice cream. "Maybe," he said. "I have to admit, I don't think Daisy and I were meant to be. Not if she can't handle my investigating things."

I nodded, spooning up the dregs of my ice cream and wishing there was more.

"And Hector *was* hiding something," I pointed out, hoping it was okay to change the subject.

Joe nodded, looking relieved to talk about this. "Cal was his best friend. His *best friend*." He paused. "Strange how that didn't come up when we talked to him earlier."

"And strange how his own criminal history never came up—only Cal's," I added.

"He could never explain why he hired Cal even though he didn't trust him," Joe said. "It seems almost like Cal had something on him."

"Like that they were both bad kids?" I suggested. "That Hector's rap sheet was just as long as Cal's? Until he reformed."

Joe cocked an eyebrow. "Unless Hector never really reformed."

We were quiet for a few seconds, letting that sink in. I thought of the articles we'd found. Hector's not wanting

Daisy to talk to Cal. All that Hector had riding on Funspot's success, and what Cal had done to derail it.

"I think we need to talk to Hector," I said.

"Hi there, boys." Hector looked surprised, and not entirely happy, to see us standing outside his Funspot office bright and early the next morning. I was sure he'd heard about Joe and Daisy's breakup from his daughter—and also, possibly, that Joe had been snooping around in his office.

So if his friendliness had lessened a little, I guess I could understand.

"We need to talk to you," Joe said simply, without hesitating. "Is this a good place?"

Hector looked from him to me. He sighed. "As good a place as any," he said, sitting back in his chair. I noticed that he didn't invite us to sit down.

"You knew Cal as a kid," I said, wanting to cut to the point as quickly as possible.

A flicker of surprise moved across his face, quickly followed by resignation. "How did you find that out?" he asked.

"A combination of the Internet and your high school yearbooks," Joe admitted. "I'm sorry for snooping. But I had the sense you weren't being entirely honest with us."

Hector looked from us down to his desk. Suddenly his expression changed to utter despair. He put his head in his hands and groaned. "I didn't want to believe he would do this," he said miserably. "I still can't believe it!"

I glanced at Joe. Poor guy. But we still needed the whole story.

"Why don't you start at the beginning?" I asked.

Hector sighed again and ran his hands through his hair. Then he sat up in his chair and seemed to try to pull himself together. "Cal was my best friend growing up," he said. "We lived in Queens. You probably know that already."

Joe nodded. "Jamaica, right?" he asked.

"Yeah," Hector said. "There were some tough guys in our neighborhood. Gang members, petty criminals. Cal and I, we both got into some trouble when we were kids. Our mothers worked, we had a lot of free time on our hands. And we were troublemakers. We gave our parents a hard time." He sighed.

"Go on," I urged.

"We started stealing cars and breaking into places when we were teenagers," Hector said. "Younger than you two. Think middle school. It was stupid of us. We almost always got caught, and by high school we both had terrible records. It was then—when I was a junior in high school—that I realized what an awful path I was on. I had to make some changes if I was going to survive. I was going to be eighteen soon, and charged as an adult if I got into trouble again. I knew I couldn't survive in prison. I wasn't that tough."

He looked down at the desk again. "So when I was sixteen, I just stopped. I retired as a criminal. I cleaned up my act. For a year or more I studied hard, I excelled in school. I pulled up my GPA to a B. When I was a senior, I applied for a scholarship for troubled kids who'd reformed themselves—and I won it. Suddenly I was going to college!"

Joe nodded. "But then . . . ?"

Hector's face fell. "Then . . . I had a chemistry teacher at the time who was really hard to please. I was never good at being on time, and one time I was late to his class—the third time that semester, I think—he announced that he was giving me a zero on the test that day. I started doing the math in my head, and I realized I could fail the whole semester—just because of being ten minutes late. Can you imagine?"

"Yeah," I admitted. Every high school seems to have a legendarily tough teacher like the one Hector was describing. Bayport actually had several—but I'd been lucky enough to stay on their good sides so far.

Hector shook his head. "Anyway. I tried to talk to the guy, but he wouldn't listen. I was furious. I told Cal what was going on, and of course he felt terrible for me. He was almost as excited about my scholarship as I was. He'd planned to work for a couple years, save up some money, and join me at college. We talked about starting a landscaping business together."

"But," I suggested.

"But," Hector repeated, sighing. "This teacher was going to ruin my chances, or so I thought. So I suddenly had this great idea. I would steal his car to get back at him."

I raised my eyebrows. Really?

"It was stupid," Hector said quickly, seeing my expression. "Of course I realize that now. But I was angry, so angry. So I did it. After school that day, I stole the guy's car—right out of the teachers' parking lot. I was planning to keep it for a few days and then return it—just to teach the guy a lesson. But he reported it missing right away. And they found the car—parked in a vacant lot right by my house."

He shook his head and sighed again.

"It was only a matter of time until I got caught. I'd been sloppy and my fingerprints were all over the dashboard. So I told Cal what I'd done, and he didn't hesitate. 'I'll take the rap for you,' he said. I tried to tell him no, it wasn't worth it, but he insisted. He said I would have done the same for him. And he said he'd take the sentence, a couple years or whatever—and then I could pay him back. Help him get into college, or find a job. He said he knew I'd make it up to him." Hector closed his eyes and shook his head.

"So Cal was arrested," I supplied. "And sent to prison for two years."

Hector nodded. "I tried to pay him back," he said in a strained voice. "I really did. But the Cal who came out of prison wasn't the same kid who'd gone in. He was different, almost broken. He struggled with drugs, he couldn't commit to anything. I set him up in community college, and he wouldn't keep up with the classes. Finally I gave up. I cut off all ties with him."

"Wow," I said. "That must have been hard."

Hector nodded again. "It was the hardest thing I've ever done. But I saw that I wasn't helping him, I was enabling him. I hoped that if I cut him off, he'd see that he had to get his act together."

He paused. "And eventually Cal did. He started working as a carnie, traveling around the country. He got good at what he did. But I don't think he ever forgave me. I tried to reach out to him, but he always ignored my calls or letters."

"Until he showed up here," Joe said.

Hector nodded. "Until I bought Funspot, and suddenly here was Cal, applying for a job. I was thrilled, thinking we would be friends again. But Cal made clear to me that he hadn't forgiven me for abandoning him all those years ago—after all he did for me. He said he just needed the job. He was tired of traveling and wanted to be closer to home."

Joe raised his eyebrows. "So you hired him?"

"I did." Hector frowned. "But first I checked him out. I found out what I told you about his former employer—about the threat against the coworker. I told Cal my concerns, and he basically told me to hire him or I would regret it. I didn't know what he meant, but I assumed it was that he would tell everyone about the car, that it was me. And I couldn't handle Daisy knowing about that. I'd worked so hard to try to set a good example for her." He paused, then leaned forward and rubbed his eyes. He looked exhausted, I realized—like he hadn't slept in days.

"In fact," he said, "what he had planned was much worse than that. And now I feel terrible, for putting those kids in danger."

We were all quiet for a minute. I felt bad for Hector, but it was hard to get around the enormity of what had happened to Kelly and Luke as a result of whatever had gone down between Hector and Cal as kids.

"What do you think he did with them?" I asked finally. In the end, that was the only thing that mattered: getting Kelly and Luke back.

Hector looked up at me. His eyes were wet and red-rimmed. "I have no idea," he said, his voice full of despair. "I realize now that I never really knew Cal at all."

"Daddy!" Daisy's sunny voice called from the lobby, and then suddenly there she was, standing in the doorway of the office. "I went to the Coffee Stop and brought you breakfa— oh, it's you two!"

At the sight of Joe and me, Daisy's face totally changed. Her eyebrows made an angry V over her eyes, and her cheeks flushed. "Daddy, what are they still doing here? I told you they can't be trusted. They've been snooping around our house, keeping things from us—"

Hector held up his hand to stop her. "Daisy, I'm sorry," he said. "It's time I was honest with you. It's me who's been keeping things from you, not these boys. They've just stumbled onto the truth."

Daisy raised an eyebrow. "Daddy . . . what are you saying?"

Hector let out a deep sigh and then launched into an explanation of who Cal was and how they knew each other. When he got to the part about what he'd done, and how Cal had taken the blame for him and things had gone south after that, Daisy's eyes widened.

"What? Is that why you told me not to talk to him?" she asked. "Because you thought he'd tell me the truth?"

Hector nodded. "I tried so hard to be a good example for you," he said. "I didn't want you to know that I hadn't met my own standards as a kid."

Daisy's expression softened. "Dad," she said quietly. "Did you really believe I'd think any less of you? You were young and stupid. You made a mistake, that's all."

Hector's eyes watered. "Oh, sweetheart," he murmured. "You make me so proud."

Daisy shook her head. "The only thing that matters right now is finding Luke and Kelly," she said. "If what you've told me about Cal is true . . . I just don't know what he might have done with them. This is really serious."

A male voice suddenly piped up from the doorway. "You can say that again!"

SIGHTINGS 12

JOE

DEREK PIPERATO STOOD IN THE DOOR-way, red-faced and furious-looking.

His brother Greg ran up behind him. "We got your message," he said, as the two of them strode into the office toward Hector. "Frankly, I'm stunned. With the amount of publicity G-Force has gotten this fleabag amusement park! The only problem with the ride right now is that it *isn't running*. If you would just open back up, you'd be rolling in money!"

Hector stood up. "Your attraction has been involved in the kidnapping of two children, and frankly, I've been horrified by your reactions to the whole proceeding. I want that thing out of my park. I want you to tear it down. Take it to Wonder World; I don't care."

Derek shook his head, too upset to speak, while Greg looked at his brother and then turned back to Hector, making a big show of looking composed.

"We've been over this," he said. "We were not involved in the creation of the secret room. There was space there, yes, but the hidden trapdoor was not part of the original design. It was your ride operator who must have altered the ride—to suit his ulterior motives."

Derek suddenly leaned forward and grabbed Greg's seersucker jacket. "Ulterior motives!" he cried. "That's perfect for the next trailer." He spoke in a deep, horror-movie voice. *"He had ulterior motives . . ."*

"ENOUGH!" Hector shouted, standing up and pointing his finger at the two brothers. "You'll be hearing from my lawyers, but our association is over. G-Force is done at Funspot."

Suddenly Frank checked his watch. "Oh, wow," he said, holding it up to me. "Look at the time. We've got about five minutes to get to school."

Daisy groaned. "That means I'm going to be late too." She glared at us. "If you two hadn't been here, I'd be at school by now."

Hector sighed. "I'm sorry, Daisy—I didn't realize how late it was. But now I have this to deal with." He gestured at the red-faced Piperato Brothers. "I'm sorry, but I can't drive you to school."

Daisy turned to us and scowled.

"It's okay," Frank said. "We're headed in that direction. Can we give you a ride?"

Was he kidding? I glared at him. Frank shrugged back at me innocently.

Daisy huffed. "I guess I don't have a choice," she said, turning from me to the Piperato Brothers to her father. She put the bag from the Coffee Stop on her father's desk and hoisted her backpack higher on her shoulder. "Bye, Daddy. I'll come by later."

She strutted out the door, and Frank turned to follow her. "Thank you for the information, Hector. Will you tell the police?

Hector sighed and nodded. "Of course."

I had little choice but to follow my brother. The three of us walked out of the administration building and out to the parking lot in awkward silence.

Nobody spoke until we were in the car—I drove, because I needed something to focus on—and pulling out onto the main road.

"Did you know that it's a myth that toilets flush in the opposite direction in the southern hemisphere?" Frank piped up suddenly.

Daisy shot him a withering look. "Are you kidding me?"

"It's true," Frank said, nodding. "A toilet flushes in whatever direction you shoot the water. It's simple physics."

I tried to focus on the drive as Frank went on to try to interest Daisy in static electricity, digestion, and whale songs.

Nothing seemed to take, and soon Daisy was glaring out the window.

We were driving down the "main drag" of town—a commercial strip filled with mini malls, fast-food chains, and run-down motels. There were a bunch of stoplights, and I was cursing our timing as we got stopped at a third light. We were going to be late for sure. I glanced out the window, trying to remember what we were doing in first-period Spanish, when suddenly a slight figure walking into a dumpy convenience store caught my eye.

"Wait a minute," I said out loud, pointing. "Frank—do you see that?"

Frank turned. The figure was wearing a baseball cap and dark glasses, but the swagger was unmistakable. "Oh, wow," he said, leaning up in his seat to see better. "That's Luke!"

Daisy startled and turned around. "Are you crazy?" she demanded.

But I was already throwing the car into reverse so I could pull across three lanes of traffic and into the store parking lot.

Daisy screamed, "WHAT ARE YOU DOING? We're already late! There's no way that's him!"

But as we barreled into the parking lot, the figure turned around, spotted us, and took off running.

REVELATIONS

13

FRANK

GET HIM!" I SHOUTED.

Joe slammed the car into park and threw the door open, forgetting for a second that he had a seat belt on. As he snapped back into his seat, I disentangled myself and sprinted out of the car after the guy. Soon I could hear Joe right behind me.

Luke was running out of the parking lot, behind the convenience store. As we drew closer he ran up to the wire fence separating the parking lot from the lot of the motel next door. He artfully inserted his foot into one of the links, launched himself up, and jumped the fence. I ran after him, scrambling up and over the fence and jumping down onto the broken asphalt with a *thud* that rattled my leg bones.

He was taking off around the nearest motel building, a

long, squat, one-story structure that looked like it had seen better days. I rocketed after him as I heard Joe climbing the fence behind me.

When I got to the front of the building, Luke was running across the parking lot, around the tiny fenced-in swimming pool, and over to the next lot, which housed a pizza joint. This lot, however, was separated from the motel by a tall plastic fence that looked impossible to climb—or jump. He stopped, looked at it for a second, and then looked back at me, seeing that I was just a few yards away.

"Give up, Luke!" I yelled. "Tell us the truth about what happened to you!"

He watched me. His dark glasses hid much of his expression, but he seemed to be considering my words. I moved closer.

Then, when I was almost close enough to touch him, he suddenly sprang back into motion, darting away from me and across the lot in the other direction—toward the street.

"Nooooo!" yelled Joe from behind me. The light had just changed, and traffic was moving by at a rapid pace.

But Luke didn't listen. He scrambled out into traffic, cars screeching to a halt and loudly honking their horns as they tried to avoid him. He reached the median, missing a pickup truck by just inches, and hopped over the narrow metal divider.

Joe ran up next to me. "Are we going to lose him?" he asked.

It was a rhetorical question, I knew. We couldn't let Luke get away after everything we'd learned. Either he was being held by Cal and had escaped by now, or there was another, more complicated, reason for his appearance.

"Let's go," I said simply, and ran toward the street.

I tried to bob and weave through the cars, but the drivers still didn't like that much. Traffic was moving around forty miles an hour, and suddenly I was trapped in a real-life game of Frogger. (That's an old arcade game. I like vintage arcade games.)

A red sports car in the second lane screeched to a halt just inches from my feet. The driver, a pretty blond lady, was so mad that she reached out the open window and threw her iced coffee at me.

Luckily, I *was* able to avoid that.

I scrambled over the median. I could hear the cars honking in protest as Joe followed me. On the other side of the road traffic was lighter, and I was able to cross without causing too much of a problem.

Luke was running around an old candy store and into the lot of another run-down motel.

He must have thought he'd lost us, because he slowed a little as he ran into the motel parking lot. He paused and looked around, and I grabbed Joe and ducked down behind a minivan in the candy store parking lot to watch. What was he doing?

When he was satisfied that Joe and I were gone, Luke casually strolled up to a motel room on the right—this motel was made up of ramshackle buildings whose rooms all faced the parking lot—and knocked. The door opened, and he disappeared inside.

"Room thirty-four," Joe observed, straightening up beside me.

"Room thirty-four," I echoed. "Do we call the police?"

Joe nodded. "Oh yeah," he said. "I'm not walking into this one alone."

He pulled his cell phone out of his pocket and hit the speed dial for the Bayport PD.

"OPEN UP! POLICE!"

Chief Olaf and an officer were crouched outside the door to room 34, guns cocked. They hammered on the door, and for a long time nothing happened. You could hear muffled voices inside, like the inhabitants were debating what to do. Just as Olaf gave the officer a meaningful glance, like they should break the door down, we could hear the scrabble of the cheap chain lock against the wooden door, and then the door opened inward.

Olaf nearly lost his balance, but he recovered quickly.

Luke was standing at the door. He stepped back, allowing the police to enter. Joe and I followed.

Inside, on one of the sunken double beds, sat Kelly, sipping a McDonald's shake.

"What's going on here?" The chief demanded, looking from one missing kid to the other.

Luke looked sheepish. He glanced behind Olaf to Frank and me, and his eyes narrowed in a glare. Then he turned back to the policemen, and his expression cleared.

"It was a hoax," he said simply.

Over the next couple of hours at the Bayport police station, Luke and Kelly told us the whole sordid tale.

"The idea was to get more publicity for G-Force, and for Funspot," he explained. "But I don't think Hector knew anything about it."

"I'm sure he didn't," said Daisy. Once the police had Luke and Kelly loaded into their squad car, Joe and I had gone back to the car to find a very teed-off Daisy. Luckily for us, she'd softened when we told her what happened.

"Tell us how this all started," Chief Olaf said.

Luke sighed and gestured to Kelly that she should start.

"A few weeks before the opening, I got an e-mail," she said. "It was from an address I'd never seen before, but the sender said he knew me and thought I might like an opportunity to help start an Internet sensation, for a lot of money."

"An Internet sensation?" Olaf repeated, like the words tasted sour.

Kelly nodded. "It was a brand-new marketing idea, was how they described it. All I had to do was pretend to disappear on the ride, and hide for a few weeks in a motel until the search died down. I'd get free meals, a few weeks off school, and a thousand dollars for my trouble."

Chief Olaf's eyes softened. "That must have seemed like a lot of money to a girl your age."

Kelly frowned at him. "It's not just that. My mom works three jobs already. I'm too young to work. I thought maybe this was a way to help out my family."

"Except that they'd go crazy with panic thinking you were missing for weeks," Olaf pointed out.

Kelly nodded, looking a little ashamed. "I know. I felt terrible about that. But I told myself it would all be okay when I came home, safe and sound. They'd be so relieved—plus we'd have the money."

"So you said yes," I said.

Kelly nodded. "Right. I e-mailed back and said I'd do it."

"How did you know what to do—what would happen when you 'disappeared'?" Olaf asked.

Kelly reached into her pocket and pulled out a folded printout. "I got this back," she replied.

The chief took the printout and unfolded it. I could read over his shoulder. There was a diagram of the inside of G-Force, like a map, with the seats numbered. *Sit in seat #6,* it said clearly. *Someone will help you out during the ride. Follow him and don't ask any questions.*

Olaf pointed to the e-mail address at the top of the page. *D@piperatobros.com,* it read. "Anyone familiar with that e-mail?"

"Derek Piperato," Joe and I said in unison.

Olaf turned to Kelly. "Does that sound familiar?"

She shrugged. "I don't know. I never met him," she said. "A guy named Cal got me out of the seat and told me what to do. When I was able to leave the ride that night, he took me to this motel. He was bringing us food and making sure we were okay, but he stopped a week or so ago." He gestured to Luke. "Luke's been taking care of us since then."

Luke nodded. "It's a good thing I had some money in my pocket."

He described a similar experience: the e-mail, the offer of a thousand dollars. He didn't mention needing to help his family—he wanted the money to put toward a new car. Like Kelly, he told himself that the pain he caused his family would be eliminated when he came home. And he produced an identical e-mail—from D@piperatobros.com.

"I can't believe this," Daisy muttered, shaking her head. "I can't believe it! Dad never would have gone into business with these guys if he knew they had this in them."

Chief Olaf looked at his officers. "We'd better get these Piperato Brothers in here," he said.

About half an hour later, Derek and Greg Piperato were dragged in, struggling and complaining.

"This is an outrage!" Derek cried. His handlebar mustache was all out of whack. "A travesty of justice! With what are we being charged?"

"Oh, take your pick," Olaf said, strolling out of the interrogation room to greet them. "Kidnapping, fraud, endangerment of a minor? Shall I go on?"

Greg Piperato looked indignant. "What are you talking about? What is the meaning of all this?"

The chief strolled over to the brothers with the printout Kelly had given him. "Does this look familiar?" He held it up in front of Greg's face.

I could see Greg's eyes moving back and forth as he struggled to take it all in.

"'Get out of the ride'?" he asked. "'You will be handsomely rewarded'? What does all this mean?"

"It means," Olaf said with a smile, "you didn't get away with it. And your little stunt backfired, because G-Force is dead in this town!"

G-FORCED AGAIN

14

JOE

IT'S GOING TO BE THE END OF THE SEASON SOON," Frank said, popping a piece of cotton candy in his mouth as we walked down the main drag of Funspot toward G-Force. "I guess this place will be dark until next season."

"That gives them plenty of time to tear down this ride," I agreed. "I'm sure Hector will be relieved about that."

"I'm sure you're right," Frank said. "Although the park has been pretty busy lately—no doubt all the publicity the hoax got."

For the last week straight the news had been obsessively covering the "G-Force hoax," featuring interviews with Luke, Kelly, Hector—even Derek and Greg Piperato, vigorously insisting that they were innocent in their bright orange jailhouse jumpsuits.

426

"I have to admit," I said, "I'm kind of looking forward to the last ride."

Tonight was G-Force's final hurrah. The Piperatos had been charged, Luke and Kelly were back with their (nonplussed, but relieved) families, and the attraction was going to be torn down starting tomorrow. But since nothing had ever been found to be wrong with the ride itself, Hector had agreed to open it for one last night. After that, surely, G-Force would just be one more strange appendix in amusement park history.

"It's a great little ride," Frank agreed, finishing up his cotton candy and tossing the paper cone in the trash. "Kidnapping, greed, and unnecessary drama notwithstanding."

We stepped around the food stands and found ourselves staring at G-Force—which was still pretty impressive, with its polished chrome sides gleaming in the late-afternoon sun. A huge line was already snaking around the clearing, excited kids and teenagers chatting eagerly about their last chance to go on the Death Ride. (Despite Hector's best efforts, the nickname had stuck.)

"This is where I wish you'd worked it out with Daisy," Frank said with a sigh.

"I know," I agreed. "I kind of wish we'd worked it out too. I miss her."

"I miss her connections," Frank added.

Suddenly I saw a familiar mane of dark hair moving toward me—and a familiar pink-lipsticked smile.

"Hi, Hardys."

Daisy was approaching, flanked by Penelope and Luke. I'd heard from Jamie that Daisy and Luke had maybe started seeing each other again; the whole scandal had brought them closer.

Which was hard to believe. Not that I'm bitter or anything.

"Hi, Daisy," I said. If our fledgling romance hadn't been saved when we solved the case, at least Daisy and I had been friendly again lately. That was a relief.

Daisy nodded. "You boys brave enough to risk the "Death Ride" again?" she asked, gesturing to the line.

"What can I say?" I asked. "We've been through so much together."

"And it *is* a great ride," Frank added.

Daisy glanced at him. "It's hard for me to forgive the Piperatos for what they did, but I guess you're right," she said, looking thoughtful. She turned back to me. "Want to ride it? With us?"

Frank jumped a little. I shot him a *Cool it* look. "You mean skip the line?" I asked.

Daisy smiled again, and her expression softened. "It's probably the least I can do, under the circumstances," she said gently.

I smiled back. "Well, we'll take you up on your offer then."

Daisy looked pleased. Penelope and Luke looked a little disappointed, but whatever. "Come with me," Daisy said.

We followed her across the clearing and up to the little platform where you boarded the ride. A new, dark-bearded operator was waiting there, wearing a name tag that said JAKE. Cal had never been found by the police—he still hadn't used his phone or credit card—and Hector believed that he would never come back. He was probably too ashamed that he'd taken the Piperato Brothers' money to do something he knew Hector wouldn't like. Hector said he would always miss his old friend, but he believed he was really and truly gone now.

Daisy smiled at Jake, and he quickly opened the gate to let us up. Then he led us to G-Force's door and let us inside. We chose seats—I didn't bother trying to sit next to Daisy this time—and Jake strapped us in. As we waited for him to let in the rest of the riders, I couldn't help staring into the little indentation where I knew the secret compartment lay. The trapdoor had been covered back up with the carpet, but I knew it was there.

After a few minutes the door opened up again and a bunch of rowdy kids entered and chose seats. I let my mind wander, trying not to listen to Daisy and Luke's chat or Frank trying to "break down" the physical properties of the ride for the thousandth time. Soon Jake backed out of the door and closed it behind him. The riders all erupted into spontaneous applause, eager to experience G-Force for one last, precious time.

The lights darkened. I instinctively grabbed onto my restraint bar as the opening chords of "Beautiful" started up and the ride began spinning. Soon images were flashing in the middle of the ride, and I felt myself being taken away. *That's what a good amusement park ride does for you*, I thought as we spun up and over and around again. *It takes you to another place—just for a few minutes.*

Too soon, the images slowed and the ride resumed its starting position. The music finished up, and the riders all applauded again. The seats locked into place. The lights came up.

"I'm going to miss it," I admitted to Frank, before a scream split the air.

"AUUUUUGGGGGGGGGGHHHHHHHHHHH!"

It was Penelope. I looked over at her, and my stomach clenched.

"It's Daisy!" she cried. *"She's missing! She's gone!"*

Oh no, I thought. *Could this really be happening all over again?*

READ ON

FOR A PEEK AT
THE NEXT MYSTERY IN THE
HARDY BOYS ADVENTURES:

*INTO
THIN AIR*

FRANK

"TELL ME AGAIN WHAT YOU HEARD," Officer Lasko said to me, crouching over his spiral notebook like it held the secrets of the universe.

I sighed. "I didn't hear anything," I said honestly, for about the tenth time. I squirmed in the hard plastic chair, wondering whether my brother and I would ever be allowed to leave. The Bayport PD had taken over the Funspot amusement park's administrative offices, which I don't think were comfortable under the best of circumstances. And these were not the best of circumstances. These were pretty much the worst of circumstances.

Daisy Rodriguez, the park owner's daughter and my brother Joe's recent lady friend, was missing.

It wasn't a normal disappearance. No missed curfews, no sneaking out after a fight with her parents. No, Daisy had gone missing off her father's most prized (and infamous) ride, the G-Force—sometimes called "the Death Ride."

Let me explain.

A couple of weeks ago Funspot reopened for the season under new ownership. Hector Rodriguez had bought the park, which had been a Bayport institution for a long time but had become pretty run-down in recent years, and wanted to totally revitalize it. Step one was hiring the Piperato Brothers, famous amusement ride designers, to create an all-new amusement ride exclusively for Funspot.

That ride was the G-Force. I first rode it on opening night with my brother, his date, Daisy, and her best friend, Penelope Chung. It was, in a word, awesome. Even now that I'd ridden it countless times, I still found it hard to describe exactly what the G-Force did. It was sleek and enclosed, like a spaceship, and it's safe to say that the seats moved around in a circle, and also up and down. Images were projected in the ride's center, and loud rock music played. But the combined effect was pretty exhilarating. Riding the G-Force made me feel like I'd climbed six mountains, skied down a black diamond slope, slain a dragon, breathed fire, and also saved humanity from certain destruction.

Like I said: awesome.

What wasn't awesome was the huge hoax the Piperato Brothers had pulled to gain publicity for the ride. That first night, a young girl disappeared while riding the G-Force, right under the nose of her watchful older sister. Her restraints had been cut, and the girl, Kelly, was gone without a trace. The ride was immediately closed down, but it reopened after inspectors found nothing wrong with it. And weirdly, kids flocked to the ride like rats to the Pied Piper.

They were encouraged by a "viral video" that the Piperato Brothers put together. It showed the ride in the creepiest light possible, asking viewers if they were "brave enough to ride the Death Ride." My classmates—along with nearly all the teenagers in a fifty-mile radius—wanted to prove that they were brave enough. The lines for the G-Force swelled, even as the police struggled to find any trace of the missing girl.

Not long after, a boy—an ex-boyfriend of Daisy's, in fact—disappeared in the same way. Parents panicked. The media pounced.

We thought we'd stopped the madness when we spotted one of the missing kids on a main street and chased him to a motel, where he'd been placed with the missing girl. These kids told an incredible story: that they'd been offered a thousand dollars to play "missing" for a couple of weeks, all to pull off a hoax and get tons of publicity for the new G-Force ride.

The hoax had been arranged by the Piperato Brothers, now in jail. The G-Force was scheduled to be torn down starting tomorrow. But since the ride had been declared safe by the inspectors, Hector had agreed to reopen it tonight for one last hurrah.

And on the first ride, Daisy had gone missing.

Unlike the others, she didn't appear to have spent any time in the tiny crawlspace in the heart of the ride, built to be a temporary hiding place as part of the Piperatos' plan. In fact, she'd left no trace whatsoever.

Hector was beside himself. Joe was freaking out.

And here I was, watching Officer Lasko chicken-scratch my answer into his notebook for the tenth time.

"Can I ask you something?" I asked.

"No," replied Officer Lasko without looking up. Aha. So this was a "bad cop" night. Chief Olaf didn't seem entirely sure how to handle my brother and me—he couldn't seem to decide whether we were friends or foes. Usually he leaned toward foes.

"Do you have any clues?" I asked. Lasko looked up from his notebook and sighed. "Did she leave anything behind? Are you thinking the Piperato Brothers are behind this, or someone new?"

Just then the door to the small office we were borrowing opened, and in walked Chief Olaf, followed by Joe, who he'd been questioning. The chief's expression was pretty grim, as was Joe's. I had the feeling that Joe's answers had been about as helpful as mine.

"I think we can let these boys go home," Olaf said, nodding at Officer Lasko "Unless you have anything new?"

Lasko shrugged and shook his head. "Not really. They didn't hear anything; the music was too loud. They didn't see anything; the ride was too dark."

Chief Olaf nodded, his lips pulled into a tight line. "All right then."

I stood up, looking at my brother. His face was pale, and he looked exhausted. I knew he had to be suffering right now. Even though he and Daisy had recently broken up—he'd decided the case was more important than getting the girl—I knew he really cared about her.

"Chief?" I asked, trying to sound as respectful as possible. "Can you tell us anything? You know we were close to Daisy. We, um—we're really worried about her."

Chief Olaf paused and looked me in the eye. I could tell that he knew there was much more I wasn't saying. He was well aware of the fact that Joe and I had helped the Bayport PD solve some pretty tricky cases in the past. He also knew that we'd gotten in trouble for our amateur sleuthing one too many times. So we'd worked out an agreement with the chief and our dad: If we followed some rules and checked in with the adults while doing our detective work, we could continue to investigate.

I think that while Chief Olaf sometimes sees us as wannabe private eyes, he knows that we're kind of good at investigating. We kind of catch a lot of criminals. And I think the chief understands, on some level, that sleuthing is in our blood.

Still watching me, he cleared his throat. "Okay," he said quietly. "I'm sure you realize that this information is for your ears only, and not to be shared with anyone. I'm telling you this because I know you were close to the victim. Understand?"

I nodded, and Joe did too. "We understand," he said, an edge of desperation in his voice.

Chief Olaf continued. "We're working on the theory that this is a copycat crime."

Joe raised an eyebrow. "Meaning?" he asked.

"Meaning that the Piperato Brothers aren't behind this," the chief clarified. "They carried out the first two disappearances and the hoax, yes. But this appears to be more serious. The kidnapper is hitting closer to home, the park owner's own daughter. We think that someone saw the Death Ride hoax in the news and was inspired to try his or her own hand."

I nodded, thinking that over, and struggling not to ask the obvious question: Why? That was the first, and hardest, question in any investigation. Figure out why the criminal did it, and you often find the criminal.

Why would anyone want to hurt Daisy? To send Hector a message? To get revenge on her or her family?

Why?

Joe wobbled on his feet, and Chief Olaf caught him roughly under the shoulder. "Sit down, son." He gestured for me to get up, and pulled my chair over for my brother to sit in. Joe followed orders, still looking exhausted and stressed.

"You boys had better get home," the chief said again. "Get some sleep. Are you okay to drive?" He looked at me.

"Sure," I said. I felt weary, but not sleepy.

He nodded. "Get going, then. We'll call you if we learn anything."

I stepped over to Joe and touched his shoulder. "You ready?"

Joe nodded. "I'm okay," he said quietly. "Fresh air will help, I think."

Chief Olaf opened the door, and we stepped out into the hallway. We could hear shouting coming from Hector's office, one room down.

Hector's office was on our way out. At the doorway, I peered in. An elegant, middle-aged lady was shouting at Hector, who sat slumped at his desk.

"You let this happen!" she cried, her voice rough with emotion. "With this terrible park! You forced that poor man to sell it to us, and it's brought nothing but misery ever since!"

At our footsteps, Hector looked up at the door. His eyes contained a deep well of sadness, more intense than I'd ever seen from him.

"Frank and Joe," he said. "Are you two okay?"

I nodded. "We're just heading home, sir. The police are done with us."

Hector nodded. He looked down, then gestured toward the woman. "Boys, this is my wife, Lucy. I don't think you've met."

Lucy, Daisy's mom, looked over at us. She looked a little embarrassed to be caught yelling at Hector. "Hello," she said.

"Frank and Joe were a huge help in finding the truth about the Piperatos," Hector said.

I nodded. "I hope we can help find Daisy, too, sir."

Hector winced and closed his eyes. My skin prickled with the feeling I'd said the wrong thing.

Finally he nodded and opened his eyes. "Get some sleep, boys."

We nodded our good-byes and walked out into the dark, silent night. Funspot had been closed for hours. Everybody had been kicked out when Daisy was discovered missing. The park always felt a little creepy when it was deserted. Most of the rides had completely powered down, but a few were still blinking their bright, aggressively happy lights into the darkness.

I closed my eyes and rubbed them. I could really use some sleep.

"Did Lasko say anything interesting?" Joe asked as we walked toward the park exit.

"Not really," I replied. "Just asked me the same questions over and over. What do you think about what the chief said?"

"About telling us if they learned anything?" Joe scoffed. "I'll believe it when I see it."

"No, about this being a copycat crime." We rounded a fence that led to the exit and were plunged into near-total darkness. A few lights shone in the parking lot, but they were still too far away to do much good. We'd left the lights of the administration building behind. I shivered, and I wasn't sure whether it was because of the sudden breeze.

Joe shrugged. "It makes about as much sense as any of this," he said. "This doesn't look like the hoaxes. They didn't find any evidence that Daisy was in the little room under the ride, for example."

"Right," I said, pausing to make sure we were going in the right direction. We had to go down "Main Street"—a now-dark and deserted stretch of souvenir shops and food stands—to get to the parking lot. I nodded at Joe and led the way.

"I just don't know what the motivation is," I added. "Who would want to hurt Daisy?"

Joe nodded. "I know. Who hates Funspot that much?"

I turned around, my mouth already open to reply, but the sound died in my throat, replaced by a scream.

A dark shadow shot from behind one of the souvenir stands—arms outstretched and headed for my brother!

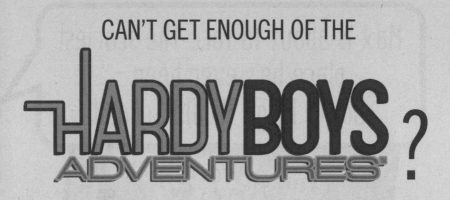
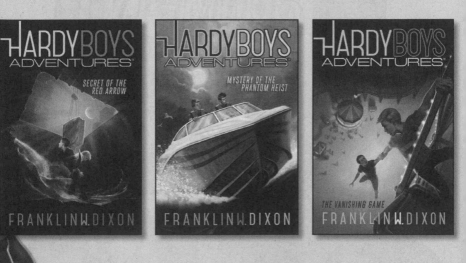
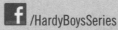